FORTUNE OF WAR
David Mack

Based on *Star Trek*® and
Star Trek: The Next Generation®
created by Gene Roddenberry

POCKET BOOKS
New York   London   Toronto   Sydney   New Delhi

The sale of this book without its cover is unauthorized. If you purchased this book without a cover, you should be aware that it was reported to the publisher as "unsold and destroyed." Neither the author nor the publisher has received payment for the sale of this "stripped book."

Pocket Books
An Imprint of Simon & Schuster, Inc.
1230 Avenue of the Americas
New York, NY 10020

This book is a work of fiction. Any references to historical events, real people, or real places are used fictitiously. Other names, characters, places, and events are products of the author's imagination, and any resemblance to actual events or places or persons, living or dead, is entirely coincidental.

™, ®, and © 2017 by CBS Studios Inc. STAR TREK and related marks and logos are trademarks of CBS Studios Inc. All Rights Reserved.

This book is published by Pocket Books, an imprint of Simon & Schuster, Inc., under exclusive license from CBS Studios Inc.

All rights reserved, including the right to reproduce this book or portions thereof in any form whatsoever. For information, address Pocket Books Subsidiary Rights Department, 1230 Avenue of the Americas, New York, NY 10020.

First Pocket Books paperback edition December 2017

POCKET and colophon are registered trademarks of Simon & Schuster, Inc.

For information about special discounts for bulk purchases, please contact Simon & Schuster Special Sales at 1-866-506-1949 or business@simonandschuster.com.

The Simon & Schuster Speakers Bureau can bring authors to your live event. For more information or to book an event, contact the Simon & Schuster Speakers Bureau at 1-866-248-3049 or visit our website at www.simonspeakers.com.

Manufactured in the United States of America

10 9 8 7 6 5 4 3 2 1

ISBN 978-1-5011-5200-9
ISBN 978-1-5011-5208-5 (ebook)

Disruptor blasts resounded inside the derelict ship.

Something exploded inside the Nausicaans' perimeter, then came the thunder of collapsing decks and buckling spaceframe. Upper decks slammed down into the corridor, kicking up dust followed by thick smoke. Wild volleys of disruptor fire screamed out of the darkness and caromed off the bulkheads, raining sparks onto Sarai and the rest of the away team.

Dalit Sarai's instinct was to shoot back, but she held her fire. There were unarmed civilians in harm's way, innocent lives she had been tasked to defend and liberate.

Another explosion filled the corridor with shrapnel. Smoky bits tore into the legs of her environmental suit, which tightened the seals at her thighs to prevent the loss of her air. Sarai flattened herself to the deck and retrieved a canister of emergency patch aerosol from her utility belt, and she sprayed it over the rips in her suit, closing them in seconds. Her suit sensed the repairs and normalized the pressure around her legs.

Riker kneeled beside her and fired off a few salvos of suppressing fire in the Nausicaans' direction. He glanced toward Sarai. *"Are you hurt?"*

"Scrapes and bruises," she said. "I'm fine."

Squatting low behind them, Modan and Sethe had drawn their phasers but seemed reluctant to fire without express orders to do so. Sethe asked, *"Orders, sirs? Do we fall back?"*

"No," Riker said. *"The mission's not done. And we don't leave our people behind."*

for the peacemakers

HISTORIAN'S NOTE

The events of this story take place in late 2386, twenty years after the *U.S.S. Enterprise* 1701-D answered a distress call from Delta Rana IV (*Star Trek: The Next Generation*, "The Survivors"), and a few months after the *Starship Titan*'s ill-fated mission to aid the Dinac (*Star Trek: Sight Unseen*).

And blood in torrents pour
In vain—always in vain
For war breeds war again.

—John Davidson
"War Song," stanza 7 (1899)

February 2366

Year three of the *U.S.S Enterprise*-D mission

One

The world was in order. All was as it was meant to be: the weak kowtowed to the strong; the dregs of the lower castes knew their place.

Escorted from his private shuttle toward the Hall of Governance in the heart of the capital, Royal Treasurer Te-Mazow felt like a master of creation. On the boulevard outside the capital, his inferiors spread their tentacles wide and flattened their bodies to the hot pavement. Te-Mazow, by dint of his office, glided above them on his antigrav pallet, his own tentacles unsullied by contact with the filthy ground, his vulnerable parts hidden from view by the jeweled platform he piloted away from his transport vehicle.

His six guards rushed to keep pace with his floating conveyance. Each of them moved on four of their seven limbs and used their rear tentacle to balance themselves. In their forelimbs, whose ends were trifurcated into nimble digits, they toted weapons to telegraph their deadly authority to all who had eyes to see.

Te-Mazow loved to watch the commoners prostrate themselves. It reminded him of how far he had come in the world, how many rivals he had bested, how much power he had amassed. This was the way of nature, the shape of life. Luxury belonged to the strong, the cruel, the quick. He had no pity for the less fortunate. *If they want what I have, they should work as hard as I do. No one is owed anything.* He felt great pride and satisfaction as his defenders kicked a pair of young grovelers clear of his sled as it ascended the incline to the royal palace. *Move aside, fools.*

The current regime had conquered and colonized a dozen worlds in the past twenty cycles, and the future promised to be even more lucrative. The frontier of Husnock space had begun to encroach upon fringe possessions of a classically weak entity known as the United Federation of Planets. The Federation, as its citizens often called it for brevity's sake, was ripe for domination by the Husnock. Its worlds were soft targets, its people timid cattle. Any culture that wasted so much time finding new ways to coddle the weak and shelter the fearful had no business pushing into the great darkness of the galaxy at large.

Exploration was the purview of the bold.

More importantly, it was profitable—and in the Husnock Star Kingdom, it was Te-Mazow who controlled the flow of wealth. Disbursements for new colonies? For new starships and space stations? For war? All had to be reviewed and approved by Te-Mazow. The king and his counselors might set policy, but Te-Mazow wielded a unique power: he told them what they did and did not have the funds to do. He told them which wars they could afford to wage.

Power had brought perquisites. Like the great majority of his peers, Te-Mazow was mated, and his estate had been earmarked for posthumous division among his registered progeny. That had not prevented him from sequestering significant sums of his personal wealth, hiding them from his legitimate heirs, so that he could maintain secondary and tertiary circles of mates and kin. He felt no shame for his actions. When he thought of the impoverished throngs who could not afford unpolluted seaside property at which to spawn healthy young, he considered it his duty to take up their burden in the propagation of the Husnock species.

Te-Mazow was nothing if not a patriot.

Inside the royal palace the shows of obeisance were even more satisfying, as everyone from supplicants to the royal court to its loyal officers splayed their bodies low to the polished floors as Te-Mazow was escorted past on the way to his office. He knew that soon, before the day was over, he would take his own turn at abasement, but the sting of this knowledge was mitigated by the fact that Te-Mazow lowered himself only before the king and his royal progeny. In a culture that numbered more than fifty billion subjects, he yielded to no more than fifty of them in total. That was a margin of magnitude he could accept.

A line of petitioners waited outside his office as his bier approached. He granted none of them the honor of his notice as he entered.

Today's line was the longest he had seen in ages. They would consume enough of his time throughout the day with their miserable requests for aid, for research funding, for handouts of the wealth accrued by their betters. He detested them. Still, some of them might make reasonable cases for how his investment in their efforts would benefit the kingdom, redound to its profit, and further burnish his reputation and enhance his power. Those he would grace with royal loans. The rest would be charged fees for wasting his precious time.

It promised to be a most profitable day, indeed.

At the entrance of his office, he collided with an invisible wall of pain.

A hideous burning sensation raged through Te-Mazow's entire body. It birthed itself deep inside his bulbous head, a fire stoked from the core of his being. Skewers of agony spiraled through his cephalus and radiated into his mantle. His hearts raced. Something was very wrong.

"Help me," he tried to say, but all his words came out slurred.

Around him his defenders collapsed, their tentacles twitching and flailing. Down the long gilded corridor, all his petitioners lay racked by spasms, froth and dark blue blood pouring from their dilated orifices. What fresh horror was this? Were they betrayed? After more than a millennium of stable rule, had another clan risen up against the Vo-Kesur?

The pain worsened. Every thought in Te-Mazur's mind shriveled like skin in lava. Screams of suffering and anguish issued from his beaked mouth, only to become lost in the cacophony of shrieks resonating inside the royal palace. It was so humiliating for him to be struck down beside the commoners, as if they deserved to die beside him like his equals.

His pain and terror redoubled—and then his body

erupted into flames, as did those of every other Husnock he could see.

Te-Mazow's world was on fire.

There was no escaping the flames.

In every city on the Husnock homeworld, and on every planet the Husnock had ever colonized, in every starship and space station manned by the Husnock, every single member of their species spontaneously combusted, consumed from within by fires of unknown origin.

Then came the voice, one more ancient than death and older than time. Its words were the last every Husnock heard as they were devoured by their personal infernos:

"For Rishon."

One mental image followed every last Husnock to the grave: a world named Delta Rana IV, set aflame by one of their starships . . . an alien female perishing in the blaze of Husnock weapons . . . then the terrifying visage of a Douwd, a being of pure energy, a peaceful creature driven by rage and grief to lay its vengeance upon them all.

Flames turned fifty billion beings to ash in the space of a breath. The skies of two dozen Husnock worlds filled with greasy black smoke . . . but there was no one left to bear witness, and no one left to rejoice. The victims of the Husnock had long since preceded them into extinction. Now the Great Silence enveloped them all. The mighty had fallen—

And the cosmos neither noticed nor cared.

September 2386

Two

It was a planet of ghosts. At least, that was what it felt like to Doctor Maxwell Theron. To all appearances it had been a colony planet before disaster struck. There was only one large city on the surface. A smattering of satellite settlements dotted the surrounding area, with the nearest seeming to be the best established and the most remote being the least developed.

One detail all the Husnock areas had in common was a sense of having been depopulated instantly and without warning. Personal transport vehicles of all kinds had crashed and strewn debris in the streets, throughout the countryside, and along the shorelines. Elegantly curving buildings stood gutted by fires long since extinguished. On the city's outskirts, fusion reactor facilities and starports lay cold and abandoned. In residences and public spaces, personal belongings had been left to succumb to the elements.

Nature had started to reclaim spaces transformed by

the now-extinct Husnock. Vines, moss, and grasses festooned the façades of empty buildings and cocooned the twisted husks of wrecked vehicles. Boulevards that once had been paved smooth now were webbed with fissures, from which flowers and fungi sprang and bent to follow the sun's slow transit of the sky. The resilience of the local flora kindled hopeful feelings in Theron. From death and destruction came renewal and rebirth. It made him reflect on the impermanence of life, the beauty of chaos, and the folly of expecting order to be anything more than a transitory disruption in entropy's march.

Heady thoughts for such a lovely morning, he chided himself. He sipped hot chai from his spill-proof mug as he crossed the expedition's campsite. His xenoarchaeology team had established its base camp along either bank of the city's central aqueduct. Though the camp had started out small, it had grown quickly. There were a few hundred people here, all of them under Theron's supervision. Only a few were xenocultural experts like himself. Their ranks comprised xenolinguists, engineers and biologists of various specialties, architects, and computer experts, not to mention support personnel including medical staff, cooks, pilots, drivers, and mechanics.

They had entrenched themselves here a few years ago, just a few months after a long-range scout ship had located this world. Starfleet had begun its low-key, classified search for the remains of the Husnock civilization twenty years earlier, not long after receiving Captain Jean-Luc Picard's after-action report detailing the *Starship Enterprise* NCC-1701-D's mission to Delta Rana IV. Summoned by a distress call, the *Enterprise* crew had found the world's surface laid waste except for a small patch of land around a pristine house occupied by an elderly couple. The woman, it turned out, had been an illusion created by the man, who in turn was revealed as a Douwd—an energy being who had confessed to the rage-driven instant genocide of the Husnock.

Thus had begun Starfleet's clandestine search for whatever remained of the Husnock, whom the Douwd had described as "a species of hideous intelligence."

The search had proved longer and more difficult than anyone had expected. The Federation had possessed no record of the Husnock prior to their attack on Delta Rana IV, and after the extinction of the Husnock their civilization had gone silent and cold, rendering them nearly invisible to most long-range detection methods. Consequently, there was nothing to indicate from what heading or region of the galaxy they had come. Further complicating matters, the Dominion War and the Borg Invasion both had interrupted Starfleet's exploration of the rimward sectors of the Alpha Quadrant frontier.

It took Starfleet seventeen years to find this isolated Husnock colony world on the edge of the galaxy's Perseus Arm. It was catalogued as FGC-779852c, and Theron had refused to let any of his colleagues from the Daystrom Institute or their peers from the Vulcan Science Academy attach a new name to it. He was determined to uncover the Husnock's designation for the planet because he was haunted by the notion that this world without a name was an unmarked grave for those who had died here.

Theron was almost inside the chow tent when Doctor Kilaris fell into step beside him. He nodded politely at the Vulcan woman. "Good morning, Doctor. On your way to breakfast?"

"I ate earlier." She handed him a padd. "My team and I have made a breakthrough."

Kilaris, like most Vulcans, was not prone to exaggeration. Theron stopped and faced her. "What kind?" She nodded at the padd. Taking her unspoken cue, he perused the top-level summary. They had unearthed a codex that contained a partial Husnock translation of an alien tome. Though the Husnock written language remained as impenetrable as ever, the alien language seemed to be one already known to the Federation. "Are you sure about this?"

"I waited until three members of my team independently verified the results. The text we found is derived from an ancient dialect of T'Kon. That suggests the Husnock at some point have had contact with an alien species whose language was influenced by the T'Kon."

All the citations checked out. Theron felt his pulse quicken. "This is a good find, Doctor. How much T'Kon text did you find, and how much was translated into Husnock?"

"The original work appears to be sizable. It should enable us to build a translation matrix for all written Husnock."

"Our very own Rosetta stone! Superb. I'll send word back to Daystrom and the VSA after I eat." His appetite asserted itself, so he beckoned her to follow him inside the chow tent. "How about spoken Husnock? Any leads on that front?"

Kilaris shook her head. "Not yet. We need to wait for the engineers to parse the Husnock's media formats." She followed him down the serving line and watched him grab a tray and a plate, which he loaded with scrambled eggs and a warm biscuit. "Have we found any Husnock DNA yet?"

"Not a speck. Whatever form the Douwd apocalypse took, it was thorough." He led Kilaris to a nearby table. They sat down across from each other. She watched him dig into his breakfast. Between bites, he asked, "Does your team need anything to speed the translation?"

"Priority access on the main computer would be appreciated."

"Done." He shoveled down another mouthful of eggs. After he swallowed, he realized she was still watching him. "Something else, Doctor?"

"My team and I will be working late tonight on the new translation matrix." A sly lift of her elegantly curved eyebrows. A subtle look around for eavesdroppers. "Shall I come to your tent tonight? Or will you await me in mine?"

Looking into Kilaris's dark brown eyes, Theron kept his expression neutral when all he wanted to do was to grin. "Mine."

She nodded, stood, and left the chow tent.

He watched her go and let himself smile.

It's gonna be a good week on the dig, I can feel it.

There was money in the big space station. Cherbegrod knew that much. Why else hide it in deep space, so far from planets? Why make it so dark? Why put traps on the airlocks?

The makers of the space station must have thought their traps clever. Well hidden. But not from Pakleds. Offworlders laughed at Pakleds. Called them slow. But Pakleds were smart. And they knew traps. How to make them, how to find them, how to take them apart.

There were a lot of traps on the space station.

The traps were invisible to the sensing units on Cherbegrod's salvage hauler, the *Gomjar*. But Cherbegrod was no fool. He sent out his engineer, Eberleg, to inspect the space station's airlock before he let the *Gomjar* dock. That was smart. Bombs and tricks and snares. Some to hurt the *Gomjar*, some to hurt him and his men. Traps everywhere.

Cherbegrod and his second-in-command, Haripog, watched over Eberleg's shoulders. The engineer took apart a delicate system with his hands, which had been fat even before he sheathed them in the space suit's heavy gloves.

The first officer grew impatient. His voice crackled from the talking widget built into Cherbegrod's space suit. *"How long to open door?"*

"Soon," Eberleg said on the same talk-channel. He poked the airlock's gears with a gadget. *"Soon."* He detached another scary-looking thing from a crevice in the airlock. *"Now."*

The door rolled open.

On the other side it was dark. Cherbegrod swatted Haripog's arm. "Make light."

Haripog fumbled with his light stick. It switched on. He pointed the beam inside the space station. Inside it was wide open, and the ceiling was so far up, the light stick's beam couldn't reach it. The three leaders of the *Gomjar* plodded inside, close together.

There were shelves and racks everywhere, long rows, as far as Cherbegrod could see. All loaded with scary things. Bombs. Missiles. Metal shapes that he couldn't name but thought would maybe go *boom* if someone hit them hard enough.

Huge mechanical arms attached to machines on the ceiling dangled but didn't move. Parked in the lanes between the shelves of exploding things were load lifters and cargo movers, and antigrav pallets lying on the deck, either switched off or out of power.

Eberleg looked at Cherbegrod and Haripog. *"Go where now?"*

Cherbegrod pointed toward a large fusion reactor control panel at the end of the center aisle. "There." He walked toward it, and his men followed him. It was a long walk. When they reached the big machine, Cherbegrod poked at its controls. A few lights blinked on the panel, then went out again. He looked at Eberleg and pointed at the console. "You fix? Make it work?"

"Will try," Eberleg said. *"Strange markings."*

As the engineer pulled apart the front of the reactor controls, Cherbegrod saw Haripog stare in wonder at the great towers of weapons. The first officer pointed at some of the parked load-lifters. *"No seats."* Then he pointed up at the giant robot arms. *"No hand controls."* He faced Cherbegrod. *"Warehouse makes itself go. That is good."*

"Yes. Less work for us." He pointed toward a wide, open passage at the end of the room. "This way."

They walked together into the next area of the space station, which was separated from the warehouse by a thick wall. On the other side was a factory. It was a maze of snaking conveyer belts, robot arms of all sizes, and sleek machines—all lying still. Weapons of war stood at attention on the conveyer belt. The ones closer to the warehouse looked almost finished. The farther back one looked along the production line, the more skeletal the warheads became.

Haripog nodded. *"No workstations. No workers. Factory runs itself."*

"And now factory is ours." Cherbegrod grinned as he imagined how rich they all would be when they started selling these deadly toys to the highest bidders. "Go tell Eberleg to make power. Then we make factory go—and no one laughs at Pakleds ever again."

Three

It was the most galling part of Dalit Sarai's weekly routine, and always the low point of any day on which it fell: her mandatory check-in with her handler. She had never resented the protocol before being posted to the *Titan* as its executive officer. When she had served as a field operative for Starfleet Intelligence, check-ins had served a number of vital functions, not the least of which was receiving updates about emerging threats and changing situations. Now the flow of information during her check-ins was strictly one way—from her to the person holding her metaphorical leash. And that was a formula for resentment.

Sarai confirmed that the door to her quarters was locked. She couldn't risk being interrupted for the next couple of minutes. With her privacy assured, she retrieved two items from the hiding place she'd devised behind the maintenance panel of her refresher nook. The first device was small and oval, similar in shape to a combadge of an earlier era, minus the familiar Starfleet delta. Seen by an untrained eye it could be mistaken for a nondescript bronze brooch. The second item was a plain metallic wand with a simplified display built into its side.

Years of training in espionage tradecraft compelled Sarai to conduct a sweep of her quarters with the wand. The compact scanner detected no hidden listening devices. She turned it off, put it away, and then tapped a well-practiced sequence on the bronze oval. The palm-sized secure comm vibrated momentarily in her hand. That signal meant the gadget was interfacing with the *Titan*'s secure computer network, spoofing the credentials of an ordinary padd or tricorder. In a matter of seconds it disabled the automated listening circuits inside her quarters and established an encrypted connection to the starship's subspace transceiver array.

It vibrated twice in quick succession; its secret channel was open and standing by. Sarai tapped a different sequence on the device, to route its encrypted channel to the computer screen on her desk. "Active. Ready."

A woman's gray-haired, aquiline visage appeared on-screen: Sarai's spymaster, Admiral Marta Batanides, director of Starfleet Intelligence. *"Report."*

"Admiral Riker continues to overextend the resources of our escort ships."

"Specifics, please."

"Since last week, Admiral Riker has dispatched the *Canterbury*, *Ajax*, and *Wasp* on headings that, in my opinion, spread them too far apart to provide meaningful tactical support to one another, or to the *Titan*, in the event of a crisis."

Batanides considered that. *"What about Captain Vale? Did she note this in her log?"*

"Negative. I voiced my concerns to her in private, but she dismissed them on the grounds that it's not my place to second-guess the admiral in matters of frontier fleet operations."

"For once, I agree with the captain. But your objections are well taken, Commander. . . . Do you have anything of note to report concerning Captain Vale?"

Sarai was reluctant to share her observations about her commanding officer, but she knew Batanides did not subscribe to the adage *no news is good news*. "Over the last seven days, she has on two occasions exhibited a questionable willingness to let Riker second-guess her orders. Neither incident had any significant effect on mission outcomes."

"The effect on crew morale is of greater concern." Batanides softened her expression. *"You've been aboard the* Titan *for eight months. How are you fitting in?"*

"The captain's trust in me remains guarded, and I suspect the admiral still harbors some resentment at my compulsory presence. As for the rest of the crew—" She wondered whether she should confide that some of them still referred to her as *the Ice Queen*, because of her aloof behavior, then she thought better of it. Instead she lied. "They recognize my authority."

"Even the chief engineer? Ra-Havreii? He has a reputation as a maverick."

The mention of Ra-Havreii rankled Sarai. "Once I made him understand that I feel no obligation as a fellow Efrosian to assuage his sexual frustrations, our working relationship improved markedly." She chose to omit mentioning the fact she had slapped him. Twice.

"And that brings us to Troi. I remain concerned about

her serving alongside Riker. Has her presence compromised the effectiveness of Riker or Vale?"

Sarai was tempted to paint a figurative target on Troi, for no better reason than the half-Betazoid diplomatic officer's empathic skills made her nervous, but Sarai's sense of honor prevailed. "I've seen no evidence of that."

"Then look harder."

The callousness and cynicism of Batanides's order upset Sarai, but she was in no position to complain. Two years earlier, she had risked going over the admiral's head to share vital intel with President Pro Tem Ishan Anjar during the Bashir-Andor crisis—a political gamble that had backfired on Sarai when Anjar's criminal past came to light. Disgrace had fallen on him and everyone associated with his scandalized run for the Federation presidency, including Sarai. She knew that had she not been recruited by Batanides to serve as her mole aboard the *Titan*, she would likely still be languishing in a do-nothing job in a munitions depot on Luna.

But that didn't mean she was willing to fabricate offenses to satisfy the admiral's obsessive vendetta against Admiral Riker and the senior officers of the *Titan*.

"If I observe anything suspect in the course of my duties, I will report it as ordered." She took secret pleasure in seeing Batanides bristle at her passive-aggressive defiance. Eager to escape the awkward conversation, Sarai added, "My shift on the bridge begins in ten minutes. So if there's nothing else?"

"Make your next report in five days." The admiral closed the secure channel.

Sarai keyed in the deactivation sequence for her

secure comm, then tucked it back into its hiding place beside the scanning wand and closed the panel. She checked her reflection in the bathroom mirror; her dark hair was secure in its regulation ponytail, and her upswept eyebrows still looked elegant and well-shaped. A deep breath, then she exhaled the tension of her talk with Batanides and exorcised all traces of emotion from her angular features.

Safe once more behind her mask of detachment, she left her quarters to start another day as SI's unofficial asset aboard the *Starship Titan*.

There was no greater gift, in Ranul Keru's opinion, than waking to face a new day.

His alarm—a gentle serenade of birdsong—sounded at 0615. Refreshed after a perfect night's sleep, Keru opened his eyes to see his beau, Bowan Radwoski, looking back at him from the other side of the bed, squinting with groggy eyes.

"Morning," Keru said.

Bowan smiled. "Hey."

There wasn't anything to talk about at that hour. It just felt good to Keru to know Bowan was there, sharing the same space and moment.

Keru rolled out of bed and plodded into the main room of their shared quarters—a recent change in their living arrangements that had been approved by the captain and effected with cheerful efficiency by the ship's quartermaster. After a few minutes of stretching and breathing to prime his body, Keru eased into his scheduled fitness routine for the morning. It was a Thursday according to the ship's chronometer, so his regimen today was yoga. Each day of the week had its own exercise plan. The day before it had been a brisk jog on a holodeck simulation of the lost beaches of Risa; the next day it would be aikido forms.

Somewhere between his salute to the sun and his warrior pose, Keru felt his tendons relax. Trickles of sweat rolled off his chest, teased his throat, and disappeared into his beard while he held a one-handed tree pose. He had only mastered the single-handstand after years of practice, and he still found it hard to hold steady. It was almost a relief when it came time for him to shift himself into the Sayanasana scorpion-pose variation, in which he balanced his inverted form on his elbows with his lower legs folded and his feet pointed toward his head.

Feeling brave, he attempted the wounded peacock pose—only to collapse in a heap. *One of these days I'll get the hang of that.* He rolled into a corpse pose to end his routine and quiet his mind. It looked like the simplest of actions—lie on one's back, don't move, and be silent. The real challenge of it, however, was with one's own unquiet mind. Today, at last, Keru let his mind vanish into the tides of his breathing. He was at peace in the now.

Soft footfalls across the carpeted deck brought him out of his meditation. Bowan stepped over him and asked on his way to the replicator, "Ready for breakfast?"

"Absolutely. But it has to be quick. I still need to shower before my shift."

"Quick is good. Healthful is better." He activated the replicator. "Egg white omelet with Swiss cheese, scallions, and broccoli. Pumpernickel bagel, toasted and buttered. Irish breakfast tea, hot." As his meal materialized with a flash of color and a wash of semimusical sound inside the replicator nook, he asked Keru, "For you?"

"Two Ktarian eggs, poached, on steamed Vulcan seaweed. Half a Terran pink grapefruit. *Raktajino*, unsweetened. And, because I can't be good all the time, a Zibalian puff tart."

Bowan removed the tray containing his order from the nook, then repeated Keru's order to the replicator. While he carried his food to the dining table, Keru toweled the perspiration from his face and arms. They ate breakfast sitting across from each other, chatting between bites as Bowan perused the morning's news feeds on his padd. After they had finished eating, Keru glanced at the chrono and sprang from his chair. "I'm late!"

He dashed through their bedroom and into the sonic shower. Even though he disliked rushing through a shower, he hated being even a minute late for a duty shift on the bridge. In under ninety seconds he had cleansed himself. He dressed in a panic, then froze as he realized he was missing—

"My combadge!" He spun in one direction, then the other. "Have you seen my—?"

Bowan stood in the bedroom doorway, holding up Keru's combadge between two fingers. "You left it in the living room. Again."

Keru plucked the combadge from his lover's hand and kissed him as he darted past him. "You're a lifesaver, Bo!" Sprinting toward the door to the corridor, he called over his shoulder, "See you tonight!" Then he was in the corridor and running for the nearest turbolift.

Everyone he passed on his way to the lift smiled at him. He wondered if they knew something he didn't. Then he caught his reflection in passing on a companel, and he realized they were all smiling because he was, from ear to ear, like a big dope.

Luck was on his side this morning. The turbolift doors were open when he arrived, and he slipped inside just before they closed. He nodded at Lieutenant Karen McCreedy from engineering. "Morning." Then, to the computer, he said, "Bridge." The lift car accelerated upward with barely any perceptible sense of movement.

As a senior officer bound for the bridge, his request superseded whatever instructions McCreedy had given the computer. It was a routine fact of life aboard Starfleet vessels, but on this occasion he felt compelled to acknowledge it with a sheepish look at the lieutenant and a humble, "Sorry."

A single shake of her head. "No worries, sir."

The doors parted with a swish, and Keru stepped onto the bridge of the *Titan*. He reached the security and tactical console, which had been manned on the overnight shift by Commander Tuvok. The Vulcan acknowledged Keru's arrival with a polite nod. "All decks report secure. Ship's status normal. No hostile contacts within sensor range."

"Acknowledged. I relieve you, Commander."

"I stand relieved." Tuvok took a step backward and relinquished the console to Keru's supervision precisely one minute before the scheduled start of alpha shift. As usual, Tuvok did not linger. He proceeded directly to the turbolift, which opened ahead of him to disgorge several passengers, including Commander Sarai, flight controller Lieutenant Commander Aili Lavena, and recently promoted bridge engineering officer Lieutenant Torvig Bu-Kar-Nguv.

Torvig gamboled to his post, which was at an aft console close to Keru's. The young Choblik, who resembled a cross between a flightless bird and a two-legged forest herbivore with a prehensile tail that ended in a set of agile robotic fingers, and whose body had been accessorized with cybernetic enhancements including two bionic arms, settled in at his post.

A few minutes later, Keru noticed on the edge of his vision that Torvig was casting a curious look his way. He met the engineer's stare. "What's up, Tor?"

"I was going to ask you the same question, Ranul."

"Why?"

"You were humming."

That caught the Trill security chief by surprise. "I was what?"

"Humming. Quite audibly." He turned apologetic. "I did not mean for you to stop. It seemed quite a happy melody."

A quick look around confirmed for Keru that other officers nearby, including Ensign Peya Fell, the new alpha-shift science division liaison, were eyeing him with curiosity. Fell cracked an amused smile before averting her gaze, leading Keru to wonder what the young Deltan woman must think of him.

Before he could feel embarrassed by his subconscious slip, Torvig asked him, "Are you really feeling that ebullient this morning? Or are you perhaps overcompensating?" He gave his species' equivalent gesture to a shrug. "I sometimes find it hard to read humanoids' emotions."

Keru stood tall, smiled, and let himself enjoy his chipper mood.

"What can I say, Tor? Life is good."

"Life sucks." Doctor Xin Ra-Havreii prowled past a line of nervous engineers who stood at consoles in the center of the main engineering deck. "And your sloppy work is the reason why." He pointed at one screen after another as he passed, doling out criticism on the move. "Meldok, your intermix ratio is off by point zero-two. . . . Crandall, distortion feedback on the starboard warp coil should never exceed point zero-three millicochranes, that reads point zero-five. . . . Damn it, Rossini, I don't want to see impurities in the flow from the Bussard collectors at more than point zero-five parts per million. . . . Tabyr, purge the EPS conduits until—"

Rossini interjected, "The specs for the Bussard collectors say the system can filter out impurities at concentrations of up to point two-five PPM."

Ra-Havreii turned back toward Ensign Paolo Rossini. Planted himself in front of the wiry young human. And glared. "I'm sorry, *Ensign*. I could have sworn that I just heard a junior engineering officer quote specs at me. As if I weren't the one who wrote the specs for this ship. Did I suffer an auditory hallucination, *Ensign*?"

Rossini snapped to attention at his post. "No, sir."

"So you *did* quote specs at me." Ra-Havreii leaned close enough that his dramatic, swooping eyebrows teased Rossini's face while he continued his reprimand. "You're still younger than some of my scars, Ensign, so let me tell you a little secret. Starship designers compile lots of recommended specs for their creations. Most of them are just educated guesswork, based on simulations and short-range test flights. No one really knows how a given system will work until long after it's deployed. And each starship is different. Within a few years of service and a couple of refits, each ship develops its own idiosyncrasies. A good engineer learns to respect those quirks. Untrained engineers"—he lowered his voice to a menacing growl—"quote specs from a manual. Do I make myself clear, mister?"

"Aye, sir."

Ra-Havreii pointed at Rossini's console. "Back to work."

He continued down the line. No one else backtalked him—until he reached the last duty station, the master status display. During most shifts he preferred to watch this post himself. However, since the *Titan*'s last refit—which had been made necessary by the beating the ship took in its battle against the Solanae at the start of the year—two veteran engineering officers had been transferred to his department by order of someone at Starfleet Command. Lieutenant Commander Aluno, a soft-spoken Catullan woman, had volunteered for the overnight shift; as a result, Ra-Havreii had barely seen her since she came aboard.

If only he could say the same about Lieutenant Commander Szevich Dalkaya. Young, smug, and maddeningly good at his job, the Zibalian was everything Ra-Havreii didn't want in a subordinate. Making matters worse, Dalkaya had the proverbial "lean and hungry look," and an air of arrogant superiority that made Ra-Havreii want to slap the tattoos off the man's face.

Dalkaya was standing in front of the master systems

display with his arms crossed and his eyebrow lifted in a show of disdain. "If you don't want your punching bags to talk back, you should get your exercise on the holodeck."

"Now I know why people call your species rude."

"Rude? Hardly. Brutally honest, perhaps." Dalkaya glanced toward Rossini, then looked back at Ra-Havreii. "He was right, you know. The specs—"

"I know what the specs say," Ra-Havreii snapped.

"Then you should update them, instead of expecting the rest of us to read your mind."

Ra-Havreii frowned and pretended to adjust something on the MSD. "I'll take that under advisement."

Dalkaya didn't seem to be fooled by the chief engineer's feigned busywork. "While you're at it, vent your angst someplace else."

"Excuse me?" He turned and put on his most intimidating glower. "Need I remind you that you're addressing a superior officer?"

Dalkaya grimaced with contempt. "Sure, pull rank. How's that been working for you? From what I see, every engineer on this ship tenses up at the sight of you. Way to boost morale."

"I won't apologize for being a perfectionist when it comes to this ship."

"A perfectionist they could handle. But you're also a micromanager and a condescending prick. And that's a step too far for most of them. And me."

Puffing out his chest, Ra-Havreii asked, "You want off this ship? Just ask."

"Not at all. I like this ship, and I like its officers and crew." He made a sour appraisal of Ra-Havreii. "Present company excluded."

Ra-Havreii's pulse quickened, and his hands turned

to fists. "Dalkaya, you do understand that insubordination is a court-martial offense."

The Zibalian appeared unfazed. "You want to rip open that bag of troubles? Be my guest. You've pissed in so many people's boots lately, I doubt there are any officers left on this ship who'd convict me on your word alone."

"Really? And just whose wrath have I incurred?"

Dalkaya swung his arm in a gesture that encompassed all of engineering. "Everyone who knows you. They won't say it to your face, but they're starting to hate you for meddling with their work and giving them advice they don't want or need."

"And I'm supposed to believe that not one of them would speak up? That you alone have the courage to speak truth to power?"

A diffident shrug. "Think what you want. But the only reason these people haven't pushed you out an airlock is they're waiting to see who you recommend for deputy chief engineer."

That news caught Ra-Havreii by surprise. He hadn't known that any of his engineers were aware that Commander Sarai had been pressuring him for months to name deputy chiefs in order to establish a clear chain of engineering command succession in the event of emergencies. He had been dragging his heels, mostly to be contrary to Sarai as payback for her spurning him, but he had justified his sloth by claiming that none of the "dilettantes" under his supervision deserved to hold such lofty titles within the department.

But apparently word had gotten out.

He pretended it was a matter of no importance. "I'll decide when I'm ready."

"Well, I'd do it sooner rather than later if I were you. The longer this goes on, the deeper their resentment's going to get. And in case you haven't noticed, you aren't making any new friends on this ship acting like a pompous twit."

And the few I used to have are getting a little more distant each day, he admitted to himself. "Anything else?"

"Yeah. Get your head out of your ass about Melora Pazlar. She dumped you. Deal with it, preferably on your time instead of ours."

Ra-Havreii grabbed Dalkaya by his tunic. "You're outta line, mister!"

A cocky smile. "I'm just trying to help. But if you don't let me go in the next five seconds, there won't be enough of you left for Doctor Ree to stitch back together. *Sir.*"

Maybe he was bluffing. It sure sounded like bravado to Ra-Havreii. But he knew enough about Zibalians to realize that he had no desire to face one in a bare-knuckle brawl. Especially not with a dozen other engineers watching to see what happened next.

He let go of Dalkaya. "You're relieved and confined to quarters until further notice."

"Whatever you say, boss." Dalkaya smoothed the front of his uniform as he backed away toward the nearest turbolift, defiant and cocksure. "Whatever you say."

Ra-Havreii watched the Zibalian depart, then he barked at the other engineers, "What? Back to work!" They all averted their eyes and retreated into their duties.

Alone in front of the MSD, all Ra-Havreii could do was brood.

He resented Dalkaya—not just because the jerk had

been right about all he had said but because, barring a massive on-duty mishap or the public murder of a Federation dignitary, Ra-Havreii was probably going to have to promote him to deputy chief of engineering.

Life sucks.

"Put it up on the companel," Admiral William Riker said. "I want to see the whole grid."

On the other side of Riker's desk, his aide de camp, Lieutenant Ssura, clutched his paws tight around a padd. When the Caitian lieutenant frowned, his whiskers twitched. "I don't think we have time for a full review right now, sir."

"Nonsense. Put it on-screen." Riker reclined his chair as Ssura relayed the latest mission priorities from Starfleet Command to the large companel mounted on the bulkhead. It was a large spreadsheet, with objectives organized by type into rows and assigned by ship into columns. In addition to listing assignments for the *Titan*, which served as Riker's flagship and mobile command post, the grid showed which tasks the Operations Division at Starfleet Command thought should be assigned to the other vessels currently under Riker's command as part of the Alpha Quadrant Frontier Exploration Group, or AQ-FEG.

Using the interface built into his office's desktop, Riker highlighted several items in the schedule. "Why are so many of the planetary surveys assigned to the *Canterbury*?"

Ssura said, "I think the rationale was the recent refit of their sensor suite."

"That's fine, but tasking them with all the surveys has them hopping back and forth all over the Carina Arm. Draft a new schedule that keeps them on a constant outward heading, then reassign whatever surveys don't fit that course to the *Wasp* and the *Ajax*."

Never a complaint or a protest from Ssura, only a compliant nod. "I'll have a new schedule ready for you by the start of alpha shift tomorrow, sir."

"Good." Riker highlighted a handful of different items in the grid. "Am I reading this right, Ssura? Gaseous anomaly surveys in the void between galactic arms?"

His aide leaned close to the companel. "I believe that's what it says, sir."

"Is that what passes for a joke at Starfleet Ops these days? Tasking my flagship with logging gaseous anomalies while sending the *Canterbury* on a possible first-contact mission?"

Perhaps sensing that the rhetorical question was a trap, Ssura considered his reply for a long moment. "I presume you'd like me to reverse those assignments, Admiral?"

"A capital idea, Lieutenant. Make it so."

Ssura noted the order on his padd, then checked the chrono. "Sixty seconds, sir."

Riker sprang from his chair. "One minute? Why didn't you tell me?"

"I tried, sir, but—"

"Move!" He almost trampled his overworked aide on his sprint out the door of his office. Though he suspected Ssura was right behind him, it was hard for Riker to tell because the Caitian's tufted paws were whisper quiet even when running on the carpeted decks of the *Titan*.

It had been a long while since Riker had really needed to run, and as he barreled through the corridors of the *Titan*, he feared that he was starting to feel his age—mostly in his knees, but also in his hips. *Have to ask Ree to take a look at that,* he decided.

Running flat out, he made a wide turn down a broad, high-ceilinged spiral ramp that connected a few of the decks in the *Titan*'s saucer section. The ramp was a nonstandard design element aboard Starfleet vessels, but the variety of alien species who served on the *Titan*, including many nonhumanoids, made its inclusion a necessity rather than a convenience.

"Make a hole, please!" Riker shouted, cueing the junior officers and enlisted personnel ahead of him to stand aside so he could pass in a hurry. It was a perquisite of his rank that he rarely employed, precisely because he had found it more effective to save it for true emergencies such as this one. *Never be the boy who cried "wolf,"* he reminded himself.

At the bottom of the ramp Riker narrowly dodged a collision with computer specialist K'chak'!'op, a massive Pak'shree female whose size and appearance—she reminded Riker of a gigantic four-eyed beetle, except for the flurry of tentacles undulating from either side of her head—made him recoil slightly. "Sorry!" He didn't wait long enough to hear the translation of her storm of angry clicking noises.

A few doors shy of his destination, Riker stopped and took a deep breath. He smoothed the front of his uniform as Lieutenant Ssura stumbled to a halt at his side. "Time?"

"Fifteen seconds, sir."

Affecting a calm demeanor, Riker continued ahead,

through the door, into the *Titan*'s education suite. On the other side had gathered several members of the ship's crew, those who had children enrolled in the on-board school run by T'Pel, the civilian wife of Commander Tuvok. The Vulcan woman was standing just inside the door, and she greeted Riker as he entered. "Welcome, Captain. Your wife is holding a seat for you up front."

"Thank you, T'Pel."

No matter how hard Riker tried not to draw attention, he found it impossible to move about the *Titan*, especially in settings such as this, without becoming the focus, even if only briefly. He smiled at other parents as he walked up the center aisle to the front row. There he settled onto a folding chair next to his wife, Commander Deanna Troi, the *Titan*'s diplomatic officer and head of its counseling division.

She made a show of checking the chrono. "Cut it a bit close this time."

"Nonsense," Riker said. "Wild *targ*s couldn't have kept me away."

The overhead lights dimmed, and a warm spotlight illuminated the small stage. From hidden speakers, classical music filled the room, and a troupe of small bodies garbed in tights and tutus pranced and spun across the stage, mesmerizing in their grace and innocence.

But there was only one who commanded Riker's attention: his daughter, Tasha, who pirouetted across the stage, showing all she had learned of ballet. *Five and a half years old and already she's the most amazing thing I've ever seen,* he marveled.

Deanna took his hand in hers. Like him, she had tears

of joy in her eyes while she watched their daughter float like a sylph in time with a melody stolen from a dream.

Will Riker loved being a Starfleet officer, and he loved exploring the galaxy. But if there were only one thing in life he knew to be true, it was that he loved his wife and daughter more.

Four

There were five words that Brunt had never thought he would entertain without irony: *It's not about the latinum.* If there was one thing every Ferengi grew up to understand, it was the foundational truth that, ultimately, *everything* in life and the universe was about latinum. Yet no matter how many different ways he manipulated the numbers on his latest undertaking, he was unable to justify its trouble or expense purely in the name of profit.

Hunched over the controls of his ship the *Net Gain*, Brunt kept his eyes on the sensor display even as his thoughts wandered through wastelands of self-doubt. Once he had been among the most feared liquidators of the Ferengi Commerce Authority. In recent years he had recovered from the financial reversals of an arms deal gone bad and clawed his way back into the upper echelons of Ferengi society. Now he was a rich and respected figure on Ferenginar, a proud

Magnus-plus-level member of the Ferengi Entrepreneurs Club.

So what am I doing at the ass end of space, lurking alone in the dark between the stars? He thought he had long ago put an end to his spacefaring days. But here he was, ensconced once more on his private ship, seeking out conflict and danger instead of luxuriating in his office, sipping on Slug-o-Cola and counting his profits in between *oo-mox* sessions with all the choicest female companions latinum could rent by the hour. By the numbers, he knew he could never explain this decision to his fellow Ferengi. They would never understand.

This wasn't business. This was personal.

New data appeared on the sensors. The Federation supply ship he was tracking had changed its heading and increased its speed. He adjusted the settings on his helm to keep the *Net Gain* in the freighter's sensor blind spot, so that if they somehow detected him they might mistake him for a sensor echo in their warp eddy.

Most small starships would be hard-pressed to pull off such a trick, but the *Net Gain* was no ordinary vessel. It was packed with improvements Brunt had acquired through years of hard work and judicious investment. Signal-boosted long-range sensors, military-grade encrypted comms, enhanced shields, and a few hidden weapon systems all made the nondescript starhopper more formidable than it appeared.

Its interior upgrades were more obvious. Creature comforts abounded; a wide, soft bunk; replicators programmed with delicacies; and several crates of prime libations concealed beneath scan-proofed deck plates were just a few of the pleasures Brunt had installed to make the *Net Gain* an environment he could stand to live in for months at a time, if necessary.

Not that he had been foolish enough to let hedonism get in the way of survivability—his ship also boasted several pragmatic enhancements: redundant battery arrays, reinforced interior force fields, intruder countermeasures, and spare escape pods, plus a survival module built into the cockpit, which could be ejected separately in the event of an emergency, all contributed to Brunt's peace of mind as he navigated alone into uncharted sectors of space beyond the rimward edge of the United Federation of Planets.

Course change completed, he surveyed the long-range scans of the sector ahead. There were no named systems this far from explored space, just notations from the Federation Galactic Catalog—strings of letters and numbers linked to bare-bones data. Though automated sensor arrays had mapped many of the sectors surrounding local space, little was known about which systems were inhabited—and, of those, which if any were populated by intelligent species.

So where is that supply ship going?

That question was part of what had drawn Brunt so far from his home and business. Sources he trusted to provide reliable information in exchange for hefty bribes had alerted him to the peculiar movements of cargo vessels in this sector. There were no known colonies in this region of space, no cultures advanced enough to engage in trade with the Federation or anyone else. If there had been, the Ferengi would already have sought them out as emerging markets.

Yet here was a ship that could carry millions of metric tons of cargo, the sort of vessel normally tasked with supporting a far-flung colony or starbase, traveling without a convoy or Starfleet escort on a heading into a place it seemed to have no business going. That meant it was either bringing something of value to an unknown port of call, or retrieving something of value from one. Either way that made a ship like this a prime target for pirates and smugglers.

Exactly the sort of people Brunt was looking for.

No one in the Ferengi Entrepreneurs Club had ever asked Brunt how he made his profits. Such questions were considered rude; inquiries of that kind were considered tantamount to attempted theft of trade secrets. How a Ferengi made his latinum was his own affair. So it was that even on Ferenginar very few people knew that Brunt was the proprietor of one of the most successful bounty-hunting operations in the quadrant.

Brunt had started as a lone operator in the *Net Gain*, tracking down criminals to collect the prices on their heads, immediately after he had turned against Gaila, his former partner in the arms-dealing trade. At first it had been easy for Brunt to gain other hoodlums' trust. His own shady reputation had enabled him to move through their ranks as if he were one of them. As a result, few of them had seen his betrayals coming until it was too late. Just like Gaila.

In time Brunt's business expanded. First he took on partners, and then he started to subcontract. Within a few years the former liquidator had transformed his one-man bounty-hunting operation into an interstellar business empire worth over a billion bars of gold-pressed latinum. He preferred not to advertise his role in the business—not because he felt any shame over it, but because violent criminals were prone to seeking retribution, and that was a hassle he wanted to avoid.

It all had gone so well . . . until the day Gaila escaped from prison. Despite having been placed into maximum-security detention on Urwyzden Alpha, the wily Ferengi death merchant had made contact with former employees on the outside, and they had paid exorbitant bribes to guards—and, Brunt suspected, the warden—to effect Gaila's unscheduled early release.

I should have seen this coming, Brunt castigated himself. *Every man has his price.*

Gaila's newfound freedom worried Brunt. What might he do now that he was on the loose? Would he seek revenge on Brunt? Would he spread the word of Brunt's occupation, thereby ensuring that every murder-minded alien in known space would come gunning for him? Or perhaps undermine his social standing on Ferenginar and deprive him of his coveted status as a Magnus-level member of the FEC? If nothing else, news of Gaila's escape from prison would smear Brunt's business reputation, even though keeping the man behind bars had been someone else's responsibility.

It was imperative, Brunt decided, that he track down Gaila before the cunning bastard had a chance to avenge himself, and return him to prison on Urwyzden Alpha.

For the sake of my reputation—not to mention the staggeringly huge bounty on Gaila's head—I will see him delivered back into the hands of the law.

He watched the supply ship speed into the void on the farthest edge of the *Net Gain*'s sensor range. Shadowing it into uncharted space was a gamble, but if, as Brunt suspected, Gaila was haunting this sector looking for easy targets, this was the sort of prey he would choose.

He set his autopilot to a stealth tracking mode and kicked back with a Slug-o-Cola.

I feel lucky. Let's roll the bones and see where they lead.

"Everyone, please grab a seat and settle so we can get started." Theron watched the expedition's two dozen department heads and deputies shuffle past one another as they looked for open seats. The Husnock hall had been laid out like an amphitheater with tiers rising in an arc around a stage, though the expedition had needed to retrofit it with seats designed to accommodate humanoid anatomy. Not all of the seats had fit neatly into the rows, a fact that sometimes made it take longer than Theron would have liked for large groups to assemble.

Waiting beside him was Doctor Kilaris. Out of sight behind the curtains they had draped along either side of the stage were a pair of security guards. Though the guards' presence at a routine staff briefing seemed superfluous to Theron, the expedition operated under strict protocols handed down by some Federation bureaucrat who, despite being more than a thousand light-years away, presumed to know what was best for Theron and his team.

Kilaris nodded at Theron. He looked out at the audience. The last few folks were easing into seats, and the aisles were clear, so it was time to get started.

"Good morning, friends," Theron said. "As promised, we have big news to share." He stepped aside and indicated with a theatrical gesture, "Doctor Kilaris, everyone."

The Vulcan woman stepped to center stage. "Thank you, Doctor Theron." She faced the audience.

"Welcome, esteemed colleagues. Yesterday, members of my team independently confirmed a discovery I made late last week: a hard-copy codex that appears to present Husnock text in parallel with lines written in an ancient dialect of T'Kon." She lifted her chin to cue her deputy, Doctor Cadman Greiss, who activated a holographic projection that filled the space behind her with a semi-transparent representation of facing pages. "As you can see, the page on the left shows Husnock script, while the one on the right is written in the ancient dialect of T'Kon that was excavated eight years ago from an archive on Delphi Ardu IV." She gestured toward Greiss, who called up the next image in the projection: the same pages, with several details highlighted in various colors. "By noting similarities in the patterns of information density and tracking the frequency of syntactic interruption, we have been able to use the T'Kon portions of the codex to perform rough translations of the Husnock text."

A hand shot up from within the audience. Theron took it upon himself to play the part of a moderator. "Yes, a question, Doctor Mukherjee?"

The architectural engineer stood and swept a few strands of her black hair from her face. "Is there a risk that we're giving the Husnock a bit too much credit here?"

Kilaris raised an eyebrow at the query. "Could you be more specific?"

"The codex you uncovered seems to be relatively new, but ancient T'Kon dates back over half a million years. If we presume the Husnock were attempting their own translation of T'Kon, should we allow for the possibility that they *mis*-translated it? And if so, might we then mistranslate the Husnock by comparing it against a factor we know well, such as T'Kon?"

If it bothered Kilaris to be put on the spot by her peers, she hid it well, Theron thought. The Vulcan tilted her head as she considered her response. "That is a risk, one we considered before announcing this discovery. However, from what we have learned about Husnock science, they were an extremely intelligent and technologically sophisticated species. And we have found other codices that seemed to contain translation matrixes, but this was the first that translated a language known to us. Based on the volume of work the Husnock have done in this field, I think it is reasonable for us to conclude that they were experienced and adept at xenolinguistics."

Mukherjee nodded and said as she sat down, "Thank you, Doctor."

"You are most welcome, Doctor." She gave another nod to Greiss, and he switched the holographic projection to a detailed close-up of a section of Husnock text. "Some of the most important elements of our discovery, as mundane as they might seem, are insights into the Husnock's use of punctuation." Kilaris pointed at numerous symbols in the text. "It is our hope that by analyzing the way that they annotate their text, we might learn to parse their syntax and grammar. Because of deficiencies in our understanding of those factors, however, several aspects of this text continue to elude us.

"First, because we have no guide for written Husnock grammar, we cannot be certain the word order in their text matches that of the T'Kon passages they translated. Consequently, we are unable at this time to construct a reliable lexicon of Husnock vocabulary. Second, because we are uncertain whether the codex is a transliteration or an idiomatic translation, our task of—"

A screeching disruptor shot interrupted her presentation.

Theron and everyone else in the room turned toward the rear of the auditorium, from whence the shot had come. Tall brawny humanoids armed with short disruptor rifles and wearing patched-together body armor and battle-scarred helmets charged in through the entrances on either side. In a matter of moments they flanked the seated scientists, none of whom stirred from their seats. Everything went quiet for a second—

Then the expedition's security guards pivoted out from behind the stage curtains and opened fire. It was a brave move but a stupid one. Their phasers, set to stun, caromed off the intruders' armor. Then the intruders returned fire, overwhelming the two security agents in barrages of disruptor pulses of unmistakably lethal setting. The last few shots ripped through the men as they crumpled to the stage, both dead before they hit the floor.

From the rear of the armored group came one figure, taller than the rest. His helmet was marked with short crimson streaks in orderly rows. Theron recognized them as the hash marks soldiers used to boast of their kills in combat. This man's helmet bore more marks than Theron could count in a glance as the decorated intruder approached the stage.

Theron stepped forward to meet him. "I'm Doctor Maxwell Theron, head of this expedition, and I surrender on behalf—"

He swatted Theron aside with a crushing backhand slap. The blow knocked Theron off his feet. He landed hard on his back, stunned and afraid for his life. In a guttural voice the painted one rasped, "Not here for you." He said to his men as he pointed at Kilaris, "Take her."

Two of his men seized Kilaris's arms. Proving her genius, she didn't struggle.

Then the leader looked at the department heads and pointed again. First at Doctor Gav glasch Pek. "Grab that one." Then at the expedition's resident computer experts, the Bynar pair 010-101. "And them." He stomped back up the aisle to the exit.

More of the thugs dragged Pek and the Bynars out behind Kilaris, who looked back at Theron, her dark eyes betraying not even an ounce of fear.

For a moment, Theron hoped the worst was over. Then he heard the painted leader growl a parting order to the rest of his men.

"Kill the others."

The command deck of the argosy *Silago-Ekon* was bathed in green light for two reasons: its Orion commanding officer, Nilat, found it restful for her eyes, and she liked that it made most of the members of her multispecies crew look more like her. Not that being painted with emerald light could hide the cranial ridges of her Klingon first officer, K'mjok, or the finlike ears of the Tiburonian communications specialist Ninivus. And Nilat was fairly certain that the coal-black skin, eyes, and teeth of their Nalori pilot Ang-Harod would look the same in any light.

All the same, every little bit helped.

She swiveled her command chair toward K'mjok, who stood hunched over the hooded sensor display, his stern face creased by a perpetual scowl. "XO, status."

K'mjok straightened as he faced her. "The merc ship just beamed up its strike team."

"Any sign they've detected us?"

The Klingon shook his head. "Negative."

"Well done, XO." Nilat made a mental note to ask management to pay K'mjok a bonus share for recommending an effective strategy to conceal the *Silago-Ekon* during this reconnaissance. On his advice they had switched to low-power mode and parked the ship above the planet's northern pole, where the magnetic fields from the planet's core would mask it from nearly all sensors. So far they seemed to have evaded being noticed by the Federation research team on the surface and the recently arrived mercenary vessel, which had just staged a commando assault against the scientists.

Ninivus looked up from the comms console. He held one hand over the ear in which he wore a wireless transceiver unit. "Commander. Receiving a distress signal from the expedition."

"Maintain comm silence and translate."

The Tiburonian furrowed his graying eyebrows. "The expedition's chief of security is signaling Starfleet with a priority alert. She says they've been attacked by a force of unknown origin. Four of their senior people have been kidnapped, and as many as twenty have been killed."

Nilat kept her expression blank, but inside she seethed. *Amateurs. Sloppy and stupid. If my people had struck first, we could've gotten in and out without bloodshed, and been light-years away before anyone knew what happened.* She nodded at Ninivus. "Monitor that channel for a reply. XO, watch long-range sensors for responding vessels."

Her weapons officer, a scar-faced Balduk named Trunch, looked up from his station. "Commander, merc ship breaking orbit. Tracking their heading on passive sensors."

"Assess their tactical strength."

He grimaced at the XO. "Same distortion that hides us, blinds us."

Even without looking Nilat felt K'mjok tense at the criticism. The Klingon and the Balduk had detested each other since the day they met a year earlier, and it had been all Nilat could do to keep them from turning her bridge into a brawlers' pit. She glared at K'mjok, a silent warning for him not to be baited, then she aimed her withering look at the Balduk. Both men backed down, deferring to her authority.

Not bad for "a skinny girl" my father said would "never amount to anything."

She rose from her chair to stand in the center of the command deck. "Helm, pursuit course. Keep the mercs at the far edge of our sensor range, and put us in their baffles."

"Pursuit course, ghost protocol," answered Ang-Harod, her long and graceful fingers executing the new heading. "Laid in and engaged."

To a stranger's eye the crew of the *Silago-Ekon* might look like undisciplined rabble, but to watch them in action was to realize they were all seasoned professionals. It gave Nilat reason to hope they might yet salvage this botched assignment.

As she sat, K'mjok sidled up to her. "Commander. A question?"

"Speak your mind, XO."

"The mercenaries are gone. The colony on the surface remains vulnerable. Why not continue our mission as planned?"

She turned a weary eye toward K'mjok, who still wore the black leather uniform and metallic sash of an empire from which he had long since been expelled. "Because the next phase of our mission would have been to abduct key personnel from the expedition and extract vital intel from them." She looked at the retreating alien ship on the main viewscreen. "Our rivals must have come here with the same plan—and I'm betting they took the very people we need to question. But even if they haven't, I don't want to risk being in orbit when Starfleet arrives."

The dishonored Klingon expatriate huffed. "So what is our plan now? Follow the hired guns and watch them claim the prize we came for?"

"Don't be such a pessimist, K'mjok. We're going to let the mercs do the dirty work. Then, once they've led us to the reward we must both be chasing, we will take it from them, and leave their burning corpses behind for Starfleet."

Five

The turbolift doors opened to reveal the bridge of the *Titan*. Standing in wait for Admiral Riker was his aide, Lieutenant Ssura. The Caitian hurried to catch up as Riker strode past toward Captain Vale's ready room. Riker held out his hand. "What do we have available?"

Ssura fell in beside Riker and put a padd into his hand. "Just the *Titan* and its AQ frontier ships, sir. The *Ajax* is the farthest out, but the *Canterbury* and the *Wasp* can rendezvous with us in sixteen hours, en route."

Riker looked up from the padd and glanced toward the bridge's center seat, in front of which stood Commander Tuvok, holding the conn. The admiral nodded once at Tuvok, who returned the simple greeting. Then the ready room door slid open ahead of Riker, and he and Ssura proceeded inside.

Awaiting them in the ready room were Vale and Sarai. The captain was seated at her desk, and Sarai stood at ease in front of it. Both officers looked up at Riker's brusque entrance. "Sorry to barge in, Captain," Riker said. He handed the padd to Vale. "But time's a factor."

"So you said." Vale, whose penchant for frequent changes to her hair color had most recently manifested itself in a multicolored dye job whose subtly layered swirls evoked the churning mists of a nebula, reviewed the report with concern. "Twenty dead, four abducted. Do we have any intel on the suspects?"

"Not yet," Ssura said. "The expedition's chief of security says the intruders disabled the camp's sensors, starting with the visual. So all we have are a few witness statements saying they were big, wore body armor and helmets, and carried military-style weapons."

Sarai asked, "How did they escape?"

"A ship in orbit," Ssura said. "It might have been picked up by one or more of the orbital sensor relays, unless they disabled those too. But if there are scans of their ship we'll be able to download that data from the relays once we reach the system."

Riker added, "All three of our sister ships are joining us, though *Ajax* might be a bit late."

Sarai looked perplexed. "Four ships? That response seems excessive, sir."

"Trust me, it's not." To Vale he continued, "We'll meet up with the *Canterbury* and the *Wasp* en route, then proceed together to—" He realized he didn't know the name of their destination. "Ssura, where'd you say we're going?"

"The report identifies it as FGC-779852c."

"Does it have a name that's more user-friendly?"

The Caitian shook his head. "None on file, sir."

"Then I'm giving it one, just for convenience. Let's call it . . . Rishon."

His suggestion stoked Vale's curiosity. "Why 'Rishon,' sir?"

Riker drew a breath as he exhumed dark memories. "Twenty years ago, while I was serving as first officer on the *Enterprise*-D, we answered a distress call from the planet Delta Rana IV. By the time we arrived, the entire planet had been laid waste—except for one small plot of grass and a single house in the middle of it. We beamed down and found two people living there, an old married couple, Kevin and Rishon Uxbridge. They claimed to be the last survivors of an unprovoked attack by a species he called the Husnock.

"But neither they nor their house were what they seemed. Kevin wasn't human, he was an energy being known as a Douwd, and he had powers on par with the Q. He confessed to us that after the Husnock destroyed the planet—and killed his wife, Rishon—he exterminated the entire Husnock species with a thought. Fifty billion of them, dead in an instant."

The first officer remained confused. "Forgive me, sir, but what does that have to do with the expedition? Or the kidnappings?"

"Uxbridge described the Husnock as 'a species of hideous intelligence,'" Riker said. "And even though he rendered them extinct in a single moment, he left behind all that they had made. Their entire civilization. Dozens of colonized worlds. A fleet of starships and a network of support facilities. Plus a stockpile of the most devastating munitions ever devised. All lying abandoned somewhere in unexplored sectors of the Alpha Quadrant, waiting to be found. If the arsenal of the Husnock falls into the wrong hands, countless lives will be in danger."

Vale put the pieces together with a grim nod. "And the expedition that got attacked—they were excavating a Husnock planet?" Noting Riker's nod of confirmation, Vale frowned. "Which means the scientists who were taken must know something that their abductors think will help them take control of the Husnock's weapons."

"That's the current thinking at Starfleet Command."

An anxious look passed between Vale and Sarai. Then the captain asked, "Mission priorities, Admiral?"

"For now, our chief objective is the rescue and safe return of all four abducted members of the expedition. You'll get their dossiers in your briefing packets. Our secondary mission is to arrest their kidnappers before they can acquire Husnock technology."

That proposition met with a dubious look from Sarai. "And if they do acquire Husnock weapons, vessels, or munitions?"

"Then we have orders to deprive them of said plunder, by means of whatever force proves necessary. I suspect there are some at Starfleet Command who'd prefer we capture any Husnock technology intact—but I'll be just as happy to see it all destroyed."

"Understood, sir," Vale said. "Number One, summon department heads for a mission briefing, and have the helm take us to Rishon at maximum warp. And start running battle drills at your discretion. If we're going to meet resistance, I want to be ready."

A quick nod from Sarai. "Aye, sir." The trim Efrosian woman turned on her heel and left the ready room at a quick step. She started snapping out orders the moment she set foot on the bridge, even before the ready room door closed behind her.

Riker said to Ssura, "Relay my orders to the *Ajax*, the *Canterbury*, and the *Wasp*. Make sure their commanders know that once our fleet assembles, Captain Vale will have operational command of the battle group."

"Aye, sir." Ssura made his own exit from the ready room.

Riker and Vale faced each other across her desk. She shook her head. "Why do I get the feeling we're about to wind up in the middle of a really ugly crossfire?"

He shrugged. "Beats cataloguing gaseous anomalies."

Vale offered a resigned smile. "I sure as hell hope so."

The kidnappers were as brusque as they were inarticulate. Apparently unwilling to trust their hostages to walk with dignity into a holding cell, the helmeted thugs insisted on pushing their captives inside their vessel's cramped and filthy brig. Kilaris was the first one over its force field threshold. She stumbled as she recovered her balance, then she sidestepped out of the path of the Bynar pair, who were shoved in behind her.

The last prisoner, Doctor Pek, struggled in his abductors' grasp. "Unhand me, you troglodytes! You vermin! I—" A gut-punch from one of the brutes silenced the Tellarite's rant. They hurled him into the cell. He landed on his belly and lay doubled over and gasping.

A low hum filled the compartment as the cell's force field activated. Kilaris approached the invisible barrier. She sensed its presence from the way the fine hairs on her forearms bent toward it. Pek grumbled curses from the deck and the Bynars huddled in a corner, cowed and silent. Kilaris eyed their captors from behind a mask of cold calm. Inside, her repressed primitive Vulcan nature raged, eager to exact vengeance on these murderers of her colleagues and her lover, Doctor Theron. It would be unseemly, she knew, to express such raw emotions; to give them voice would go against a lifetime of Vulcan philosophical instruction and discipline.

It would be illogical to deny that the feelings existed. But she refused to be ruled by them. She would let logic guide her actions. And if the time came that she needed her primitive side to bolster her strength, she would harness her dark passenger and make it serve her.

All in good time. Right now, I need more information.

The tall one who wore the decorated helmet entered and conferred with a pair of his men. The others' body language made it clear to Kilaris that they were subordinate to the painted one. If there was anything to be learned, it would come from confronting the leader.

"Kidnapping us will not profit you," she said to him, interrupting his conversation.

He looked at her. "Wrong, Vulcan. You four make us rich."

Easily distracted. Good to know. "Neither Starfleet nor the Federation will negotiate with terrorists. How do you expect to collect our ransom?"

The leader approached the force field. "Not ransom. Put to work."

"What makes you think any of us will work for you?"

"Work or die. Choose, Vulcan."

She affected a dubious mien. "If you kill us, we cannot do whatever work it is you expect of us. Perhaps you should consider a different incentive."

He leaned closer, until the edge of his helmet crackled

against the force field. "Not quick death, Vulcan. Slow. Painful. One piece at a time."

"Are you sure you possess the resolve to make good on such a threat?"

The leader bellowed, "You call me *coward*?" He pointed at the Bynars. "Bynars cowards! No *guramba*!"

"I understand now. You're a Nausicaan. That explains much."

He pulled off his helmet to reveal his ridged pate, sunken eyes, and protruding fanglike tusks, all framed by a matted tangle of coarse black hair. "You know nothing, Vulcan."

"I know your kind have long been notorious as troublemakers and criminals for hire—and that was *before* the Borg sterilized your homeworld."

The Nausicaan seemed to get taller, as if he were swelling with anger. "You call us names. Not change who we are." He barked an order at his men in their native tongue, and the others removed their helmets, revealing they were also Nausicaans. Then the leader aimed his fury at Kilaris. "I am Slokar, leader. We are Patriots of the Wind. Stand for all Nausicaans."

Pek struggled back to his feet and stood beside Kilaris, facing Slokar. "How does killing our friends and kidnapping us help you 'stand for all Nausicaans'?"

Slokar ground his teeth and his tusks. "Watch you long time. Know what you find. We find thing, too. Need what you know."

The vagueness of his boast gave Kilaris pause. "What have you found?"

"Husnock ships. Weapons."

A snort from Pek. "And who are you gonna kidnap with those?"

"Conquer new worlds. Restore Nausicaans' pride. Take back our independence." He pointed at Kilaris and Pek. "You help us."

Kilaris refused to be bullied. "And if we refuse?"

"We cut you. An ear. A finger. Your soft bits. Keep cutting until we know how many pieces it takes to *change your mind*."

Six

Riker arrived on the bridge of the *Titan* in time to watch the last few seconds of warp-stretched stars on the main viewscreen snap back into static points as the ship dropped out of warp speed.

Timing is everything, he mused.

Vale was in the center seat, reviewing information on the tactical monitor to her left. At the forward consoles were the flight control officer, Lieutenant Commander Aili Lavena, and the operations officer, Lieutenant Commander Sariel Rager. Commander Tuvok manned the tactical console, and Lieutenant Commander Keru stood watch at the security panel. Sarai was at the far side of the bridge, conferring with Lieutenant Commander Melora Pazlar at the sciences console.

The first person to notice Riker's arrival on the bridge was its engineering liaison officer, Lieutenant Torvig. The Choblik inclined his deerlike head in a humble greeting, and Riker nodded in return as he moved toward Vale. The ship's captain swiveled to face him. "Admiral."

"Status, Captain?"

"Two minutes from orbit. *Canterbury* and *Wasp* are roughly five minutes behind us. Keru is confirming beam-down coordinates with the expedition's chief of security." She swiveled a few degrees farther to look aft. "Tuvok, any sign of the attackers' ship?"

"Negative, Captain. Short- and long-range scans are both clear. However, we should be aware of a sensor blind spot above the planet's northern magnetic pole. Interference from its larger moon's magnetic field means we must rely on visual sensors for that region."

"Noted," Vale said. "Are visual scans showing anything above the pole?"

"Not at this time," Tuvok said.

Now at Vale's side, Riker said, "I'd prefer to lead the away mission, if you don't mind."

"Not at all, Admiral. Just as long as you take adequate protection."

"I *was* planning on taking a phaser."

Vale fixed him with a look of mild rebuke. "No fewer than three armed guards. Sir."

That seemed excessive to Riker. "Two, including Keru."

"We're not haggling, Admiral. If you want to leave my ship to enter an unsecured area, we'll do it by the book or not at all." In the moment that followed her ultimatum, all Riker heard on the bridge was the soft music of feedback tones and the hush of bated breath.

He acquiesced with a dip of his chin. "Aye, Captain. Three armed escorts."

"Thank you." Vale stood and stepped toward the forward

consoles. "Ops, hail the commanders of the *Wasp* and the *Canterbury*. Tell them to assume antipodal high-orbit positions and to keep an eye on long-range sensor contacts. Helm, take us into a low orbit optimized to provide tactical support for the away team in case they need it."

Lavena and Rager overlapped each other's responses of "Aye, Captain."

Returning to her seat, Vale said, "Number One, assign an away team for the admiral."

Sarai left her huddled conference with Pazlar and moved to an open console along the aft bulkhead. Calling up personnel rosters, she said, "Lieutenant Commander Keru, who do you recommend for the admiral's protection detail?"

"Sortollo, Denken, and Krotine," the security chief said.

"Have them meet you in transporter room one in five minutes." Sarai looked upward as she addressed the computer. "Bridge to Doctor Ree and Lieutenant Eviku. Report to transporter room one with tricorders, on the double. Bridge out." The first officer turned to face Riker. "Your team will meet you—"

"In transporter room one," Riker cut in. "I caught that, thank you."

"Do you have any questions about the away team assignments, sir?"

Riker shook his head. "No, it seems self-explanatory. Keru leads the criminal investigation. Doctor Ree gathers forensic evidence. Sortollo, Denken, and Krotine watch my back, and I supervise the mission and act as the point of contact with the expedition's leader pro tem." As an afterthought he asked, "Will you be joining us, Commander?"

"Not unless you or the captain orders it, sir."

"Then we're set. Good work, Commander." Riker turned to follow Keru into the turbolift, but a subtle nod from Vale made it clear she wanted to speak with him in her ready room. He acknowledged her signal and changed course to fall in behind her.

They stepped inside her sanctum—which, not so long ago, had been his—and waited for the door to slide closed behind Riker. Safe from eavesdropping, they both visibly relaxed. "Admiral, can I ask why you want to lead the away mission?"

He appreciated that she hadn't questioned him in front of her crew. "If I'm to be honest, this mission feels a bit . . . *personal* to me. I was there when we found the Uxbridges. I saw what the Husnock's weapons could do." His memory drifted back to that sad mission more than twenty years earlier. "Part of the reason Starfleet went looking for the remains of the Husnock civilization was because Captain Picard and I both knew what would happen if the wrong people found it. Jean-Luc even asked for permission to take the *Enterprise* toward the outer rim in search of whatever the Husnock left behind. But Starfleet decided we were needed elsewhere."

Vale shook her head. "What was it like to confront a being that single-handedly exterminated an entire species?"

"Terrifying. Heartbreaking. The worst part was how much he hated himself for what he had done. He had so much power, but he held it in check. Then, in a moment of grief and rage he snapped. It could have happened to any of us. But when he snapped, billions died. I can't imagine what it must feel like to carry that kind of guilt."

The overhead comm beeped, and Sarai's voice filtered

down from the speaker. *"Captain, the* Canterbury *and the* Wasp *have dropped out of warp and are assuming their positions in high orbit. Commander Lavena confirms we've entered orbit above the expedition site, and Commander Rager informs me that Admiral Riker's away team is ready to deploy."*

"Thank you, Number One. The admiral's on his way. Vale out." The channel closed with a barely audible click. Vale mustered a wan smile. "Time to get this show on the road."

"Be ready to break orbit fast." Riker backed toward the door. "As soon as we have a lead on who took the scientists and where they're headed, we're going after them."

Every member of the *Titan*'s away team except Keru was in motion the second they were free of the transporter beam. The Trill chief of security took a moment to survey the area and get his bearings. He had reviewed maps of the Husnock city and the layout of the expedition's camp, but now he was matching up the ideas of landmarks and structures with their realities. He had often found it beneficial to take a moment such as this before plunging headlong into action.

He watched Doctor Ree move through the ranks of the grieving expedition members, many of whom now had eyes bloodshot from crying over their slain friends and peers. He showed special attention to anyone who appeared to have been injured. The Pahkwa-thanh physician seemed not to notice the unease his bipedal reptilian form provoked among many of those whom he sought to help. Those he would heal recoiled when he drew near, as if they feared he might devour them rather than dress their wounds.

Admiral Riker, meanwhile, cut around the throng and made his way toward the expedition's command tents. Flanking him were *Titan* security officers Lieutenant Feren Denken, a Matalinian bruiser with a cybernetic right arm, and Lieutenant Gian Sortollo, one of the most cunning and suspicious humans Keru had ever met. Backing them up was enlisted security guard Ellec Krotine, a golden-skinned Boslic whose violet hair was pulled into a tight ponytail, emphasizing her prominent brow ridges and cheekbones.

Lingering not far from the beam-down point were Lieutenants Torvig and Eviku. The Choblik engineer gamboled in a circle as he took readings with his tricorder; the Arkenite xenobiologist pivoted in a tight circle while he did the same, his three-lobed head ringed by his slim-profile *anlac'ven*, a device that helped the aquatic-born xenobiologist maintain his balance and equilibrium on land and in zero gravity.

Keru knew from the original distress call that an attack had occurred in a nearby auditorium. Moving about the site, he located that building and assessed its tactical weaknesses and strengths. Then he formed a hypothesis for how its attackers had approached it without being intercepted by the expedition's security forces—who looked to be every bit as ineffectual as Keru had feared they would be. Patterns of disruptor damage on building exteriors and patches of open ground enabled him to trace the kidnappers' route of retreat. At the end of it, the trail went dead, just as he had suspected it would. *They beamed out from here.*

He heard footsteps and turned, his hand ready to reach for his phaser. Then he saw it was Eviku, and he relaxed. "Do you have any leads?"

"I might, sir." The Arkenite turned his tricorder so Keru could see its display. "I spoke with some of the witnesses. A few of them had high-resolution scanners comparable to our tricorders. After downloading and analyzing scans they made of the attackers, I believe we have credible evidence that the kidnappers were all Nausicaans."

It sounded plausible to Keru, but he had learned never to trust first impressions. "Good work, Lieutenant. But let's look for corroborating evidence before we—"

"Sir," exclaimed Torvig. The squat Choblik trotted to a clumsy halt between brawny Keru and wiry Eviku. With one of his bionic hands he passed a small metallic gadget to Keru, who examined it as Torvig explained, "It's a Nausicaan-made surveillance device. It appears to be linked to several others of the same design, each positioned at regular intervals around the expedition site's perimeter."

Keru noted the smug look on Eviku's face but refused to acknowledge it. The security chief handed the gadget back to Torvig. "Good find, Tor. But Nausicaan gear is pretty common on the black market, so before we—"

"I scanned it for genetic material," Torvig interrupted. "I found only Nausicaan DNA. Its rate of cellular decay suggests the traces are less than six hours old."

Now there was no avoiding Eviku's proud *I told you so* stare. Keru regarded the slender man with a feigned frown. "It would appear that the kidnappers were Nausicaan."

"Really? You don't say, sir."

Turning back toward Torvig, Keru asked, "If the Nausicaans have been watching this site long enough that they had to put in spy gear, what does that tell you, Tor?"

"That they were looking for something in particular." Bouncing forward with excitement, Torvig pointed at his tricorder data. "Or some*one*. The surveillance devices' parameters were calibrated to monitor and identify the unique signal of each expedition member's implanted bio-transponder. With that information, they could have known when all of the abductees were gathered in one place and therefore easier to take with a single action."

The more Keru learned, the greater he perceived the danger to be.

He tapped his combadge. "Keru to *Titan*."

Captain Vale answered, *"Go ahead, Commander."*

"Captain, we have evidence to suggest the perpetrators were Nausicaans. Well armed, by the look of this gear. I suggest we start scanning the planet's surface, this system, and the surrounding sector for any traces known to be associated with Nausicaan starships."

"Noted. Anything else to report?"

"Not yet, Captain. We'll keep you posted."

"See that you do," Vale said. *"Titan out."*

Keru faced Torvig and Eviku. "Follow me. We need to find the admiral."

They returned to the center of the expedition site, then used Riker's combadge signal to find their way to his side, inside the main tent of the expedition's administrative headquarters. At the far end of the temporary shelter, Riker was huddled in a corner with the expedition's chief of security, a Grazerite male named Sukorn-Eesha. Massive and hirsute, Sukorn-Eesha belonged to an ethnic minority of Grazerites whose males sported great curved horns above their ears, and his baritone carried even across wide-open distances.

"We just didn't have enough time to react," Sukorn-Eesha said to Riker. "By the time my guards in the auditorium triggered the alert, the kidnapping was already in progress. And the intruders were gone before the rest of my men reached the scene."

Keru inserted himself into the circle of conversation without regard for decorum. "Mister Sukorn, do you know if there was any link between the four scientists who were taken?"

"They were all part of the same project: unraveling the Husnock language."

Riker rolled with the new direction of inquiry. "Was that project the reason for their gathering in the auditorium?"

The Grazerite nodded. "Two of them were announcing a major breakthrough. Half the camp's been buzzing about it, but until yesterday we'd had no idea that Kilaris had found a Husnock translation of a text written in a language known to Federation science. Rumor had it she was about to make the entire Husnock language parsable by the universal translator."

That revelation widened Riker's eyes. "Would that have helped the teams working to reverse-engineer Husnock technology?"

Torvig cut in, "Almost certainly, sir."

Riker looked at Keru. "Do you think the Nausicaans knew what Kilaris and the others were working on?"

"Yes, sir. And I think they wanted it for themselves." He showed Riker the device Torvig had brought him. "They've been using a ring of these gadgets to spy on the camp. No way to know for how long. But it's a good bet they knew who they were taking, and why."

"Then we need to get after them, as soon as we can."

Sukorn-Eesha stepped forward. "Excuse me, I hate to impose, but—" He looked with great sadness toward the auditorium. "Our dead deserve to be repatriated to their kith and kin. Not buried or scattered here, strangers on an alien rock."

Riker's aspect turned sympathetic. "Of course. Do you have specific postmortem instructions for any of the victims?"

"For all of them. It was a mission requirement."

"Prepare them for stasis transport. We'll beam them up and secure them on the *Titan* until we can make the necessary arrangements to send them home."

The Grazerite bowed his head. "Thank you, Admiral. Most kind."

In a confidential tone, Riker said to Keru, "Have Doctor Ree see to the details."

"Aye, sir."

Keru's combadge chirped, and Captain Vale's voice issued from it a moment later. *"Titan to Keru. We detect no Nausicaan ships on the planet's surface, but we've picked up a faint trail of subspatial disturbance whose energy signature suggests one or more vessels made high-warp departures from this system in the last day."*

Riker hijacked the discussion. "Captain, do you have a clear heading to follow?"

"We do, sir."

"And what's the *Ajax*'s ETA?"

A short pause, then Vale answered, *"Nine minutes."*

"Plot a pursuit course for the Nausicaans," Riker said, "then beam up the victims of the attack, directly into long-term stasis. Inform the *Ajax* they'll be responsible for defending the planet after we break orbit, because we'll be taking the *Wasp* and the *Canterbury* with us."

"Yes, sir. Titan *out."*

After the channel closed, Riker looked Keru in the eye. "Get the away team ready for immediate beam up, Commander—because the chase is on."

Seven

If there was anything better than stumbling upon a fortune whose doors were standing wide open and undefended, Gaila of Ferenginar had never seen it.

It was the luckiest of lucky breaks and Gaila knew it. He had been traveling with the same dozen rank-smelling thugs for the past year inside the *Tahmila*, a rattletrap of a ship, a piece of junk so beat-up and neglected that it made the slums of Orion Prime look like the gilded halls and jeweled boulevards of the Divine Treasury. The cramped smuggling vessel reeked of fruit-scented narcotic smoke, spoiled food, synthehol, and urine. Gaila had yet to visit a planet or starport so dismal that the *Tahmila* couldn't make it look good.

He landed his decrepit ship inside an open docking bay of the mysterious facility, which he had found floating in the interstellar void, completely by chance.

Well, not completely. He had followed the dim-witted Pakleds to it. The chubby plodders weren't good for much, but they had a knack for sniffing out things worth stealing. And if there was one thing Gaila excelled at, it was robbing other thieves of their paydays.

Time for a quick check of the sensors. Gaila confirmed the docking bay's force field had engaged as soon as the *Tahmila* had touched down, and that the bay had filled with breathable air to a safe degree of pressure. *Can't be too careful.*

He switched on the intraship comm. "We're here," Gaila said. He liked the way his voice echoed inside the ship when he used its PA system. "Get out of your bunks and gear up."

From the aft corridors came the thuds, clatter, and grumblings of thugs roused from short intoxicated slumbers. The first one to join Gaila at the exit ramp was Marlik, a Brikar mercenary who was considered a runt among his species and a giant among most others. With skin that looked and felt like stone, and a body density that let him shake off most disruptor and phaser shots, Marlik was one of the best investments Gaila had ever made.

Next to arrive was Zehga, the gang's heavy-weapons expert. As a Gorn he was the slowest moving of the bunch, which was part of why he preferred ordnance that packed a wallop. If he couldn't hit with precision, he would destroy as much as possible and hope to count his foes among the collateral damage.

Close behind him was the unlikely duo of Hurq, a black-maned Chalnoth whose temper could be counted on to spark a brawl in any drinking establishment he might visit, and Zinos, an Argelian quick-draw artist who loved to end the fights Hurq started by gunning down strangers. Backing them up were half a dozen assorted lowlifes whose names Gaila didn't care to learn.

The last to answer Gaila's summons was the one he and the others needed in order to bypass the station's security and escape the confines of the docking bay: N'chk, a Kaferian whose insectoid clickings were nigh impossible to understand, but whose talent for manipulating computers was unsurpassed. He shouldered past the rest of the gang and took the lead down the ramp and across the bay to the locked door opposite the force field.

N'chk hacked it open in a matter of seconds, then stood aside to let Gaila lead the others inside the station.

Most of the facility was empty of living creatures. Gaila could see at once that what the Pakleds had stumbled upon was an automated factory, one that manufactured high-quality military-grade munitions. It was a veritable latinum mine.

And it was about to be all his.

Gaila and his goon squad turned a corner to find a band of Pakleds shuffling like incontinent geriatrics among the mountainous pallets of torpedoes, missiles, and bombs. The Ferengi ringleader pointed at the slug-witted scavengers and told his thugs, "Round 'em up."

The rest was fast and cruel.

A single wide-dispersal shot from Zehga's arm-cannon stunned half the Pakleds and sent the others waddling for cover. It took only a few minutes for Gaila's crew to round up the few Pakleds who were still conscious and march them at gunpoint to stand before the Ferengi.

As dumb as the Pakleds looked, they understood Gaila's gesture commanding them to kneel. Humbled, the craftiest of the dimwits glowered up at him. "What you want?"

"Your inventory, for starters." Gaila picked up a Pakled padd and surveyed its contents. "By the Blessed Exchequer! You really did strike the mother lode here, didn't you?" He perused page after page of itemized reports compiled by the jowly morons. Then he looked down at the one who had spoken to him. "You the one in charge here?"

"Yes," the Pakled said.

"What's your name?"

"Cherbegrod. Captain of *Gomjar*."

Gaila motioned for Cherbegrod to rise. "Stand up." The Pakled straightened to loom tall over Gaila—who cut the Pakled commander down to size by punching him in the groin. Cherbegrod wailed like a baby, then collapsed to the deck in a fetal position and whimpered. "Not to be a nitpicker, but from now on, *I'm* the one in charge here. And you—" He punished the overgrown infant with a kick in the ribs. "You're no longer welcome."

Zinos sidled over to Gaila. "Want me to ventilate 'em?"

"No, they're harmless." Gaila shouted to his Brikar henchman, "Marlik, help Hurq put 'em back on their ship—and make sure they all leave."

The two bruisers herded the Pakleds out of the warehouse. It took four of the Pakleds to carry their stricken and humiliated captain. Gaila watched them leave, then he turned to Zinos. "Take a deep breath, my friend." He inhaled with theatrical exaggeration. "Smell that?"

The mustached Argelian sniffed the air. "Metal lubricant?"

"No, you dolt. That's the sweet smell of profit. And as of now . . . it's all ours."

A heavy bundle of synthetic fabric landed in Kilaris's lap. She unfolded enough of it to see it was a heavy-duty environmental suit. Then she looked up at the Nausicaan who had thrown it at her as if it and she were both garbage. "I presume you wish me to put this on."

"Get dressed, Vulcan. We land soon." He punctuated his order by resting his hand on the grip of his disruptor pistol, which was holstered on the outside of his own environmental suit.

Kilaris saw nothing to gain by antagonizing or resisting her captors' orders, so she took off her shoes before donning the loose-fitting pressure suit over her regular clothes. "Where are we going that I'll need an environmental suit?"

"No-name planet. No air. Wear suit or die."

It was a crude but eminently persuasive rationale. Kilaris finished securing the suit and checked its built-in components. Its air reserves were full, and its radiation shields were fresh. The tool pockets, however, all had been emptied. She gave the Nausicaans credit—they weren't foolish enough to give prisoners anything that could aid their escape. "When do I get a helmet?"

"Airlock." The Nausicaan took her by the arm and pulled her from her cell. "Move."

He marched her down one corridor, then another. Doctor Pek and the Bynars had already been stuffed into environmental suits—an oversized garment for Pek, and child-sized outfits for 010 and 101. The trio stood in a huddle, watched by two Nausicaans who were also suited up for an EVA mission. Everyone's gear, captors' and prisoners' alike, looked well worn.

Slokar stood at the airlock control panel. "Brace for landing," he said.

Kilaris and her peers all found handholds along the bulkheads. Through the decks came the roar of braking thrusters. The ship lurched, rattling its hull plates against its spaceframe. An internal comm channel indicator lit up on the airlock controls as a voice spilled from its speaker: *"Bridge to Slokar. Down and secure."*

"Good," Slokar said. "Go to low-power mode. Watch long-range sensors." He looked up as the overhead lights dimmed. Then he nodded at his men, who handed EVA suit helmets to Kilaris and her colleagues. Once the prisoners' helmets were on, the Nausicaans checked their seals, then tested their transceivers. Pek's was a tricky fit; his porcine snout pressed against the faceplate—a condition that Kilaris imagined must be uncomfortable.

The Nausicaans took turns guarding Kilaris and company while their comrades fixed their own helmets into place. Slokar was the last to put on his helmet. His voice issued from the transceiver circuits inside Kilaris's helmet—and, she reasoned, everyone else's as well. *"We go single file."* He pointed at the Nausicaan who had rousted Kilaris from her cell. *"Varoh leads."* A sweeping gesture at the prisoners. *"Then you. We follow. Run and we leave you here to die."*

On that cheerful note Slokar opened the inner airlock door and ushered everyone inside. As the inner door closed, Pek asked in an aggrieved tone over the suits' open channel, *"Why land the ship? Don't you people know how to use transporters?"*

"*Too much radiation,*" Varoh said. "*Scrambles signals. No transporters. Scanners and comms only over short distances.*" He drew his weapon as Slokar depressurized the airlock.

The outer door rolled open and disappeared inside the ship's hull. Outside stretched a vista of rock formations sculpted by the wind into bizarre organic twists and spires. Dust clouds raced across the barren, rugged landscape. Overhead yawned a sky streaked with bands of green and violet, and dominated by the majestic presence of a ringed gas-giant planet.

That must be the source of the radiation, Kilaris realized.

Varoh stepped outside and led the prisoners along the jagged edge of a cliff, below which lay a precipitous drop into fathomless darkness. Kilaris stayed close to the point man because there was no trail here that she could perceive. Each step they took sent pebbles and larger stones tumbling over the edge into the abyss. One misstep would likely be more than enough to condemn her or one of her peers to the same fate.

Pek remained impatient and irascible. "*Where are we?*"

"*Quiet,*" Slokar said.

"*What are we even doing here?*" The Tellarite's temper frayed. "*Tell me you didn't kidnap us just to take us on the galaxy's worst nature hike.*"

Slokar matched Pek's ire. "*Keep walking. Talk again, I break your legs, drag you.*"

Hoping to defuse Pek's knack for confrontation, and more than a bit curious, Kilaris asked, "Can you at least give us an estimate of how far we need to walk?"

"*Just under ten* kellicams."

Kilaris mentally converted the Klingon unit of distance into Federation-standard kilometers. It was going to be a long march.

Pek clearly had made the same computation. *"Couldn't you have landed your junkpile of a ship a little bit closer to our destination?"*

"No stable ground large enough," Varoh said.

Curtains of pink dust wafted over the landing party. Kilaris listened to the patter of grit rebounding off her suit's transparent-aluminum faceplate. Austere and forbidding, the moonscape fascinated Kilaris, albeit in a morbid way. Now that she saw its unforgiving nature, she understood why the Nausicaans didn't fear their prisoners would try to escape. There was nowhere to go, no breathable air, no water to drink. Just a sand-scoured ball of rock blasted sterile by a steady bath of high-intensity radiation from its gas-giant parent world.

And us, she reflected, *trudging across it at the mercy of a band of thugs who most likely intend to leave us behind as corpses.*

For now, logic dictated cooperation. But the moment it dictated otherwise, Kilaris would act; she would show the Nausicaans the same quality of mercy they had shown Max—and she would call it justice.

"Someone get me a lock on that damn ship." Nilat paced in front of her command chair. She appreciated the irony that the main viewscreen of the *Silago-Ekon* offered her a magnificent image of a tiger-striped gas giant with a broad girdle of debris rings and an entourage of moons, yet couldn't seem to show her the one thing she was looking for amid all that splendor: the Nausicaan ship she had followed to this unnamed star system.

She circled her chair to prowl past the aft stations. K'mjok leaned on the back of Trunch's chair and observed over the Balduk's shoulder as he trained the ship's sensor array on the next closest unscanned moon. If Trunch was vexed by the Klingon XO's micromanagement, he either hid it well or was sublimating it into his work. Whichever proved to be the case, Nilat was grateful the two had stopped posturing at each other long enough to get something done for a change. She didn't expect their détente to last, but she meant to enjoy it while it did.

"I'm still waiting on an answer, you knobs. Somebody talk. Now."

K'mjok pivoted away from the sensor console. "Still looking, Commander. But the gas giant's magnetic field makes it impossible to follow ion trails within two million *kellicam*s of the planet. The moment the merc ship started its approach, we lost them."

Nilat stewed in her frustration. This, she had known from the start, was the risk involved in tailing a vessel at the extreme edge of one's long-range sensors. Following at closer range would have increased the risk of detection, but it also would have given Nilat the option of switching over to visual scanning when the planet's radiation blinded their other sensors.

She set herself against the console beside Ninivus, who looked up at her. "Commander?"

"Any comm chatter? In orbit or on the surface?"

"Which surface?" The Tiburonian jerked his head toward the main viewscreen. "We have at least four moons within easy comm range."

"Stay on it." Nilat joined K'mjok in looming over Trunch, who remained fixated upon his sensor displays. "Talk to me. Where can those bastards be?"

"We have narrowed the search to three moons," K'mjok said.

"Which already puts you one ahead of Ninivus. What else?"

The XO called up additional information on an auxiliary screen. "Moon One is a dead rock. No atmosphere." He switched to a new data set. "Moon Two is another rockball, thin atmosphere of methane and carbon dioxide, some trace elements." A final screen of data. "Moon Three is a slush of methane and liquid water under five *kellicam*s of ice crust, iron-nickel core. Tenuous atmosphere of oxygen with other trace elements."

"So . . . none are Class-M."

"Not even close." The Klingon moved closer to Nilat so he could confide in a hush, "We could hide in the planet's rings and wait to reacquire the merc ship when it moves again."

"No," Nilat said with an emphatic headshake. "They brought their hostages here for a reason. If I'm right, we can't risk letting them go mobile with whatever it is they've found. We need to intercept it *here*." What she left unsaid—at least in part because she felt it was understood by every member of her crew—was that there was more at stake in this operation than mind-boggling sums of potential wealth. If they failed in this assignment, the penalty for disappointing their masters would most likely be their lives.

Lord Srinigar is many things, but forgiving is not one of them.

Nilat tried to massage the ache from her temples, only

to be disturbed by a declaration from Ang-Harod. "Commander? We have a new problem."

The Orion sharpened her focus as she moved forward. "Talk to me, Ang."

Ang-Harod divided the main viewscreen image to show her new intel in its left third. "Three signals inbound at high warp." She superimposed an analysis filter. "Their energy signatures are consistent with Starfleet designs, and their power levels are high enough that I think we're dealing with cruisers and heavy cruisers."

"Just what we don't need right now—Federation entanglements." Nilat looked aft; she knew Trunch and K'mjok would already be working the problem. "Have they detected us?"

"Don't think so," Trunch said. "Planet hides us too."

Let's be thankful for that, at least. "Ang, what's their ETA?"

"Less than two hours." The Nalori woman added with a tone of mild surprise, "Damn, they're even faster than I remembered."

"And getting faster all the time," Nilat said, reminded of Starfleet's recent adoption of the revolutionary quantum slipstream drive. "But that just means we need to be smarter. K'mjok, program our last two recon probes to search for any sign of refined duranium or transparent aluminum, then dispatch them to the two farthest of your three candidate moons. Set them for wide-field scans from equatorial orbit. Put us in equatorial orbit of the closest moon, and execute a quick-and-dirty scan for the same factors. And make it fast, because Starfleet's coming in hot."

"Understood," K'mjok said. Then he set himself and Trunch to work turning Nilat's orders into action.

Nilat returned to Ninivus's side and leaned close to the Tiburonian. "Nin, are the signal repeaters you deployed still in play?"

"Should be, if no one else found them."

"Good. We need to keep Starfleet off our back for as long as possible." She faced the viewscreen and hoped her petty diversion would be enough. "Trigger the damsel beacons."

Eight

There were times when Captain Vale couldn't resist comparing her starship to a living thing. Her analogy du jour for the *Titan* was a bloodhound, one that could sniff out an otherwise invisible trail left in the fabric of subspace and the rarefied cosmic dust of the interstellar void. The *Luna*-class starship had some of the most advanced sensor packages in Starfleet, and its partners in the Alpha Quadrant Frontier Exploration Group possessed comparable systems.

Stars stretched and snapped past on the bridge's main viewscreen, their light distorted by the warp field that shimmered around the *Titan* like a soap bubble. Vale knew their quarry was somewhere out there, perhaps still in flight, maybe gone to ground.

Either way, we'll find you.

An alert chirped on Tuvok's console. Vale swiveled her chair toward the Vulcan, who then tapped at his panel to silence a second, then a third alert. The abrupt flurry proved peculiar enough to raise one of Tuvok's eyebrows. Vale prompted him, "Report, Commander."

"Three distress signals, Captain." He organized the data on his console as he continued. "All nearly simultaneous, yet appearing to originate from markedly different headings."

"Appearing to?"

Tuvok continued to poke at the intel on his console. "Indeed. One lies almost directly behind us. The other two would also require significant diversions from our present course."

Rager turned away from the ops panel to add, "I've analyzed the signals, Captain. All three purport to be from civilian vessels in immediate danger." With a dubious creasing of her brow she added, "And all three vessels' reported positions lie beyond the range of our sensors."

"Of course they do." She threw a look at Keru. "What do you think, Commander?"

"It seems more than coincidental," the security chief said, "that we should receive three distress calls while traveling with two escort vessels. Almost as if someone wanted to ensure there was enough distraction to occupy all three of us at once."

Vale frowned. "My thoughts exactly."

Without rising from her chair, Commander Sarai leaned toward Vale. "May I remind you, Captain, that we are required by Starfleet regulations and interstellar law—"

"To investigate all distress signals and render aid as needed," Vale said, finishing the all-too-familiar citation. "I'm well aware of the regs, Number One. But the timing and multiplicity of these Maydays is more than a bit suspect, wouldn't you agree?"

"Of course. The likelihood of these being genuine calls for aid is remote. It is far more probable that they are diversions intended to thwart our pursuit of the kidnappers. But our suspicions, no matter how well founded, provide insufficient justification to disregard the law. Even if we believe the calls to be fraudulent, we are still obligated to investigate. Sir."

And we had been getting along so well lately. "What you say is true, Number One. But the regs only require us to be responsive—not hopelessly gullible."

Sarai asked Tuvok, "Can we verify the registries of the ship's requesting aid?"

"Checking," Tuvok said as he worked.

Moments such as this reminded Vale of what she found vexing about the first officer imposed upon her by Starfleet Command. Sarai was a capable and experienced officer, but she was inflexible. Vale supposed Sarai's rigidity was a byproduct of her disgrace after the debacle with President Pro Tem Ishan; it certainly didn't comport with the sort of intellectual adaptability she had come to expect from Starfleet Intelligence field operatives, which was the division that had trained Sarai and honed her skills to a keen edge.

Tuvok looked up from his console. "The first message was too garbled for us to make out the ship's name. The other two vessels purport to hail from alien powers whose registry data is not available to us. Consequently, I cannot verify any of the vessels' identities."

The bad news didn't discourage Sarai. "Our duty remains unchanged."

"You're right, Number One. We are obligated to investigate—but just because we received three signals doesn't mean I need to divert the entire battle group."

Vale stood, to emphasize her control of the situation. "Mister Tuvok, get me Captain Scarfield on the *Wasp*."

"Aye, Captain." His labors were answered by feedback tones from his panel, and then he said, "I have Captain Scarfield on channel one."

"On-screen," Vale said. She waited until the image of warp-distorted stars was replaced by the angular cheekbones and raven hair of Captain Fiona Scarfield, the commanding officer of the *Starship Wasp*. Vale softened the news with a wry smile. "Fiona. Guess why I'm calling."

"No need. Do those Maydays look as fishy to you as they do to me?"

"More. All the same, I need you and your crew to run them down."

Scarfield nodded. *"The price we pay for being the fastest ship in the group."*

"That's the spirit," Vale said. "Plot the shortest route that'll let you scout all three signals. If any of them fails to ping on long-range sensors, rule it out and move on to the next one. Then regroup with us and the *Canterbury*, ASAP."

"Copy that." To someone off-screen, Scarfield added, *"Time to put our new slipstream drive to work. Lay in new heading one-one-six mark four, maximum slip."* With a friendly nod to Vale she signed off, *"Christine, I'll see you when I see you.* Wasp *out."*

Scarfield vanished from the viewscreen, which reverted to the view of stars. The sleek *Starship Wasp* arced across the screen ahead of the *Titan*, then it leaped away in a flash.

We have got to get ourselves one of those drives, Vale thought with mild envy.

She threw a challenging look at Sarai. "Satisfied?"

The first officer remained cool and aloof. "From a regulations standpoint? Yes."

"Wonderful. Another day, another court-martial dodged."

Vale's mild rebuke seemed to sting Sarai more keenly than she'd meant it to. The XO replied, "I am merely upholding my responsibilities as your executive officer, Captain."

"No offense intended, Number One."

I just hope you're that tenacious when it comes time to engage the enemy.

Cherbegrod felt sick. Not just from being beaten. Sick with rage. Embarrassed. The cruel Ferengi and his bullies—they did this. Made Cherbegrod hurt in his belly and his thoughts. Not right what they did. Cherbegrod found the space factory. Opened its doors. It was his salvage.

Now he had to be carried back to his chair on the *Gomjar*.

Haripog wanted to put him in his bed. Lock the door. Hide him away. But Cherbegrod knew better than that. He was smart. This was the wrong time to hide. If he crawled into his bed now, Haripog would become commander. Take away the ship. Take all Cherbegrod had left.

That would be too much for Cherbegrod. When the others had tried to put him in his cabin, he'd said, "No. Top deck. My chair. Take me." He'd kept saying it until they listened.

Eberleg and a couple of his tool-pushers set Cherbegrod in his command chair. It hurt to sit. Every part of Cherbegrod's body was in pain. He was more bruise than flesh now. If he had not been so angry, the pain would have been too much. He swallowed his hurts and stayed quiet, even though all he wanted to do was cry and scream how unfair it all was.

But there was no time for that. He had to do something. Be in charge.

"Set course," he said. "Away from the space factory. Warp speed." When no one else on the bridge seemed to do anything, he pounded the armrests of his chair. "Now!"

His fellow Pakleds scurried into action. It took them a few seconds to stop running into one another. Then they settled, and someone did as he'd said. The ship turned away from the Husnock space factory, and the stars stretched into blurry streaks on the picture screen.

Cherbegrod took a deep breath. He could still give orders. His men still did what he said. He was still captain. He knuckled a few tears from the corners of his eyes.

Haripog clomped across the deck to stand next to Cherbegrod's chair, huffing like he had just been running. His jaw muscles bulged, and a vein on the side of his head throbbed. "They took all our salvage," he said. "Months of gathering. Took it all. And half our fuel."

"We could be dead. Be glad you're not."

"Needed bigger boom," Haripog said. "More boom."

His complaining riled up the men. They surrounded Cherbegrod.

"Haripog smart," said Garagool, the pilot. "We need more boom."

Famapeg, a tool-pusher, joined in. "They took our

factory with booms." He poked Cherbegrod's chest. "Give us booms, we show the Ferengi we are strong."

"Strong and smart," slurred Uugalog, another fix-it. "Take back what is ours."

Too many lies. Too much dumb. Cherbegrod was tired of it all. "We are not strong. Not smart. We could have all the booms—they would still have the factory. And we would be dead." He hurt everywhere when he stood, but Cherbegrod needed to be seen on his feet. It was the only way his men would listen. "More boom will not help us. Boom is stupid way. Boom gets us killed." One aching, dizzying step after another, he moved through his crew, looked them in the eyes so they would know he was tough. "We are Pakleds. No good at fighting. Good at salvage."

"We salvaged space factory," Haripog said. "Ferengi took it away."

It hurt when Cherbegrod breathed deeply, but he did it to buy thinking time. "Ferengi cheat. Ferengi steal. That is what Ferengi are good at." He shuffled in agonizing steps to the forward panels. It took him a moment to find the control to switch the angle of the picture screen. He set it to look behind the *Gomjar*, then he poked the controls to make the image bigger. He looked up at the fast-shrinking image of the Husnock space factory. "We will come back. Get even with Gaila." He faced his men. "I will make this right. And make him pay."

There was no such thing, in Sarai's opinion, as a good time to be compelled into making contact with Admiral Batanides, but some moments were demonstrably worse than others. Seeing the admiral's secret code appear among the other reports on the tactical display beside her chair while she was on the bridge, in the middle of a red-alert crisis, was arguably the worst yet.

She dismissed the notice with a quick tap, knowing that her action would have three simultaneous effects: it would alert Batanides that Sarai had seen the clandestine summons, erase all record of the incoming signal and Sarai's response from *Titan*'s comm logs, and trigger the antisurveillance systems in Sarai's quarters in preparation for her secret check-in.

The hard part, Sarai knew, would be excusing herself from the bridge in the midst of the hunt for the Nausicaan ship and the kidnapped scientists without attracting undue attention. In her experience as a Starfleet Intelligence field operative, she often had found that the less one said and the fewer details one offered, the better.

She looked at Vale. "Captain? Permission to leave the bridge."

Her request puzzled Vale. "For what?"

Sarai lowered her voice. "I suspect Admiral Riker might insist on leading the rescue op. As a precaution, I'd like to retrieve some gear from my quarters, so I can back him up."

Vale nodded her consent. "Okay, but be quick, Number One."

"Aye, sir. Back in a flash."

Sarai got up and maintained her trademark calm as she walked inside the turbolift, which she directed toward her quarters. *So far, so good.*

Less than a minute later she stepped inside her quarters and locked the door. A quick check of her countersurveillance equipment confirmed that her suite remained secure from eavesdropping. She moved to her desk and opened the encrypted channel. "Active. Ready."

The face of Admiral Batanides appeared on the screen. *"We have a situation."*

"I know," Sarai said, unable to mask her irritation. "I'm in the middle of it."

"Mind your tone, Commander. And don't assume I'm ignorant of your mission status. That's precisely what makes this conversation so urgent."

Calmer but still aloof, Sarai said, "I'm listening."

"I've been reviewing Vale's and Riker's logs concerning the kidnapped scientists, as well as Riker's logs from his initial encounter with the Douwd. When analyzed in conjunction with Vale's and Riker's psych profiles, the data suggests the two of them might make . . . unfortunate *decisions with regard to this mission's priorities."*

The ominous nature of the admiral's words unsettled Sarai. "I've seen nothing to suggest either one of them would do anything to jeopardize the scientists' lives or safety."

Batanides looked skeptical. *"Exactly my concern. The admiral and the captain both seem so fixated upon the immediate issue that neither is capable of accounting for the bigger picture."*

"You've lost me, Admiral. Bigger picture?"

"The attack on the expedition represents an imminent threat to Federation security."

Sarai felt a sick churn of dread as she asked, "How so?"

"Our research into the Husnock is motivated by more than a love of pure science. As noble a goal as it might be to preserve aspects of their culture, Starfleet's investment in the project is driven by the need to keep the Husnock's military technology out of the wrong hands."

Where was the admiral going with this? "I can't imagine either the admiral or the captain would allow hostile powers to abscond with Husnock ships or weapons."

"Nor can I, Commander. My concern is that, if Husnock ships or munitions were found, Riker and Vale might be tempted to take excessive preemptive action to prevent their capture. In their zeal to preserve the status quo, they might deprive Starfleet Research and Development of the chance to study the Husnock's science for our benefit."

"Considering what the Husnock did to Delta Rana IV, such measures seem warranted."

The admiral frowned. *"That's tactical thinking. Think strategically. Consider the future."*

"But why worry about the Husnock's technology? For all we know, it's no better than anything we already have."

"Need I remind you what the Douwd called them? A species of hideous intelligence. If the Husnock were nothing else, they were dangerous." Batanides moderated her tone to one less confrontational. *"As we push farther into the galaxy, we encounter new threats. Some have abilities we've never imagined. So whether we're facing the Solanae, or the Hirogen, or who knows what else, we're going to need every advantage we can get."*

"And what do you imagine that means for me, here and now?"

"I need you to stay aware of every decision Vale and Riker make regarding Husnock ships and weapons. Don't compromise the safety of your ship or its escorts, but do all you can to persuade Riker and Vale to preserve Husnock technology for further study."

"Even if doing so presents a danger to interstellar peace?"

"The short-term risks are outweighed by the potential advances we could make in our defensive capabilities. Do whatever it takes to keep Husnock weapons out of foreign hands, but don't let Riker or Vale rob us of the opportunity to master that technology for ourselves." She lowered her chin and fixed Sarai with a piercing stare. *"Understood?"*

"Perfectly, Admiral."

"Update me when it's done. Batanides out."

The screen went dark as the admiral terminated the connection. Sarai stared at its black surface, stunned by the blatant conflict of interest Batanides had just forced upon her.

What if the captain or the admiral are dead set on destroying the Husnock's weapons, no matter what I say? What does Batanides expect me to do then? Mutiny?

She sighed to expel her frustration, then gathered up a few pieces of gear she had once used as a field agent for Starfleet Intelligence. She hoped none of them proved necessary for the rescue of the kidnapped scientists, but if they did, she knew she wouldn't hesitate to use them.

If only I could be so sure of how to handle Batanides's orders.

Exiting her quarters with a lightly packed duffel and a heavily burdened conscience, Sarai understood at last what it really felt like to be forced to serve two masters—and she didn't like it.

She didn't like it at all.

Nine

No matter how long the group trudged across the rocky moonscape, no path appeared. It was an untrammeled wilderness of dust and stone, desolate and unforgiving. Kilaris had learned to keep her eyes on only two things, in alternating turns: the ground below her feet, and the back of Varoh, the Nausicaan who had been tasked with serving as the column's trailblazer.

It had been a rough walk, but the Nausicaans had endured the hike with a minimum of fuss. The Bynars, however, had collapsed after the first two hours and since then had been carried on the backs of a matched pair of Nausicaan dullards named Motar and Zallas—an act of favor about which Doctor Pek had groused for an hour. Kilaris had gotten the impression that the Tellarite was unaccustomed to long marches or hard exercise. She, meanwhile, remained silently thankful for her upbringing in the thin air, strong gravity, and merciless heat of Vulcan: it had tempered her to face nearly any ordeal.

Now they all plodded in single file and aggrieved silence.

Have to save our air, Kilaris told herself. She wondered whether the Nausicaans had even considered supplying her or the other prisoners with enough air for the return trip. *Once we finish whatever it is they've brought us here to do, they might have no reason to bring us back.*

Varoh led them up a narrow passage through a wall of jutting rocks. The gap's sides were unnaturally straight and clean. Kilaris touched one with her gloved palm. Its surface was glassy smooth. *Cut by an energy weapon,* she realized.

As she neared the crest of the carved pass, she saw what lay on the far side.

Embedded at an angle in the planet's surface was a huge starship. Never before had Kilaris seen one of similar design, but some of the markings on its fractured outer hull were of unmistakable provenance. This wreck had been a Husnock vessel.

It had slammed into a mountainside of jagged rock formations and buried one side of itself in the stone. There were no gouges in the planet's surface leading to the crash, which led Kilaris to suspect the vessel had survived a nearly direct impact. For the ship to be even partially intact after such a calamity was most remarkable.

Varoh pointed at an open wound in the hull. His voice sounded tinny through Kilaris's helmet transceiver. *"We enter there."* He looked Kilaris in the eye. *"Then you work."*

As close as the crashed vessel appeared, it still took the group nearly an hour to reach the break in its hull. Wind-blown sand spilled into the ship in a steady flow, then vanished through cracks in the deck and bulkheads.

Varoh activated a palm beacon. Its beam slashed blue and cold through the deep shadows inside the derelict ship. *"This way,"* he said.

Kilaris had hoped that moving around inside the ship would be easier than traversing the moon's surface. Once inside she saw that was not the case. Because of the angle at which the ship had come to rest, all its decks and bulkheads were skewed at odd angles. Worse, its crash had inflicted serious interior damage. As she and the others followed Varoh deep inside the wreck, she saw bulkheads that had buckled or broken apart. Gaps in the sloped decks fell away into abysses of twisted metal, dangling cables, and shattered machinery.

Pek wondered over the open channel, *"Does he even know where he's going?"*

"Quiet," Slokar said. *"No more questions, or I bleed you."*

Though Kilaris had known the answer to Pek's question, she had kept it to herself. From the moment they had set foot inside the crashed starship, she had noted the fluorescent yellow markings painted by hand at regular intervals on the bulkheads—some in characters unique to the dominant Nausicaan language, others just simple directional notations. The symbols had glowed when the beam from Varoh's palm beacon played across them.

It was clear to her that the Nausicaans had been to this vessel before, had scouted it in detail. They likely had encountered unsafe passages, dead ends, and other hazards. Not being fools, once they confirmed a safe route through the wreckage, they marked it. Those symbols were a map out of this place. If Kilaris could avoid letting the Nausicaans know that she had discovered this, they might underestimate her at a key moment, thereby affording her a chance to put this knowledge to use. *And if it should facilitate their deaths, so much the better.*

Varoh ducked through a break in a bulkhead, then used his weapon to beckon Kilaris to follow him. She did so, and was followed inside by Pek, and then by the last two Nausicaans with the Bynars on their backs. Once they all were inside the cavernous chamber, whose center was dominated by a machine that resembled a massive pipe organ Kilaris had once seen on Earth, the Bynars were dropped to the angled deck and left to pick themselves up again.

Slokar looked at his men and pointed at a dark bank of computer consoles. *"Power."* His men hurried to the consoles and started keying in commands. As they worked, the consoles surged to life, and Kilaris was surprised to see they sported Federation-standard interfaces.

A deep hum filled the silo-like space. Kilaris searched for the source of the mellisonant vibrations and found a portable fusion generator that looked to be of Klingon design. More consoles awakened, spilling blue and orange light in all directions. As the space brightened, Kilaris saw the tangled nest of cables packed against its edges. They were a mishmash of power lines, ODN fibers, and grounding cables. By their colors and other markings she could see they hailed from a variety of sources: Cardassian, Romulan, Starfleet, and some she didn't recognize. *They must have sourced all this equipment on the black market,* she deduced.

The Nausicaans finished activating their hodgepodge of mismatched components while Slokar kept his eye on Kilaris and the others. Groaning winds resounded in the emptiness of the dead ship around them, but inside what Kilaris now could see was a multilevel, vertical cylinder of space, the peculiar machine at its heart pulsed with ever-changing hues of light and thrummed with palpable energies.

Varoh, Zallas, and Motar stepped away from the consoles. Slokar used his weapon to direct Kilaris, Pek, and the Bynars to take over where his men had left off.

"This"—he glanced at the conglomeration of cylinders—*"is Husnock computer core. You break encryption. Get us command codes for ship."* He moved to Kilaris's side, close enough that had they not been wearing environmental suits, she might have felt his breath on her neck. *"You have one hour. Then—"* He raised his disruptor to the side of her head and mimed pulling the trigger. *"Understand?"*

"Perfectly," Kilaris said, knowing it was what the brute wanted to hear.

"No tricks." Slokar tapped the side of his helmet. *"We hear what you say."*

The Nausicaans withdrew to the far side of the compartment to await the fruits of the prisoners' labors. Pek and the Bynars stared at Kilaris, as if she would know what to tell them to do next. All she knew was that she understood the Nausicaan leader's wishes all too well.

He wants us to do the impossible—and will kill us if we fail.

She breathed a quiet sigh of exasperation. *Most illogical.*

Everyone's focus was sharp on the bridge of the *Titan* as the ship dropped out of warp, followed closely by the

Canterbury. From her seat beside the captain, Sarai alternated her attention between the tactical data on her command display and the annotated imagery on the main viewscreen, which showed a ringed gas giant with several moons of varying sizes and types.

Vale leaned toward Sarai and said simply, "Find that ship, Number One."

Sarai stood. "Mister Tuvok, where does the trail lead from here?"

The Vulcan furrowed his brow at the sensor data on his console. "Difficult to say. Intense radiation from the gas giant is masking the kidnappers' impulse signature and interfering with our sensors." Tapping in new commands, he added, "Attempting to compensate."

Sarai decided to make the problem's resolution a team effort. "Rager, work with Tuvok to filter out the radiation interference. Lieutenant Torvig, stand ready to coordinate assistance from the engineering department as needed. We might need to modify the sensor array." The operations officer and engineering liaison nodded their acknowledgments of her orders, so she faced the security chief. "Keru, figure out which moons the kidnappers' ship could have landed on, then dispatch probes to scan their surfaces with optical sensors."

"Scan them old-school," Keru confirmed. "Aye, sir."

"Helm," Sarai continued, "put us in orbit of the nearest candidate moon. Ops, augment our optical scans of that moon with a narrow-frequency search for concentrations of duranium high enough to suggest the presence of a starship."

The crew settled into their tasks, and for a few minutes the bridge was quiet except for the soft music of computer feedback tones and the muted susurrus of intraship comm chatter. Sarai returned to her chair and continued to review new tactical intel on her monitor. She and Captain Vale looked up at the sound of the turbolift doors opening. They stood as Admiral Riker stepped onto the bridge and beelined toward them. "How goes the hunt, Captain?"

Vale said, "Methodically, sir."

"Well, if there's anything we can do to move things along, we—"

"Excuse me, Admiral," Tuvok cut in. "Commander? I have something. Optical scans by one of our probes have identified what appears to be the wreckage of a starship."

The captain took over. "Put it on the main screen, with telemetry."

An image hashed with static shivered on the main viewscreen. Through the digital snow and wavy lines of interference, Sarai recognized the angular shapes of a starship's hull—or, to be more precise, half of a starship's hull. The rest of it appeared to be buried in a mountainside spiked with bladelike rock formations.

Riker stared at the image, his expression a mix of wonder and horror. He spoke in a haunted whisper. "That's a Husnock ship." He looked at Tuvok. "How long has it been there?"

The Vulcan gave a small shake of his head. "Unknown, sir. Precise scans are unreliable because of the radiation from the gas giant."

Melora Pazlar swiveled her chair away from the sciences console. "Based on the erosion of the hull and the penetration of sand drifts into its ruptures, as well as the absence of any visible crash path on the moon's surface, I would estimate the vessel has been here for at least a decade, perhaps longer. If I were to offer an educated guess, I would place the time of its crash sometime shortly after the extermination of the Husnock species."

Taking a moment to review the sensor data on her own console, Sarai zoomed out five percent to survey the region surrounding the derelict. At once her eye fixed upon another glint of metal on the surface. She relayed a magnification of that object to the main viewscreen. "There's something else down there." The moment the enlarged image appeared on the forward screen, she recognized the vessel's shape. "That's the ship we've been chasing."

Intrigued, Vale asked, "Distance from the Husnock vessel?"

"Nine point six kilometers," Sarai said. "It appears their landing site was dictated by the size of their ship, which suggests they aren't carrying any auxiliary spacecraft."

"What about partners?" asked Keru. "Or rivals, for that matter?"

Rager looked up from the ops panel. "I'm not reading any other ships in the system—but with all this radiation clouding our sensors, I can't guarantee we're alone."

Tuvok switched the main screen back to the image of the Husnock ship, this time at a greater magnification than before. "There appear to be fresh footprints leading toward the ship."

That detail garnered the admiral's attention. "Can we tell how many people? Or if the prisoners are inside the ship?"

"Negative," Tuvok said. "Though there seem to be several sets of footprints, they overlap and obscure one another, suggesting the group moved single file."

"That said," interjected Keru, "we have a downed Husnock vessel, and the scientists abducted by the Nausicaans were a starship engineer, a xenolinguist who's just made a major breakthrough in the Husnock language, and a Bynar pair who have been studying Husnock computers for the past few years. If the Nausicaans haven't taken the prisoners inside that ship, I for one will be very surprised."

"As will I," Riker said. "Let's beam down an away team, on the double."

"Sorry, sir," Sarai said, "no transporters, on account of the radiation. And anyone we deploy to the surface will need to suit up for EVA. The good news is, we can land a lot closer to that wreck in a runabout than the Nausicaans could with their ship."

Riker nodded. "All right. Have the *Nechako* prepped for liftoff as soon as my away team joins me in the shuttlebay."

Sarai traded a knowing look with the captain, then said to Riker, "Admiral, this op is likely to involve close-quarters battle. If you lead the team, I'll have to insist on joining you."

"I wouldn't have it any other way. Assemble your team and meet me in the *Nechako*."

"Aye, sir." Sarai followed Riker to the turbolift as she added, "Keru, you're with me." The security chief fell in beside her as they entered the turbolift and she tapped her combadge. "Sarai to sh'Aqabaa, Modan, and Sethe: report to the main shuttlebay immediately."

Knowing that lives were hanging in the balance, Vale felt as if her every thought and action were mired in mud. Still, she did her best to present a confident façade from the center seat of *Titan*'s bridge. Around her, the other bridge officers submerged themselves into their assigned tasks, but there was naught for Vale to do but watch the main viewscreen and observe the quickly receding shimmer of the *Nechako*, which streaked toward the rocky moon and a confrontation with armed and dangerous adversaries.

Project calm, she reminded herself. *Embody professionalism.* Her mantra was interrupted by the chirp of an incoming transmission on Tuvok's console. The Vulcan silenced the alert and said, "Captain? A private transmission for you from Captain Scarfield on the *Wasp*."

Thank God—something to do. She stood. "I'll take it in my ready room."

Vale stepped off the bridge and into her sanctum—just one of the privileges of command she had learned to appreciate since her promotion to captain. Though the ready room had been hers to personalize for several months, she had yet to dress it up with personal items or creature comforts. On a certain level, she liked the room the way it was: simple, functional, and private. She settled into her chair and activated her desk's holographic comm screen. The state-of-the-art interface automatically scanned her retinal pattern and genetic profile, then opened the channel.

Captain Scarfield's face appeared inside the holoframe. *"Christine, I have good news and bad news. Got a preference for which comes first?"*

"Life is short, Fiona. Start with the good."

The dark-haired woman transferred over a packet of sensor logs on the data subchannel while she spoke. *"We tracked the first signal to a subspace repeater buoy in deep space."*

"Any idea who put it there?"

"*We have a few theories,*" Scarfield said. "*It was a patchwork piece of tech—a piece from here, a piece from there, if you know what I mean.*"

Vale nodded. "Black market. So probably the Orion Syndicate."

"*That's our guess. There's a few clever bits in the hardware and the programming, but none of it's slick enough to make me think military operators put this in the field.*" A dip of her chin. "*Check the logs I just sent. My tactical officer hacked the buoy's command-and-control.*" She continued while Vale reviewed the logs on a second screen. "*We used its transceiver to confirm that the other two Mayday calls we received came from more buoys linked to this one.*"

"And that's the good news?"

"*No, the good news is my tac guy did some kind of techno-magic that made all three buoys generate a feedback loop that fried their onboard computers. So they won't be clogging up our subspace channels anymore.*" She took a mock bow. "*You're welcome.*"

"Nicely done. And my commendations to your tac guy." She resigned herself to facing the second part of Scarfield's report. "Dare I ask what the bad news is?"

Scarfield's good mood faded. "*We've been noticing an uptick in weird activity since we fragged the buoys. Fleeting warp echoes in our baffles. Momentary pings at the edge of long-range sensors. Snippets of encrypted comm signals on ultralow subspace frequencies.*"

"You think you've picked up a tail?"

"*More than just a tail—I'd say we've picked up the whole tiger. The readings we're seeing can't all be from just one ship. We've got hits on multiple bearings, all at extreme range.*"

"Have you tried launching passive probes to extend your sensor profile?"

"Sure." The other captain shook her head. *"Hasn't worked. We're still seeing ghosts and shadows. I've put us on an evasion course—doubling back, arbitrary changes in heading and speed—but I just can't shake the feeling we're being followed by someone—or something."*

Vale couldn't pretend not to be troubled by Scarfield's news. "That doesn't sound like the Orion Syndicate, Fiona. Anyone who can play cat and mouse with a Starfleet slipstream vessel must be some sort of professional military—possibly the sort that have cloaking devices."

"My thinking exactly," Scarfield said. *"Whoever they are, I'm doing my best not to lead them back to you and the* Canterbury. *But I can only dodge 'em for so long."*

"I understand, and I appreciate what you're doing. Whoever they are, keep them busy as long as you can—but if you feel like you're getting boxed in, regroup with us immediately. If someone's looking for a showdown, we'll have better odds standing together."

"Acknowledged. If we learn anything new, we'll keep you posted. Wasp *out."*

Scarfield's face vanished, and the holoscreen went dark. Vale used the control panel on her desk to open a channel to the bridge. "Mister Tuvok, get me a secure channel to Captain Mareet on the *Canterbury*, and patch it through to my ready room."

"Aye, Captain," Tuvok replied over the comm. *"Stand by."*

It took only a few seconds before Vale's holoscreen activated again, this time to show the green-haired commanding officer of the *Canterbury*, a Catullan man just a few years older than Vale. Captain Arius Mareet greeted Vale with a warm smile. *"Captain. What news?"*

"Fiona and the *Wasp* have neutralized the phony distress signals, but they seem to have attracted mysterious and unwanted attention in the process."

"What kind of attention?"

"Let's just say I suspect this party is about to get a lot more crowded."

Ten

As encouraging as it was to be flanked by two security officers as experienced and reliable as Ranul Keru and Lieutenant Pava ek'Noor sh'Aqabaa, Will Riker still found the most reassuring companion on a dangerous away mission to be a fully charged phaser in his hand. He checked the weapon one last time as the runabout landed with a muted thump. It was set for heavy stun, broad beam—ideal for facing multiple targets in close quarters.

His breath felt warm and close inside the helmet of his environmental suit, which he found a touch claustrophobic in spite of its wraparound faceplate and excellent peripheral sight lines. When he looked back at the rest of the away team, he saw their identities superimposed above their heads, thanks to his helmet's holographic heads-up display. Keru and sh'Aqabaa checked the power levels on their phaser rifles, while computer engineer Lieutenant Holor Sethe and cryptolinguist Ensign

Y'Lira Modan were more interested in the statuses of their tricorders, both of which seemed to be on the fritz—further casualties of the intense radiation bathing the desolate moon. The two scientists, like the rest of the away team, also carried type-2 phasers, though neither the Cygnian man nor the Selenean woman looked comfortable bearing weapons.

I just hope our phasers work down here, Riker worried.

Sarai locked down the runabout's flight controls, then got up and secured her own helmet to her suit as she moved aft to join the rest of the team. Keru handed her a rifle. *"We're less than half a kilometer from the Husnock ship's nearest entry point,"* she said over the team's encrypted comm channel, *"but watch your step—it's all downhill from here, and it gets pretty steep."*

"Copy that," Keru said. *"Mind if I take point, Commander?"*

"You read my mind," Sarai said. *"Pava, stay behind the admiral. Sethe, Modan, you follow Pava, and I'll bring up the rear. Any questions?"*

"One," Riker said. "Who has the marshmallows?" A quick study of the others' blank expressions confirmed none of them had understood his cultural reference to camping. *The downside to a diverse crew.* Disappointed, he frowned. "Never mind. Move out."

Keru opened the runabout's port-side hatch and led the team out of the small starship. Just as Sarai had warned, the ground outside was rocky and pitched at a sharp angle. It took Riker a moment to find his footing and settle into a careful stride behind Keru. Small rocks and bits of debris tumbled down the incline ahead of Riker, and more rolled past him as the rest of the away team filed out of the *Nechako*. He took a moment between steps to appreciate the barren splendor of the moonscape—the sky streaked with emerald and magenta, the breathtaking curve of the gas giant's rings arcing above the horizon—but the treacherous footing forced him to turn his eyes back to the slope in front of him.

Several dozen meters later he and the others were walking atop the fissured hull of the crashed Husnock vessel. Its gunmetal-gray exterior was composed of interlocking boxy shapes and hard corners, a far cry from the graceful curves of Federation starships.

Near the designated entry point, Keru held up a fist, signaling the team to halt. *"Commander Sarai? You might want to have a look at this."*

The *Titan*'s executive officer moved forward to join Keru. Impelled by curiosity, Riker followed her, leaving sh'Aqabaa to guard Sethe and Modan. When Riker and Sarai reached Keru, he pointed inside the gash in the hull, using his palm beacon to illuminate details. *"Interiors look intact,"* he said. *"But this is a big ship. Where do we go once we're inside?"*

Riker squinted into the shadowy corridors. Footprints were everywhere. Then he pointed at something on one of the interior bulkheads. "Put some light on that."

Keru trained the beam of his palm beacon on a crudely painted symbol. *"What's that?"*

Sarai leaned in for a closer look. *"What the—? Is that—"*

"Nausicaan?" Riker cut in. "Yes, I'm pretty sure it is."

The XO and the security chief exchanged dubious looks. Keru turned an incredulous look at Riker. *"They marked their path? It can't be that easy, can it?"*

"It's Nausicaans," Riker said. "So yes, I'm pretty sure it is."

Sarai keyed in adjustments to her suit, and her faceplate became dark and nonreflective. *"No palm beacons,"* she said. *"They'll give away our position. Switch to UV and infrared, and engage motion sensors. Filter out our own signals so we don't get distracted by false positives."*

The rest of the away team did as Sarai had ordered. Sethe's catlike stare disappeared as his faceplate darkened, as did Modan's golden skin and bulbous turquoise eyes. Keru's dermal spots and sh'Aqabaa's blue antennae vanished behind their own synthetic matte-black veils.

Riker adjusted the settings on his suit's faceplate for spectrum-enhanced vision, and to eliminate unwanted reflections. At once the corridor inside the ship became clearly visible, rendered in frost-blue twilight. He was pleased to note that the Nausicaans' painted markers shimmered, making them easy to spot. "Ready," he said. "Resume formation and proceed."

The away team skulked through the dusty, tilted passageways of the decades-dead starship. Twisted bulkheads jutted into long corridors. Messes of cable dangled like jungle vines from ruptured overhead panels. Though there were no bodies—the Douwd's genocide had made certain to wipe every last trace of the Husnock from existence—Riker felt as if the ghosts of the crew whispered in the ship's darkest recesses.

It's only the wind, he told himself. He almost believed it.

Deeper inside the ship there was less dust, which made it harder to find footprints. Fortunately, the Nausicaans' pathfinder markings remained crisp and easy to follow.

Keru halted the team at an intersection of corridors. He motioned for everyone to kneel and take a moment of rest. *"There's a break in the bulkhead a few meters in front of us. I'm reading fresh heat signatures from the other side."*

Sarai asked, *"Any chance there might be safe alternative approaches? Some way we could flank them? Surround them?"*

"Maybe," Keru said. *"I see a passage that might let us get above them, and have some cover. If we split into two groups, we could pin them down and negotiate for the prisoners."*

"Sounds good," Riker said. "You and Pava take the high ground. Signal us when you're in position. Commander Sarai, you and I will stay with Sethe and Modan."

"Aye, sir," Sarai said. *"Pava, Keru, move out."*

The two security officers broke from the group and stole away into the darkness, both moving in low crouches with rifles at the ready. Riker watched the pair slip around a corner, and then he turned to Sarai. "As we humans like to say: here's where the fun begins."

Years of practice and more simulations than Keru could even begin to count—they all had made possible a moment such as this. Prowling toward an armed and hostile enemy force, the Trill kept his breathing slow and even, his hands steady; he felt light on his feet. True, the last of those sensations probably had more to do with the moon's 0.71 standard gravity, but it helped him feel ready to face whatever came next.

Moving at his side was sh'Aqabaa. The Andorian

shen seemed as cool and collected as he felt. Together they advanced up a narrow rampway to a ring-shaped level that was open on its interior side, forming a circular balcony that looked down into a space dominated by a machine composed of dozens of vertical pipes closely packed together. Voices and scraping noises of activity emanated from the level below, the same area in which Keru had detected heat signatures. He paused near the half wall that separated the ring level from the space beyond, and peeked over it. Underneath, on the lowest level, were four prisoners and four armed Nausicaans.

Keru ducked back to cover behind the wall and spoke softly as he informed the away team, "Visual confirmation. Four hostiles, four hostages. Hostiles are well armed. Hostages are in a crossfire zone. Relaying coordinates now." Signaling sh'Aqabaa with gestures, he added, "Moving to secure a better vantage for targeting. Stand by."

He and sh'Aqabaa stayed low as they crept along the ring's edge in search of a better angle from which to attack and provide supporting fire for their teammates on the lower level. Then a clenched fist from sh'Aqabaa halted Keru. She directed his attention to a shape in the darkness. It was hard to spot—its heat signature was muted, and it all but blended into the junk cluttering the deck around it. Then it moved, and Keru recognized the outline of a rifle.

"Heads up. We have a camouflaged shooter on the upper level. Moving to neutralize."

The two security officers moved apart as they circled behind the concealed sniper. In less than a minute they had the drop on him, one of them on each of his rear flanks. Keru signaled sh'Aqabaa to move in, and to watch out for traps guarding the shooter's back. They both closed to within three meters of the sniper and halted.

The longer Keru watched the sniper, the more he wondered what the shooter was doing. Whoever it was, the rifleman wasn't guarding the Nausicaans—if anything, he appeared to be targeting them, sighting them from exactly the position Keru would have chosen to use.

Deciding it was time to find out what the hell was going on, Keru trained his rifle's targeting sensor on the sniper's environmental suit.

If his gear's as fancy as it looks, he'll know we've got the drop on him.

The sniper tensed, then lowered the muzzle of his weapon. He turned and looked back at Keru and sh'Aqabaa. Through the shooter's broad faceplate, Keru recognized the flattened nose, sharp teeth, and enormous ears of a pissed-off Ferengi. The Ferengi held up an empty hand and pointed at his helmet, clearly seeking permission to adjust some setting or other. Keru nodded once but kept his weapon trained on the stranger.

The Ferengi tweaked a setting on his helmet—and then his nasal voice issued from Keru's transceiver: *"What do you think you're doing here, Starfleet?"*

"I was about to ask you the same thing. Put down your weapon."

"Drop yours." The Ferengi resumed his targeting of the Nausicaans. *"I'm working."*

The Ferengi's attitude had clearly ruffled sh'Aqabaa, who inched closer to him, her finger tensed against her rifle's trigger. *"Drop your weapon. You're under arrest."*

"Get lost. You have no jurisdiction here."

He was right, which Keru worried would only make

sh'Aqabaa angrier—and then the whole situation became moot. Targeting sensors in Keru's own suit lit up—

He and sh'Aqabaa both dived to cover as disruptor blasts exploded against the junk around them. One of the Nausicaans from below had come up to the ring level—whether on a routine patrol or drawn by their confrontation with the Ferengi, Keru had no idea—and now the balcony had become a shooting gallery.

Keru returned fire, forcing the Nausicaan to dart for shelter. Then sh'Aqabaa joined the fray—as did the Ferengi, who harassed the Nausicaan and even winged the hulking brute before they all lost sight of him in the wreckage.

More weapons fire screeched and shrieked down below. Smoke and flames climbed upward, and so many voices overlapped on the transceiver channel—Riker's, Sarai's, the Ferengi's, sh'Aqabaa's—that Keru had no idea what any of them were saying.

Then the deck underneath him and sh'Aqabaa collapsed, and the two of them plunged into free fall, through a billowing black cloud and tongues of flame, and the only voice Keru heard was his own, bellowing obscenities all the way down to an abrupt and painful landing.

Listening to the argument between Keru and the shooter he and sh'Aqabaa had confronted on the upper level, Sarai fought to resist the temptation to intrude on the conversation. She had no idea how the interloper had patched into their secure frequency, and that troubled her. *Better not give him any more intel about our numbers than he already has,* she decided. Then she saw Riker signal her, Sethe, and Modan to remain silent. *I guess the admiral feels the same way.*

She heard movement on the other side of the bulkhead. Was it the Nausicaans or the prisoners? Routine shifting from one task to another, or taking positions for a firefight? *Maybe I should move up to scout the positions of the Nausicaans and their hostages.*

Sarai suggested her plan to Riker in gestures. He rejected it with a raised palm that meant stay put. She hated doing nothing, especially in a scenario such as this, when anything—

Disruptor fire, then the whine of phasers. The Nausicaans bellowed orders, the prisoners cried out in alarm, and more disruptor blasts resounded inside the derelict ship.

Riker snapped, *"Keru! Report!"*

His order overlapped Sarai's—"Keru! Pava! Talk to me!"

Something exploded outside the Nausicaans' perimeter, then came the thunder of collapsing decks and buckling spaceframe. Upper decks slammed down into the corridor, kicking up dust followed by thick smoke. Wild volleys of disruptor fire screamed out of the darkness and caromed off the bulkheads, raining sparks onto Sarai and the rest of the away team.

Her instinct was to shoot back, but she held her fire. There were unarmed civilians in harm's way, innocent lives she had been tasked to defend and liberate. As another disruptor pulse ripped past her, she remembered her mistake from many years earlier, when, as a field operative for Starfleet Intelligence, she had fired her weapon in a crisis and struck a child bystander instead of her target. It was a fatal blunder that had haunted her ever since, a regret she would take to her grave. It was not an error she would let herself make again.

Another explosion filled the corridor with shrapnel. Smoky bits tore into the legs of her environmental suit, which tightened the seals at her thighs to prevent the loss of her air. Sarai flattened herself to the deck and retrieved a canister of emergency patch aerosol from her utility belt, and she sprayed it over the rips in her suit, closing them in seconds. Her suit sensed the repairs and normalized the pressure around her legs.

Riker kneeled beside her and fired off a few salvos of suppressing fire in the Nausicaans' direction. He glanced toward Sarai. *"Are you hurt?"*

"Scrapes and bruises," she said. "I'm fine."

Squatting low behind them, Modan and Sethe had drawn their phasers but seemed reluctant to fire without express orders to do so. Sethe asked, *"Orders, sirs? Do we fall back?"*

"No," Riker said. *"The mission's not done. And we don't leave our people behind. Modan, can your tricorder get any kind of a reading on the Nausicaans or the hostages?"*

The Selenean woman activated her tricorder, whose oscillating tones were audible even through the insulation of their environmental suits. *"Yes, sir. A faint signal, but it's clear."* She looked up and around. *"The ship's hull must be absorbing some of the radiation."*

"Thank heaven for small mercies," the admiral muttered. *"Range and bearing?"*

Modan read from her tricorder. *"Same coordinates Keru sent: sixteen meters, bearing zero-one-five mark one-one-eight."*

"Good work," Riker said. He looked at Sarai. *"How do you want to play it?"*

"Head-on," she said. "They aren't moving, so we'll go to them. You and I hug the walls and advance while Modan and Sethe lay down suppressing fire. Then we'll cover them while they move up to join us." She faced the science specialists. "Got it?" Two nods of affirmation, so she checked that her phaser rifle was set for heavy stun. "Ready."

"We go on three," Riker said. *"As soon as Sarai and I break from cover, you fire. Keep firing until we reach cover at the intersection."* He checked his own weapon, then tensed to run. *"One. Two. Three!"*

Sarai and Riker sprang from cover and sprinted down the corridor. Phaser beams sliced through the air between them, and disruptor pulses screamed past from ahead of them. They both laid down their own barrages of suppressing fire, not really aiming so much as blanketing the end of the passageway in an act of area denial. They tumbled in unison behind a dead husk of a machine at the intersection. Both of them gasped for breath—but only for half a second before they popped up again to resume firing at their unseen enemy.

Over the channel, Riker barked, *"Move up!"*

Modan and Sethe charged to huddle with Riker and Sarai behind the scorched, twisted contraption, which appeared to have long ago fallen through the decks above to rest here.

"Well done, you two," Sarai said. "Catch your breath, then we'll—"

A deafening blast and a flash of light filled the corridor, and then Sarai was falling, and the others fell with her. They tumbled through fire and shadow, smoke and bent metal, to crash down in a smoldering heap onto another deck of the Husnock ship, surrounded by debris.

It took Sarai a few seconds to shake off the blast and the fall, then get her bearings. When the fog cleared from her vision, she realized that she, Riker, and the specialists were lying in a heap, and a pair of armed Nausicaans stood a few meters away, with disruptors at the ready.

"Now you die, Starfleet," said the taller Nausicaan, over an open frequency. He aimed his weapon at Sarai—

A flurry of blaster shots peppered the corridor and raked the two Nausicaans, wounding the one who had been about to execute Sarai. Cursing and groaning, the pair retreated, firing wild shots over the prostrate away team into the darkness of the corridor beyond. Moments later the Nausicaans were gone, though Sarai heard their running steps echoing through the ship.

The team's savior emerged from the shadows to stand above them. The Ferengi shook his head and frowned in disgust. *"Never send Starfleet to do a man's job."*

Riker squinted up at the Ferengi. *"Who the hell are you?"*

"Brunt. Bounty hunter." He moved past them and continued down the same passage the Nausicaans had taken. *"What are you waiting for, Starfleet? An invitation? Let's go!"*

There was no time to argue. The Ferengi was on the hunt. Sarai scrambled to her feet, helped Riker stand, and then they got Modan and Sethe up and moving. "Let's go," Sarai said to the group, "we can't afford to lose him."

The away team hurried in pursuit of Brunt, a state of affairs that Sarai found both galling and surreal. As they caught up to him, she decided to make her feelings known. "Let's get something straight, whoever you are. Those are Federation citizens the Nausicaans are—"

"*Shh,*" Brunt hissed with a raised hand.

Before Sarai could demand an explanation, more disruptor blasts flew past her and Brunt, forcing them and the rest of the away team to fall back a few meters. Then a deep rumbling blast rocked the Husnock warship, and the ship came alive with the creaks and groans of distressed metal, and the resounding booms of more internal collapses.

A hoarse voice rasped over the open frequency. *"Starfleet! This ship—a death trap."*

Riker answered, *"We've noticed. What's your point?"*

A delay preceded the next response.

"Starfleet make deal," the Nausicaan said. *"Save lives."*

"We don't deal with terrorists or criminals," Riker said.

Sarai gripped Riker's arm and spoke to him on a private channel. "Admiral, if there's even a chance we could talk the prisoners out of here alive—"

"Trust me," Riker said to Sarai. *"I know what I'm doing."*

"Not terrorists," the Nausicaan said. *"Freedom fighters. I am Slokar, leader of the Patriots of the Wind. We fight to make a new Nausicaa. To make Nausicaans great again."*

Riker switched back to the open frequency. *"And how does murdering and kidnapping Federation citizens accomplish that?"*

"Not your fight. Starfleet never understand." Some unintelligible mumbling, then Slokar continued, *"Your people. You want? Let us go, we give them to you."*

Sarai couldn't stay quiet. "How do we know your prisoners are still alive?"

The next voice on the channel was a woman's. *"My name is Doctor Kilaris,"* she said. *"Doctor Pek and our Bynar colleagues are alive and well. Leader Slokar wishes me to negotiate safe passage for him and his men in exchange for my life and those of my peers."* After a pause, she added, *"He also wishes me to inform you that unless we reach a satisfactory compromise in the next ten minutes, he intends to blow up this vessel—and all of us with it."*

Eleven

If there was one thing Sarai had learned from her years in Starfleet, it was that nothing good ever came from negotiations conducted under extreme time pressure coupled with the threat of a fiery death. *Which probably explains the paucity of Nausicaans in Starfleet,* she decided.

Hunched down in the smoking aftermath of their commando strike gone sour, she and Riker exchanged worried looks as he did his best to keep Slokar talking. *"You've let us hear from Doctor Kilaris,"* Riker said, *"but can you offer us proof that the others are really alive?"*

"Proof of life," Slokar responded. *"Talk now."*

New voices joined the conversation. *"This is Doctor Pek."*

"Zero One Zero—"

"One Zero One, alive."

Hearing the scientists reply gave Sarai at least a small sense of assurance that the admiral's efforts weren't in vain. Then Slokar continued, *"Now you give us safe passage."*

Riker remained calm in the face of the Nausicaan's intransigence. *"My only concern is the safe return of the scientists. Let them go, and you can leave without resistance."* He noted Sarai's appalled reaction at the prospect of letting the Nausicaans escape justice, but squelched her protest with a raised hand and a look that implied, *I'm just saying what he wants to hear.*

Slokar remained intractable. *"Hostages stay with us. Resist, they die."*

Keru chimed in on the away team's secure channel. *"Commander? This is Keru. Pava and I are okay. We're flanking the Nausicaans' position."*

"Good work," Sarai said. "As soon as you and sh'Aqabaa have clear shots, hit the whole group with wide-field maximum stun."

"Including the prisoners?"

Riker gave Sarai a thumbs-up signal. She acknowledged it, then told Keru, "Affirmative. They'll wake up with headaches, but they'll be alive and free."

"Copy that. Stand by."

Growing angrier, Slokar rumbled, *"Answer, Starfleet! Safe passage! Yes or no?"*

There was genuine regret and weary resignation in Riker's voice. *"With all respect, Slokar, I can't let you leave here with those prisoners."*

"Then we all die."

The admiral regarded Sarai with a frown of disappointment. He squinted as he looked past her and then over his shoulder, searching the darkness with a confused expression before he asked over their private channel, *"What happened to the Ferengi?"*

Sarai mimicked Riker's search and confirmed that Brunt was nowhere to be seen.

Oh, no.

It was an ironic state of affairs. As much as Kilaris did not care for having been violently abducted and forced by the Nausicaans to engage in slave labor breaking the encryption keys on a Husnock computer core, she had to admit that she and her colleagues were making significant strides in their understanding of the Husnock's language and technology in a very brief period of time. Though it seemed unjust, she considered that there might be truth in the old adage: *Sometimes we do our best work with a gun to our head.*

Regardless, she still intended to kill Slokar and his men if afforded the opportunity.

She and Pek watched over the Bynars' tiny shoulders as they brainstormed their way through the final stages of hacking the decades-dormant computer core, which continued to hum along in spite of the beating it had taken in the crossfire minutes earlier. Smoke lingered in the air, and a fresh coating of dust caked the portable control panels, but neither seemed to pose an impediment to the Bynars, whose communion with the alien computer continued to deepen.

"There," Pek said, pointing at the console's main screen. *"That's the system Slokar said he wants cracked."*

010 said, *"It will take a moment—"*

"*—to remove the encryptions,*" finished 101.

Interfacing with each other via the Husnock computer, the Bynars made swift work of the encrypted data. They unlocked the file, whose raw data they routed to the adjacent workstation, which was running Kilaris's jury-rigged Husnock translation system. As soon as the new data arrived, the modified universal translator began its work.

Several seconds passed in tense silence as Kilaris and her colleagues waited to see whether their efforts would bear fruit. Then a flood of parsed data scrolled up the screen, a trove of Husnock security codes and command-access protocols, all rendered in the clear.

Kilaris experienced a moment of grim realization. *With this, the Nausicaans could seize control of intact Husnock vessels and facilities. Armed with such vessels they could slaughter billions. Perhaps we should destroy this data before—*

Pek exclaimed, *"We did it!"*

His outburst drew Slokar and Varoh to their side. *"Good,"* Slokar said. He handed Pek a data chip. *"Copy data onto this."* Pek, finally realizing the magnitude of his blunder, hesitated. Slokar drew his disruptor pistol and aimed it at Kilaris's head. *"Copy data or Vulcan dies."*

Another hesitation. As recently as the previous century, some Tellarites might not have cared about whether a Vulcan lived or died. Kilaris hoped Pek did not harbor a secret animosity toward her species—or, if he did, that this was not the moment he chose to express it.

Pek put the chip into the console and copied the Husnock security codes and command protocols onto it. When the data was finished duplicating, he ejected the chip and handed it back to Slokar, his manner restrained. *"That's all of it. Please don't hurt Doctor Kilaris."*

"Not kill you yet," Slokar rasped. *"Still need you as shields."* To Varoh he said, *"Turn off their comms. Can't let them plot."*

Before Kilaris or the others could protest, Varoh removed the transceiver relays from the outsides of their helmets, and he confiscated the cables that had let the Bynars link with the Husnock computer and each other. Now the four of them were each locked inside their own silence, waiting to see what atrocity the Nausicaans would visit upon them next.

Kilaris watched Varoh and the other subordinate Nausicaans. They moved quickly but methodically about the compartment, placing small devices topped with blinking lights.

Military ordnance was far from Kilaris's area of expertise, but even she could tell what their captors were doing: they were planting explosives around the Husnock computer core.

This is not going to end well, she speculated.

Then a devastating storm of energy pulses ripped through the compartment, their point of origin hidden by the smoke and dust in the air. One of the Nausicaans collapsed dead at Kilaris's feet, the faceplate of his helmet blown apart and his head cooked to a crisp inside. Another staggered to cover while gripping a smoldering-hot wound in his arm, his retreat covered by Slokar and Varoh, who in their haste to escape the blasts had left behind the prisoners.

Chasing the fleeing Nausicaans was a lone figure, a wild screaming Ferengi bearing a carbine disruptor rifle in each hand. He fired both weapons at once as he charged in relentless pursuit of his three much larger and better-armed opponents.

Wild shots from the Ferengi's weapons ricocheted off a bulkhead and slammed through the deck plate beneath Kilaris. It creaked, then it sagged. She and the others tried to flee to more solid footing, but it was too late—the floor fell away beneath them, and from there the only thing Kilaris could see was a blur of shadows against a deeper darkness that swallowed them all.

Phaser blasts ripped past Riker's head, all of them far too close for comfort and each one closer than the last. He had no idea who had fired first, who had fired at whom, or what in blazes was going on inside the Husnock wreck.

"Someone talk to me," he demanded. "Who's firing in there?"

Chaotic shouts and the shrieks of discharging weapons—that's all he heard for a few seconds over the open channel. Then a reply came in on the away team's secure channel. *"Sir, this is Keru. The Nausicaans are in retreat, and we've reached the civilians."*

"Who gave the order to engage?"

"It was the Ferengi, sir. He just went berserk."

Sarai asked, "Are the prisoners okay?"

"They took a spill, but they're fine. But we've got another problem. The Nausicaans set charges on the

computer, and we don't have the gear to defuse them. We've got about five minutes to get topside or we're all dead."

"Evacuate the ship," Riker said. "Skip the rendezvous point, head for the runabout."

As Riker got up to lead the exodus, Sarai asked, *"Sir, what about the Nausicaans?"*

"One thing at a time, Commander. Run!"

With Sarai, Modan, and Sethe at his back, Riker sprinted to the nearest passageway marked by the Nausicaans, then he followed the painted guides through the smoky darkness, back to the transverse corridor that led to the break in the hull. As he and the others barreled around the last corner on their way to safety, they collided with Keru, sh'Aqabaa, and the four civilian scientists, who had come by an alternative path.

Keru asked, *"Everyone okay?"*

"All here," Riker said. "Let's—"

From the shadows behind them came the Ferengi, running so hard he nearly bowled over half the away team in his haste to escape the wreck. Riker grabbed the Ferengi's arm. "You—!"

"Admiral! Thank me later, but we have to go! The ship's—"

"Going to explode, I know. What the hell did you think you were doing?"

"What your people wouldn't. And before I forget—" He pulled a data chip from his belt and pushed it into Riker's palm.

Riker held up the chip. "What the hell is this?"

Deadly serious, Brunt replied, *"My bill."*

Brunt slipped from Riker's grasp and continued his

mad dash for open air. Sarai snapped at the away team, "Don't stand there! Move!" The group ran for the exit and didn't look back. Then Sarai turned toward Riker. "Sir, let's go!"

"Lead on," he said. He pocketed the chip and followed her out, with one notion festering in his thoughts every step of the way.

I hate Ferengi.

It wasn't the longest run of Dalit Sarai's life, but it was the most desperate. She was at the back of the group, making sure no one straggled or strayed as they retreated off of the ship's hull and up the steep incline of sharp rocks. It would have been easy for her to sprint ahead of the others, take the lead, and guarantee her own survival—but she was the *Titan*'s first officer. Safeguarding the lives of her crew and the security of her ship were her chief duties, even if meant that she would be the one closest to—

A bone-shaking boom split the air as a blast wave flattened Sarai. She landed face-first, hard enough that a rock gouged a scratch across her transparent aluminum faceplate. Heat rolled over her back, and a cloud of ash, cinders, and dust roared over the away team and the rescued civilians, who all lay pinned to the slope, just like her.

She looked back. A black mushroom cloud climbed into the sickly green sky. Beneath it, the Husnock wreck collapsed into itself, its broken hull being consumed by a growing ball of fire unleashed by the Nausicaans' munitions. As the fractured, sagging hull fell inward, it started to take a swath of the hillside with it.

Sarai sprang to her feet. "Up! Move! Now!"

The others were sluggish to react, no doubt stunned by the shock wave. She pulled Riker from the ground, then Sethe and Modan. By the time she reached the civilians, they were already scrambling up the slope, following Keru and sh'Aqabaa toward the runabout.

Behind them, the slope continued to erode and showed no sign of slowing its disintegration. Stumbling up the uneven ground, Sarai opened a channel to the computer on the *Nechako*. "Computer! Start engines! Override preflight systems check! Open port-side hatch!"

The runabout's hatch slid open just before Keru got to it. He waved the others past him, and helped the civilians inside before directing them to the aft compartment.

Riker tripped over a jutting stone and landed hard on one knee. Sarai pulled him up, and then she let him run on his own once she was sure he could keep up. The admiral ducked inside the *Nechako* half a step ahead of Sarai, who knew the hillside's vanishing edge was continuing to chase her. "Computer, fire vertical thrusters in two seconds!"

She counted down in her head and dived through the open hatchway a fraction of a second before the ship lurched upward—and the ground beneath it churned into a molten slurry.

Keru pulled Sarai inside and closed the hatch manually, then he reset the ship's environmental controls. The HUD on Sarai's faceplate confirmed that a normal atmospheric mix had been restored inside the *Nechako*. She and the others doffed their helmets, and then she made her way to the cockpit, followed by Riker.

Ensconced once more in the pilot's seat, she asked Riker, "Orders, sir?"

"Back to the *Titan*," he said. "I won't risk another battle with civilians aboard."

"And the Nausicaans?"

A look of determination hardened his features. "They won't get far."

Needles of fire shot up Slokar's leg as he, Varoh, and Motar limped back to their ship. Pain did not matter. All that mattered was power, and the codes on the chip would give that to him. Give that to all Nausicaans, a people without a homeworld, a people in need of a new future.

He did not mourn the man he had left behind. Zallas was not the first to die for this cause. He would not be the last. But he had died a patriot. He was killed standing up for the Nausicaan people. Slokar vowed to make sure his name would be remembered, sung forever by his people and whispered forever by the Four Winds. Heroes deserved no less.

Motar's arm dangled limp and paralyzed at his side; he had been the first casualty of the mad Ferengi. Only Varoh had escaped the Husnock wreck unscathed. Always the lucky one—that was Varoh. But Slokar did not envy him. Who revered a veteran with no scars?

In spite of their wounds, they moved quickly across the harsh moonscape. It was good to be free of the prisoners. They had been necessary, but only up to a point. Had Starfleet or the Ferengi not interfered, Slokar could have done away with the mewling civilians as soon as they had cracked the Husnock computer. Free of their whining, he and his men made better time returning to their ship than they had on the outbound journey.

It was all for the best. Soon he and his men would be away, and once they took control of the Husnock's mighty arsenal, the future would be theirs to bend to their will.

They crested a rise in the path. Slokar grinned at the sight of his ship, the *Kaze'Noken*, parked where they had left it. Imagining the roars of acclaim that would greet their triumphant return, Slokar straightened his back and mastered the burning agony in his leg. He would face his crew with strength and pride. He would show them how a Nausicaan conquers all.

He keyed his access code into the panel beside the outer airlock door. It rolled open, and he let Varoh and Motar enter ahead of him. Once they were inside, he joined them and secured the outer door. When the airlock finished restoring the air and sterilizing their suits, the lights changed color, and Slokar keyed in his code again to open the inner door.

The three returning heroes stepped out of the airlock into the lower operations bay, where the crew stored EVA equipment and supplies. There was no one there to greet them, but that was not unusual. Slokar and his men shed their cumbersome environmental suits and stuffed them back into their storage lockers. Then Slokar stepped over to a nearby companel on the bulkhead and opened a channel to the bridge. "Yereb! We have the chip! Prepare to launch!"

He waited for his second-in-command to reply and confirm the order. No response came. Slokar was about to repeat himself when he heard the ops bay door open behind him. He and the others turned to see Yereb standing in the doorway.

Yereb fell like a cut tree and landed facedown on the deck, revealing the blade jammed deep between his shoulder blades . . . and the green Orion woman standing behind him, flanked by two men—a Klingon and a Balduk—both with disruptors aimed at Slokar and his comrades.

"Welcome back, Commander Slokar," the woman said. "My name is Nilat, and I bring you greetings and salutations from the Orion Syndicate."

Slokar and Varoh reached for their sidearms.

The Klingon and the Balduk fired.

Disruptor shots punched through Slokar's torso and Varoh's neck. The barrage continued and engulfed Motar. When the shooting stopped, Slokar and his brothers-in-arms were splayed on the deck, all three of them riddled with smoldering wounds that reeked of burnt meat.

Nilat strolled over to the mortally wounded Slokar, squatted beside him, and with delicate finesse pilfered the data chip of Husnock command codes from his clenched fist. "On behalf of my employer, thank you so very much. We truly could not have done this without you."

As she stood, the bulkhead that separated the ops bay from a vehicle bay retracted, revealing the rest of Slokar's valiant crew—all dead and stacked like cordwood.

Vile curses drowned in Slokar's blood-filled throat.

The Klingon asked Nilat, "Should we put them with the others?"

She considered it, then shook her head. "Don't bother. We won't keep this ship long enough for it to matter."

She drew her disruptor and smirked at Slokar. "Tell the Wind I said hello." She aimed and fired—and Slokar's *tegol*, freed at last from the prison of his flesh, soared with the Four Winds to the Heart of the Sky, where his ancestors awaited his coming.

Twelve

A crimson flash on the moon's surface snapped Vale's eye from her command console to the *Titan* bridge's main viewscreen. "What the hell was that?"

Tuvok checked his console. "An explosion inside the crashed Husnock vessel." He keyed in new commands. "Magnifying." The image on the screen enlarged, but there was no longer a view of the wrecked starship, only a spreading crown of black smoke obscuring the surface.

"Not helping," Vale said. "Where's the away team?" When Tuvok failed to answer immediately, she turned toward ops. "Rager, tell me you've filtered out the radiation."

The human woman looked dismayed. "Still working on it, Captain."

"Dammit." Vale stood and paced in front of her chair, growing more agitated with each passing moment of situational blindness. "Someone tell me something."

Pazlar swiveled away from the sciences console.

"I've analyzed the thermal signature of the blast, and the chemical composition of the resulting cloud. Both are consistent with high-yield explosives manufactured by the Klingons. Such munitions are frequently sold through black-market channels, which would suggest the explosion was triggered by the Nausicaans."

The next person to pipe up was Lavena. "Captain, I can adjust our orbital position to give visual sensors an oblique but unobstructed angle on the blast site."

"Do it." Vale returned to her chair. "Tactical, stay sharp. If anything moves on the surface, in the atmosphere, or anywhere else in this system, I want to know about it."

It took a few minutes for Lavena to guide the ship into an adjusted orbit. As soon as the maneuver was completed, she signaled Tuvok, who refocused the visual sensors and routed to the main viewscreen an image of a mountainside turned to fire and molten rock.

From the engineering console, Torvig asked, "Where is the Husnock ship?"

"Incinerated," Tuvok said. "It is possible the Nausicaans' explosion ignited munitions or deuterium fuel reserves that survived the vessel's crash. Or perhaps both, judging from the extent of the damage to the surrounding terrain."

The fiery wound in the moonscape stoked Vale's concern for her personnel, and for the civilians they had been sent to rescue. "Do we have any idea where the away team is?"

Rager straightened and responded with excitement, "Captain, I have a lock on the runabout. It's airborne and heading for orbit."

"Incoming message from the *Nechako*," Tuvok said. "Admiral Riker reports all personnel are aboard, plus the four civilians." New alerts sounded on Tuvok's console. He silenced them as he reviewed the incoming sensor data. "Three more ships launching from the surface. They are also heading for space, on divergent headings. One appears to be the Nausicaan ship, the other two are of unknown origin—a small starhopper and an Orion argosy."

Vale was back on her feet. "Helm, intercept the argosy. Ops, hail the runabout, tell them to go evasive until we clear them to land. Tuvok, tell the *Canterbury* to stop the Nausicaans."

He looked up from his console. "And the starhopper?"

"Let it go."

Vale hated to let any of the alien vessels slip through her grasp, but the *Wasp* was still too far out of range to assist in the roundup. While the runabout might have been able to halt the starhopper, Vale had no intention of sending the small ship into a potential combat action with civilians aboard. Either the starhopper, a small craft that carried at most a handful of passengers, or the larger Orion argosy was going to escape. Choosing to detain the larger ship might prove to be a mistake, but at this point she had to try to reel in the biggest fish that she could.

"Raising shields," Tuvok said. "Charging phasers and tractor beam."

Lavena accelerated the *Titan* out of orbit into a pursuit heading. "Closing on the Orion ship at full impulse," the Selkie said, her voice filtered through her aquatic breathing mask.

"Ops," Vale said, "open a channel to the argosy."

A few quick taps on her console, then Rager replied, "Channel open."

Vale stood to better project authority with her voice. "Attention, unidentified Orion vessel. This is Captain Christine Vale, commanding the Federation *Starship Titan*. Halt your vessel and prepare to be boarded. Acknowledge this command or be fired upon."

"They're changing course," Lavena said. "They're attack—"

Twin blasts of disruptor fire filled the viewscreen, which flared white with static as the *Titan* shook for half a second. Then the interference on the screen cleared to show a pinwheeling curtain of stars as Tuvok reported, "Direct hit, forward shields holding."

"Coming about," Lavena said. "Matching their—" She stopped and stared at her console, then looked back at Vale. "They're gone, Captain."

Tuvok added, "Captain, they appear to have cloaked."

"An Orion ship with a cloaking device?" Vale shook her head. "Who says crime doesn't pay?" She checked her command monitor. "How's *Canterbury* doing with the Nausicaans?"

"The Nausicaan ship has engaged in a series of textbook evasive maneuvers," Tuvok said. "The flight pattern suggests the ship is operating on autopilot."

Suspicion and alarm filled Vale's thoughts. "Move us closer, see if we can knock out its shields without inflicting too much damage—I want that ship captured and its logs analyzed."

"Moving to intercept," Lavena confirmed.

"Locking tractor beams and phasers," Tuvok said.

The Nausicaan ship and the *Canterbury* both grew larger on the main viewscreen, both of them locked in an erratic dance of chase and escape. Then the Nausicaan ship rolled out of its evasion pattern—and accelerated directly toward the *Titan*.

What the hell?

"They're on a ramming trajectory," Rager said. "Twelve seconds to impact."

Tuvok's console flooded with alarms. "Captain, they've dropped their shields. I'm reading no life-forms—and its self-destruct system has engaged."

Vale sat and white-knuckled the arms of her command chair. "Evasive, starboard! Fire phasers and sound collision alarm!" Alert sirens whooped over the ship's PA system but were barely audible over the sudden groaning of its spaceframe, the resonant whine of the impulse engines, and the screeching of its phaser banks all firing at once.

On the viewscreen, the *Canterbury* peeled away in a high-impulse maneuver as the *Titan*'s phaser barrage sliced through the defenseless Nausicaan ship. It exploded in a blinding flash that forced Vale to shut her eyes and look away. A shock wave buffeted the *Titan*, which rocked and shuddered. Then the glare and the tumult faded away.

Vale let go of her chair's arms and seethed. The other two alien ships had vanished into the soup of radiation pouring from the gas giant, and there was nothing left of the Nausicaan vessel but superheated gas and a quickly expanding cloud of dust. "Tuvok, report."

"Minor damage to our shield generators," he said. "All decks report secure."

"Lower shields, go to yellow alert," Vale said. "Everyone, look for anything that might tell us where the Orions or that starhopper went. Helm, take us back to orbit and recover the runabout." She stood and headed for the turbolift. "I'm going below to meet the away team and find out what happened down there. Mister Tuvok, you have the conn."

It was a relief to be free of the environmental suit. Wearing one always reminded Will Riker of how much he took his freedom of movement for granted. Returning the suit to its locker in the *Nechako*'s aft compartment, he bid it a silent *good riddance*.

He recognized the familiar pattern of a gentle bump followed by the dwindling whine of the runabout's engines. They had touched down in the *Titan*'s main shuttlebay.

Riker turned to face the four civilians, who had shed their own environmental suits and packed them into the runabout's spare storage module. "Any questions before we get out?" They shook their heads. "All right, then. Let's go."

Keru opened the port hatch. He and sh'Aqabaa were the first ones off the runabout. Sarai ushered Sethe and Modan out ahead of her, then she motioned for Riker and the civilians to go. He led the rescuees off the *Nechako* and into the *Titan*'s shuttlebay, where Captain Vale, Doctor Ree, and Riker's aide Lieutenant Ssura stood, awaiting their arrival.

Vale stepped forward and greeted the civilians. She nodded at the Vulcan woman. "Doctor Kilaris." Next she shook the Tellarite's four-fingered manus. "Doctor Pek." Then she faced the Bynars and smiled. "Doctors Zero One Zero and One Zero One. Welcome aboard the *Titan*.

Do any of you require urgent medical attention, for any reason?"

Kilaris replied, "No, Captain. None of us are injured or in distress."

"Glad to hear it. That said, Starfleet regulations require us to perform a cursory medical examination of each of you, just to ensure none of you are experiencing delayed symptoms of physical shock or psychological trauma."

The Tellarite scowled. "And if I'd rather not be poked and prodded by your lizard-doctor? What happens then?"

"You are free to refuse to be examined," Vale said. "In which case, I'll have my security chief escort you to guest quarters for a mandatory three-day observation period."

Pek harrumphed. "A perfect illustration of why I never applied to Starfleet."

Vale ignored the engineer's gripe and faced Riker. "Admiral? Are you okay?"

"Shipshape." He stepped aside and beckoned Vale with a tilt of his head. Away from the group, he asked in a confidential tone, "What was all the shooting we saw on the way up?"

She matched his discreet volume. "Three ships left the planet's surface shortly after you did. We identified one as the Nausicaans, another as an Orion argosy. The third was a starhopper with a blank transponder code. That one's still a mystery."

"Maybe not." Riker took from his pocket the data chip Brunt had foisted upon him inside the wreck. He waved to Ssura, who hurried to his side. Riker pushed the chip into Ssura's paw.

The Caitian eyed the chip. "Sir? What's this?"

"An invoice," Riker said. "From a Ferengi named Brunt." To Vale he added, "I'd wager he's the one in the starhopper."

Studying the chip, Ssura asked, "An invoice for what, Admiral?"

"Services rendered, I suspect."

A twitch of whiskers. "And what should I do with it?"

"Honestly? I don't give a damn." He turned back to Vale. "Where are they now?"

She looked confused. "Who? The Nausicaans, the Orions, or the Ferengi?"

"Any of them. All of them. Pick one."

"We fragged the Nausicaans' ship, but we didn't detect any life-forms aboard. The Orion ship cloaked, and the starhopper slipped away in the confusion."

Riker nodded as he pieced together the details in his imagination. "As far as we know, three of the four Nausicaans we fought inside the wreck escaped, and they probably had a full crew on their ship. But if their vessel was empty when you destroyed it, either they've commandeered the Orion ship, or the crew of the argosy took the Nausicaans out of play."

Before he and Vale could continue their speculations, Sarai stepped over to interrupt their private chat. "Excuse me, sirs, but Doctor Kilaris has intel you need to hear."

The XO led Riker and Vale back to the four civilians, who looked quite anxious—all except Kilaris, whose Vulcan sangfroid was truly impeccable. She stepped forward to meet Riker and Vale. "Captain. Admiral. It is imperative that you know what it was that the Nausicaans sought inside the Husnock vessel."

"We're listening," Riker said.

"Security codes and military command protocols. It seems the Nausicaans discovered the wrecked Husnock vessel and determined its computer core was intact. But without a working knowledge of the Husnock's language and technology, they were unable to access its contents."

Pek stepped up beside Kilaris. "That's why they took us."

"We assumed as much from a review of your dossiers," Vale said. "What I need to know right now is, what do the Nausicaans plan to do with the intel you helped them steal?"

"They claimed they had found an arsenal of Husnock weapons," Kilaris said, "and a fleet of their ships. Enough to let them conquer any opponent they wanted."

Riker's mood darkened as he considered the state of play. "It's a good bet whoever's on the argosy has those codes. Whether it's a Syndicate crew or the Nausicaans, it doesn't matter. We can't let them use that intel."

"Agreed," Vale said. "But until we figure out how to punch through all this radiation and strip away the protection of their cloaking device, I have no idea how to find them."

"I do," Pek said. When he realized all eyes in the shuttlebay were now on him, he puffed out his chest and stood a bit taller. "I snuck a bit of malicious code onto the Nausicaans' data chip. If the data on the chip is accessed by a networked terminal on a starship, the chip will program a detectable phase misalignment into the ship's warp coil regulators, one that will make them send out Cochrane distortion at a precise frequency of twenty-one point six MC." A faux-humble shrug. "Should make them pretty easy to track at warp, even through a cloaking device."

Sarai lifted an eyebrow. "Pretty easy? That's an understatement. Distortion like that would stick out like a sore thumb if—" An admiring nod and a thin smile as she grasped the genius of the Tellarite's sabotage. "*If* you know to look for it."

"And now we do," Riker said.

Vale said to Sarai, "Number One, escort Doctor Pek to the bridge and have him brief Commander Tuvok."

"Aye, sir," Sarai said. "Lieutenant sh'Aqabaa, you're with me."

As Sarai and sh'Aqabaa led Pek out of the shuttlebay, Riker considered a more pessimistic scenario. "Captain, it's possible the chip isn't on the argosy. Or, if it is, there's no guarantee it'll be read by a terminal connected to the ship's datanet. We need to find a way to break through its cloaking device, just in case Pek's gambit doesn't pay off."

"I'll have Xin work on it." She gently took hold of his arm and led him a few meters away from the group. This time she whispered. "How far does Starfleet expect us to take this?"

"What do you mean?"

"Say we catch the argosy, and whoever's on board won't give up the chip. What then?"

There was no point sugarcoating the truth. Orders were orders.

"In that case," he said, "we blow them to hell."

There were a great many places in which Sarai might have expected an unprovoked ambush, but the corridors of the *Titan* were not among them.

FORTUNE OF WAR

She and sh'Aqabaa had escorted Doctor Pek less than two sections away from the main shuttlebay, and the turbolift was just a few meters ahead of them, when Deanna Troi's voice called out from behind them, resounding with an almost lyrical quality: "Commander Sarai!"

The salutation made sh'Aqabaa and Pek slow their strides, but Sarai mumbled, "Keep walking," so they did. It was a childish gambit to pretend not to hear a fellow officer, but there was work to be done, and months of Starfleet-mandated counseling after Sarai's "incident" in the field a few years earlier had conditioned her to dread speaking to members of Troi's profession.

Just a few more steps to the turbolift . . .

"Commander," Troi called again, her tone unimpeachably cordial. It would be difficult to justify not stopping, but Sarai was adamant that she—"Dalit!"

Hearing her given name spoken with edge and volume stopped Sarai cold. Old feelings of guilt and alarm clouded her thinking. In a moment's reflection she realized why. *She sounded just like my mother.* It was like a shard of glass in Sarai's brain. That same castigating tone was the one Tanara Sarai had used whenever young Dalit had incurred her wrath.

Sarai turned to face the ugly music. Confused and maybe sensing her tension, sh'Aqabaa and Pek halted to wait beside her, as anxious as if Troi had called their names, as well.

Troi quick-stepped down the corridor to catch up to them. She flashed a disarming smile. "For a moment there I thought you couldn't hear me."

"My apologies, Counselor. I was a bit preoccupied." A transparent lie. Would the half-Betazoid counselor and diplomatic officer call her on it?

"We need to have a conversation, Commander," Troi said.

Sarai nodded toward Pek and sh'Aqabaa. "Now isn't a good time. We need to bring Doctor Pek up to the bridge to confer with Commander Tuvok on an urgent tactical matter."

Nothing dimmed Troi's aura of sweet cheer—a quality Sarai found cloying. "Well, I'm sure Lieutenant sh'Aqabaa knows her way to the bridge. Don't you, Lieutenant?"

"I do," said the statuesque Andorian *shen*—who stood her ground and maintained a mask of perfect neutrality as she looked to Sarai for her next instruction.

A tense moment stretched out, a silent battle of wills as the three women regarded one another with preternatural calm while the Tellarite scientist trapped in their midst fidgeted like a child with an overtaxed bladder. The longer Sarai faced off against Troi, the more she realized that the counselor's quasi-saccharine demeanor concealed a sharp and steely will. This was not a confrontation Sarai could bluff her way out of.

"Lieutenant sh'Aqabaa, take Doctor Pek to the bridge. I'll join you shortly."

"Aye, sir." The security officer took Pek's arm and led him to the turbolift, which opened at their approach. As soon as they were inside, the doors closed, and Sarai heard the faint hum of magnetic coils whisking the lift car away on its journey to the bridge.

She mirrored Troi's insincere smile. "What can I do for you, Counselor?"

"Walk with me." Troi turned and started back the way she had come without waiting for Sarai's assent, making it clear that her invitation had been an order rather than a suggestion. As soon as Sarai fell into step at her side, she continued. "We need to talk about the crew's morale."

This was not a conversation Sarai wanted to have, but decorum compelled her to hear what Troi had to say. "What about it?"

"It could be better. Long frontier assignments take their toll, on both spirit and flesh."

"And that concerns me because . . . ?"

"Traditionally," Troi said, adopting the manner of an Academy instructor, "maintaining healthy crew morale is one of the key responsibilities of a ship's executive officer. However, I've noticed that it's a role from which you appear to be utterly divorced on the *Titan*."

It pained Sarai to resist the urge to roll her eyes or grit her teeth. "You're right. I do try not to tamper with the crew's morale. In my experience, they and I are both happier this way."

They continued aft until Troi led Sarai inside the ship's ventral botanical garden, a lush green space tucked in the belly of the ship. It was a rare oasis amid the machinery of the engineering hull. Sarai wondered whether Troi had brought her here by chance, or because she thought the less synthetic environment might inspire Sarai to experience an emotional epiphany.

"No one is asking you to be the chief entertainment officer," Troi said, "or to play matchmaker for the lonely hearts. But your personnel reviews exhibit no concern for whether the officers and enlisted crew under your command are thriving in their roles, or just marking time."

"With all respect, Counselor, if any member of this crew wants to request a change of their billet or a transfer to another boat, they're welcome to ask. But

I don't have the time to micromanage the careers of over seven hundred fifty people. So if I choose to prioritize the operation of this ship, the safety of its crew, and the effective completion of our assigned missions over the professional misgivings of seven hundred strangers, that's my prerogative." She stepped in front of Troi, pivoted to face her, and stopped. "Tell me the truth, Counselor. Did the captain put you up to this little chat? Or did the admiral?"

"Neither. As the head of the counseling services division, I made this call on my own."

"Then I suggest you *un*-make it on your own. Mind your own duties, Counselor, and unless the captain or the admiral requests otherwise, keep your command advice to yourself."

Sarai stepped around Troi and left the botanical garden. She listened for the sound of pursuing footsteps or a command for her return, but she heard neither.

Her walk back to the turbolift was quiet and steeped in resentment. Riding up to deck one, she stewed in her dark mood, most annoyed by the fact that she knew, deep down, that Troi was right. Sarai had neglected a significant aspect of her role as the *Titan*'s XO—not because she was incapable of rising to the challenge, but because she didn't want to feel close to officers whom she knew she was betraying every minute of every day just by being among them.

If I felt like I really belonged here, if I thought I'd been posted here because I'd earned a return to starship service, that would be one thing, she brooded. *But the only reason I'm here is because Admiral Batanides wants a spy to watch Vale and Riker, and she thinks my tainted past makes me easy to control. I'm here because she thinks I don't deserve to be anything but a puppet.*

When she considered herself from an emotional remove and asked herself who and what she wanted to be, the answer seemed clear: she wanted to be the best first officer she could be for Captain Vale and the most loyal subordinate she could be to Admiral Riker. Both of them, in spite of whatever Sarai had been coerced into reporting about them to Batanides, were officers of good character and noble intent. They deserved better than this, she realized.

They deserve better than me.

As far as Xin Ra-Havreii was concerned, there was no better place to be when feeling antisocial than arms deep in the sensor array at the bow of the *Titan*'s secondary hull. Ensconced in the cold embrace of machines and ODN cables, he felt safely isolated from the critical eyes of his shipmates, insulated from the distractions of interacting with those who excelled at nothing so much as the finding of fault with how he chose to conduct his personal business.

He wished he could debug personal relationships with the same detachment that he brought to rewiring the ship's multispectral detection grid. Cross-circuiting isolinear slots was a simple matter of reading spec sheets and design schematics, then applying his lifetime of engineering expertise and mathematical acumen to deduce which pieces of hardware and which strings of firmware had to be adjusted to compensate for exotic radiation effects. If a tweak didn't produce the result he expected he could test it with trial and error. More than anything else, what he liked about the process was its binary nature. An action worked or it didn't; a change in the system either yielded the desired result or it didn't.

When did relationships become so ambiguous?

He dismissed the rhetorical question. *Stay focused. Just do the job.*

A soft tone issued from his padd, which was balanced atop an EPS buffer beside him. He picked up the device and perused the message. It was a summary of a bit of sabotage that a civilian engineer had snuck onto a data chip and which might aid the *Titan*'s search. He noted the specs for the anticipated millicochranes of distortion the malware would produce, then put the padd aside while he continued working. *One task at a time.*

The array's data transmission loads were almost balanced to within optimal range when he heard two sets of footfalls approaching from the corridor behind him. He hoped they would just pass on by, but instead they stopped outside his open bulkhead panel.

Ra-Havreii sighed. He looked back and made no effort to conceal his irritation at the disturbance. "Who's there and what do you want?"

Ensign Evesh, a Tellarite sensor technician who several members of the crew insisted was a female of her species, leaned her snouted black-eyed face through the gap between the bulkhead and Ra-Havreii's hip. "The captain sent us down to assist you."

Her use of a plural pronoun made the chief engineer arch one snowy eyebrow with suspicion. "You and who else, Ensign?"

"Lieutenant Commander Pazlar, sir." Evesh backed out of the tight space just far enough to let Ra-Havreii see Pazlar standing in the corridor with her arms crossed. Either oblivious of or indifferent to the acrimony and tension between the two senior officers, Evesh asked with typical Tellarite bluntness, "What do you want us to do?"

"Find someone else to annoy," Ra-Havreii said. "I have this under control."

Pazlar said, "We're here by order of the XO." Her deadpan manner telegraphed her disdain for being compelled to work with him.

Ra-Havreii pretended not to care. "Tell Sarai I don't need your help."

"You want to countermand the Ice Queen's orders? Tell her yourself."

Evesh grunted in irritation. "You're wasting time! The captain said she wants to pierce the Orions' cloak within the hour. So maybe you two can have your spat on your own time?"

Her rebuke drew shocked and reproachful looks from Pazlar and Ra-Havreii, the first time he had felt simpatico with the Elaysian science officer since their bitter breakup months earlier. Hoping to prevent the Tellarite from throwing any more fuel on the metaphorical fire, Ra-Havreii handed her an isospectral calibration tool and pointed her aft. "Open the next panel and triple the gain on the gravitic sensors for frequencies between twenty-one and twenty-two millicochranes. Compensate by compressing the curve on the signal waveform."

"Aye, sir." Evesh took the tool and moved one bulkhead aft to work.

He tried to crawl back inside the sensor assembly.

Pazlar halted him by asking, "What about me?"

Sullen and brimming with resentment, Ra-Havreii

slithered free of the machinery and confronted the science officer. "What about you?"

"Don't do this here," she said, her voice low and rich with implied threat. "Not now."

"I forgot how much you love to dictate terms." He felt her fury surfacing despite her best efforts to hide it. "Tell me: When you're done meddling with my repairs, whose work do you plan to stick your hands into next?"

"Where I stick my hands is none of your business, Commander, but I'll be more than happy to tell you where you can stick yours."

From down the corridor, Evesh griped, "Hey! I'm trying to work here. Either shut up or go find a bunk to soil in private."

Being openly disrespected by a junior officer lit Ra-Havreii's fuse. "By the hoary host! Damn it, Ensign, you're speaking to a pair of senior officers! Shut your snout and keep your eyes on your work, or so help me I'll put so many black marks on your record you'll be lucky to get a job scrubbing latrines on Rura damned Penthe!"

Pazlar tried to interpose herself between Ra-Havreii and Evesh. "Calm the hell down before you—"

"Calm down? Is that what you just said to me? Oh, that's rich. Social advice from the likes of you—that's the last damned thing I need."

Now the science officer was in his face, challenging him. "The likes of me? And what exactly are the likes of me, Doctor Ra-Havreii? What does that classification mean to you?"

"The cold and heartless." He flicked a fingernail against Pazlar's powered exoskeleton, which enabled her to function in normal gravity though her species had evolved on a low-g world. "I always used to think this was just a crutch for your brittle bones. Now I see your defects go a lot deeper than that. You're an *emotional* cripple too."

The slap of her palm across his face stung for a second. The pain of realizing he could never take back his false and foolishly chosen words, he realized too late, would last far longer.

Pazlar turned on her heel and walked away, her rage radiating from her like heat off a dying star. Ra-Havreii watched her storm down the corridor, and as she disappeared around a curve he knew this confrontation was neither past nor forgotten. It would haunt him just as certainly as did his wounded pride and desperate longing for Pazlar's lost affections.

This is rock bottom, he admitted to himself.

Evesh had left her assigned task to hover behind his shoulder. Her porcine features betrayed the slightest hint of a lascivious grin.

Ra-Havreii scowled at her. "What now, dammit?"

"I'd heard you Efrosians were a passionate lot," Evesh said, "but I had no idea you'd be so brazen in front of a former lover." She leaned closer. "I *love* brazen."

That was when Ra-Havreii remembered that among the Tellarites, heated arguments were perceived as flirting and foreplay.

Correction: this *is rock bottom.*

Thirteen

The sound of smoothly running machinery was a symphony to Gaila's lobes, and as he listened to the automated factory churning out new munitions below the control room, he felt like its maestro. *I am the conductor of the choir of profit,* he mused at the sight of robot arms assembling bombs and missiles. *Sing, Brother Supply! Sing, Brother Demand!*

Seated at the broad console in front of him, fine-tuning the settings that governed the facility's output, was his Kaferian hacker, N'chk. It mystified Gaila how the insectoid computer expert could operate the board's controls with his simple two-part claw extremities, yet somehow N'chk managed the feat with speed and precision. As many times as Gaila had been tempted to prompt N'chk to explain how he did his work, he just as often reminded himself that when something worked it was usually best not to risk messing it up by asking too many questions.

Gaila leaned closer to peer at the Husnock displays, but he found their status readouts perplexing. Unable to assess the situation for himself, he asked N'chk, "How's it going?"

The Kaferian's native language of high-speed clicks was translated in real time by a vocoder he wore around his neck. "I have restored the security measures the Pakleds bypassed. All exterior and interior defenses are now operational."

"Did you change the access codes?"

"As you requested, yes. Your executive code now grants you full control of the factory."

Gaila was pleased. "And what about the drone convoy?"

"I am having difficulty accessing their command-and-control node." N'chk pointed out a bank of displays. "I have made educated guesses concerning some of its elements. Others I will need to identify by trial and error."

Anxiety stirred inside Gaila. "How long to get it running?"

N'chk regarded Gaila with one of his wide-set compound eyes. "I am unable to say for certain. Hours. Perhaps days."

"Days?" That was not what Gaila wanted to hear. "Every minute we fail to get those drones back in service we run the risk of this factory shutting itself down again. We need to start bringing in fresh building materials *right now*."

The Kaferian seemed unmoved by Gaila's plight. "I am aware of our goals."

"Then get to work making them realities! I hired you because you're supposed to be the best xenotech hacker in the known galaxy. We only have a few hours to fix this, so don't tell me it might take you days to sort it out."

"Husnock systems are complex, Mister Gaila. I will not promise what I cannot deliver."

There was no point pushing N'chk any further. "I don't need your mission statement. Just tell me when the drones are working." He walked away from the Kaferian as much to give the hacker space in which to work as to give himself room in which to vent his frustration. He was in the middle of packing his long-stemmed pipe with Eminian sweet *sinac* when his right-hand man, Zinos, returned in a hurry from the factory floor. Gaila snapped, "And what do *you* want?"

"Aside from more money and a long vacation? How about an ETA on when we can start replenishing raw ore and ordnance compounds? This factory cranks out product like a Denebian slime devil squirts out eggs. At this rate it'll run dry of raw materials in under two hours, and—"

"I'm aware of the problem," Gaila said. "N'chk is handling it."

Zinos did not seem encouraged by that news. "You sure he's up to it?"

Gaila shrugged. "If not, he knows the consequences." He waggled his pipe.

It took a moment for Zinos to realize what Gaila wanted. Then he pulled a sparker from inside his jacket and used it to ignite the *sinac* inside the bowl of Gaila's hand-carved pipe. Gaila drew a mouthful of sweetly fragrant smoke and held it a moment to savor its narcotic effects, which were absorbed directly by his oral tissues and then his sinuses as he exhaled through his wide nostrils. "Thank you, Zinos." Another puff. "Walk with me."

Gaila ambled out of the control room, onto a catwalk that passed above the sprawl of hardworking machines that now labored for his benefit. Zinos followed him, almost at his side but always a half pace behind. The Argelian liked to say he did this as a gesture of respect, but Gaila suspected it was to give Zinos a better chance of shooting his foes in the back.

In between calming puffs, Gaila said, "Tell me, Zinos: How much of this factory did the Pakleds break when they tried to get it started?"

"Less than you might think. Vatzis says the only serious damage was in the fuel storage matrix, but he'll have it fixed within the hour." He shot a skeptical look over his shoulder, toward the control room. "Not that it'll matter, if we don't get the drone convoy running." Facing Gaila, he added, "And even if we do sort that out, what are we supposed to do with all this merchandise? We can't fit more than a few percent of it in the *Tahmila*'s hold at once."

"So? Why should that matter?"

"How are we supposed to deliver the goods to interested buyers?"

Gaila chuckled, then exhaled sweet smoke through his razor-sharp grin. "Zinos, didn't you see the outside of this factory when we arrived? Or were you not paying attention?"

Zinos looked baffled. "What are you talking about?"

"Huge missile batteries. Dozens of particle-beam arrays. Comm towers that I'll bet my last profit are designed to scramble enemy targeting sensors. And the densest grid of shield generators I've ever seen. This place is a damned fortress! And we own it!"

Understanding dawned in the Argelian's eyes. "So you're saying we'd give up the secrecy of this factory's location—"

"In order to bring our customers here," Gaila said. "Why not? We have enough firepower to pulverize a fleet. And if they try to take us hostage by destroying our supply drones, we can tweak the plant's settings to produce new ones, and then we're back in business." He stepped up to Zinos and took him by the arms, as if he were about to shake some sense into him. "This isn't just our factory anymore, Zinos. It's our damned showroom—the best in the galaxy!"

"You really think it's better to wait for buyers to come here than to take our product to where we already know the buyers are?"

Gaila grinned. "Patience, Zinos. Remember the Fourteenth Rule of Acquisition: 'Sometimes the quickest way to find profits is to let them find you.'"

The *Net Gain* was a ghost in the cosmic night. It wasn't quite invisible running in stealth mode, but unless someone searching for it knew exactly what to look for, they weren't likely to notice it. Custom-designed warp coil insulators reduced its energy signature almost to nil. As long as Brunt maintained radio silence—a requirement that was easier for him than for most, simply because he had no one to talk to—he and his ship could cruise unnoticed through the void.

On his sensor screen was the Orion argosy *Silago-Ekon*. He knew the ship well. Its crew was composed of wanted criminals from throughout known space, and in the past he had brought nearly half a dozen of them to face justice—always for a price, of course. He'd crossed the *Silago-Ekon*'s path so many times over the years that he had its energy signature stored in the *Net Gain*'s permanent sensor logs, and an alert dameon monitoring law-enforcement channels for any mention of the argosy's movements or actions.

As usual, the crew of the *Silago-Ekon* thought they were safe from detection because they were cloaked. It was almost enough to make Brunt laugh. He'd snuck aboard the ship on three separate occasions in the past seven years. On his last clandestine visit he had made a point of recording the technical specifications of their cloaking device. Now he tracked them using the same harmonic subfrequency the *Silago-Ekon*'s crew employed to operate their ship's sensors and comms through its invisibility screen. And because he had their sensor specs, he knew how to keep them from detecting his ship, even at close range.

To them, I'm just a shadow.

Brunt suspected that tracking the Orion ship would likely prove to be a roundabout path to his true quarry, but with the Nausicaans' ship blown to bits, the *Silago-Ekon* was now the only lead he had left. *If they have whatever it is the Nausicaans went to that Husnock wreck to find,* he reasoned, *then they're probably trying to get their hands on the same prize. And if I know Gaila, he's already working an angle that will turn their discovery into his profits.*

It wasn't the most farfetched plan Brunt had ever embraced. But it still contained far too many variables for his liking. What if the Orion ship headed for home, looking to sell its information rather than involve itself in the struggle to capture actual Husnock hardware? *Worse,* he thought, *what if I've misread the situation, and the Syndicate left the planet empty-handed?*

Most significantly, Brunt was not pleased with the potential costs of getting caught in a crossfire involving Husnock doomsday weapons. The greater the risk, the higher the potential return on investment needed to be in order to justify the expense and danger of continuing the hunt. *No matter how I crunch the numbers, capturing Gaila and bringing him back to prison just isn't worth it if I end up dead in the process. Pride is nice, but it's no substitute for profit.*

He had seen a lot of jobs go bad. His lobes told him this would be one of them.

Times like this almost made Brunt consider taking on a partner. A good one could watch his back and double his field of fire. Unfortunately, a partner would insist on sharing the profit.

There's always a catch, Brunt simmered.

A blip shifted on the secondary tactical screen. It was the pair of Starfleet vessels Brunt had left behind at the wreck. They seemed to be engaged in a search pattern, no doubt in an effort to locate the fleeing *Silago-Ekon* before it escaped their sensor range completely.

I could help them, Brunt mused, *but what would be in it for me?* He took a moment to check his account balance at the Bank of Bolarus. As he had expected, his invoice to Starfleet had not yet been remunerated. *They never pay their bills,* he fumed. Of late he had come to hold the opinion that the secret to the Federation's explosive growth was that it was a civilization of freeloaders who could always be counted on to default on their debts.

Secretly, he envied them. *I'd do the same thing if I could—but I'd have to face an auditor from the FCA. Unlike Starfleet, I'm held accountable for my business practices.* He shook his head. *They don't know how good they've got it.*

The Starfleet vessels veered farther from the *Silago-Ekon* while Brunt watched. In a matter of minutes, they would forfeit all chance of catching up to the argosy.

He felt no pity for the Starfleeters. They had gotten in his way inside the Husnock wreck. Had it not been for their interference, he could have neutralized the Nausicaans and rescued their hostages for a huge reward. At least, he assumed there had been a reward. If the four scientists' lives had been worth sending three Starfleet vessels into deep space to recover, then their safe return must be worth a small fortune in gold-pressed latinum.

And, of course, he would have had the data chip—and that would have brought him one step closer to capturing Gaila. *But then came Starfleet. And I kissed my profits goodbye.*

Now the ship was gone, blasted to smithereens. *So much for salvage rights,* he lamented. The scientists were on the *Titan,* and the Nausicaans had probably been vaporized with their ship, which meant there would be no bounties to collect on them.

He owed Starfleet no favors. Of that he was certain.

But the situation ahead of him seemed to be escalating faster than he had expected. The same rumors that had drawn Gaila and the Nausicaans to these remote sectors had also brought the Orion Syndicate. If pressed to lay odds on there being other dangerous factions lurking out here with an eye to capturing Husnock weapons and starships, Brunt would definitely bet *yes*.

The more players there are, the harder they'll fight. There was a fearsome arsenal at stake, the kind that would translate into tremendous military power. To

Brunt that meant he should expect more violence and greater bloodshed. That would do him more harm than good.

In a situation like this, having Starfleet around might be useful. After all, as annoying as they were, Starfleeters were at least semifriendly and not hostile by reflex. Plus, thanks to their rules and regulations, their Prime Directive and laughably quaint morals and ethics, their behavior and reactions were highly predictable. In a volatile equation such as the one taking shape ahead of Brunt, the presence of Starfleet might actually be helpful.

Unless they cheat me out of my bounty, he realized. *What if they arrest Gaila before I have a chance to catch him?* That, Brunt knew, would be a major financial setback, not to mention a stain on his professional reputation. He also had dealt with Starfleet enough times to know that those consequences weren't even the worst-case scenario. *What if those do-gooder morons wind up arresting me on some puffed-up charge? I'd be laughed out of the Entrepreneurs Club, or at the very least have my Magnus-level membership downgraded.* It was a nightmare outcome . . . until he remembered that humiliated was still better than dead.

No risk, no reward.

Brunt powered up his subspace burst transmitter. He programmed it to send an encrypted signal on a Starfleet frequency, one the *Silago-Ekon* would be unlikely to detect. After making sure his signal would be stripped of its origin metadata and bounced multiple times among several subspace radio relays—all necessary precautions to conceal its source; Brunt couldn't have anyone calling him a Starfleet stooge—he sent the *Titan* a message containing the *Silago-Ekon*'s heading, speed, and cloaking device specifications.

He shut down his transmitter and reclined his pilot's chair, curious as to what would happen next. *Let's see if Starfleeters know a gift when they see one.*

Fourteen

Precious minutes were slipping away. Vale felt a growing unease at the prospect of losing her last lead to the stolen Husnock military codes—a misstep that might soon manifest itself in the form of a devastating attack on an unprepared civilian target. That was the nightmare scenario, the one that kept her awake at night. All around her on the bridge of the *Titan*, her senior officers were doing all they could to hunt down the Orion argosy, marshaling all of the ship's formidable sensors and tactical resources—but the longer the search dragged on, the less likely it seemed that they would recover the Orions' fast-cooling trail.

If we don't catch a break pretty soon, this—

Fast beeps of alert feedback from the tactical console. Tuvok silenced the alarm and reacted with beetled brows to whatever new information was scrolling across his panel. "Captain, we've received an encrypted burst of data." The Vulcan keyed more commands into his console. "Unable to confirm the origin of the signal, but the data is . . . intriguing."

Vale stood to face him. "Don't keep us in suspense, Commander."

"It is an anonymous tip to the heading, speed, and approximate position of the Orion argosy." More tapped commands. "Also included are files that identify the vessel as the *Silago-Ekon*, an Orion argosy registered in the Ferengi Alliance, and specifications for the modified settings of its Klingon-made cloaking device."

It seemed too good to be true, and that bothered Vale. She looked to Sarai for input. "Number One? What do you think?"

"It could be a disinformation tactic." Sarai used the command terminal beside her chair to review the data Tuvok had received. "Since we can't trace the source, it's possible the Orions set up automated transmitters to cover their escape, by pointing us in the wrong direction and tempting us into adjusting our sensors to their least-helpful configuration."

That sounded implausible to Vale—but she wasn't sure she trusted Sarai's instincts. *Am I doubting her because her analysis sounds off, or because I desperately want to trust this tip?*

Not ready to give up hope, Vale faced ops. "Rager. Run another scan for any sign of the distortions Doctor Pek told us to look for." Playing a hunch, she added, "And target it along the heading that we just received." A sly look at Sarai. " 'Trust, but verify,' as the saying goes."

Her crew reacted like the well-integrated team they had become: Tuvok relayed the heading data from tactical to ops without anyone needing to ask, and Rager plugged the new coordinates into a focused sensor sweep. It took only a few moments for her to get the results. Rager shook her head. "Sensor contact negative, sir."

"Then we'll have to put our secret source's cloaking intel to work."

That was all Vale had to say to prompt Sarai into action. The first officer moved to stand behind Lieutenant Torvig at the engineering console. "How close are we to bringing Doctor Ra-Havreii's sensor modifications online?"

"They are almost done," the Choblik said. His bionic hands fine-tuned the settings on his panel. "The main array is online now, and the secondary and supplemental arrays will be back online in two minutes."

"The main array is all we need for this," Sarai said. "Engage the new mods, then plug in the details about the *Silago-Ekon*'s cloaking system."

Torvig regarded Sarai with mild anxiety even as he carried out her orders. "Commander, at this extreme range, scanning within such narrow frequency parameters will make it difficult to penetrate a cloaking device of this kind, unless we manage to aim our sensors directly at it."

"Let Mister Tuvok worry about that, Lieutenant."

"Understood, Commander." Torvig finished engaging the modified sensors. "Ready."

Sarai nodded at Tuvok, who started his tactical scan. It took only seconds for his console to chirp with a confirmation of contact. "Captain," he said, "we have detected what appears to be a cloaked starship at the indicated position and heading. Its mass, energy signature, and general configuration are consistent with our logs of the Orion argosy."

"Helm," Vale said, "pursuit course. Keep us at the edge of sensor range, and put us in their warp eddy. Make us look like a sensor echo. Mister Tuvok, relay our sensor data on a scrambled channel to the *Wasp* and the *Canterbury*."

The bridge crew set to work, and Vale headed for her ready room with the intention of briefing Riker on their good fortune—only to be paused by Sarai's voice. "Captain? A word?"

Vale turned to face her XO. "Number One?"

The first officer lowered her voice to a discreet level. "Captain, I'm glad the tip panned out, but I'm still concerned by the fact that we don't know who sent it."

"Don't we?" She beckoned Sarai with a tilt of her head, then led her off the bridge, into the ready room. When the door closed, Vale continued. "If the tip had proved false, I'd have guessed it was the Orions. But it didn't. Which leaves only one possibility." She gave Sarai a moment to process that and deduce the answer for herself.

Sarai looked almost embarrassed when she figured it out. "Brunt."

"Exactly. Brunt's a solo operator. Working this far into the Alpha Quadrant frontier, he probably thinks that keeping us and our task force 'in the game' as a check against other, better-armed players improves his odds of winning whatever peripheral gambit he's chasing here."

"Do you think Brunt's actually on our side?"

"Of course not. He's a Ferengi bounty hunter. The only side he's on is his own. But that doesn't mean his intel is wrong."

The other woman wore a look of concern. "If Brunt knows where the *Silago-Ekon* is going, he's probably following them, just as we are. Which means his motives are suspect."

"Absolutely," Vale said. "He could also be playing both sides. Either way, I have no doubt he'll stab us in the back if he thinks doing so is even slightly to his advantage."

Sarai nodded. "I'll have Tuvok and Rager start looking for Brunt's ship."

"You read my mind, Number One."

Small tools, cables, and interface adapters lay scattered across the working surfaces of the main engineering bay of the *Silago-Ekon*. Leaning at one end of the table was Nilat, who glared at her chief engineer Proat, a paunchy Denobulan with thick jowls and thicker black eyebrows. She watched him tinker with the settings on a padd, into which he had inserted the isolinear chip she had stolen from the Nausicaans. "How much longer is this going to take?"

He squinted at the padd's screen. "Not sure. How badly do you want to stay hidden?" He threaded a needlelike tool through a gap in the side of the padd. Poke, poke, poke. "This is a tricky bit of code you've brought me—and you were right, it was booby-trapped."

"I knew it. The Nausicaans always have been a twitchy lot."

Proat set down his tool and shot her a curious look from under his wild brows. "How quick you are to judge, my captain." Returning to his work, he added, "If anything, I'd say this looks like the handiwork of the Nausicaans' Federation hostages. Luckily for you, I had the foresight not to let that chip anywhere near a networked system on the ship, and I isolated this padd before using it to decode the chip's contents."

That last detail made Nilat perk up. "Then you *were* able to decode it."

"Oh, yes. Quite easily." He paused to sleeve some perspiration from his forehead and the undersides of his ocular ridges. "Whoever created the chip designed it to be self-unpacking, with a built-in universal translation matrix. Quite elegant, really. Bynar code, if I'm not mistaken."

"What about the trap? How serious was it?"

"Serious enough," he said, but his tone was dismissive. "Nothing crippling, but it would've turned our own warp coils into a beacon for anyone who knew what to look for." He isolated a string of code on the padd's screen. "I can strip it out, if you like."

"Do it," Nilat said, "but store it offline. We might have use for it someday."

A broad smile. "My thoughts exactly." A few more tweaks, and then he presented the padd to Nilat. "There you go. Clean and ready for business."

She tucked it under her arm. "Well done. If this pans out, I'll make sure you get an extra half share when we settle up with the Syndicate."

"Too kind." The engineer rounded up his tools and began cleaning the work surfaces in the engineering bay, while Nilat headed forward to a ladder.

Less than a minute later she was back on the *Silago-Ekon*'s command deck with the padd, which she handed to K'mjok. "Proat says it's working. Isolate a terminal and check it out."

Her Klingon second-in-command did as he had been

told, without asking why he needed to unlink one of the command deck's terminals from the ship's network. It was a fact of life in the Orion Syndicate that no one trusted anyone, whether they were business partners, shipmates, lovers, friends, or family. In Nilat's line of work, trusting people was the fastest way to end up incarcerated or dead. That lesson weighed on her thoughts as she and her crew prepared to make what might well be the most lucrative score of their long, shady careers.

"As we thought," K'mjok said. He shifted to give Nilat a clear view of the terminal's screen. "The Federation team made a breakthrough with the Husnock language, and the Nausicaans leveraged it to steal a set of command codes from that crashed warship."

"And those are the command codes?"

"Yes." K'mjok switched to another set of data. "I doubt they meant to use the codes on that wreck. I think they found another Husnock ship, one that's intact." He keyed in some search parameters and set up a few filters. "Before we fragged their ship, I made sure to download all their flight and comm logs. If we track their movements over the past few months—" He straightened and flashed a fanged grin. "A pattern emerges."

Nilat leaned in to study the results of the analysis. "Several round trips between the wreck and this other star system at the ass end of nowhere." She turned to an adjacent terminal and tried to punch up some charts or other data about the remote star system, only to find her ship's computer had none. "What do we know about that system? Anything?"

"Very little." K'mjok called up a page of sparse facts from the Federation Galactic Catalog. "A red giant with one small, airless rockball of a planet."

"How long to get there?"

K'mjok looked at Ang-Harod, who had been discreetly eavesdropping on their entire conversation. The Nalori woman checked her console. "At present speed, less than an hour."

"Set course for the red giant," Nilat said. "And throw in a Crazy Kahless."

"On it." Ang-Harod programmed the helm to execute the maneuver, which consisted of several rapid changes in speed and heading that, though they might seem erratic, had actually been devised to help expose the presence of starships that might be haunting one's course. It was a precaution born of paranoia, Nilat knew. After all, her ship was cloaked. What could—

"We've got a tail," Trunch reported from the weapons console. "Maybe more than one." The Balduk transferred his panel's data to the main viewscreen. "Three ships in a tight cluster. A fourth slightly ahead of them. All at the edge of sensor range, but definitely there."

Nilat tensed; she felt annoyed and alarmed in equal measure. "Starfleet?"

K'mjok heaved an angry sigh. "Almost certainly." He snapped at Trunch, "You said the Starfleet ships were moving away from us. What happened?"

"Don't know." He highlighted the lone ship traveling between the trio of Starfleet ships and the *Silago-Ekon*. "It looks like they have a friend. Maybe that's what happened."

On the viewscreen, numerous bits of data about the pursuit vessels updated: the Starfleet ships were increasing speed. It was almost certain that they knew the Crazy Kahless maneuver had exposed their presence, and now they were closing in for the kill.

A palpable wave of anxiety washed through the argosy's command deck. Nilat felt it affect all of her senior people, and she knew it wouldn't be long before word filtered down to the lower decks. This was going to be devastating to the crew's morale unless she acted quickly.

"Go to maximum warp," she said. "We need to reach that system before Starfleet does."

K'mjok ground his teeth as he considered the situation. "Even if we beat them there, it will not be by much. A few minutes, at most. That might not be enough time to finish the job."

"It will have to be," Nilat said. "Prep a boarding party. We have to be ready to act as soon as we drop to impulse." K'mjok started aft, then Nilat caught his arm. "Make sure you take the Husnock command codes. If the Nausicaans found what I think they did, you'll need them."

"Understood." He scooped up the padd on his way off the command deck.

Facing the stretch of warp-distorted stars on the viewscreen, Nilat hoped her imminent showdown with Starfleet didn't turn out to be the worst mistake of her life.

Gallows humor and nervous rumors—that was how the engineering crew of the *Silago-Ekon* coped with their fear as they learned their ship, despite being cloaked, was being chased at high warp by not one but *three* Starfleet vessels.

Proat had no time to ease the worries of his tool-pushers. They were all doing everything they could to wring just a few more tenths of a warp factor out of the argosy, even if it meant blowing half the EPS conduits along the keel. Nilat had bet their lives and freedom on a race against Starfleet, and now it was up to a bunch of half-trained youths to win the day.

Their chief engineer, however, had more pressing matters to attend.

The Denobulan had tasked all his people with more than enough busywork to keep their eyes and hands buried in the guts of the ship for the next hour. He took advantage of their distraction to slip back up to his quarters and lock the door. After a fast sweep to check for surveillance devices, he retrieved what he had told his shipmates was an urn holding the ashes of his father. Which it did, along with the ash of a few hundred cigars and an encrypted comm inside a resealable plastic shell.

He switched on the device, which had been made to sneak out ultralow-frequency bursts via the *Silago-Ekon*'s subspace transceiver. After a few fear-filled seconds, its indicator light changed from amber to blue, which meant his comrades were listening, though in accordance with protocol they would not respond.

"This is Proat. Condition urgent. Inbound with the prize. ETA forty-eight minutes. Coming in hot, pursued by three Starfleet vessels and a fourth ship of unknown origin. Recommend you prepare for hostile engagement, and proceed immediately to Phase Four."

Fifteen

No matter how complex a system appeared, Gaila often found that in the end the difference between it being operational and inert so often came down to the push of a button. Thus it came to pass that he restored the automated flow of raw materials to his newly acquired munitions factory by swiping his hand across a touchscreen whose symbols he couldn't read, but whose function N'chk assured him had been keyed to the systems they needed back online.

A flick of his wrist and the interface lit up, suddenly alive with a stream of new data. Excited but confused, he looked at his Kaferian tech guru for assurance. "Is that it?"

"Yes," N'chk said, his chittering reply filtered through his vocoder. "This facility is now transmitting power to its legion of drone supply craft, as well as its ancillary sites."

Rubbing his palms together in a pantomime of avarice,

Gaila grinned. "Good, good! How long until the first new shipment arrives?"

"Two hours," said Zinos. "After that, new loads should arrive every twelve hours or so. The system shut down with several loads already en route, so as long as the production facilities that fill the drones are automated and functional, we'll be good to go almost indefinitely."

Gaila clapped his hands once in approval. "Perfect!" He strode out of the control center and made his way down the corridor to the executive office he had appropriated. Zinos followed him, but N'chk stayed behind to monitor the facility's complicated network of machines. On the move, Gaila asked Zinos, "How are the factory's defenses?"

"Improving by the hour." Zinos tried to hand Gaila a padd but he ignored it, so Zinos pretended he hadn't been slighted, tucked the padd under his arm, and continued as if nothing awkward had happened. "Long neglect had put several systems into premature failure, but Vatzis and his boys are bringing them back online without much trouble."

"Which systems? Shields? Weapons? Be specific, damn you."

"Weapons, mostly. Nine defensive batteries in total—four topside, five below. Only three shield emitters were offline. One because of a corroded power supply, one had been struck by space debris, and the third overloaded during our systems test."

The boss Ferengi grunted as he pondered the news. "All right. Prioritize shield repairs. This factory bristles with weapons. It won't be a tragedy if a few are slow coming back into service. But we can't have any holes in our shields when clients come calling. Understand?"

"Perfectly, Mister Gaila."

"Good, get it done." Double doors parted ahead of the duo as they approached Gaila's new office. He entered the long suite, whose far wall was composed of transparent metal and therefore offered a stunning view of the cosmos beyond. Parked beside the desk of smoky obsidian was a cart that had been transferred off of the *Tahmila*. The cart was loaded with bottles of Gaila's favorite liquors, and a cluster of single-serving cans of Slug-o-Cola rested on a tray of dry ice, along with a steel bowl of fresh tube grubs whose energetic wriggling had been stunted by the coldness leaching away their vitality from below. Gaila threw himself into his executive chair—another comfort he'd had brought over to replace the office's useless alien furniture.

Zinos played the part of a dutiful underling well. He cracked open a cola, then planted the beverage and the bowl of grubs on the desk in front of Gaila. Standing back, he did his best to reclaim an air of self-respect. "When might it be appropriate for us to discuss the setting of price points for our new inventory?"

"Good question." Gaila pinched a struggling clutch of grubs from the bowl, tossed them into his mouth, and ground them into a savory paste with his fearsome teeth. "Your thoughts?"

"I feel unqualified to speculate, sir. I was hoping to learn from your business sense."

At times Gaila wondered whether Zinos had learned any of the Ferengi Rules of Acquisition other than the Thirty-third: *It never hurts to suck up to the boss.* "Without a field test, it's hard to know how to price these things. I don't want to sell a planet-buster for the same profit margin we could score on a normal torpedo. But charge too much—"

"And an angry customer might turn our merchandise against us."

"Precisely. After our tech-heads finish bringing our defenses back online, have them inspect the production line. Let's figure out how much bang we're bottling in these things."

"Understood." Once more Zinos brandished the padd. "Of course, if you're interested in seeing a live-fire exercise of Husnock munitions—" He stared at the padd and hesitated.

Never a patient man, Gaila snapped, "What are you saying?"

Zinos turned the padd so that Gaila could see its screen. "The factory's ancillary nodes track the positions and activity of Husnock ships. And their sensors have picked up what looks like an Orion vessel approaching a derelict Husnock warship in a nearby star system." Adjusting the display to show a wider area, he added, "And they're being chased by four ships, of which three are definitely of Starfleet design." A nervous smile. "So we might get a preview of what these weapons could do, and sooner than we expected."

"Assuming the Orions survive the boarding of that derelict." Gaila smirked. "I'd love to see their faces when they break in—only to discover we've already been there."

Seconds after the *Silago-Ekon* dropped out of warp Nilat saw the dark behemoth looming ahead of them, a menacing shadow in front of the mammoth orb of the red giant. Even with the main viewscreen doing its best to compensate for the star's brightness, light bled into the edges of the Husnock vessel's silhouette, rendering its shape indistinct. Below it, also bathed in ruddy light, was the lifeless planet it apparently had been doomed to orbit ever since the extinction of its owners—a story Nilat had dismissed as a myth until a few years earlier, when a smuggled Starfleet Intelligence report revealed the blood-curdling tale to be the truth.

Nilat opened a channel from her command chair to the transporter bay. "Nilat to K'mjok. We're here, thirty seconds to transport range. Is your team ready?"

"Ready to go," K'mjok responded. *"You sure transporters are safe?"*

"We're scanning for coordinates now," she said, then shot a look at Trunch, whose thick, clumsy digits poked at his console with mounting frustration and no visible progress. "Stand by."

The Balduk thumped the sides of his fists against his console. "Piece of junk!"

Nilat sighed. *This is the last thing I need.* "What now, Trunch?"

"Console frozen." He stabbed at it with his index finger, then kicked its base. "Broken!"

Before she could talk him out of what threatened to be a highly theatrical meltdown, the overhead lights flickered, and static obscured the image on the main viewscreen. All around the command deck, other senior members of the crew recoiled from their duty stations.

Ang-Harod swiveled away from the helm. "Flight controls are locked."

"All comms just went dead," Ninivus said, plucking a transceiver from his huge finlike ear. "Nothing but cosmic scratch on all frequencies."

Trunch checked a bank of auxiliary status displays. "Cloak is down. Weapons offline."

Nilat felt her temper fraying. "What just happened?" She reopened the channel to the transporter bay. "K'mjok, get back to command. Something's wrong." After a few seconds without a reply, she added with rising anxiety, "K'mjok?"

"*All* comms are down," Ninivus said. "Internal and external."

"Talk to me, Nin. Did we get hit by a cyberstrike? What's going on?"

The Tiburonian pressed his palms to his face in shock. "I have no idea."

Moving to the engineering console, Trunch stared in horror at the ship's master status display. "Airlocks opening on lower decks. Engineering crew blasted into space."

There was no longer any doubt in Nilat's mind the ship was under attack—but by whom? "Everyone, with me. We need to reach the weapons locker and arm up, right—"

The aft door opened, and a barrage of disruptor blasts screamed across the command deck. White-hot pulses ripped through Nilat's gut, Trunch's head, Ang-Harod's chest. Ninivus sprinted toward the deck's lone escape pod, but the fusillade blew out his knees before a mercy shot pierced his throat and severed his head from his body in a searing flash.

Nilat lay on the deck shivering, racked with agony from within. Her guts were numb at the center where the blast had first hit her, but its fiery torments were expanding, spreading through her vital organs and soft tissues, cooking her alive. She gasped for breath, sprawled on her back in a twisted pose. Trembling with adrenaline overload and terror, she turned her head—she refused to expire without looking her murderer in the eye.

Proat sauntered onto the command deck. He looked pleased with himself and with his bloody handiwork. In either fist he toted modified disruptor pistols. It took him only a moment to assess the situation. There was no one left to resist him. No one was conscious except Nilat. All the same, he took his time and made a slow circuit of the command deck.

He paused to fire an extra blast into Trunch's chest. "I know you're still with me, Commander." He strolled from Trunch's corpse to the smoking remains of Ang-Harod. "Since you've never made a secret of how fond you are of K'mjok, I thought you should know I beamed him and his team into space—and dematerialized them."

The chief engineer pumped a shot into the dead Nalori's skull. "I also want to say this isn't personal, or even business." He noted the separation between Ninivus's head and torso, then tapped a series of commands into the communications panel before he turned to face the main viewscreen. "This is a matter of sworn duty."

Nilat, who was sure she felt the flames of damnation creeping up her esophagus and down into her nether regions, strained to see what Proat was looking at. Then she saw it: on the main viewscreen, a ripple of distortion between the *Silago-Ekon* and the Husnock derelict resolved into the shape of a massive Breen warship.

Proat flipped her a taunting salute and smirked. "Long live the Confederacy."

Then he aimed his weapon into her face and fired.

Sixteen

Tensions were high on the command deck of the Breen dreadnought *Kulak*, but so was confidence. Standing tall in front of its center seat, projecting calm, Thot Tren bared his fangs in a broad grin inside his snout-shaped mask—the same anonymous outer face worn by all but the youngest members of Breen society. Events were transpiring much as Tren had intended, with only one minor inconvenience—but even that wrinkle had been considered and prepared for.

Pictured on the main viewscreen was the Orion argosy *Silago-Ekon*, into whose crew he had months earlier insinuated one of his Spetzkar commandos. Tren's superiors in the *thotaru* had criticized that move as a long shot, but now his gamble was paying off at last.

An alert on the communications panel. Signals officer Sevv muted it, then reported to Tren, "Incoming message from Spetzkar Proat. Audio only."

"On speakers," Tren said. He waited while Sevv re-routed the message.

"Repeat, this is Proat, on board the Silago-Ekon. *Do you read me?"*

"This is Thot Tren on the *Kulak*. Go ahead, Proat." All around the dimly lit nerve center of the battleship, the other senior officers paused in their duties to hear Proat's report.

Proat replied, *"Mission accomplished. The Nausicaans recovered the Husnock codes, as expected, and then the Orions stole the codes and neutralized the Nausicaans. I've eliminated the Syndicate crew and destroyed their copy of the codes, meaning I now possess the only copy."*

"Good work, Proat. How soon can you deploy to the Husnock vessel?"

"I'm suiting up now. I'll be ready to beam over in two minutes."

Chot Vang, the first officer of the *Kulak*, interjected, "Be advised, Chot Braz and a Spetzkar team are already on board. They've defused a number of traps someone left behind."

That news made Proat more curious than anxious. *"Traps? Left by the Husnock?"*

"Negative," Vang said. "Most of them are of Ferengi design."

"So, nothing to be concerned about—unlike our approaching visitors."

Tren regarded the tactical screens that flanked the main viewscreen. "Leave them to me, Proat." The left screen tracked the progress of the four rapidly approaching threat vessels, while the right cycled through ship profiles. All three Starfleet vessels had been identified by their energy signatures, but the fourth—a small Mancharan starhopper—was proving to be a mystery. "Deliver the Husnock codes to Chot Braz, then assist his unit in executing Phase Five."

"Understood. Proat out." The channel closed with a soft *click*.

Weapons Officer Bol looked up as the left tactical display updated with alarming new intel. "Thot Tren, the Starfleet vessels have increased speed. Revised ETA, eight minutes."

"So I see. No doubt they accelerated as soon as their sensors detected us dropping our cloak." Tren reflected on his past encounters with Starfleet, some of which predated the Dominion War. Before the war for the Alpha Quadrant, Tren would have said that Starfleet commanders had no stomachs for confrontation. Now he couldn't be so certain. Starfleet's veterans of the Dominion War could be unpredictable; many had been hardened by that conflict and tempered into dangerous blades. There was only one way for him to know which kind of officers he was facing today. "Vang, give our guests reason to reconsider their haste."

His second-in-command moved around the deck, doling out orders with quiet efficiency—first to the flight controller, Zaana; then to Bol at tactical, followed by Choy at operations; and, the last stop on Vang's circuit, the communications officer, Sevv. When his preparations were completed, he faced Tren. "Ready on your command."

"Execute," Tren said.

All his officers acted in concert. Zaana guided the *Kulak* to a new position as Sevv alerted the Spetzkar inside the Husnock vessel. Choy monitored long-range sensors as Bol dispatched a coded signal from his console—then, on the viewscreen, two more Breen warships lowered their cloaks and rippled into view, one on either side of the *Kulak*. Off of the dreadnought's port side, the heavy cruiser *Sulica*; to starboard, the battleship *Tarcza*.

Now we will see what my Starfleet counterpart is made of.

Tren asked Vang, "Any reaction from the incoming battle group?"

"Scanning," Vang replied. He moved to stand beside Bol at the tactical station. "The three Starfleet ships are diverging." Even before Vang finished his analysis, Tren saw the enemy's tactics taking shape on the left viewscreen. "They're moving to flanking positions."

Not so spineless after all. Tren settled into his chair. "Sevv, get me the commanders of the *Sulica* and the *Tarcza*, on channel one."

The communications officer acted with speed and efficiency. "Channel open."

"Commander Kran. Commander Spara. This is Thot Tren. Are you tracking the three inbound Starfleet vessels?"

"Affirmative," Spara answered over the audio channel.

"Confirmed," Kran said.

"We need to split up, but stay close to the Husnock ship until it's under our control. Each of you target one of the Starfleet ships and adjust your positions to intercept them."

Both commanders acknowledged Tren's orders, then signed off. Within seconds their hulking warships peeled off to assume more advantageous positions. From this point forward, Tren knew, the name of the game would be endurance. "Bol, raise shields, charge all weapons.

Sevv, instruct *Sulica* and *Tarcza* to do the same. Vang, sound general quarters."

All through the ship's corridors and deepest compartments, the alert sounded over the ship's internal comms. Even from his chair on the command deck, Tren imagined he could feel all his people scrambling to their duty stations and priming his ship for action. It was an electric sensation, and he felt it galvanize his ship and crew just like the surge of adrenaline in his blood.

Vang moved to stand at Tren's side. "Any engagement with Starfleet risks compromising the mission," he confided, the volume of his mask's vocoder set to a confidential level. "If they destroy the Husnock vessel before Braz and his men finish—"

"They won't." Tren envisioned the conflict to come, and he felt assured of success. "No matter how bold these enemy commanders might be, they'll be bound by Starfleet's rules of engagement. And if there is one thing I learned well during the Dominion War, Vang . . . it's how to use the Federation's nobility against it."

"*Three* of them? Are you serious?" Vale eyed the latest tactical update with frustration. "Does everyone out here except us have a cloaking device? Because this is starting to piss me off."

In under two minutes, the *Titan* and its battle group had gone from chasing a single Orion merchant ship to hurtling into a showdown with three Breen heavy warships. Seeing the situation degrade in real time left Vale feeling deflated. *The longer this mission goes on, the worse it gets.*

Looking apprehensive, Sarai sidled up to Vale and said under her breath, "Time is of the essence, Captain. If the Breen have already boarded the Husnock vessel—"

"I'm aware of the problem, Number One." Vale hoped Tuvok had better news for her. "Tactical, how's the Breen's combat posture?"

Tuvok barely suppressed a frown. "Imposing, Captain." He routed fresh sensor data to Vale's command monitor. "All three vessels are running with shields up and weapons hot."

Vale pretended not to notice Sarai's accusatory look. "All right, no one said they had to make it easy for us. Tactical, shields up, arm all weapons, and sound battle stations. Ops, alert the *Wasp* and the *Canterbury* to match our status and continue to seek flanking positions."

The red-alert siren whooped twice from the ship's PA system. After that, notice of the ship's action status was maintained by the intermittent pulsing of crimson bulkhead panels.

Swelling to fill the main viewscreen was the image of a Breen dreadnought and, behind it, a Husnock warship nearly twice its mass. Its present magnification factor had pushed the other two Breen starships off-screen, but the tactical display beside Vale's chair kept her aware of their positions and actions. "How long until we drop out of warp?"

Lavena answered from the helm, "Thirty seconds, sir."

A variety of tactical possibilities raced through Vale's imagination. "Okay. Let's see if we can end this fight before it starts. Mister Tuvok, hail the lead Breen ship."

Two taps on his console, and then Tuvok said, "Hailing frequencies open."

Vale put on her best air of authority. "Attention, unidentified Breen vessel. This is Captain Christine Vale, commanding the Federation *Starship Titan*. Identify yourselves."

She half expected to be stonewalled. Instead, the Breen's response was prompt. Its masked visage filled the main viewscreen, larger than life and twice as ugly. The metallic screech of his vocoder was translated in real time by the *Titan*'s computer. *"Captain Vale, this is Thot Tren, commanding the Breen dreadnought* Kulak. *How can we be of service?"*

Perplexed stares passed among the bridge officers, all of them as if to ask, *Since when are the Breen polite?* It was an incident without precedent, and to Vale that was a portent of danger. She stood from her chair, to better project power. "Thot Tren, on behalf of the United Federation of Planets, I need to insist you and your escorts withdraw from this sector at once."

"Captain, even if I or my government recognized the Federation's jurisdiction in this sector—which we do not—our departure would not be possible at this time."

Stepping forward to make her own countenance larger on Tren's side of the conversation, Vale asked, "And why do you say that?"

"Because this is unclaimed space—a fact acknowledged by your government and by Starfleet—and we are here conducting perfectly legal exploration. I have a mission to complete, and I will not be taking orders from you or from your lackeys on the Wasp *and the* Canterbury.*"*

Now he's just showing off, she fumed. *Proving they know who we are.* "You aren't the only ones with orders, Thot Tren. And I'm just as committed to mine as you are to yours." Without interrupting their conversation, new sensor data from Tuvok's console scrolled across the lower edge of the main viewscreen, alerting Vale that Breen life signs had been detected inside the Husnock vessel. "I'll give you one minute to get your people off that Husnock ship."

"Again, Captain, that is not possible at this time. In accordance with interstellar law, my officers are aboard that ship conducting search-and-rescue operations, just in case there are any surviving crew or passengers in need of medical assistance."

"That vessel is empty," Vale said, though she had no proof to back her claim. "We've already cleared it, and it's been marked for demolition, in the interest of interstellar security. Now pull your people off that ship, because in thirty seconds I'm gonna blast it into dust."

Out of the corner of her eye Vale noticed Sarai tense at her threat. *Odd.*

The Breen tilted his head, as if Vale were nothing more than a curious specimen he was eyeing in a laboratory. *"An idle threat, Captain. I know your Starfleet regulations as well as you do—perhaps better. And that is how I know it would be illegal for you to open fire on an unarmed, unshielded vessel when sentient life-forms are known to be aboard."*

I'm really learning to hate this guy.

More intel scrolled across the screen's bottom edge. Extracts from Thot Tren's dossier at Starfleet Intelligence. This Breen had been commanding starships for nearly two decades. His ship had been part of the Breen strike force that attacked Earth during the Dominion War, as well as a part of the Dominion fleet that had bombarded Cardassia Prime after it turned against the

Dominion shortly before the war's end. Tren was believed to have links to the Breen Intelligence Directorate and the Spetzkar—the Breen military's elite special forces. He was the epitome of a battle-scarred veteran as well as a power player in Breen politics.

My day just keeps getting better and better, Vale groused to herself.

He had called her bluff. It was time to fold or double down.

"I don't really give a damn what Starfleet regulations say. But as a courtesy, from one starship commander to another, I'm going to spell this out for you. And I'll use small words to help you understand. On behalf of the United Federation of Planets, I planted our flag on that ship. I've claimed it as sovereign Federation soil and Starfleet property. And my orders are to make sure it remains our property at all costs. Or, failing that, to keep it from becoming anyone else's—*at all costs*. And if that means I have to vaporize your boarding party, *so be it*."

Tren lowered the snout of his mask. Vale imagined fearsome eyes staring back at her from behind the narrow band of green shining inside Tren's visor. *"I admire your refusal to surrender your lie in the face of bloodshed. But my forces have been tracking your movements for some time, Captain. We know for a fact that no vessel in your battle group has ever been to this star system before. Not to plant a flag, or to do anything else. So now I will explain the terms of this encounter to you—and I will also do you the service of using small words. If any Starfleet vessel fires upon any ship under my command, or upon that Husnock vessel while my search-and-rescue team are still aboard, I will construe such violence as an act of war—and I will retaliate with appropriate force."*

He turned away, reacting to someone off-screen.

At the same moment, multiple alerts chimed on consoles all around the bridge. Vale stood like a statue while her officers scrambled into action. Sarai darted from one station to the next, collecting information on the move. Meanwhile, on the viewscreen, Thot Tren said nothing as he turned his attention once more toward Vale, as if he wanted to see what she would do next.

Sarai hurried to Vale's side and whispered in her ear. "Sir, the Husnock ship's power core just came online, and the ship has charged its beam weapons." A fearful glance at Thot Tren. "He has us outgunned, and he knows it."

Titan's two most senior officers turned as one to face Tren.

"I trust your officers have informed you of the change in circumstances." Another birdlike tilt of the Breen's head gave Vale the impression he was mocking her. *"Let me extend to you and yours the invitation you so graciously sought to impose upon me and mine: withdraw from this sector at once, Captain, or else my forces will turn your ships to scrap."*

Vale's jaw tensed, and her hands reflexively balled into fists.

Yup, this day is definitely starting to piss me off.

There was a fine distinction between a provocation and an act of war, and Thot Tren knew all too well he was close to committing the latter. On his ship's viewscreen was the face of Captain Vale, threatening escalation; through the transceiver in his helmet came reports from

Chot Braz, his Spetzkar commander aboard the Husnock starship.

"This is your last warning," Vale said. *"We can't let you take that ship."*

"My crew and I have laid claim to a derelict vessel in accordance with accepted interstellar laws of salvage. You have no legal jurisdiction to interfere."

In his ear, Braz's voice: *"We have flight control and warp capability, but no shields."*

Tren isolated his response to the transceiver channel: "Well done. Stand by." He was loath to order a first strike on the Starfleet ships. As desperate as the Breen Confederacy was for the various advantages Husnock technology might bring them, Domo Pran and the Confederate Congress had no wish to spark an all-out war with the Federation and its allies, especially now that there were rumblings within the Typhon Pact that the Romulan Star Empire and the Gorn Hegemony might not support the Breen in any conflict they were perceived to have instigated.

All the same, Tren had his orders. He was not to return empty-handed.

At tactical, Choy tensed in reaction to new intel on his panel. "The *Titan* is charging its main phaser batteries. We're being targeted."

"Hold for my order," Tren said, for Bol as well as the rest of his officers.

Bol replied, "They're firing!"

Brilliant orange beams slashed across the main viewscreen. The *Kulak*'s hull juddered from the glancing blow to its shields, which flared as they were nicked by the phaser barrage. When the shaking ceased, Bol added, "No damage to shields."

Vale reappeared on the viewscreen. *"That was a warning shot. The next won't be."*

It had been a careful, measured response. Tren suspected Captain Vale had no more desire to turn this confrontation into a shooting battle than he did—perhaps less. And he grasped the urgency of her predicament. No doubt her superiors were pressuring her to contain Husnock technology for their use with just as much fervor as his masters had shown to him. *We are two cogs in history's relentless gears, you and I. Would that I could show you mercy.*

Again he isolated his transceiver channel so he could speak privately to his Spetzkar commander. "Braz, target the Husnock ship's particle beam array on the *Titan*. Hit them just hard enough to make a point, but no harder. Is that understood?"

"As you command, Thot Tren."

The order was carried out in a matter of seconds. Searing white beams lanced from the captured Husnock vessel and pummeled the *Titan*. The Starfleet vessel bobbled beneath the assault, and as the fourth beam struck home the crackling cocoon of their shields fizzled and popped like a soap bubble. Just as Tren had hoped, Braz and his Spetzkar ceased fire the moment the *Titan*'s shields fell. Now the ship was left defenseless but not critically damaged.

Don't be foolhardy, Captain, Tren mused, hoping Vale could hear his thoughts. *We both know I have the advantage. Don't make me prove it again.*

He saw Choy collating sensor data at the operations console. "Choy, report."

"Cascade failures throughout the *Titan*," Choy said. "Engineering, life-support, tactical, all failing. The

Husnock weapons must have packed more of a punch than we expected."

That was not the outcome Tren had hoped for. A benign show of strength might have persuaded the enemy to stand down. But a crippling blow was almost certain to invite a reprisal.

Bol confirmed his suspicions. "*Titan*'s escort vessels are flanking her and extending their shields around her. . . . And they're both charging all weapons and targeting the Husnock ship."

Tren felt this crisis was about to pass a point of no return. "Braz, you're being targeted! Do you have shields up yet?"

"Negative. Half the emitters aren't engaging. They'll take hours to fix."

"Target the particle beam array on *Titan*'s escorts and—"

"Negative. Our first shot used a residual charge. We can't fire it again for five minutes."

Vang moved to Tren's side. "We can't let them destroy the Husnock ship!"

"We don't have time to break both their shields," Tren said. "Braz, do you have any other weapons ready to fire?"

"Negative. Someone raided this ship of all its munitions except one."

Bol interjected, "The escort ships are locking on to the Husnock vessel!"

"Suppressing fire!" Tren ordered. "All ships, maneuver to block their firing solution on the Husnock vessel!" Then, just to Braz: "Whatever you've got, fire it! Now!"

"Sir, the Husnock weapon is a missile, and it's tagged as 'antistellar munitions.'"

The horror of that classification froze Tren for half a breath, until his ship rocked and thundered in the wake of a brutal volley of phaser blasts and quantum torpedoes erupting against its shields. Then, hanging on to his command chair for dear life, he knew what he had to do—and he hoped this time Vale would make the sensible decision instead of the honorable one.

"Braz, arm that missile—and target it exactly the way I'm about to describe."

Seventeen

Everyone's got a plan until they get hit. That classic bit of Terran boxing wisdom echoed in Vale's thoughts as she waved away thick clouds of noxious smoke wafting across her bridge.

Everything was failing at once; the ship felt as if it were going to pieces under Vale's feet. Burning motes geysered from blackened companels along the bridge's starboard bulkhead. Scratchy comm chatter filtered from the overhead speakers, a stream of overlapping updates from the captains of the *Wasp* and the *Canterbury*, which had rallied to defend the *Titan* after its shields collapsed. Vale helped Sarai up off the deck, then she turned toward Tuvok. "Tactical, what do we have left that's actually working?"

"Not much, Captain." The Vulcan struggled to extract useful intel from his smoking console. "Engineering and ops are coordinating to reroute essential systems and bring backups online, but command-and-control systems have been damaged. If not for the *Wasp* and the *Canterbury*, we would be completely defenseless right now."

Torvig coaxed his companel back to life, then looked over his shoulder to tell Vale, "Doctor Ra-Havreii has declared an emergency on all engineering decks. Antimatter containment is destabilizing. If we can't restore full containment in the next five minutes—"

"We're all well aware what happens then, Lieutenant." Vale hunched over Rager's shoulder at ops. "Damage report."

It was clear that Rager was straining to preserve a façade of calm. "Multiple EPS conduit overloads throughout the ship. Primary and secondary sensors are scrambled, but I'm trying to reboot them." She patched in a new feed of data. "Updates from *Wasp* and *Canterbury*. The Breen are disengaging, and the Husnock ship is coming about to match their course."

"Find out where they're—"

She was cut off by Thot Tren's voice from the overhead speakers. *"I warned you not to interfere with our mission, Captain. Now I regret to be the bearer of further ill tidings. My team on the Husnock ship has been unable to override that vessel's automated defenses, and its main computer seems to have interpreted your escort ships' behavior as a hostile act. Even now it—"*

His message was interrupted by a blue streak of light emanating from the Husnock vessel. Tuvok declared, "They've fired a missile!" Everyone froze, snared by dread. Then the *Titan*'s second officer added, "It's not heading for us. Tracking its current vector." His eyes widened—not by much, but enough to tell Vale she was not going to like what he said next. "It's accelerating at high warp toward the red giant."

Oh, no. Vale jarred herself into action. "Tuvok, analyze that missile, now!"

"The missile's configuration is not one we've seen before, but its warhead contains a significant amount of trilithium. Such a munition could annihilate the star and unleash a hyperwarp shock wave. We must leave immediately!"

That was all Vale needed to hear. "Helm, set course away from the star and—"

"Captain," Lavena said, "we don't have warp speed."

Her mind raced. "How long do we have until the missile makes impact?"

"Fifteen seconds," Tuvok said. "Then thirty seconds before the shock wave hits us."

Vale all but threw herself into her command chair. "Bridge to engineering! We need warp speed in thirty seconds or we're all dead!" A sharp glance at Tuvok. "Tell the *Wasp* and the *Canterbury* to warp out of here, now!"

Before she could give more orders, Tren's voice returned. *"My comrades and I are departing, Captain. And to protect innocent lives from the Husnock vessel, we are taking it with us. For your own safety, I strongly suggest you not follow us. Tren out."*

As the channel closed, Vale wished she could strangle Tren for what he'd done.

"Captain," Tuvok said, "our escorts refuse to leave without us. Captain Scarfield wants to tow us to warp with a tractor beam."

"No," Vale said, "if we lose containment, the blast would vaporize them both. Tell them to go, that's an order!"

As Tuvok transmitted her reply, a sapphire flash on the viewscreen announced the fiery demise of the red giant, whose outer layers vanished like fog in a gale. Then the core of the star shrank into itself, collapsed to a pinpoint—then erupted in a blinding explosion that turned the viewscreen white. "Fifteen seconds to hyperwarp shock wave impact," Rager said.

Streaks of light on the screen announced the departures of the *Wasp* and the *Canterbury*. Vale was thankful she at least had been able to save—

"Containment restored," Ra-Havreii said over the intraship comm, *"warp drive online!"*

"Helm—!" That was all Vale had time to say before Lavena jumped the *Titan* to warp speed, mere seconds ahead of a shock front that portended instant destruction. As the hum of the warp drive resonated through the ship's spaceframe, Vale said to Rager, "Viewer aft."

Rager shifted the viewscreen to an aft view just in time to catch the shock front striking the system's lone rocky planet, which shattered into dust and debris that were scattered and hurled away on the blast wave's ever-expanding faster-than-light outer curve.

Sarai was back at Vale's side. "That was close."

"Understatement of the year, Number One."

The first officer picked bits of debris from her dark hair. "Now what?"

"We have to adjust our strategy and our tactics, and we need to do it fast. We've already lost control of a Husnock ship. Now we need to focus on recovering it, and avoid getting our clocks cleaned in another toe-to-toe fight. But first things first—we have to keep the Breen in our sights, because if we lose them, we're officially done."

"Well," Sarai said, "we have one thing in our favor now. Even if the Breen ships cloak, the Husnock vessel can't. And tracking something that big at long range shouldn't pose too much difficulty now that it's emitting an energy signature."

"Good, start with that." An overhead light erupted into a shower of sparks that rained down on Vale, and then the lights went out. She breathed in another lungful of bitter smoke, and its acrid sting sharpened her focus. "Helm, set course to pursue the Breen. Tactical, instruct the *Wasp* and the *Canterbury* to do the same, and to keep feeding us any intel they can scare up. Rager, Torvig, let me know when Doctor Ra-Havreii finishes putting out the fires belowdecks. Because as soon as this ship's combat ready, we're going to have a rematch with Thot Tren."

Everything on *Titan*'s main engineering deck was coming down in pieces or going up in flames. Engulfed in chaos, Ra-Havreii had spent the last few minutes darting from one crisis to the next and hoping he could stay one step ahead of calamity. As he reached through an open bulkhead to pluck out a fried board of isolinear chips, tongues of fire snapped at his arms and shriveled the fine hairs on the backs of his hands. When he finally pulled the blackened circuit board free, it was so hot he had to fling it away without concern for where it went. "Damn it!"

Ensign Meldok rushed to Ra-Havreii's side. "Sir! Are you all right?"

Ra-Havreii shook his stinging hands and blistering

fingertips. "I'm fine." He pointed past the Benzite engineer. "Bring me that dynoscanner, would you?"

"Aye, sir!" Meldok sprang away, fetched the tool, and returned.

"Thanks," Ra-Havreii said as he took the ultrasensitive molecular sensor. "Get to the master panel and shut down the starboard EPS taps until we can stabilize the—"

A deep boom and a flash of light cut him off and knocked everyone in main engineering flat on the deck. Blinking away the shock and pain inflicted by the blast, Ra-Havreii realized a key component in the warp core's matter-antimatter mix assembly had just overloaded and turned itself into smoke, slag, and shrapnel. *That's not good. Not good at all.*

"Meldok, shut down the EPS taps!" Ra-Havreii looked for the next closest member of his department and found Ensign Tasanee Panyarachun. He seized the young human woman's arm to get her attention. "Put a new control board in the coil regulator, on the double!" He pressed the dynoscanner into her hands. "And find the plasma leak in the starboard EPS manifold before it kills us all. Go!" He released her, and she took off like a streak of lightning.

A cry of wrenching metal—an overhead panel broke free high above his head and fell in a mesmerizing tumble-spin. He gauged its trajectory and knew he was clear—and then he saw it arc toward Lieutenant Indra Mondal, one of the ship's recently assigned new officers. It took him only the merest fraction of a second to realize shouting a warning would not save her; in the time it would take him to get her attention and for her to react to the danger, she would be dead.

He sprang forward and tackled her out of the panel's path. Its jagged edge tore through his left calf as it struck the deck beside them. He caged his shout of agony behind gritted teeth.

Lying on the deck in his embrace, Mondal belatedly processed what had happened. "My God," she said as he let go of her and stood. "That would have—"

"Cut off the antimatter to the mix assembly," Ra-Havreii said as he rushed away, too frantic to waste time on a pointless show of gratitude. "And make it fast, the mix chamber's overheating!" He clambered up an emergency access ladder to the ruptured component.

At the top of the ladder he scrambled onto and across a narrow catwalk to the sealed compartment that housed the premix node for the warp core. Through the sealed bulkhead door's narrow window, all he saw inside was vapor from the fractured node and smoke from the damaged banks of computers on either side of it. Then, through the gray haze, he discerned a body on the deck: one of his engineers, Ensign Crandall.

No! He keyed in the command code for the door, and its magnetic bolts retracted with a muffled *thunk*. In a blur he pulled open the heavy portal and slipped inside the radiation-shielded compartment, which was oppressively hot. He ran to Crandall and kneeled beside him. A finger to the man's carotid confirmed he still had a pulse, but it was weak. Another minute in the smoke and elevated radiation, and the ever-meticulous young human would be dead.

Ra-Havreii leaned his back against Crandall, pulled the man's body around his shoulders, then he fought his way to his feet. Sweating through his uniform, he staggered on trembling legs as he carried Crandall away from the premix node. One kick opened the unlocked portal, and Ra-Havreii stumbled out onto the catwalk, upon which he set his wounded engineer.

In between gasps of cooler air, Ra-Havreii shouted down to a cluster of blue-uniformed personnel carrying medkit satchels, "Hey! I need a medic up here! It's an emergency!"

One of them looked up and answered, "On my way!"

Meldok returned and looked up at Ra-Havreii. "EPS taps are off! Is Crandall hurt?"

"He'll live," Ra-Havreii said, hoping he wasn't giving his people false hope. Picturing the damage he had glimpsed inside the premix chamber, he added, "I need a plasma fuser!" The Benzite looked around, found an open tool box, and dug a plasma fuser from it. He lobbed the device up to Ra-Havreii, who caught it and nodded back at Meldok. "Thanks. Go help Tasanee."

"On my way." Meldok took off running to his next task.

Equipped and all too aware of the crisis still unfolding around him, Ra-Havreii went back inside the premix chamber—and this time he sealed the bulkhead door behind him.

No reason to expose anyone else to this toxic soup.

The scorching air stung his sinuses and throat as he inhaled. Each shallow breath he drew hurt worse than the one before, and as he worked repairing the cracks in the premix node, sweat drenched his long white hair and deepened the droop of his snowy mustache.

His vision blurred. Blinking, he fought to regain his acuity, but focus proved elusive. Then his guts churned with nausea, and vertigo made him feel as if the room were spinning. The elevated radiation level in the compartment was taking him down with a vengeance.

He was disappointed in himself. *Thought I could hold out longer than this.* He gulped a deep breath, and it was like swallowing fire. Two hard shakes of his head gave him back a small measure of his stability, and he kneeled to finish the last repairs on the premix node. The frantic pounding of fists against the locked bulkhead door, and the cries of his subordinates to come out and let them eject the entire warp core, only served to distract him and slow his progress.

There hadn't been enough time to suit up in radiation-resistant gear—of that Ra-Havreii had been certain the moment he saw the damage. Even as he patched and stabilized the mix assembly, he knew he had cheated disaster by less than a minute. In the time it would have taken him to don a radiation suit, the ship would either have been lost in a flash of free radicals and waste heat, or been forced to eject its warp core—a choice that would have left the *Titan* a crippled husk without warp speed or main power.

Limping away from the repaired node, Ra-Havreii felt confident he had made the best choice available to him. He unlocked the door, which was pulled open by Meldok and Mondal. Without the portal to hang on to, Ra-Havreii collapsed.

The two engineers caught him. As he lay cradled in their arms, Meldok gushed, "You did it, sir! You saved the ship!"

"I know," Ra-Havreii said in a bone-dry scratch of a whisper.

"Just hang on, sir," Mondal said. "The medics are having you beamed to sickbay."

Meldok smiled at Ra-Havreii with what seemed like a manic quality. "It was most brave of you to make that repair without a radiation suit. You're a true hero, Commander."

Ra-Havreii let go of consciousness before he could tell Meldok the truth.

I'm no hero, he realized. *I just don't care anymore whether I live or die.*

Eighteen

Even on his best day Gaila would never have been accused of being dignified. All the same, he knew it was unseemly how long and hard he had been laughing. He didn't care. He was watching his most brightly gilt dreams of avarice come true on the Husnock factory's long-range sensors.

It was utter mayhem. Starfleet ships and Breen vessels exchanging fire in a star system a few light-years away. A crippling blast fired by the Husnock derelict, which the Breen appeared to have returned to full operational status. An antistellar munition deployed to staggering effect. Each escalation of the conflict had made Gaila whoop and guffaw louder than he had before, and now he was red in the lobes, barely able to breathe, and doubled over with mirth in his chair.

A few more seconds of this and I'll pass out.

Zinos stood in the office's open doorway, his face glum as he watched Gaila contort himself with hysterics. "Good news, I presume."

Gaila decided trying to bottle up his joy would be futile, so he released it all in a victorious whoop. Then a deep breath, and he was able to answer his long-suffering right-hand man. "Magnificent news! The Breen have captured the Husnock derelict we found, and they've used it to bloody Starfleet's nose. We're off and running!"

The reed-thin Argelian widened his eyes in alarm. "Are you mad? You want to negotiate an arms deal with the Breen? A culture whose idea of haggling is arguing over how many times they'll shoot you before and after they take whatever they want?"

"That won't happen this time." Gaila pointed at Zinos. "That's why I have you." A broader gesture, at the factory around them. "And it's why I had Vatzis beef up our defenses. If the Breen come looking for trouble, we'll give them more than they can handle."

"So you say. What if they find the 'sample' you left for them?"

"What? You mean the star-fragger?"

"That's the one," Zinos said. "What if they point that thing at us?"

The cynical Ferengi sneered at the notion. "Ridiculous. First, it would be overkill. Second, when they come here, it'll be to acquire more munitions for their new armada. Blow us up, and they'll doom themselves to either a finite supply of ordnance or a costly reverse-engineering program to figure out how to make more. Third, and this is the best one of all, they *can't*—because they've *already used it!*" Gaila guffawed, unable to stop himself.

Zinos waited until Gaila had exhausted himself. "Have you considered that when the Breen arrive on our doorstep, those Starfleet vessels will be right behind them?"

Another stupid question for Gaila to dismiss. "*Pfft.* So what if they are?"

"If they find out what this facility is, they'll have every reason to destroy it."

"Every *reason*, yes, but nowhere near enough firepower. This is no rinky-dink Federation outpost, or some slapdash Orion tin can. This is a Husnock munitions plant! I used to think the latinum vaults of Ferenginar were the most impregnable places in the galaxy. Compared to this place, the latinum vaults might as well be made of Kaferian rice paper."

Unconvinced, the Argelian shook his head and paced. "I still don't like it. How can we conduct business with the Breen when we have Starfleet breathing down our necks?"

The lad had so much to learn about business. "There's no better time to extract profit from a customer than when he has a gun to his head."

"Which Rule of Acquisition is that?"

"It's not one of the Rules, it's just basic business sense. If you're selling flotation devices, you add a markup when the customer's drowning. Any Ferengi child knows that." He let out a snort of disgust. "At least they used to, before Nagus Rom and all his fairness and equality claptrap. I hear he won't even let schools bankrupt students anymore. If they can't see their classmates fail, how in the name of the Blessed Exchequer will they ever learn?"

A frown deepened the lines on Zinos's forehead. "I think we're off topic, sir."

"Hm? Oh. What were we—?" Gaila rewound the conversation thirty seconds in his memory. "Starfleet, right. Listen to me, Zinos. They're nothing to worry about.

Having them as an added pressure will speed our talks with the Breen. They'll want to re-arm their new toy in time to turn it against the Starfleeters, which means they'll have to pay whatever price we ask."

Zinos crossed his arms, a subtle signal that he wasn't buying Gaila's reasoning. "And what if the Breen decide to hold a grudge over being extorted?"

"What if they do? We'll still hold the key to their success. They can hate us all they want, but they won't be able to change the fact that they *need* us. As soon as they realize that, I guarantee you, the Breen will find themselves highly invested in our survival." He checked the sensor readouts, noted the speed of the incoming Breen ships and their Husnock spoil of war, and made some calculations in his head. "They'll be here and ready to talk business in about eight hours. Go downstairs and start prepping the showroom for our new number-one customers."

Nineteen

It had always bothered Sarai to be the last person to arrive for a meeting; it made her feel as if she were walking into an ambush. As irrational as that was, the feeling struck her again as she entered the *Titan*'s conference room, where Captain Vale and Admiral Riker faced a bulkhead companel that had been repurposed as a viewscreen. The image on the screen was divided; on the left was Captain Scarfield of the *Wasp*, and on the right was Captain Mareet of the *Canterbury*. Riker nodded at Sarai as she entered, then said to the others, "Let's get started."

Vale took swift charge of the emergency command conference. "We need ideas for how to stop the Breen, and we need them fast. Whatever crazy notions you might have, spit 'em out."

"You won't like what I have to say," Mareet replied. *"We're outnumbered and outgunned. I'd like to propose we break off pursuit and inform Starfleet Command that it needs to send in the big guns to deal with this."*

The suggestion made Riker bristle. "Absolutely not," he told the green-haired Catullan. "This mission was assigned to us, and we aren't giving it up. At least, not this easily."

It wasn't much of a pep talk, in Sarai's opinion, but it seemed to steel Scarfield's courage. *"Mareet's correct about us being outgunned, but there are other ways to hit them. They're bound to drop back to sublight at some point, and when they do, I can ram the Husnock vessel at warp speed. I don't care how strong its shields are, or thick its hull is—an impact at supraluminal speed would vaporize that thing. That's just basic physics."*

"I'd rather not jump straight to kamikaze tactics," Vale said. "Not until we've at least discussed other options that don't involve suicide." She aimed a hopeful look at Sarai. "Do the Breen ships have any known weaknesses we can exploit?"

Sarai shook her head. "None that I could find. They've made a lot of progress with their shield technology in just the last two years. And now that they're in command of a Husnock vessel, I can't even begin to tell you how much we don't know about that thing."

Mareet asked, *"Could we coax the Breen ships into separating from the Husnock vessel? Some way that we could divide and conquer?"*

"Doubtful," Sarai said. "My experience with the Breen suggests they'll stick together." She faced Riker and Vale. "Have we considered negotiating with them? Exploring a political or economic compromise?" It was a long shot of an idea, but one that Sarai knew would most please Admiral Batanides by fulfilling her desire to capture the Husnock technology for Starfleet.

Her question made Riker scrunch his brow in

confusion. "Are you suggesting we try to *bribe* the Breen into handing over the Husnock ship?"

"If that's what it takes, why not?"

Vale fixed Sarai with an incredulous stare. "And with what do you propose we tempt them? What could we possibly offer them that would persuade them to give that thing up?"

"The schematics and software for slipstream drive," Sarai said. As Riker and the captains overlapped one another's exclamations of protest, she raised her voice to continue. "We know it's something they wanted badly enough four years ago to attack the Utopia Planitia Shipyards. And two years ago they scuttled several of their ongoing spec-ops projects in a failed bid to capture an even more powerful drive system from an alternate universe." The weight of four accusatory glares made her self-conscious as she concluded, "If our mission is to relieve them of that ship at all costs, this would be one way to get the job done with minimal loss of life."

"Minimal loss of *our* lives," Riker said, "here, today. But countless more lives would be lost throughout the galaxy if we hand over slipstream technology to the Typhon Pact."

"I have to agree," Vale said. "As logical as Commander Sarai's proposal might seem on its face, depriving the Breen of one catastrophic technology by giving them another fails the spirit of our mission objective, which is to prevent disruptive technologies of any kind from falling into the wrong hands. That said, I appreciate that kind of fresh thinking. Now let's find another idea, something just as unexpected but more focused and effective."

All went quiet for a second while everyone racked their imaginations. The next person to speak was Captain

Scarfield. *"Our current conditions offer us a poor vantage from which to strike at the Breen. But what if we choose a different point of engagement?"*

A nod of understanding from Mareet. *"You're saying get ahead of them."*

"Precisely," Scarfield said. *"Right now they're in the lead, calling the shots. But if we figure out what their endgame is, maybe we can skip to that and put them on the defensive."*

"It's not a bad place to start," Riker said. "What do we know, or think we know, about what they've done so far? That might give us a clue as to what they'll do next."

Sarai picked up a padd from the conference room table and used it to call up the ship's recent logs. "So far their modus operandi appears to be to let others do their dirty work and heavy lifting, and then they swoop in and take all the loot for themselves."

A huff of cynical amusement from Vale. "That sounds like the Breen, all right."

"We've been assuming that capturing the Husnock ship was their primary objective," Sarai continued. "But their heading doesn't take them back toward Breen space—it takes them deeper into territory we believe was controlled by the Husnock. Which means they might be using that ship as a means to an end. They might be after something much bigger."

Riker's eyes narrowed. "Like an entire Husnock fleet, for instance?"

"Possibly," Sarai said. "Doctor Kilaris said she heard the Nausicaans say they had found a Husnock fleet. If the Breen knew about it, that would explain their current actions, and their reluctance to commit to a full-scale tactical engagement when we confronted them earlier."

Looking troubled, Mareet asked, *"If the Breen do have a lead on more of these ships, and they seize control of them before we can stop them, we'd find ourselves confronting a massively superior force. What would we do then?"*

Vale traded a grim look with Riker, then she sighed. "If it comes to that, I guess we'll just have to take another look at Fiona's high-warp kamikaze idea."

"Oh, well, okay then," Sarai deadpanned, "as long as we have a plan."

Twenty

Nothing was working out quite the way Brunt had expected.

Things had started out predictably enough. Though he had remained what felt like at least a few steps behind Gaila ever since he had piloted the *Net Gain* into this remote sector of the Alpha Quadrant, he had felt sure he was getting closer. The supply ships had led him to the Federation research expedition, and of course the brazen attack by the Nausicaan fringe group had proved a peculiar wrinkle. And though the ambush of the Nausicaans by an Orion Syndicate crew had seemed to catch the Starfleeters by surprise, Brunt had simply nodded. His only point of confusion up until then had been to wonder why the Syndicate hadn't acted sooner.

Then the Breen cut the Syndicate crew off at the knees, and everything had gone haywire. Brunt had come prepared to contend with small factions, such as the Syndicate and even a renegade Nausicaan militia.

But when the Breen and the Starfleet ships started exchanging fire, that was when Brunt had to admit to himself that he had become swept up in something he most assuredly was not equipped to handle. Playing two small bands of selfish opportunists against each other was old hat for the Ferengi bounty hunter, but inserting himself into what was fast becoming a large-scale military conflict was where he drew the line.

Just like my moogie always used to say: "When the great trogghemoths of the swamp do battle, the last place you want to be is under their feet."

Taking that advice to heart, he had kept his ship well out of the crossfire between the Breen and the Starfleeters. At the same time, he had performed a risk assessment concerning the continuance of his mission. Following the Breen fleet was a risky proposition. If they detected his ship, their most likely response would be to blast him to pieces.

If only they weren't my best bet of finding Gaila, he lamented.

Most surprising of all was that he felt just the tiniest sting of conscience for his peripheral role in this quickly escalating fiasco. He was watching the Breen abscond with a weapon of mass destruction, one whose technological secrets might tip the balance of power in the Typhon Pact's internal contest for political influence, not to mention their cold-war arms race with the Federation and its allies. He was almost certain he knew where they would go next, and what it would mean for countless worlds and lives throughout known space if the Breen were allowed to return home flush with the lethal bounty of the Husnock.

It was ridiculous, he told himself. There was no

reason he should feel any compulsion to intervene, or gamble his reputation and business contacts by reporting what he knew to Starfleet, or the Grand Nagus, or anyone else. *Who am I to cry foul? I used to be an arms merchant when it suited my interests. There was a time when I'd gladly have sold the Breen that ship.*

Brunt winced. There it was again—that pinprick of guilt, deep inside his stomach. He knew where it was coming from, no matter how hard he tried to deny it. His mind kept flashing back to the sight of the red giant being annihilated by an antistellar munition. He had watched its hyperwarp shock front shatter an entire world. Stone and fire had expanded, disintegrated, and merged into a superheated cloud of gas swept away by a faster-than-light wave of violence against which nothing could stand. He had witnessed the cataclysm from a safe distance, but even still the experience had left him feeling hollowed out. Gutted. Afraid.

I would never have sold such a weapon. Not at any price, not to anyone.

Was it hypocritical to seek higher moral ground after all he had done? All his life he had been taught—and had told others—that there was no greater good than profit. No deal that could not be justified so long as the return on investment was good enough. Had he been wrong?

He tried to distract himself with the minutiae of tracking the Breen while preserving his ship's stealth profile. Lurking a few light-hours behind the three Starfleet vessels, the *Net Gain* was barely able to maintain a sensor lock on the Breen ships and their stolen Husnock warship. Brunt couldn't tell whether the Starfleet ships were keeping their distance by choice, or because they lacked the ability to catch up to the Breen.

And what would they do if they caught them? It had shocked Brunt how decisively the Breen had pummeled the *Titan* into submission and cowed its escort ships. Had the Starfleeters finally inserted themselves into a situation they couldn't handle? It certainly had seemed so to Brunt back on the wasteland moon, inside the Husnock shipwreck. *What would they have done if I hadn't been there to save their asses?*

As he thought about their predicament, he lost himself in a daydream of derring-do and heroics better suited to a holonovel than a man bent on profit and survival. Part of him wished he were in a position to intervene, to somehow set his thumb on the scales of fortune and tip the balance to the Starfleeters—if only because he found them so much easier to inveigle and manipulate than he did the Breen. The Breen also had a bad habit of expressing their displeasure at winding up on the losing side of a haggle by shooting people.

Wouldn't it be grand, just once, to be the one who swings in and saves the day?

He divested himself of that absurd fantasy. The real universe was no place for heroes. Everything he had ever seen in his life had shown him that the price of courage was pain and regret, exacerbated by the loss of profit. Many of his former acquaintances, not to mention a legion of infamous and tragic figures from Ferengi history, had learned that lesson the hard way: Heroism was a sucker play, a racket, a scam with no payoff. Being hailed as a savior might look good on paper, but in practice it never seemed to work out as promised.

In the long run, vengeance well executed brought not only greater satisfaction but richer rewards. Pushing away all delusions of nobility, Brunt cleared his head and reminded himself why he had come all this way and shouldered all this risk.

At the end of the day, Brunt was in this mess to get paid.

Twenty-one

The Husnock fleet yard looked to Thot Tren like a fearsome black fractal pattern in space, with wheels on spokes radiating from other larger wheels, all linked to a central hub, with nearly every available berth occupied by a Husnock warship. It was a thing of beauty.

"Vang, order the *Sulica* and the *Tarcza* to assume defensive positions on our aft flanks," Tren said. "Bol, scan the base. Sevv, tell our boarding party to stand by with those command codes. We're about to need them. All ships, engage cloaking devices." On the viewscreen, stars stretched by warp-speed distortion rippled as the ship cloaked. "Helm, take us to impulse."

Tren tensed as his escort ships and the Husnock dreadnought dropped out of warp, with the captured vessel ahead of the *Kulak*, as a buffer between Tren's ship and the massive starport. It was a precaution dictated by the *Sulica*'s earlier scouting missions to the fleet yard.

Despite the space station having been long left derelict, its weapons systems had armed the moment they'd detected the presence of an unauthorized alien starship. The *Sulica* and her crew had narrowly escaped destruction by cloaking and retreating before the station's array of beam weapons had been able to slice them apart. Approaching the starport in the open was an error Tren knew not to repeat.

Bol reported from tactical, "The station is locking weapons on the Husnock ship."

Tren faced his signals officer. "Get me Chot Braz on a secure frequency."

Sevv opened the channel and nodded at Tren. "Ready."

"Braz, are you ready to proceed?"

"Transmitting friend-or-foe confirmation now. Stand by."

There was something familiar and comforting to Tren about the level of Husnock paranoia that would lead them to treat even one of their own ships as a threat until confirmed otherwise. It was the same level of distrust he had come to expect from his fellow Breen.

"Station's weapons are releasing their targeting locks," Bol said.

So far, so good, Tren told himself. "Braz, what's your status?"

"Logging in to the starport's control system now. Defense grid override commencing." A moment later the Spetzkar commander added, *"Defense grid neutralized. You are clear to disengage cloaking devices."*

"All ships," Tren said, patching automatically into the ships' shared secure channel, "disengage cloaking devices. Stand by to deploy boarding parties to the station." Closing the channel, he added to Vang, "See it done."

"Yes, sir." Vang withdrew to an open station on the port side of the command deck.

Tren was not given to pacing, but he felt the urge now. He was impatient and keenly aware of the danger posed by the Starfleet ships that, in spite of his warning, continued to dog his battle group. *I respect Vale's tenacity. A shame she lacks the discretion with which to temper it.*

Vang returned to Tren's side. "Boarding teams have reached the station's control center."

"Ahead of schedule. Good." He switched to the shared channel. "Braz, is the starport's comm network intact?"

"Affirmative. Initiating ping sequence. Assuming these translations of the Husnock language are accurate, we should be able to bring all vessels online in a few minutes."

"Understood. Proceed with due haste." Tren ambled toward the main viewscreen to admire the assembled Husnock fleet more closely. There were ships of many different sizes and configurations. None appeared to be larger than the one he and his crew had captured. He could only speculate as to what the various ships' mission profiles had once been. Were there minelayers? Minesweepers? Fast-attack cruisers? Might the Husnock have employed small fighter spacecraft deployed from carrier vessels? There was so much Tren yearned to know about the Husnock's long-dormant arsenal. *You'll know in time,* he promised himself. *Be patient.*

Minutes bled away while Tren waited. On the main screen the Husnock station loomed; on the aft tactical displays, sensor readouts tracked the approaching Starfleet force. He feared time might not be on his side. *Unless we secure the rest of the Husnock vessels before the* Titan *and her group arrive, we might have to settle for only half a prize—or maybe none at all.*

Pessimistic thoughts haunted him. He reflected on the recent high-profile failures of his peers. The destruction of the Salavat shipyard under Thot Keer. Thot Konar's botched assassination attempt on Federation president Nanietta Bacco. Thot Trom's failure to recover a valuable prototype wormhole-drive starship from an alternate universe. Each defeat the result of Starfleet interference, each one a scathing public humiliation for the Breen Confederacy.

Every moment that elapsed without word from the boarding parties made Tren worry just a bit more that his name would soon be added to the ranks of the beaten and disgraced.

Then came the news from Braz: *"Uplinks established and confirmed. Bringing the Husnock fleet's main reactors online now. Preparing to transmit remote command codes to all vessels. Stand by for final confirmation."*

"Well done," Tren said. "Once you have access, I want a complete inventory of our ghost fleet's ordnance for Breen Militia Command."

"Understood. I'll signal again when we have an estimated deployment countdown."

"Acknowledged." Tren closed his side of the channel and stepped back from the main viewscreen to find Vang once more lifting his snout in a subtle bid for his attention. "Report."

"The Starfleet vessels are alternately increasing speed and slowing. Either their lead ship is damaged, or they are engaged in a strategy so bizarre it defies comprehension."

"Have you warned them to cease their pursuit?"

"Yes, as you directed." Vang glanced toward the tactical displays. "They have not responded, nor have they complied."

On the main viewscreen, the Husnock fleet glimmered with signs of growing power. Under his helmet, Thot Tren bared his fangs in a grin.

"Let them come, then," he said. "If they try to stop us, they fly to their doom."

One look at the nightmarish spectacle on the *Titan*'s main viewscreen made Vale blanch. She had seen her share of lopsided battles, but this was by far the most egregious mismatch she had ever personally faced. The Husnock fleet station looked like a dandelion ready to release its downy tendrils—except the entire thing was plated with a substance so black that it nearly disappeared into the spaces between the stars. And berthed around the rings at the end of every spoke in that obscene dark flower were Husnock warships, all of them flickering to life.

Vale's throat constricted tighter the longer she looked at the alien armada. "Number One, do we know yet exactly how many of those ships there are?"

Sarai checked the tactical display beside her seat. "Two hundred eighty-six Husnock ships," she said. "Varying sizes and configurations."

From the tactical console, Tuvok added, "None of them appear to be carrying any heavy ordnance, Captain. For the moment, they appear to be restricted to particle-beam arrays."

"Just one of which easily beat the hell out of us," Vale

reminded him. "Are we reading Breen life signs inside all those ships?"

Tuvok checked his readings. "Negative. Most show no life signs. However, I am reading a cluster of life signs that match known Breen member species, inside the starport's central hub."

Brow creased, Sarai asked Vale, "Could they be piloting that many ships remotely?"

"Maybe." On the viewscreen, dozens of the Husnock starships began detaching from the station. A few were already maneuvering away to make room for other ships' departures. Vale thought back to her Academy training. "Remote piloting even one starship is hard as hell, Number One. How are the Breen mastering so many vessels at once?"

"Maybe they've accessed the ships' autopilot functions." Sarai pointed out some of the vessels. "None of them are venturing far, or moving quickly. At least, not yet."

That, Vale realized, might yet be cause for hope. "If all those ships are on autopilot, they might not be up to the challenge of combat."

Tuvok interjected, "We don't know that, Captain. The Husnock were reputed to have been wily and ruthless tacticians. If that skill set extended to their preparation of autopiloting software, their ships might in fact be capable of fairly robust defenses and counterattacks."

Sarai nodded. "He makes a good point, Captain. We shouldn't assume that the Husnock vessels are easy marks just because they're on autopilot—if that's even what's happening."

The vagueness of Sarai's warning attracted Vale's curiosity. "Meaning what?"

The first officer lowered her voice and leaned toward Vale. "When the Breen made their attempt to assassinate President Bacco—"

"I thought that was never proved."

"Trust me," Sarai whispered, "it was them. For assassins they used androids based on the designs of Doctor Noonien Soong, and they controlled them remotely using telepresence systems based on Tholian thought-wave transmitters. If—"

"How do you know all that?" Vale asked. The Efrosian woman arched an eyebrow at her, and half a second later Vale answered it for herself. "Your work for Starfleet Intelligence. Forget I asked. Continue."

"If the Breen came here with some way of making that telepresence tech work with the Husnock ships, they might have brought a huge number of extra pilots and weapons specialists. Which means each ship's navigation and tactical response might be under conscious control."

Vale felt her pulse quicken. "If that's the case, the Breen would be able to sacrifice a handful of smaller Husnock vessels just to make a point, without losing any of their people."

A somber nod from Sarai. "Unfortunately, yes." She turned an anxious look toward Vale. "I know that if I were them, that's exactly what I would do. And I'd hit us hard, and quickly."

"This is not shaping up to be our day," Vale said.

She tried to imagine some way out of this crisis. A diplomatic solution. A bluff. Anything to preclude taking the *Titan* and its two escort ships into a battle where they would be outnumbered nearly a hundred to one. But no matter what perspective from which she tried to consider the matter, she arrived at the same conclusion: the

Titan, the *Wasp*, and the *Canterbury* were all that stood between the Breen with their hijacked armada and thousands of vulnerable worlds populated by nearly a trillion innocent sentient beings.

If we fold now to save ourselves, Vale reasoned, *we'd be condemning billions to die. But if we charge into a fight we can't possibly win, the same thing will probably happen anyway. The only thing I'd be saving by taking on the Breen here would be me from my own conscience.*

At her side, Sarai asked simply, "Orders, Captain?"

Duty and honor dictated Vale's next command. "Battle stations, Number One."

"Aye, sir." Sarai left her seat and issued orders on the move, striding with purpose from one station to the next while making the *Titan* ready for combat, as insane an idea as that was.

In less than a minute the *Titan* crew made the transition from elevated alert to combat ready. Vale, ensconced in the command chair, felt the anxiety levels in the ship spike—not because she possessed any empathic gift, but because a good captain was attuned to such shifts in the tenor of the crew. As she noted the introverted somatic cues of her bridge officers, she could tell none of them harbored the illusion that the odds in this fight might favor them.

From tactical, Tuvok delivered more bad news. "The Husnock ships that have separated from the station are raising their shields and charging their beam weapons." He looked up, his trademark Vulcan stoicism slightly disrupted by a shadow of alarm. "They are forming into battle groups and deploying into overlapping defensive formations."

"Definitely not autopilot," Vale muttered to Sarai.

"Looks like you were right. The Breen have complete control over the Husnock fleet." Watching the overwhelming display of military force on the main viewscreen, Vale admitted to herself that for the first time in her career, she might have bitten into a larger slice of danger than she could possibly swallow—and that it would be her crew, her allies, and her people who would soon pay for her mistake.

Victory was at hand, of that Thot Tren was certain. All the same, he knew not to celebrate before the battle was won.

Too many of his peers had made that misstep, especially in confrontations with Starfleet. The vast majority of the *thotaru* still considered Starfleet and the Federation to be weak and therefore easy targets. Tren did not share their delusion. Long ago, when he had been young, Starfleet had been an organization of scientists sometimes called upon to defend their culture. But these days Starfleet better resembled a professional military that also happened to be one of the galaxy's preeminent scientific research and exploration agencies—a dynamic entity that only a fool would dare to underestimate. There was no doubt in Tren's mind: even when outnumbered and outgunned, Starfleet was a dangerous opponent.

He did not intend to give them a chance to prove it in action.

On the *Kulak*'s main viewscreen, he watched Husnock ships detach and navigate away from the fleet station. Concerned he had missed a vital report, he looked around the command deck for his first officer. "Vang!

The ships that are leaving the station—are they fully loaded?"

Vang moved closer and patched his helmet's transceiver directly to Tren's, to keep their conversation private from the rest of the crew. *"There was a bit of bad news on that front, sir."*

It took great effort for Tren to resist the urge to disintegrate Vang. "Explain."

"There were no munitions anywhere on the station, sir."

"None?" He gazed at the huge station and was baffled. "How can that be?"

"It would seem," Vang said, *"that the Husnock made a practice of berthing their ships and storing their heavy munitions at separate facilities. We're still not sure why, but some files Chot Braz found on the station's computer suggest it was a precaution against an accidental detonation wiping out their entire fleet in a single blast."*

Tren gave a moment's consideration to that hypothesis, and he realized it was quite plausible that a station that housed so many starships could be destroyed by a munitions-handling error. Early accounts of Breen space exploration were replete with such cautionary tales. He nodded at Vang. "Very well. Do we have any leads on where those munitions were stored?"

"Yes, sir. Husnock records mention an automated munitions plant just a few hours from here at high warp. Long-range scans suggest the facility is still there and intact."

"Good. Notify all flight controllers of those coordinates." Another look at the armada on the viewscreen. "How long until we're ready to go? Best estimate, please."

"All ships will be clear of moorings in half an hour." Vang faced the tactical screen tracking the incoming Starfleet attack group. *"Permission to pose a question, sir?"*

"Granted."

"The Starfleet ships continue to follow us. Would it not be prudent to make our stand here? Even without heavy munitions, we could overpower them with ease." He glanced at the main viewscreen. *"If we leave here before coping with the Starfleet problem, we risk leading them to the munitions factory, which would compromise its value as a resource."*

It was a valid argument. If the munitions plant became known to Starfleet, they might seek to destroy it, blockade it, or seize it for themselves—any of which would constitute a negative outcome for Tren's mission. And without the benefit of the factory's output, the Husnock ships, as formidable as their beam weapons were, would not be enough to transform the Breen Confederacy into the dominant military force among the Typhon Pact powers.

But as Tren considered the ludicrous advantage in numbers and sheer firepower that his fleet—soon to be an armada—possessed over Captain Vale and her three starships, he discovered he felt almost ashamed to exploit it. Honor had never been a primary concern in greater Breen culture, but among Tren's native people, the Fenrisal, part of being an alpha resided in not wasting one's strength fighting those who had no hope of winning. Alphas were measured by the magnitude of the risks they overcame, and judged by the strength of the enemies they defeated. Not only would Tren find no glory among his kin for winning this fight, he would be ridiculed for it.

Laughed at for not finding a battle worthy of the power entrusted to his paws.

He doubted he could explain that rationale to Vang. Though he didn't know his first officer's true species—or those of any of his personnel—nothing Vang had ever said or done had given Tren reason to think him a fellow Fenrisal. *For all I know, he isn't even a he.*

After waiting what felt like too long to respond to Vang's observation, Tren said, "I see no reason to risk losing any of our new Husnock ships in a pointless battle with Starfleet. We'll depart as soon as all Husnock vessels are free and clear to navigate."

Instead of backing away to deliver Tren's orders, Vang lingered, his body language conveying fear and suspicion. *"And if our shadows tell Starfleet about the munitions plant . . . ?"*

"Use the Husnock armada's transceivers to jam the Starfleet ships' transmissions," Tren said. "If they follow us, they won't be able to tell anyone where we go next."

"And if they chase us all the way to the factory?"

"In that case, Vang, we shall arm one of our Husnock dreadnoughts and make Starfleet see the grave error of its ways."

Twenty-two

"We're losing them," Vale said, her tone turning the observation into an accusation.

At the helm, Lavena seemed to share her captain's frustration. "There's nothing we can do, sir. Warp power is fluctuating, and our speed with it. We can't maintain maximum warp for more than a few minutes at a time before dropping back to warp six."

"For what it's worth," Sarai said, "we're still tracking that warp shadow we think is Brunt's starhopper. Even if we lose our lock on the Breen and their Husnock ghost fleet, it seems Brunt remains intent on leading us to them."

Vale frowned. "Let's all be grateful then for small mercies." She looked upward as she addressed the ship's ever-listening computer. "Bridge to Commander Ra-Havreii."

The chief engineer replied over a din of clanging and hissing, *"Yes, Captain?"*

"I need you to lock in our warp power, Xin. We keep losing speed."

"Captain, we shouldn't even be moving at warp, never mind holding top speed for any length of time." Ra-Havreii's irritation and exhaustion were evident in his voice. *"To be honest, I can't explain why the warp core hasn't completely imploded already."*

"Be sure to note that in your log. Just so you know, Doctor, we're on the cusp of another showdown with the Breen. How long until you can restore shields and weapons?"

"Best guess?" One could almost hear Ra-Havreii shrugging. *"An hour, maybe two. As soon as Doctor Ree discharges me from sickbay, I'll get you more precise numbers."*

Vale trained a withering look upon Sarai, who averted her gaze, no doubt inferring the meaning behind her captain's angry stare: *My chief engineer is in sickbay and no one told me?* In her best approximation of a calm voice, Vale said, "Keep me posted, Doctor. Bridge out."

"Something's happening," Keru said. The Trill chief of security had set himself up at a tertiary console to serve as a backup tactical officer for Tuvok. "The enemy fleet is slowing, Captain."

Tuvok checked the readouts at the primary tactical station. "Confirmed, Captain. The Breen and their ghost fleet appear to be approaching another large Husnock deep-space facility."

"Another fleet yard?" she asked. To her chagrin, the *Titan* and its escorts had been unable to approach the starport from which the Breen had hijacked more than two hundred eighty Husnock warships. Though the Breen and all the Husnock vessels had already departed, the station's defenses had locked on to the three Starfleet ships without hesitation, precluding any hope of investigating the derelict facility. Which had left them no other course of action besides continuing to shadow the Breen and their ghost fleet.

At tactical, Tuvok shook his head. "Not a shipyard. But it appears to be industrial."

Rager swiveled her chair away from the ops console. "Captain, we're reading dense concentrations of heavy machinery inside the station, all of it apparently of Husnock design. Only a few life signs, however—all of them humanoid."

"That's not all," Torvig said, the delicate digits of his bionic hands keying new commands into the engineering console. "Several telltale molecular residues suggest the facility houses a vast supply of Husnock heavy ordnance similar to that which destroyed the red giant."

Sarai leaned forward from the edge of her chair. "It's a munitions dump. Or a factory. Or maybe both." She turned toward Vale. "Captain, the Breen brought their hijacked armada here to load them up with heavy ordnance. Letting them return home with those ships would have been a disaster in itself. But if they go back to known space carrying antistellar munitions—"

"I'm aware of the danger, Number One."

"Captain," Sarai said, "this might be our last opportunity to attack."

Before Vale could answer Sarai, Tuvok interjected, "That would be most unwise. Our group remains outnumbered ninety-six point six-seven to one, and the vast majority of the threat vessels are each individually capable of outgunning us." He tapped his console, and an image of the Husnock industrial facility appeared on the main viewscreen. "It is also worth noting that the munitions plant itself possesses significant defensive capabilities. I suspect we and our allied ships would receive a most hostile welcome there, just as we did at the Husnock starport."

The turbolift doors opened. Riker strode onto the bridge and moved to Vale's side. With one hand on the back of her chair, he leaned down to ask, "How goes the hunt, Captain?"

"We have the monsters in our sights, but that's about it."

She saw the muscles in Riker's jaw tense. He eyed the image of the munitions plant on the main viewscreen. "What are we thinking that is?"

"Ammo dump," Vale said. "Best guess is the Breen mean to load up their new fleet with all of the Husnock's deadliest toys as a gift for Domo Pran."

Riker cocked one eyebrow. "Do we have a plan to stop them?"

"We're working on it," Vale lied.

Then Pazlar, bless her, chimed in. "Captain, I might have an idea for how to disrupt the Breen's remote command of the Husnock armada."

Vale, Riker, and Sarai moved to surround Pazlar at the sciences console. Eager to latch on to anything resembling hope, Vale asked, "What's your idea?"

"After considering something Commander Sarai said earlier, about the Breen using telepresence systems, I pulled up all the documentation we had on their research into that technology. And it turns out that teams at Starfleet R and D have identified a bandwidth of ultralow-frequency subspace oscillations that serve as the medium for Tholian thoughtwave radio, which is the basis for Breen telepresence. With enough time, I might be able to scrub through that range of frequencies and isolate whichever ones the Breen are using to drive those ships."

Riker asked, "How long would you need?"

"I'm not sure, but anything we can do to buy ourselves time would help."

Just then Keru declared, "The Breen-Husnock armada has come to a stop a few thousand kilometers from the munitions factory. None of them are approaching the facility."

Sarai and Vale moved together back to the center of the bridge. Intrigued, Vale asked Keru, "What's going on? Do they not have the codes for that station?"

The answer came from Tuvok. "We are detecting encrypted comm traffic between the lead Breen vessel and the station. Irregular pauses; transmissions of varying duration from each side." He furrowed his brow at some detail, then keyed a command into his console.

The image on the main viewscreen magnified to show a small area of the facility in greater detail—and then Vale saw a small starship docked at an access point on the station's hull. "Mister Tuvok, do my eyes deceive me or does there seem to be someone aboard that station?"

"I believe you are correct, Captain. And judging from the station's continuing dialogue with the Breen, I suspect that whoever is controlling that facility is haggling with them."

"Number One, order all ships to hold here until further notice." Vale aimed a hopeful look at Pazlar. "You just got yourself a bit of time, Commander. Make the most of it."

Pazlar returned the captain's smile and set herself to work. "Aye, sir."

Thot Tren had embarked upon this mission knowing he might face a variety of threats and horrors. Brutal ship-to-ship combat he could accept; close-quarters battle between small units of his Spetzkar versus alien rivals of whatever stripe would be met without hesitation. But the obstacle to his plans that now presented itself was an affront to him on every level he could imagine—personal, professional, and moral. It simply was not right that he should be compelled to contend with something as base and vulgar as this in the name of duty.

Looking back at him from the viewscreen of the *Kulak*, the Ferengi known as Gaila prompted Tren in his most condescending nasal shrill, *"Well? How much do you bid?"*

All Tren wanted was to reach through the screen and throttle Gaila. "How dare you presume to lay claim to what is rightfully ours."

His implied threat only made the Ferengi bare a fanged grin. *"Finders keepers, my dear* thot. *Now . . . let's waste no more time on insults! My factory offers a wide range of munitions, from high-speed low-yield tactical torpedoes to planet-busters to star-killers. Take your pick!"*

Was this Gaila really so obtuse? "Do you not see how many warships I control? The sheer firepower at my command?"

The grin became a sneer. *"Do you not see how many fully loaded defensive batteries this station has? Are you not aware that none of the ships in your armada have any heavy ordnance? Or that their particle-beam weapons, even en masse, are no match for this station's shields?"*

It was maddening for Tren to admit, but Gaila was right. The station's defenses were impressive, and without the bounty contained within the munitions plant, his armada was not worth half what it should be. All the same, it galled and infuriated him to be on the receiving end of terms dictated by a Ferengi. And he dreaded losing face in front of his crew. He needed to do something, anything, to salvage his faltering position.

"I did not come all this way just to barter with the likes of you."

"Technically," Gaila said, *"what we're doing isn't bartering, it's haggling."*

Tren clenched his gloved fists. On top of everything else, the Ferengi was a pedant and a jester. Hidden behind his mask, Tren seethed. He felt his nostrils flare as he huffed angrily, and a growl rolled deep in his throat. *To hell with negotiation. I want this little pest dead.*

He closed the channel to the station and returned to his post in the center of the command deck. "Bol, target all weapons! Disruptors, torpedoes, everything we have! Vang, tell the *Sulica*, the *Tarcza*, and our Husnock controllers to do the same. Hit that station with all we have! Fire!"

No one questioned him, no one asked why. It took his people less than four seconds to turn his order into an onslaught. A firestorm of energy converged upon the munitions plant. The station's shield bubble crackled into view as it dimpled and retracted beneath the fierce assault.

"Maintain fire," Tren ordered. "Bring down their shields!"

The fusillade raged on. As one volley of torpedoes after another slammed into the shield, it seemed to buckle inward. For a moment, Tren believed his forces were about to bring the station to heel.

Then the station fired back.

It was a display of raw power so unnerving that it made Tren feel hollow. Massive beams of particle energy burst from the station's weapons array and vaporized six of his Husnock ships. Then a salvo of thirty-six Husnock torpedoes streaked away from the factory at ten-degree intervals around its perimeter. Each torpedo punched through the defensive screens of a different uncrewed Husnock vessel. All at once three dozen Husnock warships were consumed from within by gouts of blue-green fire—and then they all vanished in blinding flashes that left several dozen more Husnock vessels damaged and adrift.

An incoming signal buzzed on the communications console. Sevv silenced the alert, vetted the message, then faced Tren. "Mister Gaila wishes to resume your conversation, sir."

Livid but also humbled, Tren assented with a gesture. "Put him on-screen."

The Ferengi, damn him, looked even happier and more smug than he had before. It made Tren want to gut the little grifter. *Really, Thot Tren. Did you actually think that would work? What you saw was just a small taste of what I can do with this station's armament. And those torpedoes that scrapped a decent chunk of your fleet? Apparently those are* low-yield *Husnock munitions. I just wanted to* bloody *your nose, not cut it off—but now that you know what my merchandise can do, doesn't that make it seem more valuable than ever? Not to mention, if you ever do break through my shields and hit the station . . . what do you think'll happen to you and your precious fleet when this station ignites like a sun?"* A grub-eating grin. *"Wouldn't it be more profitable for everyone involved if we could be sensible about this?"*

Every fiber of Tren's being told him to kill Gaila. But his training told him he had no choice now but to negotiate. "Very well, Mister Gaila. What do you want?"

"So glad you asked! Let's start with what you need. Two hundred forty-five Husnock vessels with varying load-outs. Judging from their configurations . . ." He made some calculations while mumbling under his breath. *"All right, I'm ready to propose a package deal to arm all your ships with what I think are their optimal complements. Sending you the specs . . . now."*

Another feedback tone at the communications panel. Sevv verified the data, then routed it to the heads-up display in Tren's helmet. As soon as Tren saw the subtotal and the final tally on Gaila's proposed invoice, his temper flared. "Are you out of your mind, Ferengi?"

"It's a fair price."

"It's nearly half the gross domestic product of the Breen Confederacy!"

"Think of it as an investment in your future."

"Your price is insane! We'll never pay that much for one round of munitions."

Gaila waved his hands and shook his head. *"No, no, no! The price I quoted you wasn't for a single load of ammunition. It was my price for relinquishing this station—lock, stock, and barrel."* A dismissive shrug.

"But, if you'd rather buy your ordnance from me a la carte, I'm happy to oblige, and to offer you a far more reasonable one-time bill."

Another beep at Sevv's console, and the invoice total refreshed in Tren's HUD. The number remained outrageously high, even for weapons of such an apocalyptic nature.

Swallowing his rage, Tren said to Gaila, "I need to present your offer to my superiors and request authorization for payment. If the Confederate Congress approves your terms, we will make the necessary financial arrangements through the Bank of Orion."

"Splendid. But I'm not a patient man, Thot Tren. Especially not when dealing with the Breen. You have thirty minutes to secure the funds. After that, you can either leave, or see your fleet blasted into dust." He made a show of checking his chrono. *"Tick-tock, thot. Gaila out."*

The channel closed, and the viewscreen reverted to an image of the munitions factory.

Vexed and hungry for payback, Tren opened a secure channel to his Spetzkar commander. "Tren to Chot Braz."

"Go ahead."

"Find a way to breach the factory and take that Ferengi out of our equation. You have twenty-nine minutes, starting now."

Twenty-three

Twenty-one minutes had elapsed since Tren tasked his Spetzkar commander with breaching the munitions station. After all the time Tren and Braz had served together in the Breen Militia, it came as a surprise to hear Braz utter opinions Tren had never before heard from him.

"My team and I have looked at this every way we know how, sir. Given the time and the resources on hand, we are forced to confirm Mister Gaila's boast: the station is unbreachable."

Tren was not ready to walk away, not when victory was so close at hand. "Are you quite certain? I'm prepared to sacrifice a few ships if it will get us inside."

"It won't make any difference," Braz said over their private transceiver channel—a precaution Tren had taken to avoid impairing his crew's morale with bad news. *"Any attack powerful enough to breach the shields runs a high risk of detonating the munitions stored on the*

station. The resulting blast would vaporize them and us, just as the Ferengi said."

To have been outwitted by a Ferengi: that was too shameful a legacy for Tren to bear. There had to be another way forward. He moved to stand with Vang at the tactical console, behind Bol. "Is there any way to conceal a cyberattack inside a comm signal to the station?"

"Theoretically," Bol said. "But we don't know enough about the Husnock systems inside the station to craft an attack. And before you ask: yes, we scoured the computers on the ships of the Husnock armada for intel on the station. They all had the same set of access codes, none of which are working now. That suggests the Ferengi and his people changed the codes."

"Smart," Vang said. He glanced at the console chrono. "Sir, we have seven minutes to answer Gaila. Should I order the fleet to assume attack formation, hold position, or withdraw?"

Denial left Tren in a state of mute paralysis. *Beaten by a Ferengi. A common criminal.*

Sevv silenced an alert on his panel. "Sir, we've just received a message on a coded frequency. Its point of origin is unknown, but the sender is hailing us by name."

Time was slipping away, and Tren was ready to seize any opportunity he could find. "Start tracing the signal. And put it on-screen. Let's all see what they have to say."

The signals officer routed the message to the command deck's main viewscreen. A bald, round-faced humanoid with a low and prominent brow slurred in a nasal voice, "*—the Pakled salvage hauler Gomjar. Please respond.*"

"This is Thot Tren, commanding the Breen dreadnought *Kulak*. Identify yourself."

"*Cherbegrod. Captain of the* Gomjar."

Inside his helmet, Tren winced. *As if dealing with a Ferengi wasn't degrading enough. Now I'm wasting precious time on a Pakled.* "What do you want, junkman?"

"*Wanted the station. Had it first. Then the Ferengi came. Stole it from us.*"

That revelation kindled Tren's interest, and he saw from the change in Vang's posture that his first officer recognized the possible opportunity the Pakleds represented. "You say you had control of the Husnock munitions factory before the Ferengi did?"

"*Yes. Our station. He took it.*" All at once a sly expression manifested on the Pakled's cherubic face. "*Now the Ferengi robs you too. Won't give you weapons.*"

A readout in the lower right corner of the viewscreen reminded Tren that he had only six minutes left to answer Gaila's demands. "Our dealings with Gaila are not your concern."

Cherbegrod shrugged. "*Just want to help you.*"

"And why would you want to do that?"

Now there was a dark shadow of malice in the Pakled's features. "*To make Gaila pay. Make him suffer. Teach him Pakleds are smart.*"

Was it possible the Pakleds really were in a position to undermine Gaila? Tren had to know. "And how, precisely, will you do that?"

Cherbegrod folded his hands in front of his chest and rested them atop the curve of his belly. "*Pakleds smart. Use shortcuts to make jobs go faster. Put shortcuts in computers.*" His eyes narrowed, betraying the

Pakled's deep cunning. *"Backdoor codes in security systems."*

Vang stepped forward beside Tren to ask Cherbegrod, "If you can penetrate the station's security, why haven't you?"

"Code only opens doors. Twelve men with Gaila. Big booms. Too many for us to fight." His sinister smirk widened. *"But you . . ."*

If what Cherbegrod said was true, it was too good an offer for Tren to ignore. "What's your price, Pakled? How much for the backdoor code to the security system?"

The Pakled nodded at one of his men. Instantly, a figure expressed in bars of gold-pressed latinum, along with a handy conversion of their value in Breen *sakto*, appeared in the heads-up display of Tren's helmet. It was a princely sum, but not an unreasonable one.

"As you see, Pakled prices are fair. Not like Ferengi's."

"Very fair." Tren relayed the figure over to Vang's helmet display. "Send us your account information and the station's backdoor code, and we'll transfer you the money."

"Money first. When we see payment, we give you the code."

Bol interrupted with a private message on Tren's transceiver. *"Found their ship, sir."*

Tren replied on the isolated channel. "Send its coordinates to the *Sulica*. If the Pakleds try to cheat us, I want their ship pulverized." Switching back to the coded Pakled frequency, he continued, "Very well. I am authorizing payment now. But be warned, Cherbegrod: my crew has a lock on your ship. If you cheat us, you will be destroyed."

"Fair deal," the Pakled said.

The countdown on the viewscreen dwindled to four minutes.

"One more condition," Cherbegrod said.

Tren grew irate. "We've already negotiated terms."

The Pakled didn't seem to care. *"Money we can give back. No promise, no deal."*

"Name it, quickly."

"The Ferengi, Gaila," Cherbegrod said. *"He must live. Kill his men, but not him."*

It was a damned odd request. Since when were Pakleds the vengeful type? "Why?"

"None of your concern. Your pledge, or no deal."

"You have my word as a Breen *thot*, my men will try their best not to kill Gaila."

Cherbegrod looked off-screen, nodded, then said, *"Deal."*

Another Pakled drifted into frame to tell Cherbegrod, *"Money received."*

Sevv turned from the signals panel. "Station security codes received."

"Testing them now," Bol said from tactical. "Codes confirmed, sir. We can override the station's security system and defensive arrays."

Tren bowed his head ever so subtly toward Cherbegrod. "A pleasure doing business with you, Captain. Now I suggest you and your crew leave. Immediately. *Kulak* out." The viewscreen snapped back to an image of the Husnock munitions station.

There were three minutes left on the countdown timer.

Under his mask, Tren was grinning again.

"Vang. Neutralize the station's security, then order

the Spetzkar to board the facility, secure its ordnance, and—if at all possible—take Mister Gaila alive."

The Spetzkar commandos deployed in silence, and none moved any more than was necessary. They all had engaged the shroud circuits on their body armor—a technology they had developed in secret after the Dominion War, one based on the natural shrouding ability of the Jem'Hadar.

To anyone watching from the Husnock station, there would be nothing to see—just an open cargo hatch on the belly of one Husnock dreadnought, and nothing in the cargo bay. But the multispectrum visors of the Spetzkar's stealth armor perceived each member of their company as a frost-blue phantom drifting through the zero-g vacuum, straight toward the station.

At the head of the formation, Chot Braz kept his focus on the station's nearest docking bay door. The plan was for the crew on the *Kulak* to mute that portal's alarms and open it ahead of the Spetzkar's arrival. As he floated closer to the massive door, Braz drew a long breath and slowed the beating of his hearts. When the time came for him to wade into the chaos of combat, he would be as calm as Pacluro Prime's frozen sea.

A text message from the *Kulak* scrolled across his visor's holographic display: *Depressurizing station docking bay. Stand by for outer door override.*

Braz and his men were just a dozen meters from the station's exterior when the docking bay doors retracted downward, into the station's dark hull. The broad portal was only half open as he and his men glided past above it, all of them holding their positions relative to one another. When the front rank reached the far wall of the bay, they halted, and the subsequent ranks followed in turn. The Spetzkar maneuvered down onto the deck and engaged the magnetic coils in their boots. As soon as Braz had his feet secure beneath him, he turned and confirmed that all of his men had made it safely inside the docking bay.

He sent back a prewritten message to Thot Tren: *All personnel are inside.*

Behind him, the outer door climbed upward and closed without any noticeable vibration. The moment it was locked, the docking bay pressurized, and its artificial gravity was restored. Braz signaled his platoon leaders with gestures, which they in turn relayed to their troops: *Disengage magnetic boots. Deploy as squads. Secure the station.* With a final pantomime to suggest oversized ears, he added, *Don't kill the Ferengi.*

One of his technical specialists unlocked the docking bay's interior hatch. Another Spetzkar checked the corridor outside with a sensor sweep and gave Braz the all-clear sign.

With a knifing thrust of one hand, Braz gave the order to move out.

Prowling the corridors in squads of eighteen commandos, the Spetzkar spread through the station while maintaining radio silence. As the station's lower levels were cleared, text messages appeared on Braz's HUD, and he sent back written instructions to continue upward.

Three levels up from the station's ventral docking bays, Braz and his squad met their first resistance. A Chalnoth and a Gorn, each toting a heavy disruptor rifle, grumbled at each other while they walked a patrol outside a munitions storage bay.

"Didn't say Vulcan food is good," the Chalnoth protested as Braz pointed one of his men at the hairy brute. "Said their food makes *them* taste good. Big difference."

The Gorn hissed, then rasped, "Vulcans. No flavor."

Braz directed another of his commandos at the Gorn.

"You have no palate," the Chalnoth said. "Vulcan is gamy. Soak it in bloodwine."

The sinewy reptilian stopped and sniffed the air. "Someone here."

The Chalnoth worked his two pairs of protruding tusks, as if he might taste a scent. "No one here. Just us." Invisible to their eyes, two Spetzkar slipped behind them, moving with the silence of a rolling fog. Then Braz gave the kill order, and his commandos each struck with a short sword whose cutting edge had been honed to a monofilament that could slice duranium.

The Gorn and the Chalnoth both stared, befuddled, as their rifles split in half just behind the focusing assembly, and the fronts of their weapons clattered to the deck at their feet. Then their heads tumbled off their shoulders, struck the deck with dull thuds, and rolled into the dark.

Spetzkar scouts advanced to the next junction, then gave the all-clear sign. Braz directed his men forward and up to the next level of the station. Unseen and unheard, they moved like vengeful spirits, agents of death creeping from shadow to shadow. Undetectable. Unstoppable.

Within a few minutes, word of six more confirmed kills in other areas of the station had reached Braz. Now he and all his men were converging upon the factory's control center and executive office. Two hostiles, a Brikar and a Kaferian, occupied the control center, whose access catwalks had all been retracted, isolating it from easy approach.

Braz opened a secure channel to the *Kulak*. "Chot Braz to Thot Tren."

"Go ahead."

"Two hostiles have isolated the control center. Should we frag it?"

"Negative. Offer them safe passage if they surrender and give us the Ferengi."

The last thing Braz would have expected from Thot Tren was a show of mercy. But orders had to be obeyed. Braz kneeled, activated his vocoder, and called out to the pair in the control center. "Attention. This is Chot Braz of the Breen Spetzkar. Surrender your position and turn over your Ferengi boss, and you can both walk out of here alive and free."

He was answered by a barrage of disruptor fire that streaked by above his head. *Glad I kept my stealth circuits engaged.* Braz scuttled to cover and poked his head out to see a squad on another catwalk being forced into retreat by an automated sentry gun. *It must be able to target based on subsonic profiles or microchanges in air density.* He raised his sonic disruptor rifle—a weapon chosen specifically for its safety of use in proximity to highly explosive ordnance—and targeted the autocannon. With a single shot he reduced the robotic sentry weapon to a sparking heap of junk. Similar conflagrations on other sides of the control center announced the destruction of other sentry weapons.

Braz opened a channel to his commandos. "We need the control center intact. Joat, lob a couple canisters of sketricine in there."

The commando asked over the transceiver channel,

"I know sketricine kills Kaferians, but will it even affect a Brikar?"

"We're about to find out," Braz said. "Fire when ready."

He waited and watched as the nerve-gas canister erupted inside the control center, filling it with lethal, dark green vapors. After more than a minute without a sound from inside the cloud, Braz decided it was time to finish the op. "Braz to *Kulak*. Can someone over there hack the station's controls and extend all the catwalk bridges to the control center?"

"Stand by," Vang replied. *"Restoring the bridges now."*

As promised, the divorced ends of the catwalks leading to the control center extended from each side and met in the middle with a metallic *clang*.

"All squads, converge on the control center."

He led his team across the catwalk bridge into the control center. Their battle suits protected them from the lingering gas, and a tweak to his visor's settings enabled Braz to see through the haze. The fragile body of the Kaferian lay crushed under the prodigious mass of the Brikar. He used his suit's built-in scanners to check them for life signs. "Dead. Someone tell Militia Command to update the specs on sketricine to include 'lethal to Brikar.'" He looked around the center, and then peered into the office beyond. "Any sign of the Ferengi?"

His men all gestured *no*.

"Braz to *Kulak*. The factory is secure, but we've lost the Ferengi."

"We haven't," Tren said. *"We tracked his ship fleeing the station about fifteen seconds ago. It just jumped to warp on a course for Ferenginar."*

"Good riddance to him," Braz said.

"Agreed. Unfortunately, we have new pests heading our way—the Starfleet variety. Get your people to work loading the armada with heavy ordnance. I'll have Chot Taan send over an engineering team to assist, and we'll get whatever help we can from the Sulica *and the* Tarcza."

Motioning his commandos out of the control center and back to the lower decks, Braz asked Tren, "How much time do we have?"

"Less than we'd like, old friend, so move with a purpose. Because as soon as those Starfleet ships arrive, I'm going to blast them all into dust."

Boiling over with rage, Gaila pounded his fists on the helm of the *Tahmila*. "What in the name of the Infernal Auditor happened back there?" He glared at Zinos, his only surviving employee. "I asked N'chk a dozen times, 'Are we secure?' And a dozen times he said we were." He gestured wildly at his rustbucket of a ship. "Did the meaning of 'secure' change, but no one told me? We had the advantage! How did we end up on the losing side of this?"

His last henchman had little to offer besides a befuddled grimace. "They found a way in."

"Oh, really. That's what went wrong? I never would've guessed! Amaze me with more of your expert analysis, Mister Zinos." Gaila locked the ship's heading into the autopilot, then he got out of his chair to confront his bewildered Argelian hireling. "We had eyes on all their ships. Weapons locked on anything that moved. And all our networks were in lockdown." Nose to chin with the slender humanoid, Gaila asked through clenched teeth, "What happened?"

Only then did Gaila see that Zinos's hand was resting on the grip of his holstered disruptor pistol. The Argelian was one of the fastest draws Gaila had ever seen, and a crack shot at any range. Now, with no one else on the ship to back up Gaila's bluster, the Ferengi realized he might, possibly, have pushed Mister Zinos just a wee bit too far for his own good.

When Zinos spoke, he sounded calm despite the dangerous glimmer in his eyes. "I checked the security myself. N'chk didn't lie, it was solid. So if it was compromised, there might have been some flaw in the system that we didn't know about. Something that was already in place when we took possession of the factory."

It was a sensible argument. Gaila chewed on that for a moment. "Maybe. Or the Breen might have found something on one of those ships they stole. Some workaround on a computer."

"Perhaps. But if the Breen had the ability to bypass our security, why negotiate in the first place? Why not approach under cloak and attack without warning?"

Damn him, that made sense. "Yes, yes, all right. So let's go back to your idea: there was a flaw in the station's security from the moment we came aboard. How did the Breen know about it? They couldn't have been here before. If they had been, they'd have left a garrison."

Zinos scratched at the lonely tuft of facial hair between his chin and lower lip. "Whoever made the flaw must have told the Breen." As he finished his statement, he looked at Gaila, as if to imply that the answer should be obvious.

And after a few seconds of contemplation it was.

"The Pakleds!" He stomped in a circle while shaking with fury, and the next dozen words out of his mouth were alien vulgarities of the most heinous kind. When he finally forced himself back into some semblance of composure, he growled like a wild animal and felt his lobes tingling with the heat of his anger. "I'll *kill* those doughy simpletons!"

"We both will," Zinos said. "But we'll need to find them first."

Gaila's mind raced, fueled now by hatred and a thirst for revenge. "If they'd given their intel to the Breen before now, the Breen wouldn't have haggled with us, they'd have just taken the station. Which means the Pakleds must've been waiting somewhere just outside our sensor range—waiting to give that information to someone they knew would be able to force us off the station." He pointed at Zinos. "They had to have been within comm range. Or maybe just beyond it, with a subspace signal buoy to mask their position." He moved to the helm, disengaged the autopilot, and changed the ship's heading. "Start scanning for that subspace radio booster. If we find it, we might be able to use it to find them."

"Or," Zinos said, "we could just put ourselves into a sensor blind spot anywhere between here and their way home." He waited for Gaila's inquiring stare, then continued. "You don't think the Pakleds would've given that intel to the Breen for free, do you? They were out here to get paid, just like the rest of us. If they gave the Breen the keys to that station, they must have gotten something of value from the Breen. And if they did—"

"Then they'll be looking to get somewhere civilized," Gaila said, following Zinos's logic. "After all, what's the point of scoring a fortune if you don't enjoy it? And since Pakleds aren't exactly known for their work ethic, it's a good bet they're already looking for a safe port of call that'll take their money." He snapped his fingers. "Pull up a star chart on the navcomp."

They hunched together over the navcomp console. Zinos summoned a chart of the surrounding sector and updated it with their position, as well as that of the munitions factory. "If we assume standard comm range, augmented by a subspace buoy—" He superimposed some circles to indicate an area with a radius of a few light-years. "If we assume they wouldn't have run deeper into unexplored space, we can probably rule out about half of this."

"A safe guess, knowing Pakleds." Gaila studied the chart. "Wherever they are, if they plan on getting back to known space, they'll have to pass through the Kineris Sector." He tapped the screen, indicating a binary system smack in the middle of the sector grid. "That's where we set up our listening post. Unless that oaf Cherbegrod wants to go a hundred light-years out of his way for no reason, he'll have to take his ship within sensor range of this system to get home."

Zinos nodded. "Yes, I think that works."

"Of course it does. I just *said so*." He cracked his knuckles. "Set our new course, Zinos. Those bumbling sacks of stupidity just cost me the deal of a lifetime, and I mean to make them pay for it in blood and latinum, even if it's the last thing I ever do."

Twenty-four

"It would seem," Keru said, his eyes locked on his tactical readouts, "that the Breen have dealt with whatever was keeping them from raiding the munitions factory."

"Confirmed," Tuvok said. "Simultaneous loading operations are under way for nearly all of the Breen-controlled Husnock ships."

It wasn't news to Vale. She watched in horror from the center seat of the *Titan*'s bridge as, on the main viewscreen, a swarm of drones ferried loads of heavy ordnance from the space station to the two hundred forty-five remaining Husnock vessels in the Breen's ghost armada. "Mister Tuvok, how long until the Breen finish loading their hijacked fleet with munitions?"

The Vulcan checked his console, then frowned. "Difficult to say. It is unclear how many pieces of ordnance the various Husnock ships are designed to carry."

In the seat beside Vale's, Sarai rolled her eyes. "Best guess, Mister Tuvok. Gauge how long it took them to arm the smallest Husnock ship, and extrapolate from there."

"Assuming that the relative sizes of the vessels correlates with their ordnance capacity and loading times"—he shot a cryptic look at Sarai—"the Husnock fleet might be fully armed in as little as another three minutes, or as long as another quarter hour."

"Either way it's not much time," Riker said. "They've already loaded enough weapons of mass destruction to lay waste to half the worlds in the Federation. We need a plan *right now*."

Vale clung to hope as she swiveled her chair toward Pazlar, who was working furiously at the science department console. "Commander Pazlar. Any luck yet?"

"I'm close, Captain, I can feel it." The platinum-haired Elaysian worked with almost feral intensity. "I've ruled out several frequencies already. I just need a few more minutes."

Before Vale could offer words of encouragement, Sarai said, "It might be too late."

On the main viewscreen, eleven Husnock vessels veered away from the munitions station to join the Breen battleship *Tarcza* in establishing a defensive formation that circled the factory on different orbital planes, while the remaining Husnock ships finished loading fresh ordnance delivered by the station's drones. "Looks like the Breen have planted their flag on the munitions plant," Vale said. "Which leaves only one question: How long until they—"

"The rest of the fleet is deploying," Tuvok interrupted.

The image on the viewscreen chilled Vale's blood. More than two hundred Husnock ships, led by the Breen heavy cruiser *Sulica* and the dreadnought *Kulak*, were accelerating away from the station and racing straight toward the *Titan* and its escort ships.

"Tactical," Vale said, "tell me they're not—"

"They are," Keru said, confirming Tuvok's dire news. "At warp nine."

"Sound battle stations, raise shields, charge all weapons." Vale didn't know if her ship would be able to survive another head-to-head fight with one Husnock vessel, never mind an entire armada. All her hopes resided on Pazlar disrupting the Breen's control of their stolen fleet, which would leave the *Sulica* and the *Kulak* facing three Starfleet vessels.

That was a fight her ship and crew might survive. If they were lucky.

Watching the unstoppable force bear down on the *Titan*, Vale muttered to Sarai, "Damn. Talk about a David and Goliath scenario."

Her first officer regarded her with disbelief. "David and Goliath? Sir, this is more like three ants taking a stand against a herd of elephants. We should retreat, while we still can."

"They'd just overtake us, Number One. And we need to give Pazlar more time."

Sarai whispered back, "She's not even close. Captain, I urge you: *retreat*."

On the screen the ships loomed larger by the second. From behind, Vale Tuvok declared, "Captain, the armada will reach us in thirty seconds."

After so many years of seeing her shipmates accomplish miracles, Vale wanted to think it could happen again—but one look at the frustration on Pazlar's face proved what Sarai had said. There were no miracles in the works. No *deus ex machina* waiting in the wings, no rabbit about to spring from some technomage's top hat.

"Twenty-five seconds," Tuvok warned.

Vale couldn't just sit and wait for the hammer to fall. "Helm, hard about! Escape and evasion tactics, maximum warp. Mister Keru, relay my order to the *Wasp* and the *Canterbury*!"

Her officers acted with speed and precision, and within seconds the *Titan* was in full retreat, its warp engines keening in minor chords through the ship's spaceframe. Then came the erratic thunder of torpedo detonations harrying their escape.

"The Breen and their armada are gaining," Keru said.

"All shield power aft," Vale said. "Fire quantum torpedoes at will from the aft launcher, random dispersal patterns. See if we can force them to break off pursuit."

"Firing," Tuvok said. "Torpedoes are impacting on Husnock shields without effect."

Lavena called back from the helm, "Captain! The *Wasp* is veering into a nearby star system. *Canterbury* is matching their heading. Should we follow?"

Vale looked to Sarai, who checked her chair's console. The first officer looked up. "The system has a dense debris ring between the third and fourth planet. It might provide cover for evasive maneuvers."

"Helm," Vale said, "take us in. Stay close to the *Wasp* and—"

A hellacious barrage rocked the *Titan*, overloading the inertial dampers and throwing the bridge crew like rag dolls from their posts. Vale landed on her belly, shaken but unhurt. Pushing herself to her feet, she said in a clear voice, "Damage report!"

"Aft shields buckling," Keru said. "Another hit like that and we're wide open."

Torvig pivoted away from an engineering panel scintillating with red warning lights. "Multiple overloads in the EPS relays and weapons arrays. Primary sensors offline."

Vale clawed her way back into her command chair. "Helm, resume evasive maneuvers. Tactical, see if the *Canterbury* can cover our—" An explosive flash on the viewscreen cut her off and yanked her heart into her throat. When the blinding glare abated, chunks of the *Canterbury*'s hull drifted into the *Titan*'s flight path. Vale felt her ship judder as it knocked aside its sister ship's debris with its navigational deflector field. "Tuvok, status of the *Wasp*!"

"They've come about on an attack heading," the Vulcan said.

Sarai was aghast. "They could escape with slipstream. What the hell are they thinking?"

"They're trying to help us escape," Vale realized, thinking aloud.

Keru shared Sarai's horror. "But there are too many Husnock ships, they'll never—"

His prediction came true in a heartbreaking flash of sickly green light as a crushing fusillade of Husnock ordnance converged on the *Wasp* and obliterated every last trace of it.

"The *Kulak* and its fleet are coming about," Keru said, almost shouting. "Right for us."

Blasts hammered the *Titan*. Lights stuttered into darkness, and bridge consoles followed them. Sparks erupted from an EPS conduit in the overhead, and then a pall of smoke filled the bridge. Keru fought to extract damage reports from his console. "Hull breaches, decks three and four. Starboard nacelle venting plasma. Phasers are offline."

"Helm," Vale said, "take us just inside the debris ring, but plot us a clean warp vector into the upper atmosphere of the fourth planet."

Her order drew a sharp look from Sarai. "A warp-hop inside a star system? Into an atmosphere? Are you crazy?"

"We can't get away, and we can't survive a stand-up fight. You got a better idea?"

Riker moved to stand between Vale and Sarai. "It can work," he told Sarai. "If we engage the metaphasic shielding protocol just before we jump, we can vanish inside the gas giant." To Vale he added, "But we'll need to cover the jump."

Sarai abandoned her objections and stood to tell Tuvok, "After we're inside the debris ring, on my order deploy half a dozen quantum torpedoes set for manual detonation. Link their triggers and the metaphasic shield change to Lavena's execution of a high-warp microjump." Tuvok acknowledged with a dip of his chin and set to work. The first officer faced Vale. "If we get the timing on this wrong by even a microsecond—"

"Instant death. What else is new?"

"Rerouting all phaser power into the shield generators," Keru said.

At ops, Rager answered, "Reconfiguring shields for metaphasic mode."

Alerts warbled on Tuvok's console. "Husnock armada is locking weapons."

"Release torpedoes," Sarai said. "Helm, stand by . . ."

"They're firing," Tuvok said.

Vale snapped, "Jump!"

Lavena tapped the helm to engage the warp drive for a tenth of a second. Thunder rocked the *Titan* and knocked out the emergency lights and main viewscreen.

Dim red lights slowly rekindled along the bulkheads. Static from cosmic background radiation faded up on the viewscreen. When the noise diminished, all that Vale could see were psychedelic swirls of color and clouds pulsing with intermittent bursts of red lightning. She sat up in her chair to project an air of authority and requested in a calm voice, "Helm, status."

Lavena adjusted her breathing mask, then checked her console's readouts. "We're inside the gas giant's upper atmosphere, Captain. Adrift but intact."

From tactical, Tuvok added, "Metaphasic shields are weak but holding steady."

Shocked and still struggling to process what had just transpired, Vale had to remind herself to breathe in, then exhale. "Number One . . . get me damage and casualty reports, plus engineering's repair estimate, as soon as you're able." She stood and straightened the tunic of her uniform. "I'll be in my ready room. You have the conn, Commander."

Vale withdrew to her sanctum, hoping each step of the way that none of her officers could see the fear in her eyes—or feel the utter despair that had taken hold of her heart.

There was a fine line between showing support to a starship captain and appearing to second-guess one. It was a tightrope William Riker had walked many times as a first officer, but the balancing act had become more precarious now that he held an admiral's rank. He had to take care not to let his concern for Vale undermine her command authority. Responsibility for the mission's outcome would ultimately rest with him, but the *Titan* was now her ship and crew, not his.

Riker did his best not to draw attention or make eye contact with *Titan*'s bridge officers as he approached the ready room door. He hesitated to press the visitor signal, unsure of what to say should Vale refuse to invite him in—or, for that matter, what to say if she bade him enter.

Sensing that his delay might draw more attention than his actions, he pressed the visitor signal and waited. A moment later he heard Vale via the door's control panel speaker: *"Come."*

The door slid open, and he entered the ready room to find Vale seated at her desk, her chair facing away from the door. She was reclined and staring out the viewport at the swirling gases of the gas giant's atmosphere, which every few seconds flashed with lightning. Riker waited for the door to close before he spoke. "Christine . . . are you all right?"

Vale sighed. "What do you think?" She swiveled her chair to face him. He saw shock in her slack expression and heard despair in her voice. "We had a plan, Will. I thought we'd outsmart them. Take them down the way we always do." She set her elbows on her desk, folded her hands together, and rested her forehead on them, like a penitent in prayer. "But it unraveled so fast. Sarai told me to retreat, but I froze. I gave the order, but then the *Wasp* and the *Canterbury* were gone before I knew what happened." She looked up at Riker; her eyes brimmed with tears of rage. "And I don't understand *why*. The

Wasp could've escaped with slipstream, left us behind. I gave the retreat order. Why didn't they save themselves?"

"Would you have left them? Or if you were commanding the *Wasp*, and I told you to leave me . . . would you have abandoned me to the Breen?"

She shook her head, then closed her eyes. "I don't know. But I can't stop thinking about all the lives that were just lost under my command."

"Not just yours." Riker sat in one of the guest chairs across from her. "I set your mission parameters. I could've pulled the plug on this op, and I didn't. This is on me too."

The air around Vale and Riker turned leaden with grief and regret. "I get sick to my stomach every time I have to write a condolence letter for a life lost on my watch," she confessed. "There's never a good way to tell people that someone they loved is gone forever. No way to phrase the news so that it doesn't hurt, so that the loss of a child, sibling, parent, or spouse doesn't leave permanent holes in their lives. Now I need to write hundreds of condolence letters, one for each person who died on the *Wasp* and the *Canterbury*. How am I supposed to do that? A form letter feels lazy and disrespectful, but how do I craft over five hundred personal notes of sorrow and regret without driving myself mad?"

"You don't. I do." He stifled her protest with a raised hand. "You had operational command of the fleet, but this mission was conducted under my flag. The loss of those lives is mine to answer for, not yours. As is the ultimate success or failure of the mission."

"So is it over? Are we cutting our losses? Or doubling down?"

It was a hard question. Riker wasn't sure there was a right answer, but he had to gauge Vale's state of mind. "You tell me, Captain. Can the *Titan* press on? Or is it time to fall back?"

"I don't know." She picked up a padd and stared at it with great intensity, as if it held the secrets of life and death. "We've got lots of damage. Most of it reparable within a few hours." She paged through the data on the padd. "No fatalities, but plenty of injured. Most of them walking wounded." Exhaustion seemed to overtake her, and she set the padd on her desk. "But we've lost both our escort ships. And even with them we weren't able to put up much of a fight." She fixed Riker with a look. "I read your reports of the Delta Rana IV mission. The Husnock's weapons didn't do this much damage to the *Enterprise*-D."

"We weren't facing a real Husnock ship," Riker said, "just a Douwd's illusion of one."

Vale nodded. "You think Kevin Uxbridge pulled his punches."

"He didn't want to destroy us. He just wanted us to go away." Riker felt Vale's burden of dread begin to weigh upon him. "One thing's for certain: the Breen won't pull their punches when they get those ships back to populated space. And judging from the beating we've just taken, I have to wonder if there's anyone or anything that can stop them now."

His grim speculation seemed to spur Vale from her chair. She stood and paced behind her desk. Then she stopped, pushed a tangle of her multicolored tresses from her face, and turned toward Riker. "We had a good plan for disrupting the Breen's control over their fleet," she said. "We just ran out of time to implement it."

"You mean Pazlar's idea—hacking into their telepresence frequency."

"Exactly. It's a viable tactic. We can't beat the Breen's ghost armada in a stand-up fight, but if we can deprive the Breen of control over the armada using stealth tactics—"

"Then we'd be looking at a relatively fair fight with the Breen."

A nod from Vale, then a frown. "But I have no idea how to get us close enough to pull this off without them blowing us to bits. And if they find a way to break through our signal-jamming, we'll be as good as dead." She regarded him with a plaintive look. "So, what's the word, Admiral? Fold our cards or go all in?"

"That's your call, Captain. Do you think your ship and your crew are up to this?"

He felt as if he could see her inner struggle play out behind her eyes, and in the corners of her mouth, and the creases of her brow. It was a battle of fear versus hope, doubt against daring. For several seconds Riker had no idea what choice Vale would make; he knew only that whatever she decided, he would back her every step of the way.

Finally, she straightened her posture and tapped her combadge. "Attention, all senior officers. This is the captain. Meet me in the observation lounge in thirty minutes. Vale out." When the channel closed, she added to Riker, "That includes you, as well, sir."

He smiled. "Understood. May I ask what you've decided?"

"You may." She returned to her chair. "Come hell or high water, I'm going to find a way to make the Breen pay for what they've done here." She called up a holographic interface to the ship's computer and began drafting what

Riker recognized as a tactical briefing memo. "Now, sir, if you'll excuse me for a few minutes, I need to write a new battle plan."

No matter how many times Thot Tren's officers told him there was nothing left of the *Titan* to find, he told them, "Look again." He wasn't asking for much. A scrap of hull. A bit of organic matter from a Federation species. Traces of any substance in the debris ring that could be connected without doubt to a Federation starship. His crew had been scouring the last known position of the *Titan* for over an hour without finding so much as a speck of its dust.

True, he had seen the ship vanish in the detonation of a Husnock munition, one whose blast had vaporized every hunk of rock in a hundred-kilometer radius. It wasn't beyond the realm of possibility that the *Titan* and its crew had likewise been rendered into vapor and free radicals. But possibility was not nearly so comforting a thing as certainty, and he wanted to know that this last impediment to his mission had been dealt with— because the nagging suspicion that the Starfleet vessel might still be lurking somewhere close by, plotting to interfere once more, threatened to sour the sweet taste of victory Tren felt he had earned.

He caught Vang by one arm as he tried to slip past behind Tren. "Anything yet?"

"No, sir. We've exhausted the primary sensor array."

"Have Bol and Choy work together," Tren said. "Try to boost the main sensor array by running subharmonic amplification scans with the auxiliary sensors. We might yet recover trace genetic material we could link to a species known to be part of the *Titan*'s crew."

The first officer looked at the weapons and operations officers, then tilted his head to beckon Tren away from the rest of the command deck personnel. "Sir, we've run every sensor protocol we can at least twice. We have analyzed our sensor logs of the last torpedo detonation using all the forensic tools available to us. There is no evidence to suggest the *Titan* survived the explosion. Based on the destruction wrought by the torpedo, the most reasonable conclusion is that their ship has been disintegrated. I respectfully suggest we terminate the search."

"I want facts, not suppositions," Tren said. "If the *Titan* was destroyed, we should be able to find something, no matter how scant."

"Not if the initial blast scattered all debris and trace material far beyond the detonation point," Vang said. "Bol has run several sims of the blast effect. They support this theory—as does the absence of any trace evidence from the asteroids that were also disintegrated."

Tren looked at the emptiness of space on the main viewscreen. He wanted to believe the mission was clear to proceed, but he also knew the risk of exposing its final phase if anyone happened to be watching. *We've come too far to lose everything when our greatest victory is finally at hand.* He looked at Vang. "Humor me. Assume the *Titan* survived that attack and escaped. Where could they be?"

"If their shields survived? They could be inside the atmosphere of the fourth planet, or even in the upper corona of the system's star." Vang stepped over to a companel and called up the armada's ordnance manifest.

"We took possession of six antistellar munitions from the factory. Assuming we're willing to sacrifice two of them, we could obliterate the star and the planet right now. If the *Titan* is sheltering in either one, they would be destroyed for sure." He stepped closer and lowered the volume of his helmet's vocoder. "Of course, we would have no way of confirming its presence or destruction in either case, and we would have to explain to Domo Pran why we wasted two-thirds of our most powerful munitions on noncritical targets."

Vang was, of course, correct in his caution. Expending two ASMs for no verifiable reason would be almost certain to draw the ire of the domo, who would be within his rights to expel Tren from the ranks of the *thotaru* for unauthorized use of Confederate Militia resources.

Sometimes, Tren realized, certainty was simply an impossibility.

"Very well," he said. "If the *Titan* still exists, it's likely heavily damaged and in hiding, and therefore poses no serious threat to the completion of our operation. Is the fleet ready to go?"

"Yes, sir," Vang said.

Tren ordered the signals officer, "Get me a channel to the *Tarcza*."

"Channel open," Sevv said.

"Spara, this is Thot Tren."

"Go ahead, sir."

"I'm about to deploy the armada. You and the *Tarcza* are to remain here with your Husnock escorts to defend the munitions plant. Do you have any questions before we depart?"

"None, sir."

"Then night and silence protect you until we return.

Kulak out." Turning to Sevv, Tren added, "Now a channel to the *Sulica*." A nod from Sevv confirmed the channel was ready. "Kran, this is Thot Tren. I want you and the *Sulica* to lead our Husnock armada home to the Confederacy. Make sure to skirt Federation space and stay in neutral interstellar territory."

"Understood," Kran said. *"Does this mean you'll be completing the mission alone?"*

"It does. But our victory will mean nothing unless you get the armada home."

"We'll see it done, sir. May darkness bring you fortune."

"And may shadow be your guide. *Kulak* out." Tren faced the viewscreen and dared to savor a moment of optimism. "Helm, set a new course. Bearing two-one-eight, mark seventeen. Maximum warp, engage when ready." To the rest of his command team he said, "Look sharp, comrades. The final phase of our mission has begun. And when it's complete . . . the rest of the galaxy will learn what it is to fear the Breen."

Twenty-five

Outside the windows of the *Titan*'s observation lounge, the smoky veil of the gas giant's upper atmosphere faded away as the starship returned to space. A passive sensor probe launched several minutes earlier had returned having found no sign of the Breen or their hijacked armada in this star system. Encouraged by that news, Vale had ordered her ship into orbit, where their remaining repairs could proceed with a minimum of complication.

She sat at the head of the conference table, with Admiral Riker on her left and Sarai on her right. The three of them watched the ship's other senior officers arrive and claim open seats around the table. Tuvok and Keru were the first through the door, followed by Pazlar. Next in was Doctor Ree. The Pahkwa-thanh physician opted to stand off to one side, since none of the room's chairs were suited to his long-tailed reptilian physiology. The last two to arrive, just seconds ahead of the scheduled start of the meeting, were Counselor Troi and Doctor

Ra-Havreii. Out of necessity, Vale had left the bridge in the capable hands of operations officer Sariel Rager, with Lavena designated as her second.

Once everyone was seated, Vale proceeded to business. "I'm sure you all know why I've called you here. We've taken a serious beating by the Breen's new Husnock toys—"

"You can say that again," Ra-Havreii grumbled.

"—and we need to regroup," Vale continued, "and devise a new strategy for stopping them from bringing those nightmares home to populated space." She aimed a sharp look at her chief engineer. "Doctor, you seem eager to speak. What's our repair status and forecast?"

The white-haired engineer looked as if he had aged a decade in the past day. "I would be lying if I said our prospects were favorable. My department's done all it can to put the ship back together, but we've run out of spare parts and working replicators. Half my personnel are currently in sickbay, and the other half haven't slept in nearly thirty hours. That said"—he read from his padd—"our warp-hop into the gas giant damaged the starboard nacelle, so we had to take a bank of subspace driver coils offline. To balance our warp field geometry, I had to disable the corresponding units in the port nacelle. So our current top speed is limited to warp seven."

Sarai leaned forward to ask, "How long until we regain full warp capacity?"

Ra-Havreii raised his prodigious white eyebrows. "Hard to say, Commander. It all hinges on our industrial replicator. If we can get that fixed in the next hour, we can restore full warp in about four hours. But that'll mean postponing repairs to the phaser banks, the EPS network in the primary hull, and the main sensor array."

The longer Ra-Havreii talked, the fouler Riker's mood seemed to become. "Doctor, can you name any system on this ship that isn't currently compromised?"

"Waste reclamation, thank the Great Bird."

Around the table, weary nods of agreement

Riker looked at Doctor Ree. "How has sickbay been holding up?"

"We're busy," Ree said. "I've seen the usual range of combat-related injuries, nothing out of the ordinary. No fatalities so far, but I have a few patients in critical condition whose luck might go either way." He added as an aside to Troi, "I'd say morale is the bigger problem."

That was news to Vale. "Counselor? Something I need to know?"

Tense, cryptic looks passed between Troi and Sarai. Then Troi said, "Just what one would expect after taking some hard hits, Captain. Commander Sarai is helping me deal with it."

"All right," Vale said. "But if this is going to be a problem, I want to know in advance."

"It won't," said Sarai. "I promise."

"Then let's get back to working the problem in front of us," Vale said. "Tuvok?"

Cool and stoic, the Vulcan said, "If we cannot currently achieve speeds greater than warp seven, and will continue to be so restricted for several more hours, it is unlikely that we will be able to catch up to the Husnock armada before it reaches the core systems of known space."

"In that case," Vale said, "we need another way to stop them. Pazlar, I still think your idea to disrupt the

Breen's telepresence control over the Husnock ships is a good one. Now that we have a bit more time, do you think you can put that into practice?"

The science officer shook her head. "Unfortunately, no. Several key systems in the primary and secondary sensor arrays were fried when we hit the gas giant's atmosphere."

Hopeful, Vale asked Ra-Havreii, "Can we fix those?"

"Not without a starbase," Ra-Havreii said. "There were a lot of delicate components in there, including a few we either can't replicate or calibrate on our own."

Keru asked, "Could we salvage the parts we need from the *Ajax*? It's still in orbit of the Husnock colony planet, less than a day away at warp seven."

"Different system specs," Ra-Havreii said, kiboshing that suggestion. "Wrong hardware, wrong firmware, all of it about two generations behind what we were using."

Vale fought to contain her mounting frustration inside a clenched fist. "We can alert Starfleet Command and share Pazlar's theory about disrupting the Breen's control of the ghost fleet, but that would mean dealing with the threat after it's already on the Federation's doorstep. If the Breen get that far, billions of people might be killed. So if anyone here has any ideas for confronting the problem before it reaches that point, now would be the time to speak up."

Concerned expressions and downcast eyes ringed the table. The exception was Keru, whose attention was fixed upon the padd in his hand. He scrunched his brow.

"Commander Keru?" Vale waited for the Trill to look up from the padd. "Found something worth sharing?"

He seemed caught off guard. "I'm not sure, Captain. It's just—" Another frown, then he tapped at the padd and transferred its contents to the large companel screen on the bulkhead opposite the windows. It was a tactical scan of the sector surrounding the *Titan*. Keru rose from his chair and moved to stand beside the screen. "This is our position," he said, pointing out the lone delta-shaped icon on the screen. Pointing to a large cluster of red triangles, he continued, "This represents the armada moving toward the Federation. And this smaller group, over here, signifies the detachment left behind to guard the munitions factory. But the one that catches my eye is this one—" He enlarged an upper corner of the scan to show a single red threat vessel icon. "This is the lead Breen vessel, the *Kulak*. It left the *Tarcza* to guard the factory, and sent the *Sulica* to bring home the armada. Both perfectly logical and expected. But the *Kulak* is pushing deeper into uncharted space, into the unexplored Eysaline Sector." He faced the other officers. "Where's that ship going? Why not stay with the attack force or the factory?"

Pazlar got up and joined Keru at the screen. "May I?" He motioned for her to take over, and she used the screen's interface to call up star charts for the surrounding sectors. "Computer, note current heading of the Breen vessel *Kulak*. Project forward along the *Kulak*'s present course and note any systems with habitable Class-M planets or moons on, or within five light-years of, that heading, and within one hundred light-years of the *Kulak*'s current position."

In less than half a second the computer's feminine voice replied, *"Only one star system conforms to the stated parameters."* It highlighted that system on the screen and indicated the *Kulak*'s most likely navigational trajectory to a standard orbit of its Class-M world.

Energized by a sense that Pazlar was onto something, Vale perked up. "Okay, so we know where the *Kulak* is headed. But do we know why? Is it another shipyard? Another munitions plant?"

"Neither seems likely," Tuvok said. "Both of the major Husnock military facilities we have encountered have been located in interstellar space. That would suggest the Husnock, for all of their aggressive tendencies, possessed at least enough of an instinct for self-preservation to segregate their formidable munitions from their population centers."

Now it was clear that Riker was intrigued. "So if the Breen aren't racing toward another Husnock military resource, where are they going? And why?"

Sarai tapped her combadge. "Sarai to bridge."

Rager answered, *"Go ahead, Commander."*

"Open a channel to the *Ajax*. Patch them through to the conference room, on the double."

"Aye, sir. Stand by."

Vale eyed her first officer. "What are you thinking, Number One?"

"Just playing a hunch," Sarai said, keying some information into a padd.

The charts on the bulkhead screen were replaced by the face of the *Ajax*'s Bolian commanding officer, Captain Atheta. *"What can we do for you, Titan?"*

"Captain," Sarai said, "have you been able to use Doctors Kilaris and Pek's work to access the Husnock computer networks on Rishon?"

"In fact, we have. Sorry to say, though, so far it's all raw data without much context."

"I'm sending you some stellar and planetary coordinates," Sarai said, keying a command into her padd.

"Can you do me a favor and see if those coordinates show up in any of the Husnock files? I don't care what it shows up as—data, metadata, whatever. I just want to know if it shows up with any regularity, especially in their communications logs."

"Hang on, my science officer is running a search for your data string now." Anxious glances were volleyed about the *Titan*'s conference room while the officers awaited the results. Then they all leaned forward as they saw the evident surprise on Captain Atheta's blue face. *"Titan, I don't know where you found those coordinates, but they are everywhere in these logs. It's one of the most common markers in the Husnock network."*

"Thank you, Captain," Sarai said. "You've been most helpful. *Titan* out." The channel closed automatically as the computer parsed her valediction, and the screen reverted to the star charts it had shown previously. Sarai wore a look of vindication. "Unless I miss my guess, Captain, I'd say the Breen are on their way to the Husnock homeworld."

Troi sounded dubious. "The Breen have never shown much interest in xenoarcheology for its own sake. So why would they care about finding the Husnock homeworld?"

"I can think of only one reason," said Keru, staring at the charts. "They either suspect or know that something on Husnock Prime represents a threat to them and their stolen fleet."

A solemn nod from Tuvok. "Logical, especially in light of our recent observations. If the Husnock really were concerned with protecting themselves from their own arsenal, it would stand to reason that they built in safeguards to prevent it from being turned against them."

Riker seemed to share his wife's doubts. "So we'd be chasing the Breen into a showdown for which we're ill prepared, on the hope that Husnock Prime—assuming that their destination is, in fact, the Husnock homeworld—contains some military or government command center that can be used to shut down the armada and its munitions?"

"That's pretty much the plan I'm considering," Vale said.

"Sounds like a mighty big gamble," Riker said.

"True, but it's also just about the only play we have left."

Sarai said, "I concur, Admiral. We can't hope to take on the armada or the battle group at the munitions factory, but the *Kulak* is traveling alone, which means we might be able to stand against it if we find a way to tilt the rules of engagement in our favor."

Before Riker could respond, Keru added, "I agree with the captain and the XO, sir. And I just want to point out that whatever is on that planet, if the Breen think it's strategically valuable, then we ought to do everything we can to make sure they don't get their hands on it."

Leaning in, Pazlar said, "Thanks to our civilian guests, we might be in a better position than the Breen to exploit whatever's on that planet. Doctor Pek and his Bynar colleagues have already written software to help our equipment interface with Husnock computers, and Doctor Kilaris is working with Modan and Tereshini to update the universal translator with a better matrix for written and spoken Husnock than they gave to the Nausicaans." She sounded almost hopeful as she concluded, "If we can catch up to the Breen and figure out what their target is, we might be able to beat them at their own game."

Riker stood and smoothed his uniform jacket with a tug. "Commander Pazlar, send your specs for disrupting the Breen's telepresence system to Lieutenant Ssura. I'll make sure he relays them to Starfleet Command with the necessary information for intercepting the Husnock armada. In the meantime, work with our civilian guests to get those new assets ready for action—we're going to need them." He faced Vale. "Captain, hunt down the *Kulak*."

She stood and smiled back, her confidence renewed. "With pleasure, Admiral."

Twenty-six

Viewed from high orbit, Husnock Prime had what Thot Tren considered an austere beauty. Gunmetal-gray seas enveloped its three ragged continents. The largest land mass was marked by a ruddy scar of active volcanoes stretching like a fiery sash from southwest to northeast. Leaden clouds tattered by wind mingled with pillars of black ash spewing from the volcanoes, giving the entire planet the aspect of a homely bride concealed behind a filthy veil.

In the shadow of such a persistent ecological threat, the Husnock somehow had evolved and flourished. Their homeworld, though now expunged of their species, remained dotted with their massive cities, most of which were linked by marvels of civil transportation infrastructure, almost all of it grand enough in scale to be visible from space.

So much potential, Tren lamented. *Such an industrious people. All wiped away by one self-righteous being that dared to think itself morally superior to those whom it murdered.*

Footsteps turned his attention away from the *Kulak*'s viewscreen. He faced his fast-approaching second-in-command. "Vang, report."

"Bol and I have located the capital city and identified the structure that houses our target." Vang nodded to Bol, who routed their findings to the main screen. An annotated map of an isolated region on the planet's surface appeared. "Ongoing analysis of intel from the Husnock ships' computers suggests this bunker is the headquarters of the Husnock fleet. Remote command authorization for all Husnock military assets' self-destruct packages should be coordinated from somewhere inside there."

Tren grew apprehensive as he studied the intel on the screen. "That's a rather large structure. How many levels does it have?"

"Three above the surface, eighteen below." Vang cued Bol with a gesture, and the weapons officer switched the image to an exploded-view schematic of the command facility. "Our scans lack interior details because the building is hardened against sensors, as well as against orbital bombardment. Passive scans have confirmed its defensive screens are still operational, and they have likely been set to automatically repel any high-energy assault."

So much for doing this the easy way. Tren ambled closer to the viewscreen. "What about a ground assault? Does the bunker have automated defenses in place for that?"

"We can't tell from orbit," Vang said. "It's possible, but certain features of the bunker's design suggest that it was made to be protected by Husnock personnel."

"That's a start," Tren said. To Bol he added, "Restore the orbital view." After the main viewscreen reverted to the high-orbit view of the planet, Tren said to Vang, "Will our cloak protect us from the planet's orbital defense platforms?"

The first officer look askance at the viewscreen. "I don't think the cloak will be necessary, sir. All scans indicate the orbital platforms are in some kind of low-power mode. None of them has responded to our probes, or to our approach."

"Very well, then. Have Zaana take us into low orbit. We'll beam down Chot Braz and the Spetzkar so they can storm the bunker and neutralize its command center."

Vang straightened, projecting pride. "I already have Taan working on the demolitions charges. Half an hour from now, that command bunker will be nothing but a molten crater."

"I look forward to that."

At the tactical console, Bol tensed. "Thot Tren, long-range sensors have detected a ship closing from aft, matching our course at high warp speed." Bol adjusted the controls on his panel, then added, "It is the Starfleet vessel *Titan*, sir."

"So . . . not gone after all. They are as tenacious as I've come to expect."

Edging closer to Tren, Vang said, "If we lead Starfleet to the Husnock command bunker, the domo will have us all killed."

"If they're tracking us, they likely already know our destination, and have transmitted it to their superiors." Tren faced Sevv. "Open a channel to the *Titan*." He waited for the silent cue from his signals officer, then continued. "Attention, Commander, *Titan*. This is Thot

Tren, commanding the *Kulak*. On behalf of the Breen Confederacy, we have annexed this sector and all star systems within it to Breen sovereign space. You are trespassing. Cease your pursuit and reverse course at once, or I will destroy your ship and your crew with it."

In the pause between Tren's challenge and *Titan*'s response, Vang asked, "Why give them the option, sir? If they comply, are we supposed to let them go?"

"If they obey, we are free to complete our mission with a minimum of complication. If they disregard my warning, they give us a pretext for war. Either way, we win." He held up his hand to silence Vang's retort as *Titan*'s commanding officer replied over the comm channel.

"Thot Tren, this is Captain Christine Vale of the Starship Titan. *There is no precedent in interstellar law for your claim of annex to a territory not contiguous with your own. Therefore, we declare your claim of sovereignty to be null and void. Furthermore, let me answer your ultimatum with one of my own. Reverse your course and attempt no landing on Husnock Prime. Do that, and I'll let you, your ship, and your crew leave this sector alive and unharmed. But if your ship is still in orbit of Husnock Prime when we arrive, or if we find any sign of your personnel on the planet's surface, I guarantee none of you will receive any mercy from us. You have two minutes to decide, Tren. Choose wisely.* Titan *out."*

The channel closed, and Tren chuckled softly inside his helmet, tickled by the human female's show of bravado. *She must know her hobbled ship is no match for mine.* Hers had been an impressive display, but not one that could make him abandon his agenda, especially not when he stood on the threshold of victory. There was only one path left to him and his crew: forward.

"Vang, proceed with my previous orders."

"As you command, sir." Vang moved about the bridge, snapping out orders like the cracking of a whip, marshaling the crew of the *Kulak* into action.

The image of Husnock Prime filled the viewscreen, and details of the scarred orb's surface resolved into ever finer levels of detail as the Breen ship accelerated toward it.

When Vang returned to Tren, it was to bring good news. "Chot Braz and the Spetzkar have deployed, and we're moving into position to launch a first strike against the *Titan*."

His report earned a nod of satisfaction from Tren. "Well done, Vang. Now steel your nerve and stir the fire in your belly—because it's time to finish what we've started."

There were good plans and there were bad plans, schemes that verged on reckless and others that crossed the line into suicidal madness. As Vale counted down the minutes and seconds until her ship would reach Husnock Prime and begin its next—and possibly its last—confrontation with the Breen dreadnought and its veteran commander, she realized the *Titan*'s current plan of action might be all of those at once.

The bridge resonated with the wail of the red alert siren. It repeated precisely three times, the call to battle stations, then went quiet. From her command chair Vale watched Husnock Prime swell larger by the moment on the main viewscreen. There was no sign of the *Kulak*, however. The Breen dreadnought had vanished from sensors and visual scanners minutes earlier. *They must be back to hiding behind their cloaking device,* Vale reasoned.

It would be a one-on-one battle, assuming Thot Tren chose to reveal his ship. Vale's only consolation at the moment was knowing that the *Kulak*, like most other starships, was unable to discharge its weapons while cloaked. No matter what Tren's reasons might be for postponing combat with the *Titan*, Vale was grateful for the reprieve. Every moment she could avoid joining that fight was another that Ra-Havreii and the engineering department had to fix just one more bit of damage on the battle-ravaged *Luna*-class starship.

Or maybe he knows as well as I do that the real battle here isn't the one in orbit. She turned almost by reflex toward Sarai, only to find the first officer's chair empty. *No way I'm taking on a Breen dreadnought without a strong XO at my side.* She swiveled her chair toward the auxiliary tactical console. "Mister Tuvok, as of now you're the acting first officer." She beckoned him with a tilt of her head toward the empty seat.

Tuvok handed off his console to a junior tactical specialist. Without question or any show of pride or trepidation, the brown-skinned Vulcan stepped forward and took his place in Sarai's seat, beside Vale's. He wasted no time reviewing the latest reports on the XO's command screen. "Commander Keru's preparations are nearly complete, Captain. As soon as the away team is ready, we should be able to proceed."

"Best estimate for the away team's readiness," Vale demanded.

"Four point seven minutes," Tuvok said.

Vale noted the disklike structures that surrounded

Husnock Prime, in high orbit above the planet's equator. "Any activity from the planet's orbital defense platforms?"

"Negative, Captain. They have remained dormant even as the Breen entered orbit."

"So much for the Husnock doing our dirty work for us." She lowered her voice and leaned toward Tuvok. "How would you rate our chances of coming out of this in one piece?"

He telegraphed his doubts with one raised eyebrow. "Suboptimal."

"Unfortunately," Vale said, "I'm inclined to agree. Mister Keru, prep the log buoy and launch it before we enter the Husnock Prime system. Set it on a course back toward Rishon, and put its subspace beacon on a twenty-four hour delay, to reduce the risk of the Breen intercepting it before the *Ajax* has a chance to recover it."

"Aye, sir." The Trill security chief carried out the command in a matter of moments, leading Vale to suspect he had anticipated her order and had placed a log buoy in standby mode hours earlier. When he looked up again, he said simply, "It's away, sir."

"Thank you, Commander."

Vale masked her mounting worry by checking the command screen beside her chair one more time. Doctor Ree had confirmed that sickbay was once again clear, he was set to dispatch medics throughout the ship, and that his triage center and surgical suite were ready to receive new patients. An update from Ra-Havreii brought much-needed good news: the ship's phaser batteries were back at full capacity, and barring any new catastrophes, the torpedo launchers would all be back online by the time *Titan* reached orbit. As for the shields . . . well, those were still anyone's guess. Vale shook her head. *So much for the myth of engineers as miracle workers.*

Under her breath she asked, knowing Tuvok would hear, "Tell me there's another way."

He seemed perplexed by her request. "Another way to what?"

"To finish the mission without resorting to violence. To bluff the Breen into surrender. Or a way to access the Breen's fleet control center remotely and end this before it starts."

Thoughtful but also reticent, Tuvok was slow to respond. "It does not appear that Thot Tren and his peers have left us any such alternatives, Captain. Nor did the Husnock, with their proclivity for paranoia and protectionism. Much as I share your desire to find a nonviolent resolution to our present dilemma . . . I am forced to conclude no such path is presently viable."

"Brevity is the soul of wit, Tuvok. Next time, you might just say, 'We're screwed.'"

"I will grant that what your idiom lacks in precision, it makes up for in concision." He looked at the image of Husnock Prime, growing larger on the viewscreen. "For what it's worth, Captain, perhaps we should be thankful we aren't facing even graver odds in this fight."

Vale saw the logic in his observation. And something more. She swiveled her chair to look at Keru. "It's almost go time, Commander. You ready?"

He keyed in his final preparatory commands with a flourish. "Set."

"And the away team?"

"They need another minute," Keru said.

"Then let's use that minute to our advantage." Vale stood and moved to stand beside Keru. Without asking him, she started keying new information into his console.

Keru backed half a step away from his console. "Sir?"

"Call it a brainstorm," Vale said. She finished outlining her idea in a flow chart, then stepped aside to give Keru a better look at it. "What do you think?"

Conflicting emotions shifted Ranul Keru's expression several times in a span of seconds. Confusion. Alarm. Sudden understanding. A malicious gleam. Then another wave of fear.

He looked wide-eyed at Vale. "Captain, this is insane. There's a hundred ways for it to go wrong and only one way it can go right."

"I know," Vale said. "Which means if it works . . . the Breen will never see it coming."

Twenty-seven

Walking while wearing an armored orbital skydiving suit was difficult for Sarai under the best of circumstances. Being forced to dodge and sidestep through the *Titan*'s main shuttlebay to avoid being trampled by an erratic procession of munitions engineers pushing antigrav pallets loaded with quantum torpedoes only intensified her hate of the skydiving suit's bulk and stiffness.

Nearly every shuttlecraft on the *Titan* had been mustered onto the deck for flight prep. Shuttle mechanics and engineers surrounded the small spacecraft in tight swarms. Flashes of light and the buzzing of tools droned over the bay's usual low thrumming of environmental systems and fuel dispensers. Work proceeded at a furious pace in every direction Sarai looked, and the air was thick with the bite of smoke and the reek of chemical fumes.

Nestled in the midst of that bedlam was a lone runabout, the *Nechako*. It, too, was being tended by a cluster of technicians, who were racing to beef up its shield emitters and strip the safety restrictions from its impulse engines to let it achieve greater sublight speeds. Sarai found it telling that most of the upgrades to the *Nechako*'s defenses and propulsion were being made at the expense of its weapons system and research modules.

It's not as if a runabout's phasers or microtorpedoes are going to make much difference against a Breen dreadnought, she admitted to herself. All the same, it ratcheted up her anxiety to know she and her away team would be hurtling into peril without any means of firing back at the enemy. *Well . . . not in space, at least.*

The other members of her away team stood in a loose line beside the *Nechako*. As Sarai emerged from the flow of bodies crowding the shuttlebay, the first of her team to see her was the senior security officer, Lieutenant sh'Aqabaa. The Andorian *shen* snapped, "Attention!"

The line straightened and everyone in it stood tall, their chins held high, with eyes front. Sarai noted their response with satisfaction. *Finally, my reputation precedes me.*

Sarai walked the line and inspected her team.

At its head stood sh'Aqabaa. Beside her was Sarai's second-in-command for this op, Lieutenant Ethan Kyzak, a Skagaran man with a lean ferocity to his features. Next was Lieutenant Kershul, their Edosian medic, who looked as ill at ease in her skydiving suit as Sarai felt in her own. Then she passed their mission specialists: cryptolinguist Y'Lira Modan, computer expert Holor Sethe, and Tarkalean combat engineer Ekaru Ithiok, whose facial ridges were so pronounced that Sarai thought they made those of Cardassians look understated.

At the end of the line were the rest of the team's

security force, which consisted of Lieutenant Gian Sortollo, Chief Petty Officer Dennisar, and Crewman Blay Chonus.

All of their skydiving suits had been prepped correctly. Sarai suspected the credit for that likely belonged to the security team. Confident they were ready to be briefed, she turned and paced slowly before them. "I trust you've all read the mission profile, yes?" Nods up and down the line. "Good. We've acquired a few bits of new intel. The most important of which is that the Breen have pinpointed our target by sending an attack force to the surface to destroy it."

Sortollo caught her eye. "Commander? Isn't that unusual for the Breen?"

"Yes, it is. I'd have expected them to separate their forces, and direct two or more diversionary units to conceal their true objective."

The follow-up question came from CPO Dennisar. "Why didn't they do that here?"

Sarai chose not to upbraid the Orion noncommissioned officer for speaking out of turn, since their deployment was imminent. "We don't know, Chief. Maybe they're under time pressure. Maybe they're shorthanded. Or perhaps they think there's no way we can stop them."

Kyzak raised his hand, then asked, "Do we have an estimate on enemy force strength?"

"At least one full platoon," Sarai said. "But we might be facing a full company." She knew what the next question was likely to be, so she added, "And no, I don't expect to face Breen regular militia. All indications are that we'll be facing Spetzkar—elite commandos."

That news did not sit well with the team, but no one let their dismay show. Instead, combat engineer Ithiok asked, "How hard a target is waiting for us down there? Do I need to bring something stronger than shaped trilithium charges?"

"I think those will get the job done," Sarai said. "We just need to punch through a weak spot to get inside the bunker, without destroying anything inside. Anything with a bigger kick than trilithium would probably shred us along with the target." Her next remarks she directed at the team's security personnel. "Our primary objective is to defend Modan and Sethe, and get both of them alive into whatever passes for that bunker's control center. Our secondary objective is to deny the Breen access to the bunker or, if they beat us inside, to neutralize them without harming the facility—and to do so before the Breen can damage the control center."

Security guard Blay lifted a hand. "Sir? Do we think that's their objective?"

She nodded at the young Bajoran man. "We do. Though it's possible they might hope to use it to seize control of an even greater number of Husnock resources, our analysis suggests it's more likely they'll try to destroy this facility in order to protect those assets they've already captured, and to deny foreign powers any means of stopping them." To the rest of the team she added, "Any more questions?" Silence and stern faces were her cues to wrap up the pep talk. "Then here's how this is going to go. We'll deploy in the *Nechako* when Captain Vale gives the order. The *Titan* and her support craft will do their best to provide us with covering fire while we make our run toward the planet. If we can reach the surface in the *Nechako*, we will. If we can't—" She gestured at her own skydiving suit. "That's what these are for. Everybody make a final check of your gear. You should each have a type-two phaser, a phaser rifle, some photon grenades, and spare power packs. And make sure your holographic goggles are working—we'll need them to see the Spetzkar if they engage their armor's chameleon circuits."

Ithiok held up her goggles and frowned at them. "Are we sure these work?"

"No," Sarai said, "but I'm positive that *not* using them will get us killed. So make sure yours is fully charged, then finish suiting up and get in the runabout."

Sarai coaxed and shepherded her team inside the *Nechako*. She knew the goggles had only a fifty-fifty chance of penetrating the Breen's shrouding armor—far better odds than the runabout had of reaching the planet's surface intact, or than the away team had of surviving a free fall from orbit followed by a low-altitude combat chute opening and high-speed landing on top of a bunker being stormed by elite Breen military operators. The only thing she really knew for certain was that her away team would be better off not knowing the odds.

For one foolish moment, Vale had entertained the optimistic side of her nature. She had dared to hope that the absence of the *Kulak* from the *Titan*'s sensors or its viewscreen might mean that Thot Tren had chosen to cloak and retreat rather than force a confrontation. Then, just before the *Titan* had finished its first orbit of Husnock Prime, the *Kulak* had emerged from its cloak dead ahead, its fearsome silhouette framed by the planet's two large moons.

So much for getting out of this without bloodshed, she thought.

"Mister Keru, angle shields toward the Breen," Vale said, knowing that the *Titan*'s power grid was compromised and unable to provide adequate protection to all sections of the ship at once. "Target all weapons on the *Kulak*. On my order, fire at will and for effect."

"The Breen are locking disruptors," Keru reported.

Beside Vale, Tuvok checked his command screen. "Helm, set evasive pattern Kilo-Red, followed by attack pattern Echo-Six." A tap on his screen opened an intraship comm channel. "Bridge to shuttlebay control. Stand by to launch all craft."

"Confirmed, bridge," answered the shuttle control officer. *"Standing by."*

Tuvok muted the channel. "Captain, do you wish to offer terms to Thot Tren?"

Vale tried to be calm, but she clenched her jaw and white-knuckled the armrests of her command chair. "No, Mister Tuvok. I think we're past the point of talking."

As if punctuating her thought, a crimson flash filled the viewscreen, then a crash of detonation against the *Titan*'s shields juddered the ship and dimmed its lights and companels.

"Shields holding," Keru reported.

"Return fire," Vale said. "Give 'em everything we've got." She looked at Tuvok to add, "Launch our fleet of pests." The Vulcan nodded and relayed her command to the shuttle control officer. On the viewscreen, the *Titan*'s phaser beams seemed to crisscross one another as they slashed across the *Kulak*'s shields, dimpling its weaker spots—which were immediately targeted by salvos of quantum torpedoes, which flared white and knocked the dreadnought a few degrees off of its course. Vale couldn't help but smirk: *You felt that, didn't you, you bastard?*

Tuvok issued new maneuvering orders to Lavena as, on the viewscreen, the narrowing gap between the *Titan* and the *Kulak* flooded with Starfleet shuttlecraft, shuttlepods, and other small auxiliary spacecraft—all speeding in wild corkscrew maneuvers toward the Breen ship, with their phasers firing nonstop. It pained Vale to sacrifice all of *Titan*'s small support craft this way, and not just because she knew how much pride Admiral Riker had taken in naming them when he had been the captain of the *Titan*. Those vessels, all named by Riker for revered Terran jazz musicians, had been integral to so many missions that Vale had come to regard them as if they were old friends—the *Mance*, the *Coltrane*, the *Gillespie*, the *Tillotson*, the *Ellington*, the *Davis*, the *Basie*, the *Marsalis*, the *Fitzgerald*, the *Armstrong*—all hurtling now in a desperate bid to buy the *Titan* and its vulnerable away team a few precious seconds of cover.

Vale nodded at Tuvok. "Now."

He thumbed open the channel to the shuttlebay. "Launch the runabout."

Too spun up to stay in her chair, Vale sprang forward. It felt good to stand. "Rager, keep a sensor lock on the runabout, we'll have to cut this way too close for it to work."

"Already tracking them," Rager said, her fingers working with grace and speed at the operations console. "Standing by for—"

"Weapons lock," Keru announced. "They're targeting the *Nechako*."

"Distract them," Vale said. "With prejudice."

Keru keyed in a command on his panel. "Triggering . . ."

Each of the shuttlecraft executed a microsecond jump to warp speed—just enough to slip past the *Kulak*'s targeting sensors and right up to its shields—where they all detonated at once, each consumed by the blue-white fire of a trio of quantum torpedoes secured inside their passenger compartments. Jolted off course and into an erratic tumble-roll by the blast, the Breen dreadnought looked almost incapacitated—

Until it resumed firing disruptors in the runabout's general direction.

"Their shots are wild," Keru noted. "They must be using manual targeting."

"Then this is the away team's best chance for escape," Vale said. "*Titan* to *Nechako*: Increase your speed. Put as much distance between you and the *Kulak* as you can!"

Sarai replied, *"Negative! We're already at top speed for atmospheric entry."*

"*Nechako*, if you don't accelerate—"

Keru cut in, "The Breen have regained targeting. They're locking on to the runabout." He tapped the firing pad for the phaser banks and harassed the dreadnought to draw their fire.

Even as phaser beams from the *Titan* pummeled the *Kulak*'s shields, Vale knew it would not be enough to stop the Breen from vaporizing the runabout. "Rager, now!"

"Trying," the operations officer said. "The Breen are jamming us! I can't get a lock!"

Tuvok reported, "The *Nechako* has breached the upper atmosphere."

"*Kulak* is charging to fire," Keru said. "We're out of time!"

Vale was desperate, and she didn't care who knew it. "Rager? Talk to me!"

"Coordinates are still fuzzy. Radowski's trying to—"

Searing beams of red energy from the *Kulak* sliced through the atmosphere of Husnock Prime and found the *Nechako*. It took only a single salvo to collapse the runabout's shields and blast the tiny starship into fire and dust. Less than a second later a black streak of smoke and debris scratched like a scar across the sky of a deserted world.

Vale felt like she had been gut-punched. It took all the courage she had to keep standing as Tuvok reported with dry precision, "The runabout has been lost, Captain."

Lavena looked up from the helm and over her shoulder at Vale. "Captain, the Breen are coming around for another pass at us. Should I initiate evasive maneuvers?"

At tactical, Keru remained stoic as he delivered bad news. "The *Kulak* is charging all weapons and targeting us. Orders, Captain?"

In her heart, Vale felt sick, paralyzed, and demoralized beyond recovery. Then she drew a deep breath and remembered who she was: not just a Starfleet officer, but a starship captain. This might be her day to die, but if it was, she planned to take her enemies into the darkness with her.

"Helm," Vale said, "evasive pattern Sierra, then attack pattern Victor. Mister Keru, tell the lower decks to keep working as ordered, and move the *Ottawa* into position. If it's a fight the Breen want, then that's exactly what they're going to get."

Even in the rarefied air of the planet's upper atmosphere, the wind that tore past Sarai roared like an avalanche, making it hard to hear the rest of her away team checking in via their helmets' transceivers. They were on the night side of the planet, which meant they were plunging through pitch-darkness without visual contact. She increased the gain on her own transmitter to compensate. "Away team," she hollered over the noise, "sound off again—after Kershul!"

She strained to hear as the remaining five members of her team answered in alphabetical order: *"Kyzak, check!"* ... *"Modan, check!"* ... *"Sethe, check!"* ... *"sh'Aqabaa, check!"* ... *"Sortollo, check!"* It was a relief to know her people were accounted for. The moment the Breen had scrambled the *Titan*'s comms and sensors, she had known they wouldn't be able to rely on help from Rager and Radowski to beam them out of the runabout ahead of the *Kulak*'s attack. That was when Sarai had given the order to abandon ship.

The evacuation had been swift and orderly. All of the *Nechako*'s science modules had been swapped out for chaff cannons to foul the Breen's sensors. Sarai had triggered the diversionary cloud of debris, then depressurized the runabout's interior before ejecting the cannons, leaving the middle section of the runabout unencumbered. Seconds later, after she and the others had moved into position, she had blown open the lateral access hatches and launched herself and the away team out of the wide-open egress points on both sides of the ship.

Now they all were plummeting like missiles toward the planet's surface, piercing like arrows through towers of gray vapor. A warning light flashed on her faceplate's holographic display—an alert that the runabout had been destroyed. She rolled in midair to look back. High above her, the remains of the *Nechako* scattered like a fiery wound across the heavens.

If the Breen think we're dead, maybe they're done jamming signals. Sarai switched her transceiver to an encrypted channel to hail the ship. "Sarai to *Titan*, do you copy?"

She had never before been so happy to hear Vale's voice. *"We read you, Number One. What's your status?"*

"Away team is clear and free-falling toward the target. ETA, three minutes, ten seconds."

"Roger that," Vale said. *"Check in with a sit-rep as soon as you touch down."*

"Understood. Going quiet for a few. Sarai out."

Dropping out of the clouds into clear air, Sarai rolled to face the ground and switched her faceplate to its night-vision setting. A quick look around accounted for all the members of her team. At a distance she couldn't tell them apart with her eyes, but their transceivers reported their positions, headings, speeds, and vital signs. So far everyone seemed to be unhurt and on target.

Below them, a vast expanse of sharp-peaked mountains and arboreal wilderness stretched away in every direction to the horizon. Directly beneath the away team was a broad plateau, one whose surface was so uniformly level that Sarai surmised it most likely had been engineered.

A large, squat hexagonal structure dominated the plateau. Its roof, unlike the land around it, was angled and crowded with subspace transmitters. Sarai adjusted her visor for a closer look at the facility's rooftop. At maximum magnification she noted that its edges were crenellated, like teeth in a gear laid out flat. Conical towers stood atop each corner of the hexagon.

She opened a channel to her team. "Everyone aim for the rear of the smaller building. Watch your grouping, don't get tangled up. Don't release until I give the order."

Projected onto her faceplate was the drop countdown. During the free fall it displayed its diminishing time in yellow. When they reached optimal altitude for chute opening, it would turn green. If they missed their narrow window it would turn orange and then red as they neared calamity. "Kyzak, do a quick sweep of the ground. Any sign of the Breen?"

"Negative," Kyzak said. *"Either they're shrouded, or we're the first ones here."*

"No way we're getting that lucky. My money says they're on the roof of the main building." Sarai checked the free fall countdown. "Stand by to deploy chutes on my mark. Three. Two. One. Mark!" She activated her main chute with one press of the control pad on the chest of her suit. The black chute erupted from its compact shell on her back and shot upward, expanding like a mushroom cloud of high-strength synthetic fabric, until it filled with air and jerked taut the carbon-fiber guide ropes connected to her suit's harness. The violent lurch left Sarai feeling like her vital organs all had been crushed into her stomach, and the momentary rush of her blood toward her legs left her dizzy and light-headed.

She shook off her disorientation. *I can't believe some people do that for fun.*

Tugs on the guide ropes enabled her to control her descent. Guiding herself into a slow spiral, she circled her designated landing point.

Then came the first shots from the main building's roof.

Disruptor pulses flashed in the darkness and screeched past Sarai and the away team. A handful of shots turned into a flurry, and then into a storm.

She drew her type-2 phaser in her right hand and

struggled to control her chute with only her left. Snapping orange blasts at the distant roof, she shouted over the comm, "Return fire!"

"At what?" hollered Sethe. *"I can't see anything!"*

"Just make them duck," sh'Aqabaa replied. *"Make it harder for them to aim!"*

Floating in chaotic circles, the fatally exposed away team fired back. Orange beams from their phasers crossed paths in midair with crimson pulses from the Breen's disruptors. Bolts of energy caromed off the far rooftop's crenellations. The away team's retaliation made the Breen assault less precise, but even still a cluster of shots ripped into Blay, who dropped his phaser and went limp as he crashed onto the rocky ground, a dozen meters away from cover.

Sarai's distance to the ground ticked down on her HUD, but she preferred to gauge her landing manually. As she reached the final meters of her jump she fired another round of suppressing fire at the Breen, then lifted her legs and bent her knees. Her heels made contact, and she jogged forward, fighting her momentum as she detached her chute.

Around her, the rest of the away team scrambled through their landings. Hectored by disruptor fire, they dashed for shelter behind the small outbuilding. As soon as sh'Aqabaa was out of the line of enemy fire, she began assembling her compression phaser rifle from the kit she had carried strapped to her left leg. Dennisar and Sortollo moved to the building's corners, each of them loading a photon grenade into a short-range tactical launcher.

Sarai summoned her specialists with hand signals. As they hurried to her side, she began assembling her own phaser rifle. "We need to get inside that compound, right now. Ideas?"

Kershul pointed toward Blay's body. "We have to try to help—"

"Forget him, he's dead." Sarai fixed the holographic targeting scope onto the top of her weapon. "We need to go forward. Ithiok, you're the combat engineer. This is why I brought you. What's your recommendation?"

The Tarkalean woman talked while assembling her own phaser rifle. "They have all the advantages right now: height, superior cover, and they're playing defense. To attack, we'll need to cross open ground, and that's a suicide play." Ithiok bit her lip while she concentrated. "And there's more bad news. On the way down I saw the main entrance had been breached."

Sh'Aqabaa scowled as she secured the shoulder stock of her rifle. "Which means the Breen are already inside the facility, possibly planting demolitions. Wonderful."

"One problem at a time," Sarai said, hoping to preserve what little esprit de corps her team had left. "Ithiok, I'm still waiting for your recommendation."

"If the *Titan* wasn't locked in a fight for its life, I'd say call down fire support from orbit. If we had more time, I'd say tunnel inside the bunker. But in this scenario, the best we can do is use photon grenades to generate smoke, then use it to cover our charge for the main entrance."

The Andorian shook her head. "We'll never make it. Those are Spetzkar. Their suits have enhancements that make ours look like toys. They'll see right through the smoke and cut us down before we get ten meters from cover."

Sethe interjected, "Sir, we might have something."

He and Modan were huddled around his compsheet—a portable computer in the form of a flexible sheet less than three millimeters thick, with a matte surface, transceiver links to the team's suits as well as to their tricorders, weapons, communicators, and a subspace comm circuit for communicating with the ship. The Cygnian turned its display toward Vale. "We have determined that the transmitters on top of the main building are active—and capable of supporting two-way communication."

Sarai stared at the complex jumble of alien symbols on the compsheet. She didn't know what they said, but she knew they were Husnock. "Sethe, are you telling me that you've hacked into the computer network of the Husnock fleet command?"

"Not its core command systems, but possibly its top-level facility controls. Though I will need Modan's help translating the interface."

"Get on it, as fast as you can." Sarai fixed the last part of her rifle into place and smiled. "Call me crazy, but I think our luck just changed."

It should have been as easy as a training exercise. The Starfleet team had been slow targets without shields, tracing circles in midair. They had all but painted targets on themselves.

But the orders from Chot Braz had said to be on the lookout for enemy personnel beaming onto the platform, and that was what Laar and his comrade Spetzkar had been doing. Crouched among the crenellations on the roof of the Husnock High Command bunker, all of them invisible thanks to the shrouding circuits in their armor, they had watched the plateau, their senses keen and searching for even the faintest shimmer of a transporter beam.

Then came flutters of wind against fabric and a stirring of shadows in the sky. Black figures betrayed only to the degree that they obscured the stars with their passage. By the time Laar and his platoon realized that a Starfleet strike team was dropping out of the sky, the enemy had nearly reached the ground, and half the unit had been in no position to fire on them.

"At least we got one of them," said Yahn, the commando manning the gap to Laar's left. "And we've got the rest pinned down. They're going nowhere."

Watching from the gap to Laar's right, Geel seemed less confident. "I still don't understand. Why didn't they show up in our visors?"

"Because we were set for infrared," Laar said to the platoon's newbie. "Their orbital dive suits are insulated to protect them during atmospheric entry and absorb excess heat as energy. If we'd been set for ultraviolet, we might have seen them sooner."

Yahn adjusted his firing stance without taking his eye off the outbuilding. "Maybe in the future we should have half the squad set IR, half on UV. Cover all our bases."

"That's a good note, Yahn. Tell me when you plan to present it to Chot Braz. It's been a while since I saw him tear a grunt limb from limb."

The ribbing turned Yahn defensive. "I'm not saying we second-guess the *chot*, I'm just saying maybe we implement the change on our own, as a precaution."

"Much smarter," Laar said, burying his sarcasm in deadpan dryness, despite knowing that by the time his words were scrambled by his vocoder and then unscrambled by Yahn's, all of his inflections would be stripped anyway. "When the *chot* says use infrared, you set UV on your own initiative. I'm sure when you save the day he'll give you a medal for original thinking."

Yahn turned his head toward Laar just for a split second, then resumed peering through his weapon's targeting scope. "Have I mentioned how much I hate you?"

"Only twice since morning chow. You're slipping."

"You're right, I'll work on—" He tensed. "Movement, both sides."

Across the rooftop, Spetzkar sharpshooters readied themselves to repel a Starfleet assault. Laar hunkered down and adjusted his own holographic targeting system, then opened a channel to the rest of his platoon. "Look sharp. Shooters on the flanks, watch for anyone with tactical launchers. We can't let them put a photon grenade on the roof."

From down the line, someone announced, "Here they come!"

Orange light slashed the darkness above Laar's head. He tracked one beam's source and tried to lock in a target. Then a photon grenade exploded—in the middle of the open ground between the bunker and the outbuilding.

Geel shouted, "They're just making smoke!"

"Engage your haze filters," Laar said. "If they think smoke's going to help—"

Another blast, a deafening thunderclap that knocked the Spetzkar shooters away from the crenellations. Laar found himself on his back, his ears ringing and his guts feeling bruised. He scrambled back to his post. "Hold the line! Suppressing fire!"

He unleashed barrages of disruptor pulses at any sign

of movement in the open, any flinch of motion near the outbuilding. Cool night air flowed through his helmet's damaged filter, thick with the reek of ozone and the bite of smoke and hot dust. Worst of all, however, was the tinnitus. Laar could barely hear his own weapon discharge, and reports coming in through his helmet's transceiver sounded like echoes from a light-year away.

Which was why he didn't so much hear the machines coming alive around him and his men as he felt a vibration in the rooftop. Before he had a chance to determine what was causing it, his holographic visor fritzed along with his comms. Then, in spite of his suit's insulation, a galvanic prickling stung the back of his neck—

Right before a searing flash of green light erased him from existence.

A wall of smoke blocked Sarai's view of the bunker. Though she had no direct view of the six Husnock gun batteries, their deep buzzing roar felt like a drill chewing into her gut, and she saw the drifting fog of war set aglow by erratic flashes of green light.

Wind parted the gray curtain between Sarai and the bunker, revealing the Breen's dire fate. Hounded from all sides by antipersonnel cannons mounted in the conical towers at the corners of the bunker, the Breen had nowhere to run. Every defilade that offered protection from one tower was exposed to another. A few Spetzkar jumped over the crenellations, only to be picked off in the air as they fell. Their bodies struck the rocky ground in smoldering pieces.

Kyzak crouched behind Sarai to peek around the

corner at the carnage. He shook his head. "I almost feel sorry for those guys."

"I don't," said sh'Aqabaa, who observed over his shoulder. "Not one bit."

The massacre ended with a final staccato burst, followed by eerie silence.

Sethe poked at his portable compsheet, then angled it toward Modan for confirmation. The Selenean tapped at the screen, then nodded to Sethe. The computer specialist met Sarai's expectant stare and nodded. "Roof's clear, Commander."

"So I'd gathered. But what happens to us when we approach the bunker?"

Ithiok leaned in to join the conversation. "If their targeting system sees us as friendlies, we'd be free to move in and out of the bunker. Can you teach it to accept our IFF transponders?"

"That would take at least an hour," Sethe said.

Sarai shook her head. "The Breen are already inside the bunker, we can't spare the time. What other options do we have?"

"I could just turn off the guns." Sethe tapped the screen of the compsheet. "Like so."

A sour mood settled over Kyzak. "Are you serious? Next time, lead with that."

"Enough," Sarai said. "Advance in pairs; I'll be the odd man out. Fan out, in case they have a shooter inside the entrance. Regroup along the bunker's wall to either side of the main door. We'll make our way inside using standard two-by-two cover formation. Move out."

The team darted away from the outbuilding, into the wide-open space that yawned between it and the bunker. Sarai sprinted a short way ahead of the team to take point, her phaser rifle held in a low ready position. The meters separating her from the bunker felt stretched by her fear of running headlong into a trap. She was only partially encouraged by the knowledge that if the area in front of the entrance had been mined by the Breen, any hidden ordnance would have been detonated by Sortollo and Dennisar's photon-grenade barrage minutes earlier.

Half a minute later she and the others all reached the bunker and pressed their backs to its outer wall while they caught their breath. Sarai was to the left of the entrance with sh'Aqabaa, Kershul, Ithiok, and Sethe. On the other side of the main door were Kyzak, Dennisar, Modan, and Sortollo. Sarai leaned forward to tell Ithiok, "Sensor sweep the first corridor."

Ithiok pulled her tricorder from its pouch on the right leg of her dive suit. Because the device had been configured for combat operations, it was silent while she scanned. "I can't get a clear reading past the door." She pulled a small sphere from another pocket of her suit and lobbed the marble-like device to Sarai. "Roll that inside for me."

Sarai pivoted around the corner and in a single motion gently bowled the tiny sphere through the cracked-open main portal. The orb made almost no sound as it rolled across the floor and disappeared inside the pitch-dark bunker.

Ithiok adjusted her tricorder. "Okay. Main corridor clear. Low-level signal dampening looks to be built into the structure. No sign of active interference." She put away her tricorder. "Good news is, any Breen inside the bunker probably didn't have contact with the ones on the roof. Bad news is, once we go past the first corridor, we'll be cut off from the *Titan*—no comms or transporters can reach us in there. And if we want to stay in touch with each other, we'll either need to maintain line of sight, or set up signal relays at every corner and level change."

"Stay focused on the positive," Sarai said to the group. "We'll be on our own, but we'll have the advantage of surprise. Let's do whatever we can to make the most of that." To Ithiok she added, "Make sure you scoop up that marble of yours on the way in. I get the feeling we'll need it again as we get closer to contact with the enemy." She turned the corner and prowled toward the entrance, her rifle braced against her shoulder. "Let's go."

The others fell in behind her. She opened the main doors so the team could begin the process of advancing with cover. Last to the door was sh'Aqabaa, who asked Sarai, "You do know we'll be outnumbered in there by about six to one, right?"

"One problem at a time, Lieutenant," Sarai said. "One problem at a time."

Twenty-eight

Every hit that rocked the *Titan* felt to Riker like a punch in his gut. No matter how many times he reminded himself that he was an admiral, that the *Titan* was Vale's ship to command now, when the vessel was under attack his possessive impulses came to the fore.

The overhead light in the turbolift car stuttered on and off as the ship thundered from punishing impacts on its shields and outer hull. The lift's normal low hum turned sickly as its magnetic propulsion system struggled to maintain power. In spite of all that noise, Riker heard the ship's spaceframe groan as it was put to the test by high-impulse combat maneuvers.

Beside him in the lift, his aide, Ssura, clutched the safety rail. The Caitian's tufted ears lay flat against his skull, and the fur on the nape of his neck stood up as if drawn by an electrical charge. He shot a worried look at Riker. "Admiral, we should really return to your quarters."

Another blast made the ship lurch and pressed them against the back wall of the lift car. Riker was sure he caught a suppressed growl rattling deep inside Ssura's throat. "I need to know what's happening, but the comms are down, so we're going to the bridge. That's final."

"Yes, sir." A booming roar of collision was followed by a momentary fluctuation in the ship's artificial gravity. For a moment Ssura looked as if he might vomit, then he recovered.

The lift's doors opened to reveal a scene of surprising calm on the bridge. Riker strode onto the bridge, and Ssura stumbled out of the lift behind him.

Standing in the center of it all, Vale doled out orders with speed and clarity. "Evasive, starboard. Keru, aft torpedoes, spread Tango. Ops, divert auxiliary power to the aft shields. Torvig, switch to a chroniton-based scrambler, keep fouling their targeting locks." Out of the corner of her eye she noticed Riker. "Sir, you should be in your quarters."

"Not until I know what's—" He was cut off by the din of high-energy detonations hammering the *Titan*'s shields. Consoles along the aft bulkhead went dark, and a backup EPS conduit ruptured in the overhead, raining white-hot sparks on him and Ssura. They both scurried clear of the firefall, then Ssura swatted smoldering motes from his mane and his uniform. Even after the last phosphor was extinguished, the bitter stink of burnt fur lingered in the air.

From the first officer's chair Tuvok reported, "Warp drive is offline."

"That's fine," Vale said, "I wasn't planning on running, anyway."

Torvig looked up from his console, his large eyes full of sadness. "Casualties in engineering, Captain. Two dead, eleven injured."

That news robbed Vale of some of her swagger. She asked Keru, "How much longer?"

"Thirty seconds," Keru said. "Assets are in position." He muted an alert on his panel. "The *Kulak*'s coming around on our port side, locking weapons—"

"Helm," Vale said, "turn to face them, full impulse. Rager, angle all shields forward. Keru, phasers, continuous fire. Torpedoes, full spread, pattern Bravo."

Riker couldn't stand being a spectator any longer. He rushed past Keru to stand at Vale's side. "Head to head with a Breen dreadnought? Are you crazy?"

Vale's glare was as hard as dilithium, her tone as sharp as a Klingon's *d'k tahg*. "Sir, with all due respect—shut up or get off my bridge." She stepped away from him as the main viewscreen filled with phaser beams and the blazing streaks of quantum torpedoes.

Torvig finished a task on his engineering panel and faced the captain. "Sensor blind ready."

Vale acknowledged the report with the barest hint of a nod, then said in a voice for everyone, "Okay, folks, just like we planned. Helm, first pass of the nearest defense platform in exactly one minute from . . . now." She turned and looked at Tuvok, who got up and walked past Riker on his way to the turbolift without any reaction from the rest of the bridge crew.

The Breen dreadnought filled the viewscreen, and for a moment Riker feared Vale might actually intend to ram the *Kulak*. All Riker could do was stare, dumbfounded.

What the hell is she doing?

"On my mark," Vale called out. "Three. Two. One. Break! Roll to port!"

The impulse engines whined in protest as Lavena pushed the ship into a rolling turn to avoid a collision with the much-larger dreadnought. Then came the gut-quaking concussions of more disruptor blasts pummeling the *Titan*'s overtaxed shields—followed by a resonant, echoing boom that Riker knew from bitter experience meant the hull had been breached.

"Hull breach, deck sixteen starboard," Keru said. He looked up to add, "Hangar four."

"Viewscreen aft," Vale said. The image switched to reveal a cloud of debris and cargo containers that had been ejected from the *Titan*. "All right, go evasive, full impulse, keep the port side and aft quarter toward the Breen. Give me a fast orbit of the planet, and try to use its moons' magnetic fields to keep them from getting a target lock. Angle shields aft and port."

Keru fired the phasers several times in quick succession. "The Breen are dropping back."

Vale reacted without hesitation. "Helm, reduce speed, three-quarter impulse. Switch to evasive pattern Alpha. Keru, ease up on phasers."

Now Riker was sure that Vale had lost her senses. At the risk of being forcibly escorted off the bridge, he approached her and said under his breath, "What do you think you're doing?"

"My job." She shouldered past him and rested her hand on Rager's shoulder. "Stand by." To Lavena she said, "Second pass at the platform in thirty seconds, then retrace our steps." A pivot toward Keru. "What do you say? Ready for this?"

The Trill flashed a bright smile from behind his beard. "Gonna be a real close shave."

"As if you'd know what one was," Vale quipped. "Look sharp, people. Here we go."

Ssura sidled up to Riker and directed his attention toward a nearby tactical display. "Admiral . . . we're flying directly into the *Kulak*'s firing solution."

Riker shot a look at Vale. "Captain, if you don't break off, we're all dead."

She answered his concern with a thin smile. "One problem at a time, Admiral."

A meter shy of the next intersection in the bunker corridor, Sarai put her back to the wall while Ithiok shot a fingernail-sized adhesive comm relay into the corner. The devices were only a temporary solution to the problem of the bunker's impenetrability to signals; each one had a battery that would keep the relay active for up to a day. Sarai had to hope she and the away team would not be inside the bunker long enough for that limitation to come into play.

She looked back at Sethe, who had been tracking their progress with his tricorder, and asked him in a whisper, "How close are we?"

"Around the corner, on the left, six meters." He adjusted the tricorder's settings. "No life-signs, but I'm tracking air disturbances. Someone's moving in there." Another tweak. "And I'm reading trace particles from standard-issue Breen military demolitions."

Ithiok pulled up her own custom-modified tricorder. "Confirmed. Jamming their detonator frequencies . . .

now." She tucked away her tricorder and hefted her rifle. "What's our next play, Commander?"

"We need control of the Husnock's fleet command systems," Sarai said.

"And the Breen know that," Kyzak said. "Even if we suppress their demolitions, they can still just shoot the hell out of that control center."

That didn't sit well with sh'Aqabaa. "If ever there was a time we needed backup—"

"Backup!" Sethe interrupted. He fought to contain his excitement and keep his voice down. "That's it, sir." He pulled out his compsheet, unrolled it, and set to work as he continued. "The Husnock didn't mess around when it came to systems redundancy. When I was looking for this control center, I thought I saw—" He turned the compsheet toward Sarai to show her a floor plan. "An auxiliary control center, six levels down, off the central lift column."

His enthusiasm was dimmed by Sortollo's caution. "What if the Breen are already there?"

"I don't think they are," Sethe said. "If they were, the most direct route would have been down the core access ramps, past two blast doors, both of which still read as closed." The lithe Cygnian pivoted toward Sarai. "Commander, if Modan and I can get down to auxiliary control, we can patch you into the same systems the Breen are looking to destroy up here."

It was a long-shot plan, but what it lacked in detail it made up for in audacity, and that was good enough for Sarai. "Okay, the two of you head down to auxiliary control. Dennisar, you're with them. If you meet resistance don't do anything crazy, fall back to us."

"Copy that, sir." Dennisar took off down the corridor,

past the intersection, with Sethe and Modan close at his flanks. Within seconds the trio had finessed open a blast door and disappeared into the deeper levels of the Husnock bunker.

Sarai addressed the other members of the team. "The rest of us need to keep the Breen busy up here as long as we can. Any second now they'll figure out we're jamming their remote detonators, at which point I suspect they'll go for their backups—molecular detonators. If we're still in the room when those go off . . . I'll just say it's been an honor serving with all of you."

Sortollo braced his rifle's stock against his shoulder. "Let's do this."

The others followed his lead. Even Kershul, the combat medic, had her rifle in position. Sarai tried to signal her to stand down. "You should hang back, Kershul, in case we—"

"Unless you order me not to join you, sir, I'm going in."

"Then I order you to hold position here, at the doorway," Sarai said. "Give us covering fire and watch our six. Make sure the Breen don't sneak in reinforcements behind us."

No argument, just a quick nod. "You got it."

"Okay, move up to the doorway, then Kershul covers as we enter. I'll take point. Go." Crouched low, Sarai jogged around the corner and headed for the doorway. With every step her heart slammed like a war drum inside her chest, its frantic tempo driven by adrenaline. The rest of her team moved with her, everyone falling into place with near-silent precision. Sarai was the first to the doorway, with Kershul at her back. She waited until everyone else was with them against the wall. Once the corner was turned, there would be no chance of avoiding a fight.

With a gesture she queried her team: *All set?*

In unison they signaled back, *Good to go.*

There was no time for second-guessing, no room for doubt. Sarai willed herself into action, turned the corner, and moved inside the control center.

It was a crescent-shaped space with four wide, curved tiers of workstations facing a wall of long-dark viewscreens. Thanks to the shroud-penetrating filter built into the helmet of Sarai's orbital skydiving suit, she saw the frost-blue apparitions of more than thirty Spetzkar inside the facility. Most of the Breen were in groups of three, four, or five, with a few lone stragglers tending to tasks in the far corners of the large, high-ceilinged space.

Sarai reached cover behind a meter-thick bank of dormant computers without being noticed. Less than four seconds later sh'Aqabaa was on her left and Sortollo on her right.

As Kyzak darted through the open doorway, one of the Breen spat a buzzsaw din of vocoder noise, an electronically scrambled shout. Then came a wild barrage of disruptor shots, all hounding Kyzak on his mad dash to safety behind a different bank of workstations.

Then Kershul returned fire from the doorway, splitting the Breen's focus.

Sarai spun about and got up in a crouch to fire over the top of her impromptu barrier. Sortollo and sh'Aqabaa did the same. As the Spetzkar leaped for their own places of cover, Ithiok darted through the doorway to take position beside Kyzak.

Sortollo squatted low and reached for his last photon

grenade. Sarai seized his arm to stop him. "Are you crazy? What're you doing?"

"Trying to even the odds!"

"By setting off their demolitions with *us inside the room*?"

Thwarted and annoyed, Sortollo tucked the grenade back onto his belt. Phaser shots from Kershul raced over his and Sarai's heads, to harass Breen on the center's upper tiers. He and Sarai resumed peppering the room with arbitrary scourges of phaser fire. "Commander," the human said, "I don't mean to be critical here, but we're outnumbered five to one. Did you even have a plan for this when we came in here?"

"Of course I did," Sarai said as she picked off two Spetzkar with a double headshot. "Fight 'em 'til we can't."

One more good hit and we're finished. It was one thing to have faith in the officers under one's command, but for Will Riker it was a test of his nerves to stand by and say nothing as he watched them steer what once had been his ship toward its apparently imminent destruction.

All of his decades of experience told him that no good would come of interfering in Vale's command during a pitched battle. The survival of the ship and its crew hinged on the efficacy of its chain of command. If he meddled, he would not only undermine her authority as the *Titan*'s commanding officer, he might endanger the ship at a crucial moment.

But standing at the rear of the bridge, all he could do whenever the ship trembled from another blast by the *Kulak*'s disruptors or its torpedoes was fear for the safety of Deanna and their young daughter, Tasha. They both no doubt were huddling in their quarters, deep in the best-protected sections of the ship, but that gave little solace to Riker as he envisioned the *Titan* erupting into a cloud of superheated gas the moment the Breen landed one more lucky shot.

He knew exactly what he would do if he were in command. He—

No, he told himself. *Not your command. Don't get in Christine's way.*

Damage reports flew by Riker as quickly as the sparks from erupting consoles, and a momentary fault in the inertial dampers threw him and the rest of the bridge crew to starboard. He landed hard on the deck, but when Keru moved to help him, he said only, "Mind your post!" The security chief took Riker at his word and put his full attention back on the battle, where it belonged. This was no time for Vale's senior officers to suffer from divided focus.

Thunder and dimming lights, another violent lurch—now Riker was tossed aft, against a bulkhead. As he fought his way off the deck yet again, he heard Rager report from ops, "Aft shields collapsing, hull breaches on decks fourteen through sixteen, sections eleven and twelve. Main power dropping, tapping impulse to compensate."

"Helm," Vale said, rising from her chair. "Take us around the platform again, best speed. Keru, all phasers aft—I want them to be the only thing the Breen can see."

"Aye, Captain," Keru said. "Watch me razzle as I dazzle." Keying in commands with speed and dexterity, Keru orchestrated a masterful barrage of phaser fire—one that, as Riker had feared, struck the *Kulak*'s forward shields without result.

On the main viewscreen, the Husnock orbital defense station swelled as the *Titan* sped toward it, then it seemed to turn on its side as the *Luna*-class starship rolled its starboard side toward the planet's surface and away from the Breen's steady fusillade of return fire.

Watching the scene unfold, it felt to Riker like déjà vu. *This was where the Breen blew a hole in our side last time,* he realized. *And now Christine's making all the same errors again.*

It made no sense to him. He knew her tactical training was better than this.

A debris cluster blurred past on the viewscreen, and then Riker saw Vale shoot a nod at Keru, who tapped his console twice. The image on-screen switched to an aft view of the pursuing Breen dreadnought—just as it was engulfed in a flash that whited out the screen.

Then the shock wave of the explosion slammed into the *Titan*, and everything went dark. If not for the glow of falling sparks, the bridge would have been as black as the inside of a fist.

Lights and power came back in fits and starts. By the time the main viewscreen flickered back to life, only half of the bridge's consoles were functional.

Riker watched the *Kulak* drift out of the fire cloud with its bow tilted upward, and the ship was in a slow roll and tumble that suggested it had lost its ability to maneuver, even if just for a few seconds. In that moment Riker saw that the dreadnought's ventral hull had been torn open in multiple places, many of which were venting plasma and vapor.

Keru declared with pride, "Her shields are down!"

Just like ours, Riker thought, but he couldn't help but be impressed by the trap Vale had set. She had feigned taking a hit so she could secretly mine the theater of combat with quantum torpedoes disguised as debris, and then Keru had armed and triggered them at the last second.

He was about to cross the bridge to congratulate her when, on the viewscreen, the *Kulak* righted itself and shifted course to resume its straight-on attack heading.

Vale turned a hopeful look at Keru. "Tactical, status."

"Shields and weapons offline," Keru said.

Still not betraying the least sign of dismay, Vale settled into her seat. "Helm, report."

Lavena answered, "Impulse coils overloaded, warp drive offline." She looked back, and even through her aquatic breathing mask Riker could discern her fear. "We're dead in space."

A warbling signal on the tactical console. Keru silenced it.

"Thot Tren is hailing us, Captain."

She pushed her multicolored hair off her brow and lifted her chin. "On-screen."

The image of the Breen commander appeared on the viewscreen, albeit behind a hash of static and other interference. Behind the universal translator's interpretation of his words, Riker could still hear the machine-noise of the Breen's vocoder.

"Captain Vale . . . don't you think this has gone on long enough?"

Vale projected cool defiance. "Maybe I think it's not nearly done."

"That would be a fatal mistake, Captain. I will grant you credit for a palpable hit with your hidden torpedoes, but now your ship stands defenseless before mine. Recall your team from the planet's surface, and let my

personnel complete their mission free of your interference, and I will leave you, your ship, and your crew intact to fight another day."

The captain made a fist of her left hand and folded her right hand over it—a gesture that Riker recognized as Vale suppressing the urge to pummel someone who was in dire need of an ass-kicking. "I know you think you're being generous, Thot Tren. But I'm afraid I'll have to tell you to take that offer and choke on it."

The Breen tilted his head, as if his perception of Vale had suddenly gone askew. *"I admire your spirit, Captain."*

"But let me guess: You regret having to kill me?"

"No. That would be unprofessional. But I will speak well of your memory. Tren out."

The channel closed, reverting the viewscreen to the image of the *Kulak* bearing down on the *Titan*, its weapons array ablaze with fearsome energies.

Riker moved to Vale's side as he contemplated their imminent shared demise. "I don't suppose you have another ace up your sleeve, do you?"

"How many times have I beaten you at poker?" A mischievous smirk as she tapped her combadge. "Vale to Tuvok: open fire."

It was not a plan that Tuvok would himself ever have proposed, but over the course of a long career in Starfleet he had learned to trust the instincts of his commanding officers.

So it was that he had found himself in an environmental suit, standing beside computer engineering specialist Lieutenant Reyfin Omal, a Tyrakhean woman whose pale complexion was accentuated by her prominent and symmetrical black facial tattoos, on the exterior of an orbital defense platform high above the equator of Husnock Prime.

Omal had been working from Doctor Kilaris's translation key for the Husnock language, filtered by Doctor Pek's parsing matrix, and refined by Lieutenant Sethe's Starfleet-standard interface and Modan's intuitive improvements to the universal translator's handling of Husnock syntax and grammar. She had patched a portable compsheet into the defense platform's controls, and was transmitting to the holographic HUD in Tuvok's faceplate an animated guide to operating the manual targeting console for the platform's massive particle cannons.

Before restarting the platform's primary power generator, he asked her, "You are certain these steps are correct? And that there is sufficient power to operate the system?"

"Positive," she had said over the coded transceiver. *"Punch it."*

Following the step-by-step guide she had programmed, he had awakened the platform's long-dormant reactor core and begun charging its firing modules, while keeping its targeting systems offline. He had feared it might take several minutes or even an hour to bring the station's systems to full power, but once roused, the weapons systems had charged to full power in under a minute. Tuvok regarded the Husnock's technology with a grudging respect. As distasteful as he found their culture's amorality, their achievements in engineering had been remarkable.

"Here they come," Omal had said, at the first sign of the *Titan*'s latest pass.

Knowing time was running out, Tuvok had adjusted the platform's IFF—identify friend or foe—circuits to treat the *Titan* as a nonhostile vessel. After that, all he had been able to do was wait and hope to hear Vale's order, the one for which she had sent him here to prepare.

And then the order came.

"Vale to Tuvok: open fire."

He locked the platform's weapons onto the *Kulak*, targeted the central power coupling in its weapons array, adjusted the Husnock particle cannons' power levels to just above the bare minimum needed to cripple that part of the Breen ship . . . and then he fired.

It felt like using a hammer of the gods to swat an insect.

A single blast reduced the dreadnought's tactical grid to a smoldering mess and left the *Kulak* rolling slowly to starboard. The wounded ship vented atmosphere in a cloud that quickly dispersed into the vacuum of space.

Omal looked at Tuvok, her silver eyes wide. *"No wonder the Breen wanted to capture this tech. It hits like a* torga *beast!"*

"I will have to take your word for that comparison," Tuvok said. "As for the Breen . . . let us hope their instinct for self-preservation outweighs their desire for domination. Because I would prefer not to fire this weapon again—but if they force me to, I will."

Flames ringed the command deck of the *Kulak*. Damage-control personnel scrambled to douse the flames, but one look at the blackened panels and slagged circuitry left behind by the blazes made it clear to Thot Tren that his ship had suffered a crippling blow. This fight was over.

He struggled to stand. If the spinning inside his head didn't betray him, he feared his left leg would. He called up his medical scan on his helmet's HUD. The injury in his leg was only a hairline fracture, not a break. He would soldier on until his ship was clear of danger.

The main viewscreen fritzed and failed repeatedly to hold a steady image. As it stuttered in and out of service, Tren saw the *Titan* still sitting dead ahead, its battle-ravaged hull looking at least as sorry as that of the *Kulak*. He was sure they hadn't fired the shot that had hobbled his ship—so who had? He limped in a half circle until he saw his weapons officer was back at his post. "Bol, report. What hit us?"

"A Husnock defense platform, sir." He checked his malfunctioning console before he added, "They're still locked on to us, and they're charged for another shot."

Choy looked back from ops. "One more hit from that thing—"

"I know," Tren said. Favoring his good leg, he moved to confront his first officer. "Vang, you told me those platforms were dormant."

"Our scans said they were."

"Scans? You didn't send engineering recon teams to check?"

"There wasn't time, sir. The *Titan* was already entering the system, and we needed to prioritize the strike against the command center on—"

Tren cut him off with a fast-draw snap shot from

his disruptor. The pulse burned through the front of Vang's mask and cooked his head to a cinder inside his helmet.

The body slumped to the deck at Tren's feet. "Choy. You are first officer now. Assign a new operations chief, then get me damage and casualty reports."

"As you command." Choy left his post and beckoned a relief officer to take his place.

Tren was still considering his next move when Sevv said, "We're being hailed."

"Put her on-screen," Tren said.

Just as he had expected, he was once again confronted by the face of Captain Vale. Her pale countenance resembled those of the Paclu, and her multihued hair reminded Tren of a Silgov's colorful tresses. *"Thot Tren. Reverse your course and leave this system immediately. If you fail to comply, I will give the order to have your ship destroyed. Choose now."*

"I need time to recover my personnel from the planet's surface."

Vale shook her head. *"No. Their fate is up to me now. This is your last warning."*

Bol interjected via Tren's private transceiver channel, *"Engineer Taan confirms we have lost all shields and weapons. He will need at least a day to begin repairs."*

Tren nodded once, as much for Choy as for Vale. "Well played, Captain. Until we meet again, may darkness bring you fortune. *Kulak* out." The channel closed, and Tren pivoted away from the viewscreen. "Helm, set course away from the *Titan*, then out of the system, best speed."

Choy stepped into Tren's path. "Sir, we can't just abandon our Spetzkar on the planet."

"We haven't abandoned them, Choy. As of now they're either prisoners or casualties. In either case, they are beyond our help." He shouldered past his new XO. "I'm going down to medical." He gestured at the still-smoking corpse of Vang. "Clean that up before I get back."

Twenty-nine

Even as the Breen warship turned away and accelerated into retreat, Vale refused to let herself believe she had won. Too many times she had thought she had the Breen beaten, only to find they had lured her into a snare. Now her ship was a smoke-filled wreck barely able to maintain life-support. Watching the *Kulak* jump to warp, she clung to her skepticism. She would not fall victim to overconfidence again.

Then Keru announced, "They've set a course to rendezvous with their fleet and are retreating at warp eight point six." The bridge crew greeted the news with a modest cheer and a smattering of applause, while Vale was happy just to be able to exhale.

Riker clasped her shoulder. "You won."

"I know what winning feels like," she said. "This isn't it." She slipped free of Riker's hand. "Keru, hail Sarai. Find out what the hell's going on down there."

Her throat tightened while she waited for the channel;

if the Breen had succeeded in destroying the command center before Vale and her team could use it to neutralize the Husnock armada, then all of this pain, suffering, and death had been for nothing.

"Channel open," Keru said.

"Number One, what's your status?"

Over the banshee screeches of weapons fire, Sarai replied, *"Busy! What's yours?"*

"All secure in orbit. Have you neutralized the Husnock fleet?"

"Negative! The main control center's toast!"

Vale felt the bridge crew's anxiety rising. "Do you need backup?"

"Yes!" More high-pitched noise was followed by incoherent shouts and a rumble of detonation. *"We're falling—"* Another interruption of phaser fire. *"Falling back to auxiliary control on sublevel eight."*

"Do whatever you have to, but don't let the Breen take aux control. Reinforcements are on the way. *Titan* out." Vale turned to Keru, who was already handing off his console to a junior officer. "Get down there, and take everyone we've got! Move!" As he dashed into the turbolift, she faced Rager. "Strike teams to all transporter rooms, beam them to the bunker entrance."

"Sending the coordinates to all transporter consoles now," Rager said.

Her crew swung into action without doubt or delay, but while Vale wanted to feel pride, all she could sense was a twisting knot of dread deep in her gut. This was why she had known not to celebrate the *Kulak*'s retreat. The battle with the ship had only ever been a diversion, an obstacle to halting the Breen's real mission on the surface.

Not so long ago, I'd have been down there leading the fight, Vale brooded. *Now my place is here.* She pushed back against her guilt at being expected to stand apart from the fray while waiting to learn the fates of all those she had just ordered into danger.

Then Riker was once more at her side. He said nothing—but he rested his hand on her shoulder in a firm but gentle manner that conveyed a simple comfort: *I know how you feel.*

She acknowledged his silent encouragement with a nod, then faced the viewscreen with a stoic expression while she awaited the resolution of a crisis that was now out of her hands.

Give 'em hell, Number One.

Whatever substance the walls inside the Husnock bunker were made of, it had the perilous quality of deflecting energy blasts rather than absorbing them—a fact Sarai and her team had discovered only after the shooting had started inside the main control center.

Each shot that had missed its intended target, and failed to blow holes in one of the tiered banks of workstations, had caromed around the room in a working definition of reflective optics until it slammed into a person, a computer, or the floor. For one fleeting instant Sarai had thought she and the away team might turn this quirk of Husnock architecture to their advantage. After all, how often would one get to fire a beam weapon around corners?

Unfortunately, whether by accident or preparation, the Breen had hit upon the idea first. All it had taken was a single shot to either side of the open doorway, and the area where Sarai and the others had hunkered down had become a frenzy of unpredictable ricochets. And it didn't help that there were so many Breen commandos. They had filled the control center with a storm of disruptor pulses bouncing every which way.

That was when Sarai had given the order to fall back.

She and her five shipmates had fallen over one another while searing blasts grazed their arms and legs. They had been lucky to get out the door with their lives, even though every one of them had emerged from the control center wounded.

Not that retreating did any good.

The walls in the corridors were composed of the same reflective compound, which meant the passageways were nothing more than glorified kill boxes. Every shot that slipped through the doorway at even a slight angle volleyed back and forth, giving it two or sometimes even three extra chances to hit one of them before it careened down the corridor into the shadows. The away team crawled on their bellies, with wild shots blurring past only centimeters above them.

Sarai stopped and reached out to grab Ithiok's arm. "If Modan stops blocking the Breen's remote detonators, can you trigger them with your tricorder?"

Baffled, the Tarkalean woman asked, "Yeah, but why would I do that?"

"Trust me," Sarai said. She tapped her combadge. "Sarai to Modan! Do you copy?"

"Go ahead, sir."

"Stop blocking the Breen's detonators."

"But—"

"That's an order! Do it!" She looked back at Sortollo,

who was closest to the open doorway. "Photon grenade, minimum yield, now!" As he prepped the munition, she told the others, "Get ready to run!" Another swarm of disruptor blasts filled the corridor, forcing them all to plant their faces against the floor. "Sortollo! Now!"

The security officer lobbed the photon grenade through the doorway without looking to see where it would land. Set for minimum yield, it would at best deliver a mild stun to the armored Spetzkar commandos—but more importantly, it would buy the away team a few seconds to escape.

A blue-white flash and a bone-rattling boom inside the control center shook the bunker. "Move!" Sarai shouted as she sprang to her feet and sprinted for the accessway that led down to the bunker's deeper sublevels. The others followed close behind her, with Sortollo acting as the rear guard to discourage the Breen from pursuing too closely.

As they raced down the spiral ramp, disruptor blasts screamed down from above and peppered the floor between them. Sarai hollered over her shoulder, "Ithiok! Trigger their detonators!" The combat engineer lifted her tricorder and pressed one button.

The blast felt like an earthquake, as if Ithiok had just unleashed a synthetic apocalypse. Smoke, dust, and flames poured into the accessway from the command level above the away team, and rained tiny bits of debris—including pieces of Breen armor—upon their heads.

Then more crimson disruptor bolts tore out of the smoke and ricocheted down the silo-like space around the spiral ramp, hectoring the away team with a chaotic barrage.

In the midst of that bedlam, Sarai's transceiver warbled inside her helmet to indicate an incoming signal from the *Titan*: *"Number One, what's your status?"*

Sarai dodged another shot from above. "Busy! What's yours!"

"All secure in orbit. Have you neutralized the Husnock fleet?"

"Negative! The main control center's toast!" She thought it wise to omit from her report that she had just been the one who had destroyed it.

A wild shot took a crazy bounce and burned a hole through Sortollo's right knee as Vale asked, *"Do you need backup?"*

"Yes!" She stopped and returned fire upward at the handful of Breen who had escaped the main control center and were still hounding them into the bowels of the bunker. "We're falling—" A near-miss showered her head and shoulders with shrapnel from part of the metal walkway above. "Falling back to auxiliary control on sublevel eight." She waited until sh'Aqabaa and Kershul carried Sortollo past her and Ithiok, then she directed Kyzak to take up the rear guard as they continued their descent.

"Do whatever you have to," Vale said over the comm, *"but don't let the Breen take aux control. Reinforcements are on the way.* Titan *out."*

The channel closed as Sarai followed her teammates onto sublevel eight. She plucked their second photon grenade off of Sortollo's utility belt, then motioned for the team to keep moving. "Ithiok, take point. Get them to aux control. I'll buy us a few more seconds." As the team hurried onward, she adjusted the settings on the photon grenade. Medium yield. Proximity trigger, five-second delay. She set it on the ramp beside the open doorway and armed it.

Then she ran like hell.

She scrambled through the door into auxiliary control just before she heard the blast, which put a crack through the ceiling and rained dust on her and everything else in sight. "This is it," she told the team. "Last stand. We can't let them get a shot through this doorway. Dennisar, take point with sh'Aqabaa. Anything moves out there, light it up. Kyzak, you and I have their backs. If one of them goes down, we take over. Kershul, patch up Sortollo. Ithiok, do whatever you have to, but make sure the Breen can't trigger any demolitions on this level." At last she turned toward Sethe and Modan, who were hunched over a Husnock command terminal they had coaxed into service. "As for you two, I don't mean to rush you, but—"

"We just need another minute or two," Modan said.

"A minute we can give you," Sarai said. "More than that—"

Sethe added with conviction, "Just give us that minute, sir."

Sarai checked her rifle's charge, then moved up to the ready line. "All right, team. You heard the techsperts. Whatever it takes, let's give them that minute."

The room and the corridor outside fell strangely quiet. That felt like a bad sign to Sarai. It meant someone was hatching a plan. "Den? Pava? Anything?" The security guards shook their heads. Was it possible her trap with the second photon grenade had thwarted the Breen's pursuit? Or had neutralized the last of their personnel? Or was it more likely the Breen were using their armor's shrouding ability to launch a stealth assault?

"Fire," Sarai whispered.

Dennisar squinted in confusion. "But there's nothing out—"

"Light up that corridor," Sarai insisted. "All of it. Now."

Phaser beams crisscrossed in the darkness, rebounded off the walls, and turned the narrow hallway outside the auxiliary control center into a three-dimensional lattice of deadly energy—that instantly fried two shrouded Spetzkar, wounded another, and sent five more scurrying back around the corner to cover. Then they started to return fire, flooding the corridor with disruptor pulses bouncing in all directions and coming damned close to slipping through the open doorway. With trial and error, Sarai knew her people could get a shot around that same corner to hit the Breen—but would the Spetzkar's luck prove better?

From the back of the room, Modan called out, "Commander! We've got it!"

"Hold the line," Sarai said to Kyzak, then she ran to confirm Sethe and Modan's work. "Show me. What are we looking at?"

"These are the Husnock High Command's executive systems," Sethe explained, walking Sarai through the interface on the screen. "Just as we hoped, the Husnock High Command had a protocol for preventing their fleet from being used against them."

"So can we shut them all down from here?"

"Yes," Modan said. "And we can do more that that."

At the doorway, a Breen disruptor pulse blasted through Dennisar's shoulder and laid him out flat on the floor. Kyzak pivoted into Dennisar's place and continued firing at the Breen.

Sarai directed Modan's fearful eyes back at the Husnock computer screen. "What else can you do? Tell me, now."

"We can self-destruct the entire Husnock armada," she said. "Every ship, every munitions factory, every fleet station. All you need to do is give the order."

Sarai was about to do exactly that, and then she recalled the conflict in her mission agenda, the divided loyalty that had haunted her ever since she had come aboard the *Titan*.

Admiral Batanides was very clear, she remembered. *She wanted the Husnock fleet captured for study by Starfleet R and D. But my orders from Admiral Riker and Captain Vale are just as clear: they want this threat to galactic peace neutralized. If I destroy it all, Batanides will end me. But if I don't destroy it while I have the chance—*

In a crimson blink, sh'Aqabaa was down, a smoking hole in her left ribs. Ithiok pulled the wounded *shen* away from the door, then moved up to take her place.

All this bloodshed for nothing if I make the wrong choice.

"Sethe, can you locate all vessels in the Husnock fleet with this system?"

"Easily."

"Find a ship at the farthest rimward edge of space, as far from here and the Federation as possible. Isolate that one ship and shut it down cold except for a command code you set. Then arm the self-destruct packages on every other Husnock military asset in existence." Out of the kindness of her sensitive Efrosian heart, she added, "Set a two-minute delay, and make them broadcast a warning to anyone who can hear to get to safe distance."

Modan and Sethe keyed in commands with lightning speed. Then Sethe entered the final command with a flourish and smiled at Sarai. "Countdown under way."

It was a moment that felt like triumph—until the barrage at the doorway intensified, and within seconds Ithiok and Kyzak were both struggling to hold their ground after taking two hits each. Sarai ran back to the doorway, pulled Kyzak out of the line of fire, and took over for him, filling the passageway outside with death. Out of the corner of her eye she saw Kershul pull Ithiok back from the doorway, and then the Edosian medic was holding the line beside Sarai.

This will be a good death, Sarai told herself. *No shame dying in a stand-up fight.*

Then came multiple concussive blasts from around the corner, and the echoes of phasers not hers or Kershul's. Reinforcements from the *Titan* had arrived.

The Breen's barrage halted.

Sarai's combadge warbled. *"Keru to Sarai. Please respond."*

"I'm here, Keru."

"Mission status?"

She looked to Modan for confirmation. The Selenean woman gave her a thumbs-up.

"Accomplished. Do you want to tell the Breen, or shall I?"

She imagined she could almost hear his grin. *"I think you've earned it."*

Leaning close to the doorway, she called out, "Attention, Breen personnel. Who currently has command of your unit?"

After a short delay, a harshly translated voice replied, "Chot Vixx. I have command."

"Well, Vixx, I have bad news for you. The *Kulak* has left the system without you. And we've just destroyed the entire Husnock armada from auxiliary control. Your mission is a failure. It's also over."

From beyond the smoke, Vixx asked, "And what will happen to me and my men?"

"That's up to you. You've got ten seconds to make up your mind. Call it."

It took only five seconds for Vixx to make his choice, but they felt to Sarai like the longest five seconds of her life.

Then she heard the clatter of metal against the floor, and saw half a dozen Breen disruptor rifles sliding out of the smoke, to a stop near her doorway. To her great relief, none of them were emitting the telltale whine of a weapon on a buildup to an overload—and when she looked closer she saw that their power cells had been removed, rendering them inactive.

"Hold your fire," Vixx said. "We've laid down our weapons. We're coming out."

Sarai could hardly believe what she had heard was real. In every engagement against the Breen's elite special forces she had ever read about, the Spetzkar had died fighting to the last soldier rather than permit themselves to be taken as prisoners of war. She didn't know what sort of changes were brewing in the Breen Confederacy to have made the commandos' surrender possible, but whatever they were she was grateful for them.

"Commander, hold your position," Keru said to Sarai over her helmet's transceiver. *"My team'll take it from here. Stand by for medical evac."*

"Acknowledged." Sarai slumped against a wall and sank to the floor, overcome by a wave of exhaustion and relief. She activated her subspace transceiver. "Sarai to *Titan*."

Vale answered, *"Good to hear your voice, Number One."*

"Good to be heard, Captain."

"So what's the word, Commander?"

"Mission accomplished, sir. And tell security to prep the brig: we're bringing home some unexpected guests."

Thot Tren's last hope for a victorious end to his mission had rested upon the capabilities of Chot Braz and his Spetzkar on the surface of Husnock Prime. Their mission had been one of simple demolition: destroy the command-and-control centers of the Husnock High Command before Starfleet found a way to exploit them against the captured armada.

The *Kulak* had not yet passed the outer bounds of the Husnock Prime star system when Tren returned to its command deck after a brief visit to the ship's medical bay. As he arrived, Sevv turned from his console to report, "Sir! Distress calls from the *Sulica* and the *Tarcza*."

That was all Tren needed to hear to know his mission had failed. "Split screen," he said, "shared channel." Now he and his subordinate commanders would be able to see one another.

Kran appeared on the left side of the viewscreen, Spara on the right, both talking over each other. Tren silenced them with a raised hand. "Kran, report."

"Automated warnings from the armada, sir. All ships to self-destruct in two minutes."

Spara added, *"We've heard the same warning, from our support ships and the factory."*

"Disengage all telepresence pilots and move your ships to safe distance."

"I have three dozen personnel inside the factory," Spara said. *"I can't evacuate them in two minutes unless there's a way to get a transporter beam through the station's hull."*

Tren knew that trying to beam through Husnock armor was a lost cause, and he had no intention of losing an entire ship for a futile effort. "Leave them behind," he said. "Your first duty is to your ship. Both of you, move your vessels to safe distance, now. Then patch your screens through to mine."

The two commanders delegated Tren's order to their seconds-in-command, and then the images on the *Kulak*'s viewscreen switched from the command decks of the *Tarcza* and the *Sulica* to their views, respectively, of the munitions factory and the Husnock armada. In the lower left corner of the *Kulak*'s screen a timer counted down the final moments to detonation.

In near-perfect synchronicity, the armada and the munitions factory erupted in supernova blasts, explosions a billion times brighter than the average star but gone in less than a second. When the flash was gone the images from the *Sulica* and the *Tarcza* both crackled with interference from faster-than-light pulses of subspace disruption unleashed by the antistellar munitions that had been destroyed in the conflagration.

Choy stepped into view by Tren's side. "The domo won't be pleased with us, will he?"

"I wouldn't be concerned about that," Tren told his new first officer.

"After what he did to Thot Keer? And Thot Trom?"

"I promised we would not return empty-handed," Tren said, "and we haven't. We have extensive sensor data from our field test of an antistellar munition, and we have schematics downloaded from the automated factory."

"A fleet ready for war would have been a far more valuable prize," Choy said.

"True. But even if it takes our scientists decades to unravel the secrets in the Husnock's designs, this mission will have been more than justified. Consider, Choy: What have we really lost? Fewer than a hundred lives, for a start. And how can we say we lost the armada or the factory when we never really had them? Starfleet, on the other hand . . . they've lost two starships with hundreds of personnel each. A score of prominent scientists. And by sacrificing the Husnock military arsenal, they've deprived themselves of the opportunity to learn its secrets." Tren regarded the warp-stretched stars on the viewscreen, and he felt no anxiety whatsoever about the homecoming he and his battle group would receive. "Have no fear, Choy. Our mission has been a success, and we will be welcomed home as heroes, blessed by the fortune of war."

October 2386

Thirty

Hammers broke Cherbegrod's dream of creamy food and endless foot rubs. He startled awake in his bunk. Banging echoed in his quarters, shook his ship. Not hammers—explosions. Then the alarm on the wall started to cry, whooping up and down, and orange lights flashed as he pulled on his coverall. The noise chased him as he left his cabin and waddle-jogged through the corridors of the *Gomjar* to reach his chair on the top deck.

Haripog and Eberleg were behind him as he plodded down the last stretch. More banging hits made the lights go on and off. Sparks and smoke jumped from wall panels and stung Cherbegrod's face. He swatted the hot bits from his face and arms and kept moving.

The three Pakleds were almost to the top deck's main hatch when a bright light filled the corridor in front of them. Too bright to look at. Cherbegrod squinted his bleary eyes, lifted his hand, and turned his face away. Then came the pretty sound, like music. When the droning and the light faded, Cherbegrod lowered his hand to see who had beamed aboard his ship.

Gaila pointed a disruptor pistol at Cherbegrod, and the skinny man next to him pointed his weapon at Haripog and Eberleg. The Ferengi bared his fangs in a grin that even Cherbegrod knew wasn't friendly. "Hello, Cherbegrod, you sneaky little tube grub." An upward jerk of his weapon. "Hands up, you backstabber."

Cherbegrod raised his hands over his head, and so did his men. "Why you here?"

"Why do you think, moron? I know it was you who sold me out to the Breen." He took a step forward. "You undercut my price and gave them some kind of backdoor code you and your lazy pals snuck into the security system."

"Not lazy. Smart. Do more work with—"

"Shut up!" Gaila thrust the muzzle of his weapon closer to Cherbegrod's face. "I know the Breen must have paid you a fortune for that station. Which I'm betting makes you the richest junk hauler in the quadrant. But that station wasn't yours to sell. So whatever the Breen gave you? You're going to hand it over to me. Right now."

Anger made Cherbegrod's face warm. He narrowed his eyes and stood taller so that he towered over the Ferengi. "Sold codes to Breen. Codes ours to sell. What Breen did with codes? Not our business." He was done being afraid of bullies. He leaned forward and put his own head against the end of Gaila's pistol. "Not paying you."

"Then you're in for a long and very painful ordeal, my chubby friend. I will make you and your crew pay for every mind-numbing conversation I've ever had with your dull-witted species; for every time your kind shortchanged me on a deal; for every time your ilk has tried to double-cross me. Then I will kill you and revive you as many times as it takes to break you. And when I'm done, and you've handed over the money that was rightfully mine, Zinos and I will sell you and every last one of your idiot underlings into hard-labor slavery."

He ended his rant by shooting Cherbegrod in the foot.

Cherbegrod wailed in pain. It hurt so much, like fire creeping in his bones. He fell down and wanted to clutch his smoking foot, but it was agony to touch it. Tears streamed down his face as he spat at Gaila. "Not paying you!"

The Ferengi shook his head. "I didn't think it was possible, but apparently you really are dumber than you look. I'm going to enjoy—" He shut up as his man Zinos fell dead beside him, his eyes wide and his throat gushing blood from a fresh slice.

Gaila started to turn around, then stopped when someone else's disruptor was pressed to the back of his head, just behind his left lobe. A figure stepped out of the shadows behind him—another Ferengi by the name of Brunt, a strangely polite member of his species who had come aboard the *Gomjar* a day earlier as a paying guest, for reasons Cherbegrod hadn't understood.

Brunt gestured with the bloody knife in his other hand for Gaila to put down his pistol. "Set it on the deck, nice and slow, or I'll fry your skull from lobe to lobe." Gaila did as Brunt said. Then Brunt added, "Now kick it over to the Pakleds."

A tap of Gaila's foot sent the weapon across the deck to Eberleg, who picked it up and pointed it at Gaila.

Haripog helped Cherbegrod stand up, and he supported him so Cherbegrod could keep his wounded foot off the deck.

Gaila glared as Brunt searched his pockets and relieved him of various small devices. "You're making a mistake, Brunt. Join me and we can split the take off these Pakled chumps."

"Split it, eh? Fifty-fifty?"

"I was thinking more seventy-thirty, seeing as—"

"Shut up." He clubbed Gaila on the back of his head with the grip of his disruptor. Gaila crumpled to the deck, and Brunt stood over him, like a Balduk cage fighter taunting his beaten foe. "No more deals, Gaila. I'm taking you back to Urwyzden."

"For what? Some measly bounty?"

"That's right," Brunt said.

"But I'm offering you a thousand times that bounty! A world of profit!"

Brunt put his knee into Gaila's back and pinned him to the deck as he slapped a pair of magnetic manacles around the gunrunner's wrists. "Profit isn't everything."

Hearing that put a look of horror on Gaila's face. "What kind of a Ferengi *are* you?"

Brunt the bounty hunter pulled Gaila to his feet and prodded him down the corridor, toward the transporter bay. "The kind who's taking you back to jail."

Sequestered behind the locked door of her quarters on the *Titan*, Sarai faced the grave visage of Admiral Batanides via her clandestine subspace channel. The flag officer's simmering anger was so vivid and palpable that it seemed to transcend the boundaries of the holographic transmission.

"So, as I noted earlier," Sarai said, "the *Titan* is scheduled to remain here at Starbase Mainzer for at least another week while we arrange transports for the remains of our dead and finish repairs. One reason the work is proceeding slowly is that I've granted Commander Ra-Havreii a temporary leave of absence while he receives needed therapy." She deliberately omitted the detail that his therapy was psychiatric in nature, in the hope that Batanides would assume the chief engineer was receiving medical attention for the wounds he had suffered in action. "Fortunately, before he left he appointed Lieutenant Commander Dalkaya as the new deputy chief of engineering, and that transition has been effected without incident."

"That's not the intel I'm expecting from you, Dalit, and you know that." Batanides didn't try to disguise the suspicion in her eyes or her voice. *"Get on with it."*

Sarai paused to let Batanides feel her resentment in kind. "If you're referring to Captain Vale and Admiral Riker, you should be pleased to learn that they're both settling into their respective roles in accordance with established Starfleet protocols."

The admiral did not seem convinced. *"Is that so?"*

"In fact it is. Throughout the operation in Husnock space, the admiral exercised great restraint and impeccable discretion with regard to the chain of command. He set strategic objectives but delegated tactical command of the fleet to Captain Vale, as per regulations. He also refrained from spending an inordinate amount of time on the bridge, and he gave no indication of second-guessing Captain Vale's tactics or command prerogatives."

"That sounds like quite a reversal of their past dynamic."

"I can report based only on what I saw, Admiral."

The steely-eyed, gray-haired woman on the other side of the subspace channel studied Sarai. When she spoke again, a note of irritation crept into her voice. *"Let's put aside for the moment my concerns about Vale and Riker. We need to talk about what you did."*

"I carried out my orders in good faith," Sarai said. "Nothing more, nothing less."

"I'm not sure I'd agree with that." Batanides leaned in so that her face dominated the holoscreen. *"I told you that we wanted to capture the Husnock fleet for our own research."*

"I left you a Husnock battleship completely intact. Study it all you want."

"One ship? I read the after-action report, Commander. You could have disabled the Husnock arsenal without destroying it, but you self-destructed all but a single vessel—which, I might note, sits at the farthest end of Husnock space, nearly a year's travel at high warp from the Federation. I presume you think choosing to spare that *ship was funny?"*

"Well, I certainly don't think it was sad. I saw what kind of munitions the Husnock used. Weapons of mass destruction like those have no place in Starfleet."

Batanides scowled. *"That wasn't your call to make."*

"As the one who led an away team that free-fell from orbit and survived a firefight with an entire company of Breen commandos to secure the assets in question, I think it was. If you disagree with my assessment, you can lead that mission yourself next time."

The admiral's anger turned cold. *"Need I remind you,*

Commander, that I can scuttle your career whenever I like?"

"Be my guest. But if you do, you'd better be ready to explain to Admiral Riker why you took it upon yourself to plant an unauthorized spy aboard his flagship." She watched the admiral's reaction to that threat and was pleased to see it made Batanides back up just a bit.

"Don't get overconfident," Batanides said. *"I redacted the worst parts of your service record before I had you transferred to the* Titan. *If you suddenly develop an attack of conscience, I'll make sure Admiral Riker and Captain Vale get to see the least flattering version of your dossier—right before you spend the rest of your life in a Starfleet Intelligence black site. Do I make myself clear, Commander?"*

"Positively transparent, sir."

"Your next report is due in five days. Get me new intel on Riker and Vale, or else." Without a farewell or the least concession to courtesy, Batanides closed the channel.

The holoscreen went dark. Sarai sighed and let her shoulders slump. "What now?"

Leaning against the wall on either side of her desk, out of the field of view for the holoscreen's sensor, Captain Vale and Admiral Riker exchanged troubled looks.

"Now," Riker said, "we find a way to get you out of this mess with your career intact."

"And then," Vale added, "we show Batanides she just messed with the wrong crew."

Acknowledgments

My sincere thanks go out to those folks whose support and assistance proved invaluable during the writing of this book: my wife, Kara; my agent, Lucienne Diver; my friends and fellow authors James Swallow and Kirsten Beyer; my editors, Margaret Clark and Ed Schlesinger; and our indefatigable licensing liaison, the great John Van Citters. You are all rock stars.

About the Author

David Mack is REDACTED.

Buy his novel *The Midnight Front*, coming in January 2018.

Learn more on his official website:

davidmack.pro

Or follow him on Twitter:

@DavidAlanMack